The Honourable M

The Honourable Member for Pepynbridge
by
Peter Morrell
ISBN: 978-0-9954805-4-4

Also by Peter Morrell

Fiction
The Rector of Pepynbridge
The Islamist of Pepynbridge

Non-Fiction
The Russells of Thornhaugh

The Honourable Member for Pepynbridge

Copyright Peter Morrell 2016

All rights reserved. No part of this publication may be reproduced, stored in a retrieval system or transmitted in any form or by any means, electronic, mechanical, photo-copy, recording or otherwise, without prior written consent of the copyright owner. Nor can it be circulated in any form of binding or cover other than that in which it is published and without similar condition including this condition being imposed on a subsequent purchaser.

This novel is a work of fiction. Whilst some living where it is set may recognise similarities between Pepynbridge and Medborough and actual places in the East Midlands of England, names and characters of the living characters who participate in the narrative, rather than being incidental to it like David Cameron, are the product of the author's imagination and any resemblance to actual persons, living or dead, is unintended and entirely coincidental.

Scripture quotations are taken from the New Revised Standard Version Bible, Anglicized Edition, copyright © 1989, 1995 National Council of Churches of Christ in the United States of America. Used by permission. All rights reserved.

The right of Peter Morrell to be identified as the author of this work has been asserted in accordance with the Copyright Designs and Patents Act 1988.

A copy of this book is deposited with the British Library

Published by

i2i Publishing. Manchester.
www.i2ipublishing.co.uk

The Honourable Member for Pepynbridge

*"Can I just say I live for the day when
gay clergymen can be openly gay,
and when there will be gay marriages,
which will be paid for, in Lichfield Cathedral
and all the other cathedrals in England
and the rest of the United Kingdom,
in a liberal nation."*

Michael Fabricant, MP for Lichfield,
during questions to Caroline Spelman MP,
Second Church Estates Commissioner,
in the House of Commons, 5 May 2016.

PLAN OF PEPYNBRIDGE

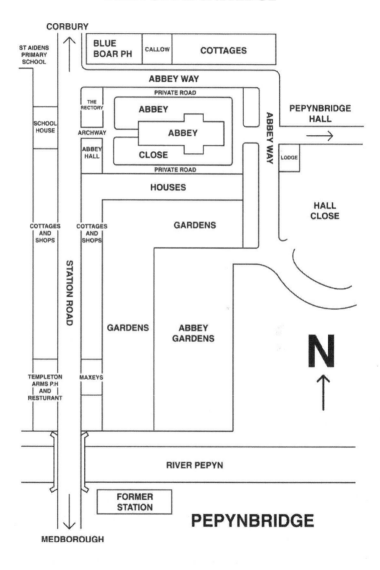

Acknowledgements

Creating *The Honourable Member for Pepynbridge* has required research into issues surrounding homosexuality and same-sex marriage, the attitude of the Church of England towards both, the passage of Private Members' Bills through the House of Commons, the organisation of Constituency Conservative Associations, the selection of Conservative prospective parliamentary candidates, and the cultivation of wheat. I acknowledge the assistance I have received from three publications in the public domain and individuals from whom I sought help in person.

Publications

William R Rice, Urban Friburg & Sergey Gavrilets, *Homosexuality as a Consequence of Epigenetically Canalized Sexual Development* (The Quarterly Review of Biology, Volume 87, No. 4, December 2012. The University of Chicago)
Alan Wilson, Bishop of Buckingham, *More Perfect Union? Understanding Same-Sex Marriage* (London. Darton, Longman & Todd. 2014)
Matthew Vines, *God and the Gay Christian* (New York. Convergent Books. 2014)

Individuals (in no particular order)

Bishop John Flack on an overview of the position of the Church of England on same-sex marriage; **Michael Ellis MP**, Member of Parliament for Northampton North and **Ray Boyd**, one-time Conservative Constituency Agent, on the process of selecting a Conservative prospective parliamentary candidate; and on local

7
The Honourable Member for Pepynbridge

Conservative constituency organisation; **Fergus Reid**, House of Commons Clerk, on the procedure regarding the passage of Private Members' Bills through the House of Commons; **Nigel Smith** on security issues; **Tim Webster**, Senior Cattle Auctioneer, Melton Mowbray Market; **Charles Rearden**, on career threatening injuries in rugby football; and correcting my French; **Len Brookes**, farmer, on wheat cultivation and the use of GPS; and **Charlie Harman** who kindly read and advised upon the passages that describe the thoughts and concerns of a homosexual contemplating the prospect of disclosing his sexual orientation to his family and the wider public.

My thanks are also owed to **Lionel Ross** of **i2i Publishing** for his continuing support; and to my wife, **Mary** for her patience and constructive comments on the draft of *The Honourable Member for Pepynbridge*;

8
The Honourable Member for Pepynbridge

PREFACE

The Honourable Member for Pepynbridge is the third novel in the Pepynbridge series.

As readers of one or both its predecessors will know, each addresses controversial social, religious and ethical issues within the environment of a quintessentially English rural community, Pepynbridge. *The Honourable Member for Pepynbridge* is no different, exploring, as it does, homosexuality and same-gender marriage, and the place of both within contemporary English culture and Christian thought and practice.

In all three novels, a vehicle was needed to harbour, articulate and act upon the prejudices, or strong oppositional views if the reader prefers, that invariably erupt when such issues are confronted within the wider community. In each novel, that vehicle is Alfred Wicken, a farmer in Pepynbridge.

I number farmers amongst my friends and whilst I have encountered the attitudes ventilated by Alfred Wicken in a number of folk, whom I decline to identify, I have never done so amongst my farming friends.

I should not wish it to be thought, therefore, that I suggest farmers are any the less sophisticated, tolerant and progressive than any other decent, fair-minded member of English society. In my experience, if anything the opposite is the case.

Peter Morrell
North-East Northamptonshire
3 August 2016

NOTE

Unless otherwise stated, times in the narrative before 27 March 2016 are in Greenwich Mean Time; and afterwards in British Summer Time. Times in France and Spain are stated to be in Central European Time ("CET"), which is always one hour ahead of Greenwich Mean Time and British Summer Time.

11

The Honourable Member for Pepynbridge

BILL

TO

Permit the Church of England to conduct marriages of same sex couples in accordance with its rites.

BE IT ENACTED by the Queen's most Excellent Majesty, by and with the advice and consent of the Lords Spiritual and Temporal, and Commons, in this present Parliament assembled, and by the authority of the same, as follows:—

1. Extension of same sex marriage according to religious rites: compulsion to solemnise

(1) Subsections (3) (4) and (5) of Section 1 of the Marriage (Same Sex Couples) Act 2013 are repealed.

(2) In paragraph 1 of Canon B 30 of the Seventh Edition of the Canons of the Church of England omit—

(a) "one man with a woman", and insert

(b) "one person with another person".

2. Amendment of Canon B 30 of the Seventh Edition of the Canons of the Church of England

(1) Omit paragraph 2 of Canon B 30 from the Seventh Edition of the Canons of the Church of England.

3. Extent, commencement and citation

(1) This Act extends to England only.

(2) This Act comes into force on the day on which it is passed.

(3) This Act may be cited as the Marriage (Same Sex Couples) (Amendment) Act 2016.

12
The Honourable Member for Pepynbridge

THE HONOURABLE MEMBER FOR PEPYNBRIDGE

PROPOSAL

Tuesday, 29 December 2015

"Pascal and I have decided to get married."

Rays of low, mid-morning, winter sunshine were straying obliquely into the Reverend Herbert Onion's study in Pepynbridge Rectory. They silhouetted the head and shoulders of the Rector, sitting behind his desk, his back to the east-facing window. They lit the finely drawn, clean-shaven features of Ralph Waters, QC, MP, sitting on one of two dark brown leather wing armchairs, placed obliquely in front and to each side of Herbert's desk. Wearing a light grey, two-piece, Givenchy wool-mohair suit, a pink cotton shirt and a dark blue silk tie, Waters' gaze was fixed on Herbert.

Aged fifty-five, Waters had been elected at the General Election of May 2015 as the Conservative Member of Parliament for the constituency of Pepynbridge Forest following the retirement of his well-regarded, septuagenarian, Conservative predecessor. In medieval times, Pepynbridge Forest had been a royal hunting forest. Now the constituency encompassed a stretch of rural East Midlands, just shy of the maximum permitted 5,000 square miles, comprising Corbury, with a population of around 10,000, several smaller towns, some fifty villages, the largest of which was Pepynbridge with some 2,000 residents, and isolated farms and hamlets.

In the other wing armchair, wearing magenta needle-cord trousers and a dark blue, roll-neck, cashmere sweater, sat Pascal Legrand, a retired *Top 14* French Rugby Union player. In his mid-thirties and black, Legrand's physique filled the chair. In shadow, his face was lost in the darkness of surrounding leather. Despite his bulk, he was trim and ran a fitness centre in Gray's Inn Road, London, bought and financed by his partner sitting opposite him.

Herbert looked at the lawyer and politician, weighing him up. By contrast with Legrand, Waters' figure barely occupied the wing armchair. Small, delicate and silver haired, Herbert noted fine and carefully manicured hands resting on the chair's leather arms. The announcement Waters had just made had been delivered in a forensically precise and lightly pitched tenor.

"Yes?" enquired Herbert, wondering what was coming and hoping it was not what he feared. But it was.

"Rector, Pascal and I would like you to marry us in the Abbey."

"Mr Waters…" started Herbert.

"Please call me Ralph," interrupted the other, pronouncing it "rayf".

"Thank you, Ralph, I shall. Ralph, in your position, surely you know that same-sex marriages cannot be solemnised by the Church of England."

"Indeed, I do, Rector…"

Herbert smiled.

The Honourable Member for Pepynbridge

"Ralph, please call me Herbie."

"Thank you, Herbie."

Waters' features failed to acknowledge the gentle humour latent in the exchange.

"I am well aware of the law," he continued. "Same-sex marriages in the Church of England are prohibited by a combination of Section One of the Marriage (Same Sex Couples) Act Two thousand and thirteen, and Canon B Thirty of the Canons of the Church of England."

Herbert nodded. Waters' familiarity with the legislation left him unsurprised by what followed.

"And Herbie, I am going to try and change the law."

"How?"

"By a Private Member's Bill I'm piloting through the House of Commons."

"But Ralph, when I was an ordinand, I was taught that Parliament does not legislate for the Church of England. It leaves that to General Synod."

"It usually does, Herbie. But only by convention. There is nothing to prevent Parliament from legislating independently for the Church of England. And that's just what I am about."

"Forgive me, Ralph, but are you doing that just for yourself..." Herbert paused, before adding, "...and for Pascal, of course?"

"No, Herbie. Certainly not. That would be an abuse of my position as a Member of Parliament. I'm doing it for all gay and lesbian Anglicans. It's totally unacceptable that the Church of England holds to the line it currently does on homosexuality, epitomised by its refusal to conduct same-sex marriages in church. Not only is it a scandal, but it runs counter to public opinion. Times have changed, Herbie. You know what the polls say?"

"Well, I've read about it in the papers and on-line. But, Ralph, you can remind me, I'm sure."

Waters reached inside the jacket of his exquisitely tailored suit and drew out a sheet of paper. Donning readers, he unfolded it.

"In two thousand and fourteen, a study by Ipsos MORI found that sixty-one percent of those intending to vote Conservative and fifty-four percent of those intending to vote UKIP supported same-sex marriage. And that, overall, sixty-nine percent of people in this country believe that gays should be allowed to marry. And that figure rises to eighty-eight percent of those polled aged between eighteen and thirty-four."

Waters re-folded the paper and restored it to the inner recess of his jacket.

"Herbie, I have been an observant Christian for as long as I can remember and an observant Anglican since I converted from Roman Catholicism at university. I still am."

Herbert nodded.

"Ralph, I know. You took communion in the Abbey at Midnight Mass last week."

"As did Pascal, Herbie. The Church of England is our national church. It's supposed to be for all our people. And yet, whilst you may welcome Pascal and me Herbie, institutionally the Church of England does not. In the light of the figures I've just read out, are you surprised that so few young people come to church?"

When in May 2014 Herbert had been inducted as the Rector of Pepynbridge, he had encountered a church community riven by differences over theology and liturgy. A group of life-long residents had been determined to continue the parish's tradition of *Book of Common Prayer* liturgy dating from the Restoration, it having previously sided with Parliament in the Civil War. There had been others in Pepynbridge who had chosen instead to worship in neighbouring parishes that used the contemporary Anglican rite of *Common Worship*. Sunday attendances in St Aidan's Abbey, Pepynbridge's parish church, were often in single figures. Its roof required repairs, estimated at a million pounds. The parish was failing and the diocesan bishop, Julian Ross, had told Herbert that it was his charge to rescue it. He was the parish's last chance. Herbert, wedded to Anglo-Catholic tradition and an outstanding musician, had re-established and trained up the choir and, helped by local solicitor and organist, Jack Driver, had introduced a choral High Mass on Saturday evenings. It had proved successful and Herbert had moved it to Sunday mornings, attracting ever burgeoning congregations. He continued to celebrate *Book of Common Prayer* Holy Communion earlier on Sunday mornings for the traditionalists. On Herbert's arrival in the parish, they had been referred to as The Puritan Tendency. More recently, they had become marginalised and had morphed into The

Puritan Remnant. As a result of Herbert's reforms, to the irritation of neighbouring parishes from which St Aidan's Abbey drew worshippers, its eleven o'clock Sunday morning High Mass was attended by hundreds, including many young people. On major festivals, there was barely room for everyone in a nave that seated 500. As Herbert had intended, the attraction of the Abbey's worship lay with the practised elegance of its liturgy and the outstanding quality of the music that accompanied it. Smaller village churches, less well resourced, struggled to attract congregations, particularly the young.

Herbert acknowledged that the Church of England's attitude to homosexuality was a hindrance. So was he surprised that, across England, young people were deterred from attending worship in Anglican churches?

"No, Ralph, I am not in the least surprised. And as I'm sure you're aware, the Archbishop of Canterbury is as concerned about it as you are. But, unlike the Pope, he can only do so much on his own initiative. A newly elected General Synod was inaugurated last November and will meet for its next session in February. Whether it will decide to go down the path of same-sex, or as I prefer, same-gender marriage remains to be seen. Only if it does, can the policy be changed."

"Unless my Bill succeeds."

"Unless your Bill succeeds. Will it, though?"

"Herbie, let me tell you something about the passage of a Private Member's Bill through the House of Commons. At the beginning of every new Session, there's a ballot to determine who may claim a Second Reading for a Private Member's Bill and in what order. For the current twenty fifteen to twenty sixteen Session, the ballot was held last June. I was drawn seventh, giving me a good chance of a Second Reading debate on my Bill. The First Reading, a mere formality, was in June. The Second Reading is crucial because, at that stage, any Member can talk it out. That's what often happens unless it has the open or tacit support of the Government. If a Member tries to talk a Bill out, its sponsor can call for a vote on it. Only if at least one hundred Members vote in support is the filibuster defeated and the Bill survives to go on to the Committee Stage. There it can be amended, but not defeated. After that, it comes back to the full House for its Report Stage and Third Reading, which often occur on the same day. If it passes then, it goes to the House of Lords, where it is subjected to a similar process."

Herbert nodded and smiled.

"So, at what stage is your Bill, Ralph?"

"The Second Reading will be on Friday, the twenty-second of January. If it passes, the Committee Stage will be some time in February and it should really complete its stages in the House of Commons by the eleventh of March."

"Why?"

"Because, Herbie, Parliament will be prorogued next May and my Bill must be passed by both Houses of Parliament by then to become law. Otherwise, it falls."

"Will it have been passed in both Houses by next May?"

The Honourable Member for Pepynbridge

"Herbie, impossible to predict. However, I have been informed that the Government is anxious for General Synod to address same-sex marriage again and, with a view to encouraging it to do so, it has decided to support my Bill, certainly through its Second Reading."

"Which it will survive?"

"Yes, it will. Conservative Members will learn through the usual channels that HMG is supporting my Bill and the necessary numbers will be whipped to defeat anyone intent on talking it out. With the help of a supportive speech from a Government minister during the debate, it will survive. Then it will go to Committee."

"And after that?"

"We'll have to see. If there is no time for it to be passed by both Houses in this Session and HMG continues to support it, then HMG might re-introduce it as a Public Bill in the new Session, which begins next May, and await the outcome of the meeting of General Synod in York at the beginning of July."

"Would the Government do that, Ralph?"

"Hard to say, Herbie. I just don't know but I hope so. That's all I can do."

"I understand."

Herbie drew a deep breath.

"So, Ralph, when do you wish to be married?"

"As soon as possible, Herbie. In fact, if my Bill survives its Second Reading, we should like you to consider whether to turn a blind eye to Canon Law and marry us in the spring. We would go thorough a civil ceremony first, but you could conduct a full formal marriage ceremony in the Abbey afterwards."

Herbert regarded Ralph Waters thoughtfully for a moment before, eyebrows raised, he switched his gaze to Pascal Legrand.

"Yes, Father," nodded the Frenchman, speaking softly in fluent, but faintly accented English. "That's right. That's what we want you to do for us, please."

Waters and Legrand stared expectantly at Herbert, who looked up at the Abbey, reflected in the looking glass above his study door through the window behind his desk, and pondered his legal responsibility as Rector. Finally, he lowered his gaze and glanced alternately at each of them.

"Ralph and Pascal, I shall have to consult. I have some sympathy for what you're asking me to do, but if I do it, and I'm not promising I shall, I need to carry my bishop and the Parochial Church Council with me."

Waters smiled and nodded.

"Thank you, Herbie. At this stage we can expect no more."

He paused and Herbert expected him to rise to leave, but instead Waters said,

"I gather a million pounds has been raised to repair the Abbey roof?"

As well as introducing more widely accepted worship, in 2014 and 2015, Herbert had arranged for two CDs to be recorded of recitals of sacred music by the choir, accompanied by organ and instrumentalists, which had been bought by the thousand, both on-line and from shops.

The Honourable Member for Pepynbridge

And he had introduced ticket-only concerts in the Abbey, which had sold out. By Christmas Eve 2015, five days ago, £950,000 had been raised, which had been made up to a million by Alistair and Augusta Templeton-Smith of Pepynbridge Hall, and by Alice Burton, Augusta Templeton-Smith's older half sister and a churchwarden, who lived in the nearby hamlet of Summerhay. Herbert had previously obtained quotations for the repair of the roof, and the authority of the Parochial Church Council to accept the lowest. In round figures it had been a million pounds and on Boxing Day, on behalf of the churchwardens, Herbert had emailed Corbury Construction, accepting its tender. That morning, before Waters and Legrand had come to see him, Herbert had received an email in reply. The work was to start in March and would last six months.

"Indeed. We have been very fortunate. The repair starts this spring."

"Will the Abbey be useable?"

"Oh, yes. You will remember, I think, that the nave and chancel have a stone-vaulted ceiling?"

Waters nodded.

"Well," Herbert continued, "it's the wooden and copper roof above it that requires restoration. The builders will erect a water-proof canopy over the Abbey. The work won't affect services beneath."

"And what's your next project, Herbie?"

Waters had informed himself of Herbert's achievements since Herbert had arrived in Pepynbridge and he correctly judged that the Rector was not one to let matters rest with the roof. The previous July, Herbert, together with Joshua Cohen, a friend from when they had studied together at the Guildhall School of Music and Drama and now an artist manager, had arranged for the second Choir CD to be recorded and marketed. One track had been the *Spatzenmesse* or Sparrow Mass by Mozart, for which Herbert had hired professional musicians to play the parts for trumpets, trombones, timpani and strings. To his and Jack Driver's irritation, the organ could not be used, because it was tuned to a pitch that was incompatible with orchestral instruments.

"Well, Ralph, since you ask, I should like to have the Abbey organ retuned."

"Why?"

"Why? Because the organ, which together with the choir stalls was installed in the late nineteenth century during a flirtation by the then rector with the Oxford Movement, is tuned a semi-tone higher than instruments used in orchestras or brass bands."

"Would retuning it be expensive?"

"It would Ralph."

"How much, Herbie?"

"I've been quoted just shy of a quarter of a million pounds."

"Herbie, if all goes well and you marry Pascal and me in Pepynbridge Abbey, I shall mark the occasion by paying for the retuning. You know that I can, don't you?"

Before his election to Parliament, Ralph Waters' practice had been in the Commercial Court in London, where the advocates' fees reflected the importance of the cases in which they appeared, disputes between international corporations, involving millions, sometimes billions of pounds, dollars or euros. Over his thirty years at the Bar, Waters had amassed a fortune which he had invested in London property and the fitness centre managed by Pascal Legrand. Herbert had learnt something of this from Gordon Slim, another barrister who lived in Pepynbridge.

"Ralph, I assume so from what I have heard about you. The household of God in Pepynbridge would be enormously grateful if you did. But let's just wait and see what can be arranged. All right?"

Waters and Legrand rose. Smiling, they shook hands with Herbert and left. As he returned from the hallway to his study, Herbert pondered. Was that a bribe? Yes, it was. Do I mind? No I don't. If that's the will of the Holy Spirit, why should I question it? But arranging their marriage in the Abbey was going to present a challenge. A serious challenge.

Herbert tapped numbers into the telephone on his desk and spoke in turn to his two churchwardens, Alice Burton in Summerhay and Richard Maxey, a retired general practitioner who lived in Pepynbridge with his wife, Mary, in a cottage towards the bottom of Station Road, near the River Pepyn. Outlining briefly the nature of the challenge with which he and they had been presented, they arranged to meet at Alice's the following Tuesday.

◆◆◆◆◆◆◆◆◆◆◆◆◆◆◆◆◆◆◆◆◆◆

The Honourable Member for Pepynbridge

New Year's Eve, 2015

Settled long before the Norman Conquest on the north bank of the gently-flowing River Pepyn, Pepynbridge is dominated by St Aidan's Abbey. When the Benedictine monastery was dissolved in 1538, the village was already sizeable and Thomas Cromwell, Lord Great Chamberlain and King Henry the VIII's chief minister, decided that, unlike other abbey churches in nearby East Anglia, St Aidan's should be left intact as its parish church. Built between the twelfth and fifteenth centuries, its massive square tower, standing proud above nave, chancel and side aisles, is visible for miles around. The Abbey sits in Abbey Close, bounded on the south by stone cottages, on the west by a long, Tudor brick- and stone-built building comprising the Rectory at one end and Abbey Hall, used for meetings, at the other, and on the north and east by Abbey Way. Opposite the Abbey's east end, through gates and past a lodge, a lime avenue leads from Abbey Way to Pepynbridge Hall. Built in the late sixteenth century by Francis Templeton, a courtier of Queen Elizabeth, its fifty metre wide, stone-built front, interrupted by two mullioned bay windows reaching up to its eves, is pierced by an imposing wooden door in the middle that opens into an entrance hall, two storeys high. Doors lead off left and right into reception rooms and a wide staircase ascends to a balcony along its back and sides, serving bedrooms and bathrooms. Double doors at the back of the entrance hall open into the Long Gallery, stretching the whole length of the ground floor. Beyond a ha-ha behind Pepynbridge Hall, lies the broad sweep of Hall Park, with a cricket square and a pavilion. Along a track to the left of the Hall and concealed by woodland, is Coronation Cottage, let to Ralph Waters and used by him at weekends as his constituency base.

Twice married, William Templeton, father of Alice and Augusta, had died without a son. When the Roman Catholic Alistair Smith had married Augusta, he had linked his surname with hers, hence Templeton–Smith, and the Anglican Augusta had converted to Rome. In the past, Alistair and Augusta had worshipped in a Roman Catholic church in the City of Medborough, the county town some 10 miles to the east of Pepynbridge and seat of its eponymous diocese. However, since Herbert had improved the liturgy in the Abbey as spectacularly as he had, Alistair and Augusta attended Anglican High Mass there every Sunday whenever they could. Blessed with four children, on their deaths and subject only to the impact of inheritance tax or its replacement, the future of Pepynbridge Hall and its estate, comprising several thousand acres, appeared secure.

As was their custom on New Year's Eve, Alistair and Augusta Templeton-Smith were hosting a dinner in the Long Gallery. A table had been set up, at which were sitting Alistair and Augusta, their children, Edgar, Joseph, Martha and Antonia, aged twenty-four, eighteen, sixteen and fifteen respectively, Alice Burton, Herbert and Julie Onion, Richard and Mary Maxey, and Gordon and Sylvia Slim. Next to Alistair, as guest of honour, sat Ralph Waters.

The Honourable Member for Pepynbridge

Pascal Legrand was at the other end of the table, flanked by Augusta and Edgar.

Crystal chandeliers shed soft light over crystal glasses, silver cutlery and Meissen china, and, on the walls, upon paintings dating from the seventeenth and eighteenth centuries. In pride of place was an El Greco collected by Francis Templeton's son, William, who had succeeded his father as a courtier, but to King James I. Conversation flowed with the wine, served with the food by Cyril the butler, assisted by caterers' staff hired for the occasion.

Alistair Templeton-Smith, aged forty-eight, tall, straight-backed, square-shouldered with long rectangular features crowned by thick black hair closely brushed to his scalp, had been commissioned in the Blues and Royals before joining an investment bank in the City of London, to which he commuted several days a week.

Augusta Templeton-Smith, aged forty-five, was shorter than her husband. Her friendly, pretty face, with amused blue eyes, a small straight nose, round cheeks and a generous mouth, was framed by thick, fair, wavy hair that coiled under her chin and around her neck. An enthusiastic and active member of Pepynbridge Tennis Club, her taut athleticism recalled her time as a county player.

Over the main course of roast partridge, stuffed with aubergine, basil and pine nuts, and accompanied by old claret, Waters mentioned to Alistair that he was sponsoring a Private Member's Bill through the House of Commons.

"Really? How interesting. And what does it set out to do, Ralph?"

The Honourable Member for Pepynbridge

As Ralph Waters explained, Alistair's features clouded and he weighed his response carefully. He had first met Waters after the General Election the previous May, when Waters had come to see him about renting Coronation Cottage. Alistair had learnt then that the MP was gay and that Pascal Legrand was his partner.

When Waters paused, Alistair, anxious to preserve social harmony, remarked,

"Ralph, you do know, don't you, that Augusta, our children and I are Roman Catholics?"

"Alistair, indeed I do. Although you were all in the Abbey on Christmas Eve for Midnight Mass."

"We were. We choose to worship there, because Herbie's liturgy is so beautifully executed. So much better than the dreary stuff on offer in our own churches in Medborough and Corbury. But because I worship in an Anglican church does not mean that I have abandoned my Roman Catholicism. And you know what Rome teaches about homosexuality, don't you?"

"Alistair, I do. I too was raised as a Roman Catholic. I converted at university when I realised that I was gay. The Church of England's record on tolerating homosexuality is not good as it demonstrated just the other day when the Bishop of Winchester refused the retired precentor of Salisbury Cathedral permission to officiate as a priest in the diocese because he'd married his male partner of thirty years. But Rome's attitude is a damn sight worse, as events last October demonstrated."

The Honourable Member for Pepynbridge

"You mean the sacking of that Polish priest in the Vatican just before the start of the synod that Pope Francis summoned on family issues? What was his name?"

"I do mean that. Krzysztof Charamsa was the priest. And I also mean that same synod's restated hostility towards same-sex marriage. Charamsa went on, you may remember, to embark upon a campaign to change the Church's teaching on homosexuality."

"But in coming out and demanding a change in the Church's attitude towards homosexuality, as he did at a press conference in Rome and later in his letter to the Pope that he released to the BBC, he went against the *Catechism of the Catholic Church*."

"Which pronounces that homosexual acts are, and I'm familiar with the text, 'acts of grave depravity' and 'intrinsically disordered'."

"Correct, Ralph. So you converted."

Waters nodded.

"And am I right in surmising you want to change the law against gay marriage in the Church of England so that you and Pascal can be married in church?"

"Well, not just us. I want to change the law for all gays and lesbians. But yes, we are hoping to be married in the Abbey."

As this exchange had progressed, the table had fallen silent.

Alistair looked at Herbert.

"Are you aware of this, Herbie?"

"Yes, Alistair, I am. Ralph and Pascal came to see me about it the other day."

"Problems, Herbie?"

"Big problems, Alistair."

"Not surprised. Let's have a straw poll. Do we think that same-sex marriages should be conducted in church? Augusta?"

"No, Alistair, I do not."

As Alistair enquired around the table, the division of opinion was generational. Alice Burton and the Maxeys, all in their seventies, were against. Gordon and Sylvia Slim, in their forties, declared themselves uncommitted. Tactfully Alistair did not ask Herbert Onion, but his wife of ten months, Julie, aged thirty-seven and head teacher at Saint Aiden's Church of England Primary School in Pepynbridge, was in favour. Leaving his own children to last, they provided Alistair and Augusta with an unexpected and unwelcome surprise. All four firmly supported the right of gay couples to be married in church in the same way as straights.

"You see, Alistair," said Waters, "that's just what public opinion polls disclose. Overwhelmingly, the young are in favour. Christian and secular young are anyway."

Alistair decided to change the subject and his conversation with Waters moved to the state of the Labour Party following the election of Jeremy Corbyn as its Leader.

At the other end of the table, Augusta turned to Pascal Legrand, admiring his massive presence, even greater than Edgar's. There was, she noted with an interest that she admitted to herself later, owed something to sexual attraction, a physical gentleness about him and a diffidence in his speaking.

"So, you used to play rugby, Pascal. Am I right?" Revealing two rows of perfectly set white teeth, Pascal's lips drew apart in a broad smile that lit up the whole of his face. Augusta suppressed a sudden erotic yearning with a smidgen of guilt. God, she thought, he may be black, but he's seriously beautiful.

"You are..." Pascal replied, adding after a barely perceptible pause, "... Augusta."

Alistair had established the use of first names with Ralph Waters and Pascal Legrand, but Pascal felt uncomfortable with it. He would have preferred to use surnames and, if he had been in France, "*vous*". Even today in France, polite people did not generally *tutoyer* each other beyond their circle of family and close friends.

"Who did you play for, Pascal?"

Pascal named a well-known club in South West France.

"It is one of the *Top Quatorze*," he added, helpfully.

Sitting on the other side of Pascal, Edgar Templeton-Smith observed his mother gently shaking her head and frowning quizzically.

"Mum, it's like the Aviva Premiership over here."

Augusta continued to shake her head.

"It's like the top division in a league."

"You mean, the best club sides, Edgar?"

"Yes, Mum, I do. The club Pascal played for is one of the best in France. But you never won a cap, Pascal?"

The Honourable Member for Pepynbridge

Now it was Pascal's turn to look puzzled.

"You never played for France?"

"No. Perhaps…but I suffered an injury to the neck and accepted medical advice to retire."

"Surgery?"

Pascal nodded.

"Are you okay, now?"

"Yes, Edgar. I already knew Ralph and when I recovered, we became partners. Now I am the *patron* of his fitness centre in London…"

"Pascal," broke in Augusta, "Edgar used to play rugby."

"Union?"

"Yes, Pascal," said Edgar.

Over drinks before dinner Pascal had noted Edgar's athletic frame, all of one metre ninety tall and carrying not a gram of surplus fat so far as he could see. Now he understood. It made sense. A scintilla of interest entered his mind. I wonder if he's gay. Probably not. But if he was…Pascal dismissed his train of thought.

"He won a Blue at Oxford," continued Augusta.

Now it was Pascal's turn to shake his head.

"He played for Oxford University, Pascal."

Pascal turned and, raising his eyebrows, he looked at Edgar.

"That's right, Pascal, I did. But when I came down…"

Pascal's brow knitted.

"…when I left Oxford," Edgar continued, "I gave up rugby to pursue a career in politics. Currently, I work in the

Conservative Research Department in Millbank. You know
where I mean?"

Pascal nodded. Some who came to his fitness centre
worked there.

"I'm looking to get elected to the House of Commons.
I've just been accepted onto the Approved List."

Pascal again looked puzzled.

"The list of people the Conservative Party has approved
to stand for Parliament," explained Edgar.

"Aren't you rather young? How old are you?"

"I'm twenty-four. But I wouldn't expect to be chosen for
a winnable seat first time round. More likely for a seat with
a big Labour majority. The next General Election will be in
twenty twenty, when I shall be twenty-eight. After that,
with luck, I'll be adopted in a safe seat and elected in
twenty twenty-five, when I'll be thirty-three. So not so
young by then."

"Have you got a..." Pascal paused, lost for the right
word.

"A constituency?"

Pascal nodded.

"No, but I'm applying for interviews and what with that
and my work in the Research Department, there's no time
to play rugby to the standard I should like."

"Pity!"

"It's a question of priorities."

"Ah, voilà. C'est toujours une question de priorités."

"Exactement."

"Please may we stick to English?"

"Of course, Mum."

"Did you learn French at university, Edgar?"

"No, Pascal, at school. I'm not that good at it. At Oxford, I read..." Edgar paused and substituted "...studied politics, philosophy and economics."

"And you got a First darling, didn't you?" announced Augusta proudly. Edgar smiled.

By now, pudding had been served with a sauterne and the meal drew to a close. Alistair did not follow his father's custom of inviting the women to leave while the men chatted over port, fruit and cheese. They all rose and went into an exquisite drawing room at the front of the Hall, appointed with eighteenth century furniture and a collection of paintings by George Stubbs and John Frederick Herring Senior, where vintage port and vintage brandy awaited. Cyril served them and Alistair turned on a television and set it to mute. Edgar and Pascal sat together on a sofa and discussed rugby union.

On another sofa, Sylvia Slim was telling Herbert and Julie Onion about the novel she was writing.

"It's an historical novel based on the life of a man called John Russell."

"Any relation to the dukes of Bedford?" asked Herbert.

"Yes. A direct ancestor and the founder of the Russell fortune. He came from Dorset, became very friendly with King Henry the Eighth and married a woman called Anne Sapcote who owned estates in this part of the world. When Henry dissolved the monasteries, the king parcelled out the monastic estates between himself and his favourites. John

Russell, as well as keeping his head, acquired more monastic land than anyone else except the king."

"But not this monastic land," said Herbert. "Pepynbridge, I mean."

"No, not this. I understand that was bought from Queen Elizabeth by Alistair's ancestor, William, the father of Francis Templeton, who built the Hall."

Herbert gestured at the walls of the drawing room.

"And the stones from the refectory and the cloisters are all around us,"

"And how is your novel coming along?" asked Julie Onion.

"I'm about half way through."

"Have you found a publisher yet?"

"No, Julie. It's very disappointing. I've sent a synopsis and, whenever invited, the first three chapters to dozens of publishers and agents, but I've only had rejections. Polite, but rejections all the same."

"I'd be interested in reading it."

"Really, Julie? How encouraging. When I've finished it, I'll print it off and drop it into the Rectory, if you like?"

"Yes, please Sylvia. I would like."

On a third sofa, Richard and Mary Maxey and Alice Burton were discussing Waters' request to be married by Herbert in the Abbey. They agreed that it was fraught with problems.

"And how will Alfred Wicken react?" asked Mary, referring to a local farmer, renowned for his bigotry.

Richard and Alice responded wordlessly, shaking their heads.

"Alice, you and I are meeting Herbie at the Mill to discuss it next Tuesday, aren't we?"

"Richard, we are. I shall be interested in Herbie's take on it."

Their conversation moved on.

Drawn together by their shared profession, Ralph Waters and Gordon Slim, each holding a cup of coffee, were standing and admiring a painting by Stubbs. After the usual exploratory sallies concerning their respective practices and sets of chambers, Gordon asked,

"The Commercial Court doesn't sit in August and September, does it Ralph?"

"Only to hear urgent applications, Gordon. I don't stay in London over the Long Vacation. Pascal and I spend all of August and the beginning of September in Spain."

"Oh, really?"

Gordon was not just being polite. He was and sounded interested.

Waters nodded.

"I own a house there."

"So do Sylvia and I."

"Where?"

"In the Marina Alta. In the mountains inland from Javea, Denia and Moraira."

"Know it well. My house is near Granadella."

The Honourable Member for Pepynbridge

Granadella is a small bay between Javea and Moraira, all but enclosed by steep, rocky cliffs, with villas built above it on a headland called Cabo de la Nao.

"Oh yes," acknowledged Gordon. "We've snorkelled in the bay."

"It's good for that. My house is built on a cliff a hundred metres or so above the sea. When you sit on my terrace, it's like being on the bridge of a ship. All you can see is the Mediterranean."

"Sounds lovely."

"It is. When do you go out there, Gordon?"

"Same time as you, Ralph. In August."

"You'll have to visit us. When I was at the Bar, we used to go out for a short break between the end of the Easter Term and the beginning of the Trinity Term. That roughly coincides with Parliament's Whitsun Recess from late May until the beginning of June. About ten days. This coming year, Pascal and I plan to go out then. What about you, Gordon?"

Gordon shook his head.

"No, Ralph. My practice is mainly in the Crown and County Courts where no heed is paid to legal terms. If my clerk gets it right, I shall be busy in court in May and June. But thank you, all the same. I'm sure Sylvia, Roger and I would like to meet up with you in Spain later in the summer. Out there, we're only about half an hour's drive away."

As they were exchanging email addresses and UK and Spanish telephone numbers, Alistair turned up the sound on the television and the chimes of Big Ben rang out. Cyril entered with a magnum of Pol Roger. Glasses were charged and drained, good wishes, hand-shakes and kisses exchanged and the guests departed, leaving the Hall to the family and staff.

♦♦♦♦♦♦♦♦♦♦♦♦♦♦♦♦♦♦♦♦♦

Monday, 4 January 2016

For longer than anyone alive could remember, there had been a pheasant shoot on the Pepynbridge Estate on the first Monday after Christmas. However, Monday, 28 December, had been a Bank Holiday and Alistair had given his estate staff, who doubled-up as shoot beaters, the day off, postponing the shoot to the first Monday in January.

It took place over land owned by the Templeton-Smiths and Alfred Wicken. Alfred's family had farmed in Pepynbridge for generations, which Alfred claimed reached back to the time of the Commonwealth. Apart from fattening a few steers, Alfred was an arable farmer. He rented some of the land he farmed from Alistair and let the sporting rights over his own fields and woods to Alistair. In return, as well as receiving rent, he was invited to join the Templeton-Smiths on their Christmas Shoot.

A heavily built man aged forty-two and of medium height, Alfred's face bore the legacy of excessive drinking since he had been a Young Farmer until the previous autumn, when he had cut down. Clad in tweed breeches, a green Schöffel shooting coat and tweed cap, he was standing with his back to a wood, staring up at a yellow

The Honourable Member for Pepynbridge

strip of ripe maize in front of woodland lining the skyline. It was overcast, with a fresh westerly breeze that would ensure that the pheasants would fly fast and curl, presenting good sport.

Alfred lived with his wife, Marigold, aged thirty-four, and their only child Sophie, aged sixteen, in a farm-house a mile outside Pepynbridge on the road to Corbury. After giving birth to Sophie, Marigold had been unable to have more children and Alfred, bitter that there would be no son to carry on the farm when he retired, had rejected Sophie, whose only interests, as she grew up, had been ballet and music. That had changed last year, when Sophie had fallen in love with a seventeen, now eighteen, year old South Asian, Ash Malik. In March 2015, Ash, together with his father, Abi Malik, a consultant psychiatrist, his mother, Sabi, and his younger sister, Leela, had moved into Abbey Gardens, Pepynbridge. After meeting Sophie and spending time with her on Alfred's farm, Ash had become utterly absorbed by farming and had resolved to go to agricultural college in September 2016, after taking A-Levels at Medborough Academy. Alfred, who numbered racism amongst his many prejudices, had found it hard to accept Ash at first, but when Ash and Sophie had announced they would marry as soon as Ash had finished college and that Ash wanted to carry on the farm, reluctantly Alfred had warmed to him.

Another factor that had assisted Alfred's grudging acceptance of Ash was that the previous September, terrorist outrages in England planned by an Islamist group calling itself *IstishhadUK* had been foiled when Ash, one of its recruits, had disclosed the plot, initially to Herbert Onion, and then to the police. Nineteen terrorists had been arrested and were now on remand in HMP Belmarsh, awaiting trial at Woolwich Crown Court, fixed for 6 June. In exchange for telling the police about the plot and agreeing to give evidence against the others, Ash had been granted immunity from prosecution. At the trial, he would be the principal witness for the Crown.

It had been partly the prospect of Ash marrying Sophie and carrying on the farm that had persuaded Alfred to moderate his excessive drinking. But there had been something else. Marigold had left him in December 2014 because of his abuse of alcohol and hostility towards Sophie. Changing both, he had correctly anticipated, might induce her to return, which she had done in September 2015.

Alfred belonged to the Puritan Remnant and was a member of the Parochial Church Council that was next to meet on Monday 18 January when Waters and Legrand's request to be married in the Abbey would be discussed. However, as Alfred stood waiting for pheasants to fly towards him, the agenda for the meeting had not been circulated and he had heard nothing about the proposed same-sex marriage.

Standing next to Alfred in the line of guns was Ash. Dark-skinned and of above average height, his lean, athletic frame was concealed by his shooting coat. Unlike the other guns, he was wearing no cap or hat. Thick black hair framed a broad forehead, dark brown eyes, an aquiline nose, a generous mouth and a pointed chin. Close behind Ash stood a middle-aged, open-faced man, dressed in outdoor clothing like everyone else. An armed police officer, Craig Miller was detailed to protect Ash from retaliation by Islamists for his betrayal of *IstishhadUK*. Although Ash had never shot live game before, before Christmas he had practised shooting clay pigeons behind Pepynbridge Farmhouse. The presence today of a trained firearms officer at his shoulder carried the additional benefit of ensuring that Ash would be safe with the shotgun Alfred had lent him, putting no one else present at risk of injury. The previous summer, when playing for Pepynbridge Cricket Club Firsts, Ash had demonstrated that he was an outstanding all-rounder and he had been offered a professional contract by Northants for 2016. With good hand to eye co-ordination, the other guns did not doubt that he would prove a competent shot.

A further incentive for Ash to be safe with the shotgun was the knowledge that Sophie, who had previously demonstrated no interest in either the farm or shooting, had today, for the first time in her life and as a gesture of her love for Ash, volunteered to be one of the beaters, who were now approaching the guns in the cover above them. As Ash watched and waited, gazing upwards, his mind went back to the afternoon last August, when he and Sophie had made love on the strip of mown grass between the maize and the wood and Ash had decided to marry Sophie, to farm, and to betray *IstishhadUK*. Something he had done shortly afterwards to Herbert Onion in his study at the Rectory.

The other guns were Alistair, Edgar, Joseph and Martha Templeton-Smith, Richard Maxey and Gordon Slim. Alistair had invited Ralph Waters, but the House of Commons was to resume sitting the next day and, accompanied by Pascal Legrand, Waters had returned to London. That had been his excuse, but Waters had rarely shot and not well when he had done, so he was relieved not to be a guest at Alistair's shoot.

The guns could hear the tapping of sticks and low calls of the beaters walking through the wood and the maize above them. Then came the whirr of the wings of a cock pheasant as it emerged from the bottom of the strip of maize and soared to clear the wood behind the guns. A crack rang out and it fell, shot dead by Alistair. More pheasants flew from the cover and sounds of more shots rang out. Some birds were missed. Injured ones were collected and despatched by pickers-up with dogs, waiting amongst the trees behind the guns.

A pheasant flew high towards Ash. As he had practised at clay pigeons, he raised his gun, swung through the bird until he could no longer see it beyond the end of the barrels and, continuing to swing, squeezed the trigger.

"Well shot, Ash," said Craig Miller quietly. "Stone dead."

◆◆◆◆◆◆◆◆◆◆◆◆◆◆◆◆◆◆◆◆◆◆

The Honourable Member for Pepynbridge

Tuesday, 5 January 2016

Early the next morning, Edgar Templeton-Smith parked his VW Golf in the long-term car park at Medborough Station and caught a train to Kings Cross to start work at Millbank at 9.00 a.m. As he journeyed south, Edgar thoughts turned to Ralph Waters and Pascal Legrand. On New Year's Eve, their presence in Pepynbridge Hall had unsettled him.

Although Edgar had dated girls at school and later at Oxford, the encounters had led nowhere and, after each, privately and with disappointment, he had acknowledged that his companion had not attracted him physically. The girls had been good-looking, as indeed he was. They had been enthusiastically receptive of him and good company, but even when a kiss had been shared, he had felt no hint of arousal.

And there'd been a boy at school, Tristram, with whom, from the age of fifteen, Edgar had embarked upon an intense and enduring relationship that had progressed to mutual sexual experimentation. It had aroused him physically in a way he had never experienced with a girl, but had bequeathed a legacy of guilt that his supposed faith had inhibited him from sharing with his confessor, and which had haunted him for a long time afterwards. When Edgar had left Beaufort School, he had broken off contact with Tristram, hoping that their relationship had been but an adolescent crush, but often since he had regretted doing so. There had been other boys at school to whom he had felt sexually drawn and, at Oxford, a rugby blue, tall, classically sculpted, dark haired with aquiline features and dark, almost black, eyes, to whom he had once made a tentative approach, brusquely rebuffed.

His blue eyes stared out of the carriage window from a face resembling Alistair's, rectangular, square jawed, with a straight nose and broad forehead, but, in Edgar's case, crowned by an unruly shock of thick, blond hair, inherited from Augusta. On New Year's Eve, Edgar acknowledged, he had been erotically drawn to Pascal Legrand and this morning, reluctantly, he finally concluded that his sexual preference was not, and never would be, for the opposite gender. That left him with a choice. Either celibacy, or an intimate relationship with a man. For the moment, he was content with the former, but could not foresee how long that would suffice. He sighed deeply and turned his attention back to *The Daily Telegraph* that he had bought at Medborough Station.

Edgar had been at his desk for two hours, when Herbert Onion and Richard Maxey separately drove to Summerhay, arriving at Alice's within moments of each other. Alice Burton, Augusta's older half-sister and widow of John, a career diplomat, had spent most of her married life abroad. There had been no children and, twelve years previously, when John Burton had died, Alice had transferred her half interest in Pepynbridge Hall to Augusta. Since then Alice had lived in a converted watermill spanning the River Pepyn at Summerhay, some two miles to the south of Pepynbridge and reached down a narrow lane from the main road to Medborough. As well as the Mill, bought by Alice and John as their English retreat, Alice owned the four cottages that, together with the Mill, made up the hamlet of Summerhay, as well as several acres of land and woods to the east of the Mill, bordering both banks of the River Pepyn.

The front door of the Mill opened to reveal a tall, slim, elegant figure. Aged seventy-two, Alice Burton's grey, naturally wavy hair framed strong features, piercing blue eyes, a wide, narrow-lipped mouth and skin rendered leathery by over-exposure to the tropical sun.

"Good of you to come. Do come in."

The voice was deep and richly melodious.

Herbert and Richard followed her upstairs to a room on the first floor of the Mill that extended its whole length. Once the milling hall, it was now a drawing room and study, with a large desk and chair at one end and, at the other, two sofas facing each other across a low table. Stairs led up to bedrooms and bathrooms. A big window looked out onto the River Pepyn, flowing slate grey under a leaden sky. A tray laden with a silver coffee pot, a jug of milk, a bowl of sugar and china cups and saucers lay on the table between the sofas.

"Coffee? Yes? Milk and sugar?"

They sat back on the sofas, cradling cups of coffee.

"This," started Alice, "is not going to be easy."

"If you would permit me to say so, Alice," observed Richard Maxey drily, "that must be the understatement of the year."

The Honourable Member for Pepynbridge

The others smiled at him. The same age as Alice and wearing the dependable manner of the respected general practitioner he had been before he had retired and moved to Pepynbridge, Richard Maxey's bulky frame recalled the days when, as a medical student, he had played rugby for his hospital. True, his ruddy features betrayed some additional weight, his blue eyes half buried in creases of flesh, but he rightly regarded himself as reasonably fit for a man his age.

By contrast, Herbert, aged forty-one, was slightly built. Under a tangle of black curls, dark brown eyes were magnified by outsize black-rimmed spectacles, below which a slender nose led down to full lips and a narrow chin. It was the sensitive face of an artist or, Alice sometimes reflected, even of a saint, given how calmly Herbert had coped with all that fate had thrown at him since his arrival in Pepynbridge in May 2014.

"Well, Herbie," enquired Alice. "What's your position on Ralph Waters' request?"

"Alice, instinctively I'm sympathetic. I've not had to think seriously about what I prefer to term same-gender, rather than same-sex, marriage before. I've been on-line and discovered two books that deal with it. One was written by the Bishop of Buckingham, a man called Alan Wilson, and the other by an American called Matthew Vines. I've ordered both and I really need to read them before making up my mind. I hope to do so before the PCC meeting on the eighteenth of January and before I approach the bishop. But, as I say, instinctively I'm sympathetic."

"Some won't like it," observed Alice firmly. "Not Alfred Wicken, nor his father Reg, nor Peggy."

Peggy Taplow was a single woman in her seventies who farmed outside the village.

"And probably not Norman, either," she added.

Norman Callow, head teacher at St Aidan's Church of England Primary School for forty years, had retired in 2012 to a cottage in the village.

"The Puritan Remnant," cut in Herbert, gloomily.

"Yes," said Alice. "I hope we can be rid of them at the next PCC elections, but at the moment, we're stuck with them."

"When are they up for re-election?" asked Richard Maxey.

"At the Annual General Meeting, Richard. That will be…"

Alice rose, went to her desk, collected a diary, returned and flicked though it. She found the page she was looking for.

"…on Sunday, the twenty-fourth of April in the Abbey after Sung Eucharist."

"Can't we postpone the issue of same-sex marriage until after then?"

"No, Richard. It has to be addressed now. Don't you agree, Herbie?"

"I do, Alice. It would be wrong, in my view, to keep Ralph and Pascal waiting until the end of April. We owe it to them to try and sort something out sooner."

"Well, Richard, as you made clear at the Templeton-Smiths, you're not in favour."

"Alice, it's not that I'm hostile. It's just that I'm not persuaded. On New Year's Eve, that was my instinctive and immediate reaction. I am, I hope, a reasonable, pragmatic sort of chap with an open mind and I've thought about it a bit since then. However, try as I might, at the moment I cannot reconcile myself with it. Scripture is against it. And I'm seventy-two now…"

"Same as me," interrupted Alice.

Richard smiled and continued,

"Until nineteen sixty-seven, homosexual acts even in private were criminal in England and Wales. And, I seem to recall, even later than that in Scotland and Northern Ireland. At my preparatory and public schools, homosexuality was not tolerated. The head of my single-sex public school used to say, as he put it, that 'anyone caught mucking about with his own or anyone else's body', would be sacked. I appreciate it's widely accepted now, but I still have a problem with it. I am aware that sexual preference is largely innate, although recent research in America suggests that environmental elements during childhood may also contribute. My psychiatric colleagues tell me that it's incurable clinically and the Royal College of Psychiatrists disapproves of so-called conversion therapy. Nevertheless, I can't get over the fact that Genesis makes it clear that men and women were created to complement each other and not those of the same gender."

"And I'm not persuaded either," observed Alice firmly.

The Honourable Member for Pepynbridge

"Look," said Herbert, "I suggest that I do some research and then we'll discuss it again. The next PCC meeting is on the eighteenth of January and I am duty bound to put Waters and Legrand's request on the agenda. Do you agree?"

Alice and Richard did.

"I'll read those books before then, but whether we have a full-blown discussion on the eighteenth is something I'd like to think about. It might be better afterwards."

"What, straight afterwards, Herbie?"

"No, Alice. If I think it would help, I might suggest that everyone, who wants to, reads the books I've mentioned and then we can discuss it at a later date."

"Sounds sensible to me, Herbie," said Richard Maxey.

"I agree," added Alice Burton.

They continued to chat for a while before Herbert and Richard left. As they walked to their cars, Richard enquired, "I'm right, Herbie, aren't I? Scripture is against it?"

"On the face of it, it is, Richard, but I've read somewhere that the relevant passages in the Old Testament may have been misinterpreted."

"Misinterpreted?" Richard's voice rose with mild incredulity. "And what about what Saint Paul says about it?"

"To be treated with caution, Richard. He'd been a Pharisee and may merely have been adopting or repeating what the Hebrew Bible said about it. Give me time to look into it, okay?"

"All right, Herbie."

They climbed into their cars and drove back to Pepynbridge.

◆◆◆◆◆◆◆◆◆◆◆◆◆◆◆◆◆◆◆◆◆

Friday, 8 January, 2016

Ralph Waters was sitting in a Parker Knoll armchair opposite his mother. Perched on a Windsor chair, Elsie Waters was eighty, slim and short, with neat features that reflected Ralph's, silvery wavy hair and bright, kind, green eyes. She was wearing a close-fitting cashmere jumper and blue slacks that emphasised a still elegant figure, and black court shoes on tiny feet.

It was just after 11.00 a.m. Between mother and son, a low table bore two cups of coffee and a plate of cupcakes. A window looked out across a sunlit lawn to a large, brick-built, country house. Elsie Waters had lived for five years in her custom-built, modern bungalow, with its small combined sitting and dining room, tiny kitchen, double bedroom and en-suite shower. It was one of twenty, clustered like satellites about Temple Grange, a newly-rich merchant's mansion built in 1895 in extensive grounds on the outskirts of Saint Albans. A restaurant, television lounge, hairdressing and cosmetic salon, library and indoor plunge pool were sited within the mansion, which was also home to a permanent staff of nurses, carers, cleaners and cooks, who looked after their mainly elderly clients, as they were taught to call them.

Elsie Waters was twenty-five years older than Ralph, her only child, whom she had raised following the death of his father in a road accident when Ralph had been just five years old. Elsie had not remarried and, during her long widowhood, the bond between mother and son had deepened.

"So, how's it going, Ralph?"

"Well thanks, Ma."

Elsie had greeted the knowledge that Ralph was gay, disclosed to her by him when he was at university, with mixed feelings, feelings that had endured. There was a part of her that would have welcomed a new generation of Waters, but another that did not relish sharing Ralph with another woman. She had come to accept Pascal, whom she knew was outside in Ralph's car, although she was unhappy that he was black and appreciated her son's sensitivity in minimising contact between them.

Ralph, who visited his mother most Fridays, but had not done so on New Year's Day, described the dinner party he and Pascal had attended at Pepynbridge Hall on New Year's Eve.

"Sounds pretty posh to me, Ralph," commented Elsie when Ralph had finished.

Ralph smiled, privately acknowledging the shared history that lay behind her remark. His parents' circumstances had been modest. Derek, his father, had been employed as a borough clerk in South London. Elsie had worked as a secretary in the same office before the birth of their son.

Following the death of Derek Waters, the proceeds of a generous life assurance policy had funded Ralph's education at a private Roman Catholic day school. At eighteen, Ralph's prodigious intelligence had won him a scholarship to Oxford, where he had read Law, graduating with a first class honours degree. Thence had been but a small step to a prestigious set of chambers in Lincoln's Inn, specialising in commercial law, where, following a pupillage, Ralph's rise had been meteoric. He was gifted, his head of chambers had once remarked, with "rocket factor". Courteous but never obsequious towards his wealthy and powerful clients, the incisive ferocity of his advocacy, when he needed to deploy it, intimidated opponents and he was much sought after. Appointed Queen's Counsel at thirty-five, Ralph had spent the next twenty years earning millions, before he had tired of it all. Unbeknown to his contemporaries at the Bar and on the Bench, Ralph Waters had long been a generous giver to numerous charities, his favoured one being the Saint Martin in the Fields Christmas Appeal for the homeless in London. Having amassed a fortune, his instinct for public service had induced him to try his hand at national politics. The Conservative Party had greeted his application to go onto its Approved List with delight and, on 7 May 2015, it had been an easy ride for Ralph Waters to succeed the retiring Member for Pepynbridge Forest.

"Why become an MP?" Elsie had asked him after his adoption.

"Because I've had a lot of fun at the Bar and accumulated a lot of money and I think it's time I put something back into a society that's treated me as well as it has. And anyway, after over thirty years in practice, I'm bored with the Bar. And I've no wish to go on the Bench."

"But won't being gay worry you as an MP, darling?"

"No, I don't think so. Since you were young, Ma, times have changed."

Elsie Waters had nodded knowingly. He was a good boy, was her Ralph. After all, he paid the £1,000 a week it cost to keep her at Temple Grange as well as settling her monthly bill for meals in the restaurant when she ate there, rather than cooking for herself. She didn't know why he was gay. She was unaware there was an innate element in sexual orientation and hoped that it was nothing she had done that had brought about his gayness. But then she mused, not for the first time, perhaps it's not such a bad thing. He's happy and so am I, so why worry?

Ralph and Elsie chatted as they sipped coffee and nibbled cupcakes until, at noon, Ralph glanced at his watch and rose.

"Well, Ma. Time to be off."

"Yes, darling. Same time next Friday?"

"Of course."

She rose, agile for her years. As she had done ever since he had been an infant, Elsie took her son's now silvery crowned head between her palms and kissed him on the lips.

"Take care, won't you, darling?"

"Shall do, Ma. You too."

Ralph left the bungalow and climbed into the front passenger seat of the Range Rover parked outside.

The Honourable Member for Pepynbridge

"Thanks, Pascal."

"To Pepynbridge, Boss?"

"To Pepynbridge, Pascal."

Ralph liked Pascal Legrand calling him "Boss". It reflected both the status of their relationship and the affection that underpinned it. Pascal drove out of the grounds of Temple Grange and, after a few miles, joined the A1 at Hatfield and headed north.

Since Alfred Wicken had turned over a new leaf in August 2015, he only went to the pub on Friday evenings and Sunday lunchtimes, although he still enjoyed a generous whisky every evening before bed. Daily since his teens, Alfred had frequented the Blue Boar on the corner of Station Road and Abbey Way in Pepynbridge. He had not been discouraged from doing so by his father, Reginald, aged seventy-one, who was sitting with Alfred at their usual table in a corner of the bar. With watery blue eyes beneath a thatch of wiry, tightly-curled, grey hair, Reginald's rust coloured features bore witness to the life-long heavy drinking that had served as an example to his son.

The third man at the table was Norman Callow. Aged sixty-nine and widowed four years previously, he was thin and sad-faced, with a few strands of sandy hair carefully arranged across a shiny scalp. His left eye was slightly lower than his right, his mouth sagged to the left and his speech was faintly distorted, legacies of a minor stroke he had suffered the previous year. For a while, Herbert and

The Honourable Member for Pepynbridge

Julie Onion had wondered whether they should arrange for Norman to live in a care home, but there was iron beneath Norman's skin that had driven an adequate recovery and he was now well able to look after himself.

"What do you think of our new MP, Son?"

"Bloody hell, Dad, he's a queer. Bent. Blokes like that should be strung up."

Alfred paused briefly, before adding,

"After their balls have been chopped off. And you know what, Dad?"

"What's that, Son?"

"I'd chop them off myself if I had the chance."

"What do you think, Norman?"

"Reg, like you, I'm of the generation that finds the modern attitude to homosexuality hard to take."

Norman's laboured way with words betrayed the pedagogue he had been most of his adult life.

"I'm afraid I agree with Alfred," said Reg. "For me it's not a question of 'hard to take'. I simply can't abide it."

Norman Callow decided to disengage.

"And you know what?" Alfred's voice rose, thick with anger. "What's worse is that our MP's got a wog boyfriend. Have you seen him? Bloody great nigger, he is, straight out of the jungle."

Norman Callow's instinctive liberalism could not let that pass.

"Alfred," he protested, "he's a Frenchman."

"That makes it worse, not better."

"When he was younger, he was a top class rugby union player…" Callow paused, before adding, "…in France."

"So what? He's black and he's a bugger."

"Alfred," called the landlord from the bar, "watch your language, please."

"Sorry, Fred."

"Well, Alfred," observed Norman Callow wryly, "the moderation of your drinking doesn't seem to have affected your…" he toyed with "bigotry", but instead substituted "…outlook on the world."

"Norman, there were good reasons last year to change how I behaved, but none to change what I think."

Norman and Reginald remained silent. They knew that Alfred's reform had been driven by his wish to persuade Marigold to return to live at the farmhouse as well as by the fact that Sophie's South Asian boyfriend, Ash, offered the only hope of continuing the Wicken family farm. But Alfred left them in no doubt that he had not abandoned his long-held and floridly expressed prejudices.

Alfred took their empty pint glasses to the bar to be refilled. When he returned to the table, the talk turned to farming and politics. Like many other arable farmers, Alfred Wicken's harvest in 2015 had been high yielding, but the prices he had received had failed to cover the cost of production.

"It's being in Europe," Alfred announced.

"How's that, Alfred?"

"Norman, if we weren't in Europe, our Government could subsidise production. Pay us so much a ton to cover the cost of cultivation with a bit more to reward us. But the CAP doesn't do that."

"But there are subsidies, aren't there?" objected Norman Callow.

"Yes, but they're bloody complicated and pay no attention to the prices we receive. It's the prices that should be subsidised."

"But, Alfred," protested his father, "we're producing too much food in the world."

"Yes, I agree Dad. But relying on food from Russia and places like that will be no bloody good when every farmer in England has gone out of business."

"True, Son."

"We need to win this referendum to get out of Europe."

"There," observed Norman Callow, "I'm inclined to agree with you."

"So do I," added Reg.

"I've joined UKIP, you know," said Alfred.

The others nodded. They'd heard it before from Alfred.

"Last November. Went on-line and joined. On the Wednesday before Christmas, I went to a joint meeting of the Pepynbridge Forest and Medborough Branches in Medborough. It meets in Medborough on the fourth Wednesday of the month. Nice crowd. Hearts in the right place."

"Better than the pub, Alfred?"

"Yes, Dad, much better. And I'll tell you this. Since Labour went off its trolley and chose that chap...what's his name?"

The Honourable Member for Pepynbridge

"Jeremy Corbyn, Alfred?"

"Yes, that's him, Norman. Since they chose him as Leader, support for UKIP in this constituency has been rising. If anything happened to that ponce, Waters, UKIP reckons it would win a by-election, especially if it occurred before the EU Referendum. And that would give a boost to the Leave.EU campaign. I've been on-line and joined that as well."

Callow was unsure whether he followed Alfred's logic, but what he said was,

"What do you mean, 'if anything happened to that ponce, Waters'?"

"Oh, just speculation," sighed Alfred. "Mind you..."

He gazed ruminatively at the bottles mounted on optics behind the bar, but decided not to add to what he had said.

Reginald Wicken observed his son and wondered about him. Alfred was apt to fall prey to impetuosity, as a disastrous foray into dairy farming in the noughties had proved. He wouldn't put it past him to do something stupid, but maybe what he had been saying about Waters had just been beer talk. He hoped so and decided to move the conversation on.

"How are things doing on the farm, Son?"

"Oh, not too bad so far. We'll have to see..."

Alfred's voice tailed off, although he was not entirely clear in his own mind whether he was referring to his crops or to Ralph Waters QC, MP.

It was past closing time when Alfred climbed into his Land Rover Discovery and drove an exaggeratingly careful course the mile or so along the Corbury road to Pepynbridge Farm. Marigold was accustomed to her husband arriving home from the pub the worse for wear. She couldn't imagine how he had never been caught when he drove back from the Blue Boar. Perhaps because the local police were almost invisible, what with cuts in their resources and staff. But at least Alfred only arrived home drunk now on Fridays and Sundays and she tolerated that. By the time he arrived, she was in bed, feigning sleep to avoid an alcohol-fuelled and unconsummateable romp. She listened to him unsteadily mounting the stairs. No romping tonight, she thought with relief and, as Alfred noisily cleaned his teeth in the shower-room adjoining their bedroom, she fell asleep.

◆◆◆◆◆◆◆◆◆◆◆◆◆◆◆◆◆◆◆◆

Sunday, 10 January 2016

Following High Mass, coffee and chat in the Abbey, the six Templeton-Smiths, together with Ralph Waters and Pascal Legrand, walked out of Abbey Close, across Abbey Way and down the lime avenue to Pepynbridge Hall. As they approached the front door, Ralph Waters turned to Edgar Templeton-Smith.

"Edgar, we're driving back to London this afternoon. Would you like a lift?"

Edgar thought: It won't matter if the Golf isn't at Medborough Station next Friday. There's a bus I can catch from Medborough to Pepynbridge.

"That's very kind of you, Ralph. What time?"

"We'll be leaving at four."

That would give Edgar time to have lunch in the Hall.

"What are you doing for lunch, Ralph?" asked Alistair.

"We'll have a snack at the cottage and a proper meal when we get back to London. That way, there's no problem about one of us driving. If that was an invitation Alistair, thank you. But no, I hope you understand."

"Perfectly," replied Alistair, relieved. He did not want Waters and Legrand to become regular Sunday features at the Hall.

"Okay, Ralph. I'll be at Coronation Cottage by four."

"No, no, Edgar. We'll pick you up from here."

They had reached the front of the Hall and so it was left.

At 4.00 p.m. Edgar climbed into the back of Waters' Range Rover. As Pascal drove south, there was little conversation, but at Apex Corner Waters twisted around and asked Edgar where he lived.

"I share a house with friends in Clapham. And you?"

"We live in Barton Street, behind Westminster Abbey. Why don't you stay with us tonight? We'll be going to a little restaurant in Victoria Street. You don't have to eat much if you don't want to, but we could chat and I'd like that. We can lend you pyjamas and things."

Edgar's mental antennae quivered. This, he thought, may be an opportunity I should not miss.

"Thank you, Ralph. I'd like that too."

Later they were sitting at a table in a small Spanish restaurant in Victoria Street, a hundred yards or so from the marble and stone column opposite the west entrance of

The Honourable Member for Pepynbridge

Westminster Abbey, designed by George Gilbert Scott to remember the alumni of Westminster School who had fallen in the Crimean War and Indian Mutiny.

"How do you like working in the Research Department, Edgar?"

"Oh, it's alright."

Edgar paused, sensing a fly may have been cast over him. Well, no harm in rising to the bait, if that's what it was.

"Actually, to be frank, Ralph, it's pretty boring. All routine stuff. Analysis of policy options, that sort of thing. But miles removed from what's actually happening at the political coal-face."

"Edgar, I've had a word with one of the Party's vice-chairmen. You're well regarded. Bright, interested and, when the situation requires, refreshingly original. You're not likely to be elected next time, but if you play your cards right, you could be in the Commons by twenty twenty-five. You don't need to continue in the Research Department to achieve that. How does becoming my parliamentary assistant grab you?"

So, I was right, thought Edgar. It had been a fly. And a welcome one, too.

"Ralph, that's tempting, but what about the Research Department? I don't want to let the people there down."

"Don't worry about that, Edgar. I've spoken to Angus and you would come to me with his blessing."

Angus Morris was the Party vice-chairman in the Research Department to whom Edgar reported and who supervised his work. If Angus had given Ralph a green light, then it should be all right. But Edgar thought: I'd better check with Angus myself, just to make sure.

"Thank you, Ralph. Could you just give me a day or two to think about it and to take advice?"

Edgar's caution impressed Waters. He'll go far, he thought, if handled aright.

"Of course, Edgar. Shall we say by Friday?"

"Fine by me."

They ate for a while in silence before Waters broke it.

"Edgar, forgive me for being personal, but it's a good idea to know something about those who work with me. Have you got a girlfriend?"

Edgar forked his last mouthful of *cerdo iberico al horno* past his lips and chewed, conscious of the gaze of his companions upon him. They're both gay and may suspect that I am too, he thought. Well, maybe this is the time for me to say so. And maybe these are the guys to tell. He swallowed the mouthful.

"No, Edgar, I don't…" he paused, then added, "…and I'm not likely to. I'm gay."

As the words left him, relief flooded through him. There, he'd said it. For the first time. It was out. Out at last. But what would these two do with it? He looked at Waters, who was smiling sympathetically.

"That was hard for you to say, wasn't it, Edgar?"

Edgar nodded.

"First time?"

Edgar nodded again.

"Did you suspect me?"

"We wondered."

"Will it matter?"

"Not at all," replied Waters. "Look at me. Attitudes have changed vastly over the past few years. There are Members of the House of Commons who are openly gay, including some Government ministers. It'll do you no harm at all. Better to be open about it than trying to dissemble. If you try to cover it up, then after you're elected, whenever that happens, the Press will accuse you of being less than frank with your electorate. Got a boyfriend?"

Edgar shook his head.

"No, celibate."

"Ever had a boyfriend? Any skeletons in the cupboard?"

"No, none."

"What did you tell the Parliamentary Assessment Board?"

Waters was referring to the body comprising senior Conservative Party volunteers and MPs that decides whether an aspirant candidate has, or has the potential to have, the skills and aptitude looked for by the Conservative Party to make a good MP. If the candidate passes the Board, their name is added to the Approved List of Conservative Candidates.

"I wasn't asked."

"What, not at all?"

"No. I was asked if I was married or was planning to marry and I said, truthfully, that I was not. That's all. If you don't mind me asking, Ralph, did the Board ask you?"

"Didn't need to. I came out years ago and, as a high profile QC, it was public knowledge. Okay, Edgar…"

Waters passed a card across the table.

"…give me a ring or email me by Friday?"

"Will do."

"And if you're up for it, we'll meet and discuss terms, pay and things like that."

A waiter approached the table, cleared away the empty plates and left menus for the next course.

♦♦♦♦♦♦♦♦♦♦♦♦♦♦♦♦♦♦♦♦♦

Monday, 11 January 2016

Gordon and Sylvia Slim had moved from London to Pepynbridge in 2014. Both were tall, slim and good-looking. Whilst Gordon was fair-skinned, fine-featured, blond and blue-eyed, by contrast Sylvia's colouring was Mediterranean. Thick, long, dark hair tumbled around an oval, olive coloured face, with dark eyes, a straight nose and generous mouth. They were deeply fond of their only child, Roger, and were sad that their attempts to have more had not born fruit. Now that Sylvia was forty, it was becoming less and less likely. They had considered, but rejected adoption. Roger was a dayboy at Corbury School, ten miles west of Pepynbridge, to which Sylvia took him every week-day and Saturday mornings during term-time and from which she collected him each afternoon, or occasionally in the evening if Roger was involved in after-school activities. Gordon's practice was on the South

Eastern Circuit and tonight, as he did whenever he needed to, he would be staying in the flat he rented in Gray's Inn.

On this Monday morning, when Sylvia arrived home from Corbury and stepped through the front door of their five-bedroom, modern house in Hall Close, she collected a pile of envelopes from the doormat. As well as junk mail, there was an A4 white envelope that felt bulky and was embossed with the name of a publisher to whom she had submitted a synopsis and the first three chapters of *A Tyrant's Best Friend* just before Christmas. Sylvia went into the kitchen, threw away the junk mail, made herself a Nespresso coffee and took it and the envelope to where her laptop lay on the kitchen table.

She sat down, took a sip of coffee and, opening the envelope with a kitchen knife, drew out a letter addressed to her and a stapled wad of paper. As she read the letter, warmth spread through her. They liked her novel. They believed it would sell well and they were prepared to publish it. A contract was enclosed. But when Sylvia read the contract, the warmth evaporated. As well as the usual clauses about ownership of copyright and the like, the publisher would only proceed when she returned the contract signed, accompanied by the complete typescript and a cheque for £7,000.

Sylvia suppressed an urge to scream and finished her coffee, deep in thought. Then she tapped Herbert's number into her mobile.

"Hello? Reverend Onion, Rector of Pepynbridge."

"Hello Herbie, it's Sylvia."

"Oh, hello, Sylvia. How can I help?"

"Herbie, do you know anything about publishing?"

"Books or music, Sylvia?"

"Books."

"Well, I know a bit about publishing music, but not books. Why do you ask?"

Sylvia explained about her novel, the offer she had received that morning and the price being demanded.

"Herbie, do you think I should accept?"

"Sylvia, if you don't mind, I'd rather not discuss this over the phone. Why not drop over and we can have a chat. I'm free until twelve."

It was a short walk from Hall Close to the Rectory and ten minutes later Sylvia was sitting in a wing armchair across from Herbert behind his desk.

"Yes, Sylvia?"

Still sitting, Sylvia twisted and leant across the desk towards Herbert, proffering him the large white envelope. As Herbert reached forward to take it from her, Sylvia's sensuous, olive beauty recalled Roger. Not as Roger was now, but as he had been when, in July 2014 and aged thirteen, Herbert had first set eyes on him. His mind went back to that evening in the Abbey when he had been overwhelmed by an androgynous beauty he had never previously encountered in a boy. Suddenly, it was not Sylvia, but the younger Roger looking at him, expectantly holding out the envelope, and Herbert experienced once again the barely manageable compulsion to enfold the boy in his arms that had plagued him all that summer and autumn.

"Herbie, the contract is in here."

With an impatient shake of his head, Herbert recovered the present. Roger was fifteen. His voice had broken and he was nearly as tall as his father. Conscious of his enduring predilection for young boys, Herbert rejoiced that Roger's pre-pubescence was but a distant memory. He had grown handsome and would attract to be sure, but not Herbert. With a deep breath, Herbert took hold of the envelope.

"Thank you, Sylvia."

Sylvia watched as Herbert removed and read its contents. Then he looked up.

"As I told you, Sylvia, I know nothing about book publishing, but Josh may be able to help. Remember him?"

Sylvia nodded.

Herbert tapped a number into a telephone on the desk and put the handset to his ear.

"Josh? Hi, it's Herbie. You all right?" A pause, then, "Yes, fine thanks. Got a moment?" Another pause. "You have? I wonder if you could help a friend of mine." Herbert went on to explain. There followed a longer pause while, Sylvia guessed, Cohen was talking. Herbert was making notes on a pad in front of him. Finally, "Josh, thanks. Very helpful. I'll tell her." Then he paused again, before saying, "You would? That's very kind of you, Josh. I'll tell her that as well. 'Bye." Another pause then, "Shalom."

Herbert replaced the handset and looked up at Sylvia.

"Josh says, don't touch this with a bargepole. He knows about book publishing. It's part of his work as an artist manager. This is what he's told me."

Herbert glanced at his notes.

"This offer you've got is from what's called in the trade a vanity publisher. Let's start at the beginning. These days, it's very difficult for a first-time author to persuade a publisher to publish a book, especially a novel."

Sylvia nodded vigorously.

"Herbie, don't tell me about it."

Herbert continued,

"Publishers have lost money and are risk averse. On-line buying has completely changed the nature of their business. Mainline publishers rarely publish anything that hasn't been written by someone who is already successful, or if it's history or biography, by a qualified academic or respected expert. When it comes to a first-time novel, however good it is, whether or not it succeeds is a matter of chance. As you have discovered, it's well nigh impossible to find a publisher like Random House, who'll take it on. There are other routes. There's self-publishing. The author…" Herbert paused as he looked through his notes "…E L James, originally self-published *Fifty Shades of Grey* as an e-book."

He looked up.

"Know what that is?"

Sylvia nodded.

"It's proved to be a publishing sensation, as have its sequels, but she had to take a chance and publish it herself.

Presumably because no one else would. Now she's been taken on by Random House. So self-publishing is one way you could publish your novel. What's it about?"

Sylvia explained.

"And what's it called?"

"*A Tyrant's Best Friend.*"

"Sounds good. Then there are so-called vanity publishers, like this one."

Herbert gestured towards the white envelope and its contents on his desk.

"As the description implies, they prey upon human vanity. They exploit a writer's obsession to see their book in print over their name. They charge more than they need to print it. They usually price it unrealistically and then persuade the unfortunate author to buy the unsold stock at that exorbitant price. In short, they prey upon weakness and gullibility."

"What about agents? I've tried to interest a number of them in my book, but with no success. Like many publishers, some won't even accept unsolicited manuscripts."

"Josh mentioned agents. They're risk averse too. Josh says there are literally thousands of books being written by all sorts of people these days. It's commonly observed in the trade, he told me, that everyone has one good book in them, which is generally where it should stay."

Sylvia smiled.

"So what options, if any, are there between a mainline and a vanity publisher?"

"Well, as I mentioned, there's self-publishing."

"Yes, I know about that. I've looked on-line at a number of ways to self-publish."

"And?"

"It's complicated, Herbie, especially if you want to market a physical book, rather than an e-book. Some authors are happy to go down that road. But I'd rather have a publisher to look after the formatting, artwork, printing and distribution. And maybe help with the marketing."

"Josh says that there is a middle way. It's called collaborative publishing. Although purists argue that it still exploits an author's vanity, Josh thinks that's unfair. A collaborative publisher will ask for a modest contribution towards the cost of publishing, but will format the book, look after any artwork needed, have it printed, price it realistically and manage its distribution. The marketing is down to the author. Josh says a collaborative publisher will ask for a lot less than seven thousand pounds. He's going to email me a list of some which I'll forward to you, Sylvia."

"Herbie, I really am grateful. Thank you."

"Well, let's see how we get on, shall we? And good luck, Sylvia."

They exchanged warm smiles across Herbert's desk and Sylvia left.

As Sylvia closed the study door behind her, Herbert's mind went back to the moment when she had reminded him so shockingly of the younger Roger. Herbert was happily married to Julie. He valued their love-making. She understood his problem which, Herbert reflected, had not troubled him since Roger's voice had broken. No other young, attractive boy had since crossed his path. Is my deviancy diminishing? he wondered. Can't be sure. Mustn't let my guard down.

He reached for *The New English Hymnal* to select the hymns that would be sung in the Abbey on Sundays in February.

♦♦♦♦♦♦♦♦♦♦♦♦♦♦♦♦♦♦♦♦♦

Saturday, 16 January 2016

After Angus Morris had given him a fair wind, Edgar had emailed Ralph on Friday morning that he would like to work for him. Now, at 6.00 p.m. on Saturday evening, he and Ralph, each holding a glass of claret, were in armchairs in the sitting room at Coronation Cottage.

"There are various categories of employees in an MP's office, Edgar. The one below the topmost is called a parliamentary assistant, or, in the jargon of IPSA, 'Research Two'."

"IPSA?"

"The Independent Parliamentary Standards Authority. I'm surprised you didn't know that. It's an independent body set up by Parliament, largely in response to the expenses scandal in two thousand and nine. Amongst other things, it regulates the amount an MP can pay members of his immediate family. You're not in that category, but the IPSA scales give a good idea of what fair remuneration would be for each employee grade."

Waters picked up a piece of paper from a small table beside his armchair and glanced at it.

"The IPSA scale for a family member employed as a parliamentary assistant ranges from twenty-three to thirty-four thousand pounds a year. Edgar, in my estimation, you're worth thirty thousand."

Waters replaced the paper on the table and looked up.

Edgar smiled. It was considerably more than he was being paid in Millbank.

"Sounds good, Ralph. What would it involve?"

"You would work full-time in my office in Westminster, Mondays to Thursdays. And on Fridays, either at home or sometimes in London, for example, when I'm piloting my Bill through the House. Jane, my secretary, manages my diary and deals with correspondence and things like that. You would carry out research, both at my request and on your own initiative, draft press releases and mail shots for my approval, attend functions with me and stand in for me when I'm unavailable. That'll be good practice for you, Edgar. And you'd liaise when necessary with Government Departments, foreign embassies, charities and the media on my behalf. All right?"

"Ralph, sounds great. I can't thank you enough."

"Not at all, Edgar. I think you're destined for great things. You're just the sort of youngster we need in the House and it's a pleasure to help you on your way. If you agree to join me, Research has agreed to release you. I suggest that you start the week after next on Monday, the twenty-fifth of January. There are certain formalities to be completed, like written terms of employment and the tiresome business of getting security clearance so you can be issued with a parliamentary pass. Jane will email you about all that on Monday. All right?"

They drained their glasses, and Pascal, who had been hovering with a glass carafe through the doorway, promptly entered and refilled them.

"I'll be issuing a Press Release announcing your appointment in the constituency. In fact, drafting it can be your first task. Do you want to be described as gay, Edgar?"

"Tricky, Ralph."

"Why?"

"My parents don't know that I'm gay. As you know, we're Roman Catholic and although I don't take religion that seriously..."

"You mean your faith comes and goes like the reception of Magic FM in the Chilterns?"

Ralph Waters smiled at this well-worn joke. It was new to Edgar.

"Who said that?"

"David Cameron did. He claims that Boris said it first."

"Well that's about how my faith is, but Mum and Dad are devout and they won't welcome the fact that I'm gay one bit."

"But Edgar, it's got to come out at some stage. Better sooner than later."

Privately, Edgar acknowledged the soundness of this, but he hesitated.

"Okay," continued, Waters. "Not just yet then, eh?"

Edgar's features betrayed relief. I'll face up to it one day, he told himself, but, as Saint Augustine of Hippo, when he had prayed to God to make him chaste, had added, "Not yet."

"So that's agreed, is it Edgar?"

"Yes, Ralph, it is. And once again, thank you."

"Not at all. It's a pleasure. Welcome aboard. Oh, and Edgar?"

"Yes, Ralph?"

"I said you'll start working for me on Monday, the twenty-fifth, but Research has agreed that you should be in the Commons next Friday, when I expect my Bill to receive its Second Reading."

"Sure, thing, Ralph."

"And one more thing, Edgar?"

"Yes?"

"You can stay with us in Barton Street any time you wish."

They smiled broadly and raised their glasses.

After Edgar left to walk back to the Hall, Ralph Waters went into the small dining room, sat at the table that Pascal had laid for dinner and poured a glass of claret each for himself and Pascal from the freshly filled carafe. Pascal brought two plates in from the kitchen, placed one in front of Ralph and the other across the table and sat down. Ralph took a mouthful, chewed, swallowed and remarked,

"Delicious."

"*Porc braisé aux pruneaux, Patron.*"

The Honourable Member for Pepynbridge

As well as playing rugby union, Pascal had learnt to cook in France and it was a feature of their domestic arrangements that, when they ate in, Pascal was the chef. He loved cooking and excelled at it. He also shopped for everything from food to lavatory rolls, although Ralph employed cleaners in London and Pepynbridge. It was a domestic arrangement that suited them both very well. They chatted about Edgar.

"Nice lad, don't you think, Pascal?"

"*Très agreeable. Très aimable.*"

Ralph spoke French and occasionally they lapsed into Pascal's second language. Born in the Congo, Swahili was his first and English his third. Pascal continued,

"*Il va devenir premier ministre d'Angleterre?*"

"*Peut-être.*"

"*Vraiment?*"

Ralph chuckled and shrugged his shoulders.

"*On ne sait jamais.*"

They continued to eat in companionable silence. The pork was followed by fresh fruit and cheese. When they had finished and the carafe of claret was empty, Pascal cleared away.

Ralph glanced at his watch.

"Pascal, I'm going to have an early night, if you don't mind?"

"*Pas du tout, Patron.* But, there's a programme on TV I'd like to watch at nine o'clock?"

"Okay. Oh, Pascal? Which wheelie bin do we need to put out before we leave tomorrow?"

The Honourable Member for Pepynbridge

Tuesday was bin collection day.

"The green one. I'll do it, Boss. No worry."

"Thanks. I'm going for a short walk before bed. I'll see you upstairs later."

Ralph left the table and, while Pascal washed up, he put on a cap and a coat and went outside. The night was clear and frosty. Ralph walked along the track to Pepynbridge Hall and then down the lime avenue. He paused when he reached Abbey Way and took in the beauty of the medieval sacred building, bathed in eerie light shed by the three-quarter moon. After a while, Ralph retraced his steps. Back at the cottage, he looked in on Pascal watching television in the sitting room, then climbed the stairs, undressed, put on pyjamas, cleaned his teeth and climbed into the outsize double-bed that replicated the one in Barton Street.

When much later, after dragging the green wheelie bin the hundred metres to the Hall, Pascal entered their bedroom, Ralph was still, breathing regularly. Pascal slipped in beside him and he too was soon asleep.

The Honourable Member for Pepynbridge

ENGAGEMENT

Sunday, 17 January 2016

It was 11.00 a.m. and the Puritan Remnant was gathered in Peggy Taplow's farmhouse on the outskirts of Pepynbridge. Peggy's family had farmed her land, she claimed, since the time of Cromwell. Aged seventy-two, her father had been a churchwarden at the Abbey for forty-four years before he had died and her mother, also dead, had been lead soprano in the choir. An only child, Peggy had never married. Heavily built with mannish, square, weathered features, a determined mouth, piercing eyes and a mass of grey, curly hair clinging close to her scalp, she was sitting at the head of the kitchen table. Sitting along from her were Alfred and Marigold Wicken, Reginald Wicken and Norman Callow. Norman Callow's grandmother, daughter of Alfred Wicken's great-grandfather, had been instrumental in the establishment of St Aidan's Church of England Primary School before the First World War. Until 2014, there had not been a time within living memory when a Wicken and a Callow had not been involved in the life of Pepynbridge Abbey, whether as bell-ringer, churchwarden, chorister or member of the Parochial Church Council.

With the arrival of Herbert Onion in 2014, the context of church life in Pepynbridge had utterly changed. Herbert's Anglo-Catholic style of liturgy was anathema to those sitting around Peggy Taplow's kitchen table. For them, the *Book of Common Prayer* had sustained the Church of

England since the reign of King Edward the Sixth and was all that Christian England needed. They regarded anything else with deep suspicion and condemned the modern *Common Worship* liturgy as papist. Except Marigold Wicken, they were members of the PCC and had been since long before Herbert had arrived in Pepynbridge. But they were acutely aware of, and deeply resented, their subsequent loss of influence. In the face of Herbert's popularity and their open disapproval of him, none of them, they thought, stood much chance of being re-elected to the PCC when their three-year terms expired in April.

On the previous Thursday, Herbert had circulated an agenda for the PCC meeting on Monday, 18 January. A copy lay on the table before each of those gathered in Peggy Taplow's kitchen.

"Item Five," recited Peggy. "Request by Ralph Waters QC, MP..." she spat out the suffixed letters contemptuously "...and Pascal Legrand to be married in a ceremony conducted by the Rector in the Abbey."

It was that which had led Alfred the previous evening to telephone the others present, suggesting that they meet at Peggy Taplow's on Sunday morning after they had attended *Book of Common Prayer* Holy Communion.

"Scandalous!" pronounced Peggy. "Do we agree?"

"We do," chorused Alfred and Reg Wicken.

Marigold Wicken and Norman Callow sat silent.

Peggy looked at Norman Callow.

"Norman, I see you've brought a Bible with you. What does that say about homosexuality? It's against it, isn't it?"

The Honourable Member for Pepynbridge

"It is, Peggy."

Norman Callow opened his Bible, adorned with coloured highlighter flags, and, in his slightly distorted speech, he began to read.

"Leviticus, chapter eighteen, verse twenty-two. 'You shall not lie with a male as with a woman, it is an abomination'. Leviticus chapter twenty, verse thirteen. 'If man lies with a male as with a woman, both of them have committed an abomination. They shall be put to death; their blood is upon them'."

"Quite right," broke in Alfred. "Put 'em to death, both of them."

Callow ignored the interruption and turned towards the back of his Bible.

"Romans chapter one, verses twenty-six to twenty-seven. 'For this reason'," he read out, "'God gave them up to shameless passions.' Paul," Callow explained, "is writing about pagans." He continued, " 'Their women exchanged natural intercourse for unnatural, and in the same way also the men, giving up natural intercourse with women, were consumed with passion for each other. Men committed shameless acts with men and received in their own persons the due penalty for their error'. And there are similar passages in One Corinthians, chapter six, verse nine, in One Timothy, chapter one, verse ten, and in Jude, verse seven. This is what we're going to discuss tomorrow. Frankly, I think it's blasphemous even to put it on the agenda. Onion should have refused outright to marry them and that would have been that."

"God knows," observed Reginald Wicken, "we've had to put up with more than enough from that man, and now this. What do you think, Son?"

"In Cromwell's day," growled Alfred, "he'd have been burnt at the stake."

"Who, Alfred?"

"Herbie Onion, Peggy. And it's a bloody shame we can't do the same today. And if I had my way, I'd do the same with that MP and his black boyfriend. Disgusting! That's what it is. Bloody disgusting!"

Peggy, who, like the others, had previously experienced Alfred's ranting, decided to move the conversation on.

"Is there anything we can do about it before tomorrow?"

They were silent for a moment. Then Norman Callow said,

"We could alert the local Press."

Another silence, as this was digested. Then Callow added,

"And if the local Press decided it was newsworthy, they might pass it on to the nationals."

"Great!" yelped Alfred, his voice pitching higher than usual. "*The Daily Mail* and *The Sun* would make a meal of it."

"Steady on," warned Peggy Taplow. "Let's see if we can dispose of this quietly, without bringing the village into the public eye."

And, in a reference to the national coverage of Ash Malik's foiling of the terrorist plot,

"We had enough of that last year."

"Ash was a brave lad," objected Alfred.

"Of course he was, Alfred. I'm not saying he wasn't. But we don't need any more exposure like that for now. Let's see what happens at tomorrow's meeting and meet again after that if we think we need to."

"Okay Peggy," said Alfred, echoed by the others.

And so it was left.

High Mass in the Abbey had ended and worshippers were gathered at the west end of the nave for coffee and gossip. Until Jack Driver had read the agenda for the PCC Meeting, he had not known of Ralph Waters and Pascal Legrand's request to be married in the Abbey. Herbert approached him.

"Jack, could you spare me a few moments in the Rectory?"

"Yes, of course, Herbie."

A few minutes later, they were in Herbert's study, sitting across from each other in the leather wing armchairs. Jack Driver refused a drink. He would be driving back to Medborough and the house he shared with his wife for lunch.

Jack Driver was the same age as Herbert. Their friendship dated from when they had studied music together at The Guildhall School of Music and Drama. A solicitor living and working in Medborough, in May 2014 Jack had been recruited by Herbert as the Abbey organist, since when they had worked closely together and their friendship had deepened. Despite Jack living in

Medborough, he had worshipped in the Abbey since May 2014, entitling his inclusion on the Parochial Electoral Roll. In turn, that had enabled his co-option onto the PCC in place of Marigold Wicken, who had resigned after she had left Alfred in December 2014. Tall, with a spare bony frame, large square head, bland pale features and short grey hair, Driver's grey eyes appraised Herbert thoughtfully.

"I can guess what this is about, Herbie."

Herbert recounted his meeting just after Christmas with Ralph Waters and Pascal Legrand.

"But, Herbie, it's against the law."

"I know that, Jack, but Waters intends to change the law."

"How?"

When Herbert explained, Jack raised his eyebrows in surprise and exhaled slowly and audibly through pursed lips. The friends studied each other, each wondering what the other made of the MP's request.

Jack Driver broke the silence.

"Even if his Bill succeeds in the Commons, it would have to go to the Lords, where instinct tells me it will founder. And even if it doesn't, it won't be law until next year, so why are you bothering with it now, Herbie?"

"Jack, if Waters' Bill survives its Second Reading later this month, he has asked me to conduct a full marriage service for them soon afterwards."

"In the Abbey?"

"In the Abbey."

"But that can't produce a legally binding marriage, Herbie. You know that."

"Indeed I do, Jack. They would go through a civil ceremony first."

"Two issues, Herbie. Would the PCC approve of same-sex marriage? And if it does, would it condone the breach of Canon Law if you were to conduct a marriage service in the Abbey?"

"Precisely, Jack. And it's about same-gender marriage that I'm anxious to know what you think. So far as the second issue is concerned, as you may be aware, there are incumbents who, presumably with the agreement of their PCCs, are ignoring Canon Law and conducting full marriage services in church for same-gender couples. I'll run that possibility past Bishop Julian before inviting the PCC to discuss it. But it's on the first, the principle of same-gender marriage, that I want the PCC to come to a decision now."

Jack Driver sat silent for several moments. Finally, he said,

"You know, Herbie. I've never had to think seriously about same-sex or same-gender marriage before. I'm the same age as you and we were brought up in a very different social environment to our parents. If they were alive, and sadly mine aren't, they would be appalled, as I expect Alice Burton, Richard Maxey and the Puritan Remnant will be…"

"Well, your parents might have been, Jack," interrupted Herbert. "As you know, I never knew my father and hardly my mother. But what do you think, Jack?"

"I'm not against it, Herbie. I'm far from comfortable with it, but in two thousand and thirteen, Parliament passed a law permitting it. The Church of England has to move with the times. It's hard enough to encourage youngsters into church these days. I recall the Archbishop of Canterbury saying a year or so ago that young people equate our Church's current attitude to homosexuality with racism."

"Your memory does not deceive you. It was in the autumn of twenty thirteen. Those may not be the archbishop's actual words, but he said something like it in an address to the Evangelical Alliance. So, on the issue of same-gender marriage...?"

"I'll go with it. But what about Canon Law, Herbie?"

"As I just mentioned, I'll have to discuss that with Bishop Julian, but I doubt I'll get anywhere with him."

Herbert paused, letting silence hang between them in the study, before resuming with,

"Jack, there are two books I've read that support same-gender marriage."

Herbert rose, collected two volumes from his desk and handed them to Driver before settling back into his wing armchair.

"I'm going to suggest tomorrow that everyone on the PCC reads them too. Then, I'll adjourn the meeting for four weeks when we'll resume our discussion."

The Honourable Member for Pepynbridge

Jack Driver turned each book over and read the blurb on the back covers.

"Herbie, I've not heard of these. Could you lend them to me?"

"I could, Jack, but I should prefer to keep hold of them myself until after tomorrow's meeting. Anyway, I'm going to suggest that you all order copies from Amazon."

"Fine, by me." Jack paused. "But what about the bishop?"

"Well, even though I doubt he'll consent to my conducting a same-gender marriage service, out of respect for Waters and Legrand, I think it's important to have a discussion in the PCC on the principle of gay marriage, because there may be a compromise."

"And what would that be, Herbie?"

"It's complicated, so bear with me."

"Of course."

Herbert rose, sat behind his desk and opened a folder.

"The Episcopal Church of the United States, in short the American Anglican Church, has devised a service called *The Witnessing and Blessing of a Lifelong Covenant*. Despite the name, to all intents and purposes, save legal, it's a marriage service. There are Presenters, adopting the roles of best man and chief bridesmaid. There are vows of covenantal, exclusive and faithful love. Rings are blessed and exchanged and then a pronouncement made that the couple, and I quote, 'are bound to one another in a holy covenant so long as they both shall live'."

"So, if the PCC approves same-sex marriage, what's the problem?"

"There are two, Jack. Firstly, Ralph Waters won't wear it. He's fighting for the principle. Nothing less than a full marriage service in church will do."

"And the second problem, Herbie?"

Herbert looked again at the folder.

"The House of Bishops' *Pastoral Guidance on Same Sex Marriage*, issued on the fifteenth of February two thousand and fourteen. After recalling its pastoral statement issued in two thousand and five that, and I quote, 'clergy should not provide services of blessing for those who registered civil partnerships', the House of Bishops goes on to state, 'The same approach as commended in the two thousand and five statement should therefore apply to couples who enter same-sex marriage'. And it adds that 'Services of Blessing should not be provided. Clergy should respond pastorally and sensitively in other ways'."

"Not legally binding, Herbie."

"No, Jack, it's not. It's guidance, not law, but I might be in almost as much hot water with Bishop Julian if I disregarded it as I would be if I conducted an appropriately adapted *Common Worship* or *BCP* marriage service. That's something else I need to explore with him. Frankly, there's no theological, as opposed to a legal, difference between the text of the American blessing service and the text of the Church of England marriage ceremony."

"I follow that. I doubt whether Bishop Julian will approve of you breaking Canon Law but he might turn a blind eye to the compromise, provided it didn't attract publicity."

"And I'm sure he wouldn't be the first bishop to do so, Jack. But let's see, shall we? Thanks for sparing me the time."

"No problem, Herbie. And Herbie?"

"Yes?"

"Good luck with it."

"Thanks, Jack, I'll need it."

Jack Driver left.

◆◆◆◆◆◆◆◆◆◆◆◆◆◆◆◆◆◆◆◆◆

Monday, 18 January 2016

When Sylvia Slim returned from Corbury and opened her Microsoft Outlook inbox, she found an email from Herbert, forwarding one from Joshua Cohen with the names of collaborative publishers that he suggested were worth an approach. It concluded,

I don't know exactly how much each of them charges, but friends in the trade tell me they're all worth a try. Wish your friend 'Good Luck' from me. Shalom, Josh.

Sylvia emailed a reply to Herbert, asking him to thank Joshua. She then went on-line to the websites of the publishers Joshua had suggested. Scrolling through them, she hesitated. Then she decided to finish the novel first, so she could submit it entire. She closed the internet and, in Word, opened *A Tyrant's Best Friend* and sat for a while, pondering the title. Was it right? Would it help to sell the novel? She shook her head. She really didn't know. Surely that's for the publisher to decide? Her mind cleared and she scrolled down to where she had finished typing on Friday.

As John walked through the door, Wolsey greeted him with, "Welcome back, John."

Sylvia typed,

"It's good to be here, My Lord. Bologna's a lovely city, but I'd rather have seen it in less trying circumstances..."

By the time Sylvia left to collect Roger at 4.30 p.m., she had completed another 3,000 words. She was pleased and would revise them the next morning. As she drove out of Pepynbridge, she calculated that she should finish the first draft by the end of February. Only if she was happy with it, would she look again at Joshua's email. Anyway, she'd like to know what Julie thought of it before submitting it to yet another publisher.

At 6.00 p.m. in Abbey Hall, the southern part of the long, narrow Tudor building that divides St Aidan's Abbey from Station Road, Herbert Onion, sitting at the head of a long rectangular table, opened the meeting of the Parochial Church Council with a prayer. Also at the table were Alice Burton, Richard Maxey, Gordon and Sylvia Slim, Julie Onion, Jack Driver, Peggy Taplow, Alfred and Reginald Wicken and, farthest away from Herbert, Norman Callow.

It was nearly an hour before agenda item five was reached. Herbert, adopting a neutral tone, gave an account of his meeting with Ralph Waters and Pascal Legrand just after Christmas. Then, as Jack Driver had done in his study the day before, Herbert identified the two issues at stake.

He continued,

"So far as concerns the second, namely whether I should conduct a marriage service for Waters and Legrand in the Abbey before it is lawful, I don't want to discuss that this evening. A number of rectors and vicars are ignoring the law and conducting same-gender marriages in church and I shall talk to Bishop Julian about that. What I should like us to consider is the first issue, namely whether, in principle, we are in favour of same-gender marriage. At the moment, I remind you, same-gender marriage is lawful, but conducting it in an Anglican church like the Abbey, is not. If we decide as a PCC that we are in favour of same-gender marriages, then it follows, I suggest, that we should permit them to be conducted in the Abbey if and when they become lawful. Until then, however, there is a possibility that we could allow the blessing of a same-gender marriage in the Abbey. Do you all follow me so far?"

Around the table, heads nodded.

"But Herbie," objected Alfred Wicken. "Why do we need to discuss same-sex marriage at all before it becomes lawful?"

"Because Mr Waters and Mr Legrand have asked me to conduct their marriage. In addition, Alfred, you may or may not be aware that Ralph Waters is piloting a Private Member's Bill through Parliament to make the conduct of same-gender marriages in Anglican churches lawful."

Alfred shook his head angrily.

"For those reasons," Herbert continued, "I am firmly of the view that, out of respect for them, this PCC should discuss and decide whether or not we are in favour of same-gender marriage. If we are, then I can canvass with Bishop Julian what sort of service I can conduct in the Abbey, acknowledging and blessing their union."

Alfred still shook his head.

"You don't agree, Alfred?"

"No, I don't. I think it's wrong to discuss it at all."

"Does any one agree with Alfred? Reginald, you do. And Peggy. Any one else?"

Herbert looked down the table at Norman Callow, who raised his eyebrows and gave a slight shrug of his shoulders.

"No? All right, we'll make a start. But before we do, we need to recognise that discussing same-gender marriage will be difficult and potentially embarrassing, touching, as it inevitably will, upon certain aspects of intimate physiology."

"What do you mean by that?"

Alfred's tone was hostile.

"Sexual intercourse, Alfred."

"Buggery, you mean Herbie, don't you? What we need is plain speaking."

"Alfred, I hope that our discussions will indeed be frank. But they also need to be properly informed."

"Informed?" exploded Alfred. "Informed? Buggery is buggery. And buggery's wrong, Herbie. It's unnatural, that's what it is. It's a deadly sin. The Bible says so. In this country, we used to hang people for buggery. It's a shame we don't still. If we did, all this nonsense about same-sex marriage would never have raised its head. Herbie, we're supposed to be a God-fearing country. But we're becoming a sin-loving country..."

Herbert held up a hand.

"Alfred!"

His tone was uncharacteristically sharp. Alfred clamped his lips.

"Alfred, not everyone shares your views. And it may be that not everyone around this table does. Or will do. Last week, in order to prepare for our discussion, I read two books. One is called *More Perfect Union?* by Alan Wilson, Bishop of Buckingham, and the other *God and the Gay Christian* by an American, Matthew Vines. Both make a strong theological case for taking a fresh look at those passages in Scripture that apparently condemn homosexuality..."

Alfred, his face flushed even deeper than usual, opened his mouth to speak. Herbert raised his hand again.

"No, Alfred. Please let me finish."

"Go on, then," conceded Alfred, grudgingly.

"Thank you Alfred. Both authors argue persuasively that same-gender attraction is a given, rather than a chosen life style. And that it is not in fact condemned by Scripture. Consequently, they make out a strong case for accepting same-gender marriage."

"So what conclusion have you come to, Herbie, then?"

Peggy Taplow's tone was suspicious, rather than hostile.

"Peggy, for the moment, I would rather not say."

"Why not?"

"Because I would first like to hear what the rest of you think."

"Well, that's easy. Just ask us."

"Not now, Peggy."

"Why not now, Herbie?"

"Because I want us to come to an informed conclusion. This is a very important decision for this PCC."

"Why?" demanded Alfred.

"Because, Alfred," said Herbert patiently, "the request to be married in the Abbey has been made by our Member of Parliament who in addition is an eminent lawyer..."

Alfred again opened his mouth to speak.

"No, Alfred. Please let me continue. Ralph Waters is not only an MP and a QC, but he's trying to change the law that forbids same-gender marriage in Anglican churches. He's high profile and, once the controversy he stirs up becomes public, the eyes of the nation will be on us."

"Not again," remarked Peggy in disgust.

"Yes, Peggy, I'm afraid so. So we have to take his request very seriously and not just dismiss it out of hand, as I suspect some here this evening would like. Isn't that right, Alfred?"

Now looking subdued, Alfred nodded.

"Good," continued Herbert. "My suggestion is that we adjourn this discussion to a later date and continue it when those of you who choose to, have read one or both the books I've mentioned."

The Honourable Member for Pepynbridge

Peggy stared expressionlessly at Herbert, but said nothing. Herbert glanced at the rest. Alfred and Reginald both avoided his gaze, their heads sullenly inclined towards their agendas on the table in front of them. Norman Callow looked out of the window at a street-light, shining in Station Road. The remainder wore expressions of interest.

"Where can we buy them?"

"On-line, Gordon."

Herbert looked down at some papers.

"On Amazon..." He read out the prices of the books in both paperback and Kindle editions and concluded,

"Because this issue is so important, I suggest that the parish reimburses anybody who buys them but doesn't want to keep them."

"I'm happy with that, Herbie."

The speaker was Gordon Slim, the Treasurer.

"Thank you, Gordon. Every-one else agree?"

Although some registered mute unhappiness, there were no dissenting voices.

"Good. I've printed off copies of the relevant pages from Amazon's website."

Herbert passed them around the table and discussion moved on to the next agenda item. When they reached "Time and date of next meeting", it was fixed for Monday, 15 February, at 6.00 p.m.

"And I suggest," said Herbert, "that those who have read one or both books meet here to discuss them at four o'clock the same afternoon. All right?"

It was agreed.

The Grace was said by all and the meeting closed.

As Herbert walked past the archway to the Rectory, to his surprise Norman Callow joined him and said that he would like to have a private discussion with him when it was convenient. They arranged to meet in the Rectory the next morning at 10.00 a.m.

Alice Burton, Richard Maxey, Jack Driver and Gordon and Sylvia Slim accompanied Herbert and Julie to the Rectory where Mary Maxey was waiting for them. Leela, Abi and Sabi Malik's sixteen-year old daughter, was baby-sitting Alice, Herbert and Julie's four month old daughter, generally referred to as Little Alice to distinguish her from Alice Burton, after whom she had been named.

"Is Little Alice asleep, Leela?" asked Julie.

"Yes, Julie. Such a sweet child."

"Yes. Thanks, Leela."

Julie handed Leela an envelope containing cash and Leela left to walk the short distance to her parents' home in Abbey Gardens.

Herbert, Alice, Richard, Gordon and Jack remained in the sitting room drinking wine and fruit juice, while Julie, Mary and Sylvia laid out a buffet supper in the dining room.

"If you don't mind me saying so, Herbie, you handled that well."

"Thank you, Richard. But that's only the beginning. Plenty of squalls ahead. And what I did not tell any of you this evening, because, if you'll forgive the pun, I did not want the waters to be muddied, is that if the marriage service happens, Ralph Waters has offered to pay for the re-tuning of the organ."

Jack Driver whistled softly.

"That's a quarter of a million pounds, isn't it?"

"It is."

"Shrewd."

"But Herbie, it's a bribe," objected Alice Burton.

"Alice, call it what you will, but it's not illegal. It's entirely normal for people for whom the Church has provided highly cherished service to reward it with a gift."

"But not to that extent, Herbie."

"Alice, Waters is a rich man. Don't forget the widow's offering. Luke chapter twenty-one, verse three. She gave all that she had, did she not? Compared with her offering, given his wealth, Waters' gift would be little more than small change."

"You old Jesuit!" exclaimed Jack Driver and they all laughed.

"But I should prefer you kept that to yourselves until after the adjourned meeting of the PCC on the fifteenth of February."

"Of course," they assured Herbert.

"Supper's ready," called Julie.

Alfred was driving back to Pepynbridge Farm. Because it was Monday, true to his self-imposed ordinance, he did not stop at the Blue Boar, although he certainly could have done with a drink. By God was he cross. The thought of that fancy ponce Waters doing unmentionable things with that nigger. What was his name? Can't remember. But the thought of it. Or worse still, the thought of that big black ape buggering Waters. The image of a Spanish fighting bull mounting a white spring lamb came to mind.

On Monday evenings Marigold took Sophie to ballet in Medborough, so when Alfred let himself in, the house was empty. He looked at the wall clock in the kitchen. 8.00 p.m. Marigold and Sophie would be leaving Medborough about now and, as always on a Monday, supper would be at half past. Marigold would have left it ready in the warm oven. Alfred sat at the kitchen table, resisting the temptation to pour himself a large whisky. He'd put that off until after supper. Instead he brooded. As he did, dark thoughts crowded his mind. If, in some mysterious way, something were to happen to that poncey MP, a number of problems would disappear. First of all, what they had been discussing earlier in the PCC meeting would never happen. Secondly, in the event of a by-election, as he had predicted in the Blue Boar the other day, there was a good chance that Pepynbridge Forest would elect a UKIP Member of Parliament. Thirdly, that would make it more likely that, in the EU Referendum, the UK would vote to leave. And fourthly, Godly Pepynbridge would be rid of a poisonous presence, a cancerous tumour. All of which would be really, really good. But how could Waters be got rid of?

An idea began to form in Alfred Wicken's mind. Shaking his head and smiling, he dismissed it outright. But, as the minutes dragged on while he waited for Marigold and

Sophie, the thought returned and Alfred began to toy with it. He heard tyres crunching on the gravel. Well, he thought, I'll think about it. Plenty of time to make up my mind, one way or another. I'd have to be careful, though. Mustn't get caught. And then, just as Marigold and Sophie walked in, Alfred mused, Funny, if I'd been boozing in the Blue Boar this evening, I don't suppose the idea would even have entered my head.

"Hello, Alfred. Everything okay?"

"Yes, thanks, Marigold. Hello Sophie."

"Hello, Dad," replied his daughter, kissing him on the cheek, reassured that there was no alcohol on his breath. PCC meetings, she knew, always stressed her father.

"How did the meeting go?"

Alfred recounted the discussion that had taken place on agenda item five.

"Golly!" exclaimed Marigold. "It's not going ahead is it?"

"Couldn't say, at the moment. But not," announced Alfred emphatically, but with a scintilla of guilt, "if I have anything to do with it."

Marigold was by nature a gentle woman. Of medium height and slim, with dark hair pulled back into a bun that accentuated her angular features, she looked older than thirty-four, the legacy of coping for years with a demanding, bullying and drunkard husband. She avoided controversy whenever she could. All she had ever wanted to do was to get on with life, without arguments, which is why she had tolerated Alfred's boorish behaviour for as long as she had. Both leaving him and returning had been difficult decisions for her. She thought for a few moments and decided that if Mr Waters and Mr Legrand wanted to get married, why shouldn't they? These days, lots of gay men and women did. She looked at Sophie.

"What do you think, Sophie?"

"Mum, me and my friends are in favour of gay marriage. We had a discussion about it in RE at the Academy the other day."

Alfred shook his head sadly.

"That's what they say on the telly."

"What's that, Dad?"

"That the young are in favour of it. It's beyond me."

"Well, let's talk about something else," suggested Marigold, not wanting supper to be spoiled by controversy, accompanied, as she knew from experience it would be, by Alfred's ranting.

In the light of the thoughts that had lodged in Alfred's mind before Marigold and Sophie had arrived home, he also decided that it would be wise to change the subject. He'd keep such mischievous notions strictly to himself. In fact, I won't disclose them to anyone in Pepynbridge, not even to Dad. If I do decide to do anything, he told himself, which I haven't, but if I do, I'll go further afield.

As they ate and Marigold and Alfred chatted, Sophie kept quiet, watching her father and wondering what he had meant by, "Not if I have anything to do with it." From the years when he had subjected her to what her therapist had termed "emotional abuse", Sophie was only too well aware of her father's capacity for causing harm. But he wouldn't do anything illegal, would he? She wasn't sure, but was just a little afraid. She did not want anything to disrupt her plan to marry Ash when he finished agricultural college and began working on the farm. But that could only happen if Dad was still around. And he wouldn't be if he did anything seriously silly. And, you know what? she admitted to herself. He's quite capable of that. There's a bit of madness in my dad. I should know.

♦♦♦♦♦♦♦♦♦♦♦♦♦♦♦♦♦♦♦♦♦

Tuesday, 19 January 2016

From wing armchairs, Herbert Onion and Norman Callow surveyed each other across Herbert's study.

"I'll read those books, Herbie."

Herbert raised his eyebrows in surprise.

"Herbie, homosexuality repels me. When I first read the agenda for the meeting, I was cross, as Alfred, Reg and Peggy would confirm. But Herbie, for the whole of my professional life, I was a primary school teacher. What that taught me is that culture changes. Year after year, there's a new intake of children, each bringing with them the cultural assumptions of their parents who, for the most part, are only twenty or thirty years older than them. Cultural assumptions that, as the years passed, became increasingly at odds with my own. But it was not for me to instil out-dated social attitudes in my pupils. My job was to prepare them for the world as it was going to be when they were older, not the world that I wished it still was. So, despite my distaste, I am prepared to learn about homosexuality and same-sex marriage. As is plain to all, they're now inescapable features of twenty-first century life in this country, so maybe the Church of England has to move with the times. I'll read those books and see whether what they say makes sense within the modern context."

"Thank you for that, Norman. Please borrow mine."

Herbert rose, collected the books from his desk, handed them to Callow and resumed his seat.

"Thank you Herbie. I don't own a computer, so I can't order books on-line. And after my stroke, I'm not allowed to drive, so it's difficult for me to get to a bookshop. But tell me, Herbie, what was your view about all this before you read these books?"

"Norman, I was uneasy. I didn't know what to think. But one thing is very clear in my mind. People with unconventional sexual preferences are usually not to blame for them. We are all children of God, to be treated with respect. The overwhelming message that emerges from those two books is that there's no such thing as bad love. All self-giving or sacrificial love is good and is sanctioned by God. If a person can only love a member of their own gender, then their love is as valid as my love is for Julie and as yours was for your wife, when she was alive."

"Herbie, are you saying that it's genetically programmed?"

"No, Norman. Not quite. But, after Ralph Waters came to me with his request, I decided to do some research. It's easy these days you know. On-line?"

Herbert's voice lifted interrogatively and he looked at Norman, who nodded.

"If you say so, Herbie. I wouldn't know."

"The current scientific consensus is that same-gender attraction is not genetically determined as such, but there is a recent well-regarded study suggesting that it is epigenetically influenced."

Norman raised his eyebrows.

"As I understand it, Norman," continued Herbert, "and I'm no scientist, epigenetics is where a gene carries with it a chemical marker that influences the way in which the gene behaves…" Herbert paused before adding, "…or expresses itself."

Herbert rose and sat behind his desk. He reached towards a wire tray stacked with papers, riffled through them and drew out a stapled bundle headed, *Homosexuality as a Consequence of Epigenetically Canalized Sexual Development* from *The Quarterly Review of Biology*, published by the University of Chicago, which he had copied on-line. The paper was dated December 2012. Herbert found where he had marked it.

"This research suggests that these chemical markers can be inherited from a parent, but…" and Herbert turned over several sheets before adding, "…as I understand it and it's not easy, they may also be transmitted to a foetus in the womb. In other words, whatever the mechanism, pre-disposition towards same-gender orientation is either transmitted generationally or arises spontaneously. It is not a life-style choice."

"Fascinating, Herbie. You know, it doesn't altogether surprise me. I've sometimes come across same gender attraction in primary school children."

"And there's also some evidence," Herbert went on, "that environmental or relational factors in childhood may play a part. In other words, if a person is innately predisposed towards homosexuality, it may emerge as dominant anyway. Or it may take an event or events in childhood to precipitate that orientation and over-ride social norms. But, Norman, what is absolutely clear is that there is no so-called cure for it. Extensive psychological programming to alter sexual preference has never been recorded as succeeding."

"I'll read these," Callow held up the books, "and return them when I have done. And I'll come to your discussion at four o'clock on the fifteenth of February."

"Thank you, Norman."

"But I'll wager Alfred won't be amongst them."

"Indeed not. Nor Reginald. And probably not Peggy, either."

They smiled, stood and shook hands.

After Callow left his study, Herbert breathed a sigh of relief and offered up a brief, silent prayer. He entertained the hope, albeit short of expectation, that Norman Callow might change his mind about homosexuality in general and same-gender marriage in particular.

◆◆◆◆◆◆◆◆◆◆◆◆◆◆◆◆◆◆◆◆◆◆

The Honourable Member for Pepynbridge

Wednesday, 20 January 2016

It was sunny but cold when, shortly before 11.00 a.m., Herbert drove into the grounds of the Bishop's Palace in Medborough. In his study, Bishop Julian greeted him warmly. Married with five adult children, Julian Ross was tall and lean, with aquiline features and a full head of grey, straight hair, a lock of which fell boyishly across his forehead. Kindly blue eyes beneath pepper and salt eyebrows stared out through rimless spectacles. His was the face of a pastor and scholar, which he was, but set upon the frame of an athlete, which once he had been, winning a Blue at Cambridge as a middle-distance runner. Socially liberal and Anglo-Catholic by persuasion and training, he was enjoying his time at Medborough and would be well pleased if that was where he ended his active ministry.

In 2014, Julian Ross had taken a risk when he had encouraged Herbert to apply for the vacancy in Pepynbridge. Herbert's father had left his mother before he was born. His mother had been an alcoholic and, at the age of four and lacking any other close relatives, Herbert had been placed in local authority care. His mother had overdosed and died two years later. When Herbert was ten, he had been moved to a children's home in Leicester where he had suffered persistent sexual abuse by its principal. And he had been encouraged to groom newly arrived boys for the same purpose. Herbert's sexual and emotional development had been arrested, leaving him with a fondness for pre-pubescent boys. Herbert had not indulged his deviancy since he was fifteen, when he had left the children's home and lodged with fosterers in London while he studied music at The Junior Guildhall School of Music and Drama. Ross had known all this and had judged that Herbert was master of his problem and would not succumb to temptation. Ross had been uneasily aware that, were he proved wrong, his own position would come under scrutiny, given current public concern about pædophilia in general and sacerdotal sexual abuse of children in particular, but his judgement had been vindicated. As well as achieving much for the parish of Pepynbridge, rescuing St Aidan's Abbey from near certain redundancy, last year Herbert had married Julie Swift and they now had a daughter. Whilst that was no guarantee against future transgression, Ross knew from all he had heard and read about Herbert since his move to Pepynbridge, that relapse was extremely unlikely. So, in Bishop Julian's book, Herbert Onion had succeeded against the odds in more ways than one and Julian Ross was considering whether to appoint him a non-residential canon of Medborough Cathedral.

After chatting about the state of his parish, Herbert disclosed the challenge with which Ralph Waters had presented him. Ross held Herbert's enquiring gaze with affection.

"Herbie, whilst the law is as it is, I cannot approve of you conducting a same-sex marriage ceremony in Pepynbridge Abbey. Could I turn a blind eye if you did? I am well aware that some incumbents in this diocese have conducted same-sex marriages in their churches, but it has been done discreetly. My permission has not been sought.

No complaint has been made to me. I've had no reason to investigate and, if appropriate, to discipline the priest in question. But Herbie, what chance would there be of you conducting such a ceremony out of the public eye, involving as it would an MP and QC intent on changing the law and a retired French senior rugby union player? None at all."

"Bishop, I agree."

"And you are aware, I trust, of the House of Bishops Guidance of two thousand and fourteen on formal services of blessing?"

"Bishop, I am."

"As I'm sure you know, there is an authorised order for *Prayer and Dedication after a Civil Marriage*."

"Indeed, Bishop, but that falls far short of a marriage ceremony. There is no exchange of vows, or of rings. I'm afraid that given his present state of mind, there's no way that Ralph Waters would agree to that."

"Well, Herbie, Mr Waters has put you and Pepynbridge in a difficult position, but I'm afraid that if you did conduct a ceremony of marriage and it came to my notice, as inevitably it would, I should have to discipline you. Without prejudging the issue, in such circumstances it would be well-near impossible for me to maintain you as the Rector of Pepynbridge."

"I understand, Bishop. But what about if Waters' Bill gets through the House of Commons?"

"Canon Law would remain unaltered unless and until his Bill is approved by the House of Lords. And I can tell you from my experience of sitting in the Lords, it's unlikely to survive there, if for no other reason than their Lordships would be very chary of contravening the convention that such matters should be left to General Synod."

"And what about General Synod?"

"I could not possibly say. What I can tell you is that, in my view, and it is just my personal view, the House of Bishops by a majority would support same-sex marriage in church. But I have simply no idea what the Houses of Clergy and Laity would do, even if it was brought before Synod."

"Will it be?"

"I suspect it will be before much longer. But not this February. It's not on the agenda."

Bishop Ross contemplated Herbert thoughtfully. Then he swivelled his chair and looked out of his study window at a frost-dusted lawn stretching to a shrubbery, backed by a high stone wall some fifty yards distant. Herbert waited patiently, wondering what was coming. He guessed something was and he was right. Julian Ross liked Herbert, was even fond of him, and if he could provide him with some comfort, he would. He swivelled back to face Herbert.

"Herbie, there is something that I am willing to disclose, provided I can rely unequivocally upon your confidence?"

"Of course, Bishop. Need you ask?"

Julian Ross looked at Herbert for a few moments, weighing him up. He decided he could trust him.

"Herbie, there are some small groups, commissioned by Canterbury and York, currently charged with confidential consideration of same-sex marriage and whether to recognise it. I am participating in those discussions. I ask, please, that you treat what I have just said in total confidence. Not even Julie should know."

"Bishop, you have my word."

"Thank you. The discussions are going well," Julian Ross continued, "and the current plan is that there should be a closed debate about it at General Synod next July. In my estimation there is a reasonable prospect of the Church altering its approach, probably sooner, rather than later. But as matters stand, Herbie, I cannot be of more help. You and I are prisoners of events, the outcome of which we shall have to await."

"Bishop, thank you for telling me that."

Herbert paused, wondering how far he could press Julian Ross. Ah well, he thought: Nothing ventured, nothing gained.

"Finally, Bishop, if you don't mind me asking…"

Bishop Julian smiled and shook his head gently.

"…what would your reaction be if I conducted a service of blessing?"

Julian Ross paused for what seemed to Herbert to be an age. Finally, his face a mask,

"Herbie, we both know what guidance says. Let's wait and see what happens and cross bridges when we come to them, eh?"

The discussion over, courtesies were exchanged and Herbert left.

Well that's clear then, he thought, there's nothing I can do except, as Julian Ross just said, wait upon events. Did I detect some Episcopal ambivalence regarding a service of blessing? Perhaps. Can't be sure. Take nothing for granted. Play my cards carefully.

He climbed into his car and drove back to Pepynbridge, wondering how and when he was going to explain the position to Ralph Waters and Pascal Legrand. But it would be helpful, very helpful, if he could persuade the PCC to approve the principle of same-gender marriage being conducted in the Abbey. It would be the first step along a way that, Herbert hoped, could lead to some sort of ceremony in the Abbey that would have the support of the PCC and the approval of Ralph Waters and Pascal Legrand. And even, perhaps, the benefit of an Episcopal blind eye, if not of Episcopal approval. Not forgetting the retuning of the organ.

◆◆◆◆◆◆◆◆◆◆◆◆◆◆◆◆◆◆◆◆◆

Friday, 22 January 2016

Shortly after 9.30 a.m., Edgar was sitting in the Strangers' Gallery, or Visitors' Gallery as it is now termed, of the House of Commons, as below him a clerk sitting in front of the Deputy Speaker intoned,

"The Marriage (Same Sex Couples) (Amendment) Bill."

Ralph Waters called out,

"Now, Sir."

"Mr Waters," announced the Deputy Speaker.

Ralph Waters rose to his feet.

The Honourable Member for Pepynbridge

"Thank you, Mr Deputy Speaker. I beg to move that the Bill be now read a second time."

Waters, speaking without notes, introduced his Bill, citing opinion polls to demonstrate the high level of public support for the change he was asking the House to enact and emphasising the injustice that the Church of England's inability by law to conduct same-sex marriages was doing to devout Anglicans who were in same-sex relationships. The fifty Members in the Chamber, more than the quorum needed for a valid vote, listened patiently.

A Member, to whom Waters gave way, rose to object that the subject of Waters' Bill was a matter that, by long standing convention, should be left to General Synod, pointing out that only after that would it be for Parliament,

"...to pass or strike down a Measure presented to it by General Synod which sought to amend the law as the honourable and learned Member's Bill sets out to do."

Waters responded,

"I thank my honourable Friend for his not unexpected contribution to this debate, but at present, there is no proposal before General Synod to do what the Bill seeks to achieve. Hence, the injustice will be perpetuated unless and until this House and this Parliament makes clear to General Synod that its present stance is unacceptable, unjust, and inconsistent with the role of the Church of England to serve the whole nation. The role, I remind honourable Members, that was established by its founder, Her Majesty Queen Elizabeth the First. In the final analysis, it is for Parliament and not General Synod to represent the nation and to correct injustice wherever and whenever it finds it."

Waters continued with his opening remarks for a while longer. When he resumed his seat, a number of speeches followed from Members, both for and against, before an Under-Secretary of State rose from the Treasury Bench.

"Firstly, I congratulate my honourable and learned Friend, the Member for Pepynbridge Forest, on bringing this important Bill before the House and on his excellent speech. Whilst the Government entertains significant reservations about the propriety of this House and another place legislating directly upon matters concerning the government and theological practice of the Church of England, nevertheless it recognises that the legalisation of the conduct of valid same-sex marriages in Anglican churches is one that attracts majority public support in England. For this reason, if for no other, the Government is minded to allow this Bill to go forward unless and until the issue has been addressed afresh by General Synod. The Government will keep its position under review during the passage of this Bill through this House and another place in the light of any deliberations of the General Synod of the Church of England."

Such remarks from a Government minister signalled that if any Member in the Chamber tried to talk the Bill out, there were sufficient Members elsewhere in the Palace of Westminster willing to respond to the division bell and carry a vote of closure. After several more speeches and interventions from other Members and short closing remarks by Waters commending his Bill to the House, the Deputy Speaker announced,

"The Question is that the Bill be read a second time. As many as are of the opinion say 'Aye'."

There came a chorus of "Ayes".

Then,

"Of the contrary, 'No'."

Shouts of "No", following which the Deputy Speaker called,

"Clear the lobbies."

Two minutes later, after the appointment of four tellers, the Deputy Speaker again put the Question to the House and received the same responses, after which he announced the identities of the tellers. The Members left the Chamber for the division lobbies, drifting back in ones and twos after they had voted. Eight minutes later, the Deputy Speaker ordered,

"Lock the doors."

After which the last Member to leave the voting lobbies could be heard calling faintly,

"All out."

The tellers approached the table in front of the Deputy Speaker and, after a clerk had transcribed the voting figures, the senior teller announced,

"The 'Ayes' to the Right, thirty-two. The 'Noes' to the Left, nineteen."

This was repeated by the Deputy Speaker, who concluded,

"So the 'Ayes' have it. The 'Ayes' have it. Unlock."

The House moved on to consider another Bill.

Ralph Waters had arranged to meet Edgar in Central Lobby, where Edgar congratulated him.

"Thank you, Edgar. Now, on Monday…" and he gave Edgar details of where to present himself in the Palace of Westminster and how to secure his accreditation as Waters' parliamentary assistant.

"After that, Edgar, come to my room in Norman Shaw North."

Ralph explained where to find it.

"See you on Monday."

"Thanks, Ralph. Until Monday."

Because Ralph had known that, with Government support, his Bill would receive its Second Reading, he had made provisional arrangements for it to be considered in committee on 3 February. He now confirmed those arrangements before leaving the Palace of Westminster. Later, on the way to Pepynbridge, the hands-free mobile rang in the Range Rover.

"Yes?"

"Is that Ralph Waters, MP?"

"It is."

"Oh, hello, Mr Waters. *BBC Radio Four Today Programme* here. The editor would like to know if you would do an interview tomorrow morning in the light of your success today in the House of Commons."

"Yes, of course."

"Okay, it'll be…" and the voice at the other end of the connection mentioned the name of a presenter.

Ralph thought for a moment.

"Could I call you back?"

"Of course, but soon please?"

"Yes, of course."

The voice mentioned the number displayed on the screen in front of Ralph. The call over, Ralph found Herbert's number in the mobile's memory and rang it.

"Hello? Reverend Onion, Rector of Pepynbridge."

"Herbie, it's Ralph."

"Oh, hello Ralph. How did it go today?"

"It passed."

"Good news. So how can I help?"

"The *Today Programme* wants to interview me about my Bill tomorrow morning. Are you able to tell me what the position is with the bishop and the PCC?"

"Ralph, I'm afraid Bishop Julian will not consent to my conducting a full marriage ceremony in the Abbey whilst it's against Canon Law."

"Not surprised. But what about the PCC?"

Herbert disclosed the exercise its members were undertaking, that it would meet again on 15 February to discuss same-gender marriage and, he expected, would then come to a decision as to whether, if it became legal, it would condone Herbert conducting the marriage of Ralph and Pascal in the Abbey.

"And what do you think the outcome will be, Herbie?"

"I am quietly confident, but I'd rather you didn't quote me on that. If you do so on air, it could antagonise any who are currently undecided."

"Okay, Herbie, and thanks."

Ralph Waters rang the *Today Programme* and explained that although he was willing to be interviewed the next day, for the reasons he explained, he thought it would be better postponed until after the Committee Stage on 3 February. And preferably after 15 February, when the Pepynbridge Parochial Church Council would decide whether it would support him being lawfully married in the Abbey. The voice at the other end of the line agreed.

"If the editor is okay with that, we'll be back in touch after the fifteenth of February, Mr Waters. 'Bye."

◆◆◆◆◆◆◆◆◆◆◆◆◆◆◆◆◆◆◆◆◆

Sunday, 24 January 2016

It was the Third Sunday of Epiphany and in St Aidan's Abbey High Mass was in progress. The sacred space beneath the stone-vaulted ceiling had been pervaded by swirling coils of incense and Haydn's music, sublimely executed by choir and organ. Communion had been distributed, the Post-Communions said and now choir and congregation were shaking the Abbey's ancient pillars with the great hymn, *"Alleluia, sing to Jesus..."* to the tune of *Hyfrydol*, composed by Rowland H. Prichard. Finally, as the reverberating cadences resolved into echoes, Herbert pronounced the blessing from the High Altar, followed by,

"Go in peace to love and serve the Lord."

Which was greeted by a rumbled,

"In the name of Christ. Amen."

The Honourable Member for Pepynbridge

The choir recessed from the east end of the choir stalls down the chancel, preceded by the crucifer and followed by Herbert, resplendent in a gold-embroidered white chasuble, while Jack Driver played the opening bars of J S Bach's Toccata and Fugue in D Minor. When at the crossing Herbert turned into the south transept, most worshippers resumed their seats to hear out the Bach, before moving to the west end of the nave where refreshments awaited.

A little apart from the rest, Ralph Waters and Pascal Legrand, holding mugs of coffee, were chatting together. Herbert approached them.

"Good morning, Ralph."

"Good morning, Herbie. Lovely service."

"Thank you."

"And the Bach, like all the music, was outstanding. Who's the organist?"

"Jack Driver..." and Herbert explained how Jack Driver and he had been students together at The Guildhall School of Music and Drama, how Jack had qualified as a solicitor and moved to Medborough where he was now a partner in the law firm, Driver & Sickle, and how Herbert had recruited him as the Abbey organist.

"Like everything else about the Abbey, Herbie, outstanding."

"Thank you, Ralph. Ralph, could you spare me a moment at the Rectory in a little while?"

Herbert looked at his watch. 12.15 p.m.

"Say at a quarter to one?"

"Sure. And Pascal too?"

"Of course."

Half an hour later in his study, Herbert disclosed, in greater detail than he had on the phone the day before, the progress of the PCC meeting and his conversation with Bishop Julian.

"The bishop was sympathetic, you say?"

"Yes, Ralph, that was my impression. As I've just said, in his opinion, the House of Bishops may support same-gender marriage in church. Whether the Houses of Clergy and Laity would do likewise, he could not say. Any more than I can."

Ralph Waters thought for a moment.

"Herbie, Edgar Templeton-Smith is joining me tomorrow as my parliamentary assistant."

"I didn't know that, Ralph. A good move, I'd say, from both points of view."

"Thank you, Herbie. One of his tasks will be to liaise with outside bodies of interest to me in my parliamentary work. Do you think Bishop Julian would be willing to talk to Edgar about my Bill?"

"I couldn't say Ralph, but no harm in trying. He's very approachable."

◆◆◆◆◆◆◆◆◆◆◆◆◆◆◆◆◆◆◆◆◆

Monday, 25 January 2016

At the beginning of each new Parliament, long-serving Members are allocated a room in Portcullis House on the corner of Bridge Street and Victoria Embankment, opened in 2001 and overlooking the River Thames. More recently elected Members, like Waters, are lodged in Norman Shaw North. Overlooking the Victoria Embankment and built between 1890 and 1906, Norman Shaw North comprises one half of what until 1966 had been the headquarters of the Metropolitan Police Service, famously called New Scotland Yard. Ralph's room afforded just enough space for three desks and chairs.

Ralph was sitting at one desk. His secretary Jane, in her twenties, slim, single and pretty with long light brown hair and grey eyes, was at the second. Edgar was at the third. Through the one window, Big Ben was visible.

"Edgar?"

"Yes, Ralph?"

"I was chatting to Herbie Onion yesterday. He told me that the Bishop of Medborough may be sympathetic to same-sex marriage. It would be very helpful to me if I had a contact in the House of Bishops. Follow me?"

"I do, Ralph."

"HMG may be supporting my Bill now, but I need to be prepared if it wavers. To have some privileged access to the mood of General Synod could be useful in negotiations with the Minister of State. Edgar, could you please set up a meeting between you and the bishop and discover whether he would be willing to help in that way?"

"I'll try, Ralph."

Edgar went on-line to the Medborough Diocese web-site and composed an email to Bishop Julian's secretary. After Waters had approved it, Edgar pressed *"Send"* and waited. The answer was not long in coming. Yes, Bishop Julian would be pleased to have a chat with Edgar in the Bishop's Palace, Medborough, on the following Friday, 29 January, at 11.00 a.m. Would that suit Edgar? It would, Edgar replied.

"Well done, Edgar. Just make yourself known to him and see if you can gauge how he feels about the issue. Okay? If I need to meet him, you'd be well placed to arrange it."

♦♦♦♦♦♦♦♦♦♦♦♦♦♦♦♦♦♦♦♦♦♦

Wednesday, 27 January 2016

Since Marigold had moved back to Pepynbridge Farm in September 2014, she spent Monday mornings and, whenever necessary, Wednesday and Friday mornings in Alfred's office, doing his books. When she walked in this morning, Alfred was out on the farm. Sitting at his desk with a pile of invoices, she noticed two paperbacks. She drew them towards her and read their titles. *More Perfect Union?* by an English bishop called Alan Wilson, and *God and the Gay Christian* by an American, Matthew Vines. Whatever is Alfred doing with these? she wondered. She saw that some pages in *More Perfect Union?* had been flagged with page markers. So, he's studying them, she thought. Not like Alfred. He may have a degree in agriculture, but he's no academic. Mentally idle, he is. Or at least, has been for years. When he's not on the farm, or in the pub, or out at a meeting, he sits in front of the television.

She browsed and saw that both books were about homosexuality and gay marriage. Well! So he's preparing himself for the next session of the PCC. He must be taking it seriously if he's bothering to read up about it. She pushed the books back to where they had lain. Shall I ask him about them? she wondered. Better not. It'll only create trouble, she decided.

She began to leaf through the invoices, entering details from each into Alfred's accounts on the screen in front of her.

That evening, Alfred went to a UKIP meeting in Medborough. There was a discussion about provisional plans for campaigning for a "No" vote in the East and West Medborough and Pepynbridge Forest Constituencies when the date of the EU Referendum was known. Alfred volunteered to speak as a farmer at public meetings in the evening, but added,

"I won't knock on doors, if you don't mind. Too much to do on the farm. Mustn't neglect that."

◆◆◆◆◆◆◆◆◆◆◆◆◆◆◆◆◆◆◆◆◆

Friday, 29 January 2016

Edgar enjoyed his first week working for Ralph. He spent most of his time in Norman Shaw North, but on Wednesday morning he had been in the House of Commons for Prime Minister's Questions. Edgar's appetite had been whetted. He had longed to be on the green benches, cheering his Party Leader on. Waiting another nine years for a fair wind when he could join in was going to be hard to bear. And by then it wouldn't be David Cameron either. Edgar speculated briefly on the future leadership of the Conservative Party and gave up. Time would tell.

On Monday morning, Edgar had left his VW Golf in Medborough Station car park. He knew that Ralph visited his mother on Friday mornings and, as Edgar had explained, except when he was needed by Ralph in London on a Friday, he preferred to be back in Pepynbridge by Thursday evening. Yesterday, Edgar had travelled from Kings Cross by train, retrieved his Golf and driven home.

This morning, Edgar drove to the Bishop's Palace in Medborough and, at 11.00 a.m., he was shown into Bishop Julian's study. Edgar did not know what to expect. He had been educated at Beaufort School, attached to a Roman Catholic Benedictine monastery in Yorkshire, where his brother and sisters were still pupils. In Edgar's day, the Abbott had been the headmaster and, on the few occasions when Edgar had been in his study, its walls had displayed a crucifix and pictures of the Blessèd Virgin Mary, Saint Benedict and Popes John Paul II and Benedict XVI. There was nothing like that in Bishop Julian's room. It was lined with laden bookshelves. A large bay window looked out onto a well-tended lawn. Bishop Julian was sitting behind a large desk. There were two upright chairs on its other side, on one of which Edgar sat at the invitation of the bishop. Also in the room, Edgar saw, were a sofa, two easy chairs and a low table bearing stacked copies of *The Church Times* and *The Tablet*.

The conversation was cordial. Yes, Julian Ross was aware of the Bill that Ralph Waters was promoting in the House of Commons. In principle, he was in favour of same-sex marriages being conducted in Anglican churches. However, whilst he could not sanction Herbert Onion conducting an unlawful marriage service,

"...there is nothing to prevent him from conducting the authorised Anglican order of *Prayer and Dedication after a Civil Marriage*, marking the relationship between Mr Waters and his partner. However, I gather from Herbert Onion that Mr Waters would not be satisfied with that?"

"No, Bishop, I'm afraid not."

Despite reiterating his own support for same-sex marriage, Bishop Julian added that he could not forecast when, and, he added carefully, if ever the Church of England would authorise its celebration in church.

"Bishop, Mr Waters would like a point of contact, an informant if you like, within the House of Bishops, independent of any bishop liaising on this issue with HMG. At present, the Government is supporting his Bill, but if there is a change of mind, Mr Waters would like access to an in-house assessment of the current mood of General Synod. Something that will not necessarily be evident from its public deliberations. Bishop, Mr Waters has sent me to ask you if you would you be willing to help him in that narrow way?"

Julian Ross reflected. He warmed to this personable young man, obviously destined for a political career. He could detect no risk in agreeing to his request provided Edgar was discreet. And he was confident Edgar would be.

"I can see no harm in that, Edgar. We have your email address. I'm not one of those in touch with the Government about same-sex marriage or Mr Waters' Bill, but if I provide you or Mr Waters with any information, it must be on a strictly non-attributable basis."

"Of course, Bishop. And thank you. Mr Waters will be grateful."

Julian Ross decided not to reveal the existence of the ongoing, discreet discussions within the Church of England hierarchy on same-sex marriage. Edgar was there on behalf of Ralph Waters and it would be unfair to burden him with information he could not pass on to his employer. Entrusting it to Waters in the expectation that he would not disseminate it would be tempting Providence too far.

"Goodbye, Edgar. And please give my regards to your father."

"I will, Bishop," responded Edgar, tilting his head and raising his eyebrows quizzically.

"His bank looks after the finances of this diocese," Julian Ross explained.

The meeting was over and Edgar left.

Later, in the knowledge that Ralph was back from St Albans and would not be conducting a surgery in Corbury that afternoon, Edgar called in at Coronation Cottage and reported his conversation with the bishop.

"Was he sympathetic, did you think?"

"Ralph, he's certainly in favour of same-sex marriage, but he's playing his cards very close to his chest. He is well aware of your Bill and is avoiding any public discussion about it."

"Don't blame, him, Edgar. But Pascal and I are not interested in the order of *Prayer and Dedication after a Civil Marriage*. I've researched that. It's marriage in church we want and its gay church weddings I'm campaigning for."

"I told Bishop Ross that, Ralph. But he is willing to keep us informed as to the inner workings of General Synod and the strength of sentiment there."

Ralph Waters nodded.

"Can't ask for more at the moment. Having made the connection, I think you should liaise with Bishop Ross. Okay?"

Edgar walked the hundred or so metres back to the Hall. After a light lunch with Augusta in the conservatory overlooking the Park, Edgar went for a walk and then to his room and his laptop. It was the custom of the Templeton-Smiths to gather in the drawing room for a drink before dinner. They did not dress formally, as had happened in the time of Alice and Augusta's father, but Cyril would be on hand to serve drinks, which lent the occasion a measure of formality. At 7.30 p.m., Edgar went downstairs. Dinner was at 8.00 p.m. and Edgar expected his mother and father to be in the drawing room. But when he entered, to his surprise there were present only Augusta, sitting on a sofa, and Cyril, hovering by the drinks table.

"Where's Dad?" Edgar asked.

"He's attending a meeting at the Pavilion. He should be back by eight."

A younger Alistair had played cricket for Oxford University, for Combined Services and, as an amateur, for Northants. He was President of the Pepynbridge Cricket Club and had been for several years. The Club played in the park behind the Hall.

Edgar collected a gin and tonic from Cyril, took it to an armchair and sat facing his mother.

"Anything more, Madam?"

"Not for the moment, Cyril. I'll ring if there is."

"Very well, Madam."

Cyril left the room.

"So, Edgar, what's it like working for a homosexual?"

Edgar was under no illusion as to what his mother, and his father for that matter, thought about homosexuality. He knew what the *Catechism of the Catholic Church* said about it and suspected his parents would not admit to any personal deviation from that, unless and until it was sanctioned by the Pope.

"Mum, it's just like working for anyone else. Of course, his Bill means that sometimes we discuss homosexuality and same-sex marriage objectively, but the fact that he's gay doesn't intrude into our work."

Augusta gazed down into her gin and tonic, swirling it gently around in the glass, and said nothing for several seconds. Then she made up her mind.

"Edgar, forgive me for mentioning it, but your father and I are disappointed that you don't have a girlfriend. You never have had, have you?"

"Not a steady girlfriend, Mum. No, I haven't."

"Is there a problem?"

Edgar thought: If I'm going to come out, it's going to be in my time and no one else's, especially not at my parents' behest, much as I love and respect them.

"No, Mum. Early days yet. I'm only twenty-four."

Augusta eyed her son, of whom she was dearly fond, and decided to leave the topic where it lay. The conversation moved on to other things until Alistair arrived and they went straight into the dining room, where Cyril awaited.

Later in bed, Edgar pondered the earlier sally by his mother. Had his father put her up to it? If he had, it meant that they suspected the truth about him. Sleep eluded him. He needed to talk in confidence to someone other than Ralph or Pascal. Then an idea came to him, which, the more he examined it, the sounder it seemed. He drifted into peaceful slumber.

◆◆◆◆◆◆◆◆◆◆◆◆◆◆◆◆◆◆◆◆◆

Saturday, 30 January 2016

The telephone rang in Herbert's study.

"Hello? Reverend Onion, Rector of Pepynbridge." A pause, then, "Yes, Edgar, of course. When?" Pause. "I'm free at the moment." Pause. "Good."

Herbert went to the study door.

"Julie?"

"Yes?"

"Edgar Templeton-Smith is coming to see me. Please may we have two coffees?"

"Coming up."

Ten minutes later, Herbert and Edgar were sitting opposite each other in the wing armchairs, nursing mugs of coffee.

Herbert listened expressionlessly as Edgar disclosed his sexual orientation. Privately, he was intrigued at how Providence was coincidentally drawing into his hands disparate threads of the same tapestry.

"So, Father, whilst I shall have to come out eventually, I want to do so in a way that causes the least amount of distress to those I love, like Mum and Dad. I don't think my brother and sisters will mind much, but Mum and Dad will."

Herbert nodded. With his Anglo-Catholic background and familiarity with Roman Catholic doctrine, he understood Edgar's dilemma.

"How is your faith, Edgar?"

"Not very strong, Father…"

Herbert interrupted him.

"Everyone calls me Herbie, Edgar."

"Thanks, Herbie. About my faith. I attend Mass in the Abbey on Sundays to please Mum and Dad, but I don't really believe."

Edgar decided not to repeat the line about Magic FM and the Chilterns.

"I'm sorry," he added lamely.

"You needn't be," responded Herbert, cheerfully. "I don't care why people come to Mass on Sundays, so long as they come. What with the music and the liturgy, it's a good place to encounter God, if they want to."

They exchanged smiles. Then Herbert said,

"I don't see any need for you to come out, as you put it, until you have to."

"Which would be when, Herbie?"

"As I see it, Edgar, it operates on two levels, the public and the private. At the public level, you've told me that Ralph has said you should disclose your sexuality to a constituency selection panel. That may be right, although, if I were you, I'd only do so if and when you're short-listed. And even then, only if you are asked about it. If you're not asked, it's safe to assume that the panel is not bothered whether you're gay. The private level concerns your parents and your friends. It seems to me that you only need to tell them that you're gay when you have no choice."

"What do you mean, Herbie?"

"If it becomes public knowledge, they'll find out anyway. If it doesn't, then you'll only need to come out if and when you enter into a committed gay relationship. As you've just told me, there's no one on the horizon at present. It's wholly wrong for people to assume that someone is gay simply because they do not have, and don't seem inclined to have, a partner of the opposite gender. Celibacy is a respectable life-style choice, adopted by both men and women."

That, thought Edgar, suits me fine. For the time being, anyway.

"Thank you, Herbie."

"Not at all, Edgar. Please don't hesitate to come and see me again. Any time, okay? Have you been selected for anywhere yet?"

"Not yet, I keep sending in my CV."

"Well, good luck."

"Thanks."

They smiled at each other, finished their coffee and Edgar left.

◆◆◆◆◆◆◆◆◆◆◆◆◆◆◆◆◆◆◆◆◆

Monday, 1 February 2016

Ralph, Edgar and Jane were sitting in Ralph's room in Norman Shaw North, with mugs of coffee on their desks.

"Another poll for you, Ralph."

"What's that, Edgar?"

"It's in today's *Daily Telegraph* and on the *BBC News* website. Here, I've downloaded and printed it."

Edgar handed a sheet of paper to Ralph who read that in a poll of 1,500 Anglicans conducted by *YouGov*, forty-five percent responded that same-sex marriage was right and only thirty-seven percent thought it wrong.

"Interesting," observed Ralph. "Three years ago, it says that the percentages were thirty-eight for and forty-seven against."

He read on and added,

"And seventy-four percent of Anglicans aged between twenty-five and thirty-four are in favour of gay marriage. Edgar, the tide is flowing our way."

"Indeed, Ralph. But how fast?"

"Well, it reports and I quote, 'A spokesperson for the Church of England said it was holding Shared Conversations on the issue', whatever that means, 'and would continue to do so at General Synod this summer'. I do find that encouraging. I expect Herbie Onion knows about it, but Edgar, could you please email him this report?"

When Herbert received and read it, he nodded. He had already picked up the same news that morning from the review of the day's papers on the *Today Programme*. Shared Conversations were not so secret after all, which he took to be a good sign.

◆◆◆◆◆◆◆◆◆◆◆◆◆◆◆◆◆◆◆◆◆

Wednesday, 3 February 2016

Shortly before 2.00 p.m., Ralph and Edgar made their way to Committee Room Nine on the Committee Corridor in the Palace of Westminster. Ralph Waters took his seat with the Conservative Members of the Public Bill Committee across the horseshoe-shaped table from Opposition Members. At Waters' suggestion, Edgar sat behind the Press at the right hand end of the area reserved for the general public. Waters asked a member of the Commons staff, sitting on a chair against the wall behind him, to act if necessary as a messenger between himself and Edgar.

The Chair opened the discussion by welcoming everyone present and congratulating,

"...the honourable and learned Member for Pepynbridge Forest on getting his Bill to this stage".

The Chair reminded the room that a committee considering Private Members' Bills does not receive oral or written evidence. However, he referred to a letter received from Lambeth Palace, copies of which had been circulated to all present, expressing unhappiness with the Bill on the grounds that, by convention, Parliament does not legislate of its own motion for matters concerning the Church of England and that the subject of the Bill should be a matter for General Synod.

A lengthy list of amendments had been tabled by members of the Committee, although none by Waters. The amendments had been grouped by the clerks into topics and, turn by turn, the Chair called upon the proposer of the lead amendment to speak to it. Then the Chair invited Members sitting on opposite sides of the table to contribute. So far as Edgar could discern, the amendments proposed to a Bill so short of detail were instruments in an elaborate game of verbal jousting, enjoyed by its participants, but arcane and confusing to the newly initiated, like himself. Despite the coherence of the contributions, in terms of engagement the procedure resembled a leisurely five-day Test Match rather than eighty minutes of robust and incisive rugby football.

None of the amendments debated were pressed to a vote.

The proceedings ended when Ralph thanked the Chair and the members of the Committee for their participation in the proceedings and it was resolved, without a division, that the Bill was to be reported to the House un-amended.

On the way out of the Palace of Westminster, Ralph remarked,

"A good experience for you, Edgar. You'll be contributing in there one day."

"It all seemed a little pointless to me, Ralph. Your Bill is so short. Surely it could have gone through on the nod?"

"It could have done, but that's not how the House of Commons works. The right to subject any legislative proposal, however short, to debate is a guarantee against tyranny. We do it as a matter of principle to demonstrate our independence."

"But EU directives are made on the nod, Ralph," Edgar protested.

"True, Edgar. But you will be aware from your studies at Oxford that the scope for amending a statutory instrument giving effect to an EU Directive is very limited. I hope that will change when the Government has concluded its current negotiations for a looser relationship with Europe."

"When will the Report Stage and Third Reading be?"

"I have named the fourth of March. It's the next Friday set aside for Private Members' Bills. I had to do that but I can defer it if necessary."

They walked on silently for a while.

"Edgar, in the strictest confidence, last week I had a private discussion with ..." Ralph named a Government minister, "...who has indicated that HMG does not want to antagonise the Church of England. It's willing to wait and see whether General Synod reconsiders the Church's position on same-sex marriage when it meets in York in July. As you know, it's not on Synod's agenda for its meeting on Monday week. If no significant progress is made in July, then the Government will re-introduce my Bill in the Commons in the next Session and support it. If it passes, it will go to the Lords."

"Will it pass in the House of Lords?" enquired Edgar. "Bishop Ross thought it unlikely."

"I couldn't say. If it doesn't pass in the Lords, there's nothing more I can do about it unless I come near the top of another Private Members' Bills ballot."

By now, Ralph and Edgar had crossed Bridge Street and were walking up Parliament Street towards Norman Shaw North.

"Pascal's not here this weekend," remarked Ralph.

"No, Ralph. I imagine he'll be going to Paris to watch the Six Nations match on Saturday between France and Italy."

"That's right, Edgar. He's leaving tomorrow for a reunion dinner at his old club in South West France. He suggested to me some time ago that he might invite you to go with him, but I told him that I needed you here. I wasn't sure whether the Committee Stage would spill over into another day. I hope you don't mind?"

"Not at all, Ralph. And he'll be in Paris next weekend as well, won't he?"

"Why?"

"It's France against Ireland."

"Has he asked you, Edgar?"

"No, Ralph, but please don't worry about it. We hardly know each other."

"Mmmm...I think he has it mind to invite you to go with him to Paris at least once to watch a Six Nations match. He said something to me about it. He's quite shy, you know."

"Yes, I realise that. If he did invite me, would you mind my going?"

"Of course I wouldn't, Edgar. I trust you both. But would you go if he asked you?"

"I would, Ralph."

"Okay. I'll tell him. After the one next week, are there any more Six Nation matches in Paris this year?"

Edgar laughed.

"You bet. England against France on the nineteenth of March. It's the final match of the Championship and it could be the decider."

"So you and Pascal would be supporting opposing teams."

"We would be, but no problem. But it would be difficult for me to return the favour. I'm a Twickenham debenture holder, which entitles me to just one ticket per match. When I go, I meet up with old rugby friends who are also debenture holders and we arrange it so that we sit together. I couldn't buy a ticket for Pascal to sit with us."

"Don't give it a thought. Pascal and I usually attend international matches at Twickenham together, but I don't go with him to Paris. I prefer to stay in this country at this time of the year. We'll be at Twickenham on the twenty-seventh of February to watch England beating Ireland."

"I wish, Ralph. I wish."

They chuckled and turned into Norman Shaw North.

◆◆◆◆◆◆◆◆◆◆◆◆◆◆◆◆◆◆◆◆◆

Monday, 15 February 2016

On 11 February, the House of Commons had risen for a week's recess. Edgar decided to spend it at home in Pepynbridge, working on various projects for Ralph. Ralph remained in London. On Friday, 12 February, as Edgar had guessed he would, Pascal Legrand had travelled to Paris to watch the match on Saturday between France and Ireland which France won by just one point.

At 4.00 p.m. on Monday, Herbert Onion, Alice Burton, Richard Maxey, Gordon and Sylvia Slim, and, Herbert was pleased to see, Norman Callow, were sitting at the long rectangular table in Abbey Hall. Jack Driver would have been present had he not been working in Medborough. Julie Onion was next door in the Rectory, caring for Little Alice. She had read the books by Alan Wilson and Matthew Vines and had assured Herbert that, at 6.00 p.m. when Leela would come and baby-sit, she would attend the PCC meeting and support same-gender marriage in church. Herbert was confident that Jack Driver would do likewise.

The absence of Alfred and Reginald Wicken and Peggy Taplow did not surprise him.

Herbert opened the meeting.

"Thank you all for coming. Shall we start with a prayer?"

Herbert said a short prayer, asking for God's guidance in the discussions that were to follow. Then, after mentioning the *YouGov* poll of Anglicans in which forty-five percent supported same-gender marriage and only thirty-seven percent were against it, he continued,

"I suggest that we look at the passages in Scripture that apparently condemn homosexual acts. Genesis, chapter nineteen, verses one to twenty-six, Leviticus, chapter eighteen, verse twenty-two and chapter twenty, verse thirteen, and, in the New Testament, Romans, chapter one, verses twenty-six to twenty-seven, One Corinthians, chapter six, verse nine, One Timothy, chapter one, verse ten, and Jude, verse seven. Content?"

The others assented.

"But before we do that, we need, I think, to consider two other passages from Genesis in chapters one and two."

Herbert reached in front of him for a copy of the Anglicised edition of the New Revised Standard Version of the Bible, adorned with flags. He opened it at the first flag.

"There are two accounts of the creation of Adam and Eve, both of whom are stated to have been made in the image of God. After the second account, the author adds this. 'Therefore a man leaves his father and his mother and clings to his wife, and they become one flesh'. The text states that God did this because Adam was alone, and I quote, 'It is not good that a man should be alone. I will make him a helper as his partner'. God created Eve because there was no other creature that could fulfil the role of helper. In chapter one, God told Adam and Eve, 'Be fruitful and multiply, and fill the earth and subdue it'. Note," commented Herbert, "that there is no mention of love. Eve's role was to help Adam and, with him, to procreate. If the human race is to survive, that was and remains an overarching imperative. Some argue that the self-evident physical complementarily of men and women militates against love between people of the same gender. I hope we can agree that, within the Christian context, love is a covenantal, self-giving relationship that can exist between any two people regardless of gender. Any comments, anyone?"

Around the table, heads shook.

"Good. What we need to address this afternoon is not love between persons of the same gender, but its physical expression. Having read Alan Wilson and Matthew Vines as we have done…"

Herbert paused and noted nods around the table.

"…can we agree with them that the passage from Genesis, chapter nineteen and the two passages from Leviticus should be interpreted in the light of the social context prevailing at the time when they were written?"

"You are referring, Herbie, are you," offered Richard Maxey, "to the historically cultural, unequal status of men and women?"

"Thank you, Richard; indeed I am."

A discussion followed, examining the proposition advanced by Wilson and Vines and supported by secular texts contemporary with the biblical passages in Genesis and Leviticus, that in the Ancient World, including Israel and Judea, men were regarded as superior to women. Women were seen as inferior human beings who had failed to develop fully in the womb.

"And the passages from Leviticus," observed Gordon Slim, "need to be read in that context, don't they? Sexual activity between men was okay in the Ancient World provided it didn't involve sexual intercourse where the passive partner adopted the inferior status of a woman. In doing so, he was betraying his God-given masculine and, therefore, superior nature."

"That's how I read it," responded Herbert.

He continued,

"In Leviticus, chapter eighteen, the relevant passage follows prohibitions of sexual activity between related men and women, reproduced by *A Table of Kindred and Affinity* in the sixteen sixty-two *Book of Common Prayer*. The passage we need to consider reads, 'You shall not lie with a male as with a woman.' Note the use of the expression 'lie with'. It is a prohibition against the specific act of sexual intercourse, not against other sexual activity that was widely practised between men at the time. Leviticus twenty, thirteen is couched in precisely the same terms."

"Difficult to take, Herbie."

"Yes, Richard, it is, given the attitude that prevailed in this country until very recently. But were we right? That's the question. Today's young think we were dead wrong."

Norman looked up.

"But what about sodomy, then?"

"Well, Norman," countered Herbert "it's one prohibition in Leviticus amongst many that are not observed these days. For example, the way that men were meant to cut their hair or the dietary rules. If we don't regard transgressing those as sinful, why should we focus on sodomy as the only one that remains?"

"But," persisted Norman quietly, "in Genesis, chapter nineteen, the mob at Lot's gate were demanding to sodomise the two male guests in his house. So wasn't sodomy the reason why Sodom and Gomorrah were destroyed?"

"I don't think so," responded Herbert. "The men of Sodom were under a sacred obligation to offer strangers hospitality and sanctuary. Lot was a stranger. His guests were strangers. And they were also angels, not human beings. Instead of treating them with the respect to which they were entitled as guests, by demanding that Lot send them out to be raped, the men of Sodom were seeking to humiliate them. And Lot along with them."

"But what about Lot's offer to the mob of his two virgin daughters to be raped instead?" demanded Sylvia indignantly.

"It's the context, again, Sylvia."

"What do you mean, Herbie?"

"His guests were male. His daughters were women," cut in Norman Callow sourly, "and therefore inferior. He offered them to protect his male guests. Appalling!"

"Outrageous!" exclaimed Sylvia.

"Yes," agreed Herbert, "it was. But understandable in the context of the time, I'm afraid. The sin of Sodom was not sodomy, but the willingness of its men to violate Lot's sacred duty of hospitality and sanctuary. That's why Sodom and Gomorrah were destroyed. The story is an allegory to demonstrate the importance of treating strangers well."

"That's not what Jude wrote," objected Norman Callow, opening a copy of the Bible he had brought with him. "In verse seven, Jude writes that 'Sodom and Gomorrah and the surrounding cities, which…indulged in sexual immorality and pursued unnatural lust, serve as an example by undergoing a punishment of eternal fire'."

"Yes, Norman," remarked Herbert approvingly. "But…" and Herbert reached out to a copy of *God and the Gay Christian* and turned up a flagged page, "…Vines points out that the Greek phrase Jude actually used for 'unnatural lust' was *sarkos heteras*, literally 'other' or 'different' flesh, not same-gender flesh. *Sarkos heteras* referred to the angels who were Lot's guests and weren't human. Jude was not referring to sexual activity between men, but between men and angels. Rather different. The reason Sodom was destroyed was because they treated Lot and his guests badly. Jesus made that clear."

"Did he? When?"

"Yes, Norman, he did."

Herbert reached out to his Bible and opened it at a flag.

"In Chapter ten of Luke's Gospel, Luke records how Jesus sent seventy of his followers on ahead of him, instructing them to take nothing for their journey, but to stay as guests. He told them that if they were not made welcome in a town, they were, and I quote, to 'go out into its streets and say, "Even the dust of your town that clings to our feet, we wipe off in protest against you. Yet know this: the kingdom of God has come near".' And Jesus concluded, 'I tell you, on that day it will be more tolerable for Sodom than for that town'. The sin of Sodom was not sodomy, but its failure to welcome strangers."

Norman Callow nodded thoughtfully.

Herbert opened *More Perfect Union?* at another flag.

"Regarding same-sex relationships, Alan Wilson writes, 'Once gay relationships are no longer seen as intrinsically disordered, they can be tested by exactly the same moral criteria as others. Do they display virtues of permanence, stability, mutual love and fidelity? Relationships are better judged by their fruit than by their configuration.' Vines makes precisely the same point, quoting Jesus from Matthew's Gospel."

Herbert opened his Bible again, and read,

" 'A good tree cannot bear bad fruit, nor can a bad tree bear good fruit…thus you will know them by their fruits'."

"That does make sense," said Alice Burton, speaking for the first time.

"And," continued Herbert relentlessly, "we should bear in mind the research that suggests that tendency towards same gender attraction is determined prenatally. Post-natal environmental factors, such as parent-child relationships, may merely trigger an innate pre-disposition that experience has demonstrated therapy cannot change…"

"Clinically, that's right, Herbie," interrupted Richard Maxey. "In two thousand and fourteen, the Royal College of Psychiatrists declared that gay conversion therapy is unethical and potentially harmful. I found that on the web just before I came out."

Herbert smiled broadly at him.

"Thank you, Doctor."

Richard returned the smile.

"Not at all, Rector."

"Theologically," Herbert went on, "it leads to the intriguing conclusion that if, as our faith teaches us, men and women are made in the image of God, that's as true for gays as for straights."

"You mean that God can be gay?"

Alice sounded incredulous.

"Alice, God is neither male nor female. God is neither straight nor gay. As Saint John wrote, God is love. Every human being, whether born straight or gay, is created in that image, with the capacity to love another, regardless of gender."

Alice paused before responding,

"I follow that Herbie."

"So what about the passages from Paul's letters, Herbie?"

"Norman, the social context in which Paul was writing was unchanged from what it had been when Leviticus was written. Women were still regarded as inferior to men. Listen to what Paul wrote in his first letter to the Corinthians, chapter eleven, verse seven."

Herbert opened his Bible.

" 'A man ought not to have his head veiled, since he is the image and reflection of God. But woman is the reflection of man'."

"He didn't write that did he, Herbie?"

Sylvia's voice registered outrage and disbelief.

"I'm afraid he did, Sylvia. To continue…"

"Sorry, Herbie," interrupted Sylvia, "but I do find that shocking."

"And, I have to say, so do I," remarked Alice.

"I'm not surprised. In Colossians," continued Herbert, "Paul insisted that wives should be subject to their husbands. It lends weight to what Wilson and Vines argue. Moving on, in Romans, Paul was condemning idolaters. Pagans in other words. The punishment for idolatry was humiliation by 'shameless acts'. By un-natural intercourse, where un-natural meant socially unacceptable. Paul says nothing in Romans about covenantal love between people of the same gender. Or about sexual intimacy between them, short of intercourse."

He paused, waiting for comments, but none came.

The Honourable Member for Pepynbridge

"Regarding the passages in One Corinthians and One Timothy," Herbert went on, "the essence of what Paul writes relates to the social context we've already looked at. For a man to adopt the traditional female role during sexual intercourse was regarded as humiliating, degrading and contrary to God's creative design. But Paul also condemned other socially unacceptable practices, like men with long hair, women talking during worship and women not covering their hair or wearing it braided."

Herbert paused again but still no one spoke. He sensed the mood of the meeting was moving behind him and that it was time to draw the discussion to a close.

"What neither Paul nor Leviticus addresses is covenantal, stable and faithful love between people of the same gender. That is never condemned in the whole of Scripture. Not even by Jesus. Nor is sexual activity, short of intercourse, between people of the same gender, whether they are male or female. How do we feel about that?"

Herbert glanced around the table. Some nodded cautiously. Richard Maxey was expressionless. When Herbert's gaze fell on Norman Callow, his response was,

"So what's your view, Herbie?"

"Norman, as I told you when we met the other day, before I read Alan Wilson and Matthew Vines, I was in two minds. I was born in nineteen seventy-five, when homosexual acts were already legal. Nevertheless, the stigma clung, evidenced by the passing of Section twenty-eight in nineteen eighty-eight, which prohibited schools from promoting same-gender lifestyles. More recently, in the light of comments two years ago by the Archbishop of Canterbury and the evidence that young people are in favour of intimate same-gender relationships, I had begun to question my own attitude towards them. Even when Ralph Waters and Pascal Legrand came to see me just after Christmas, I was unsure. But, having read Wilson and Vines, my mind is made up. Our Christian faith demands that we celebrate and support any truly loving relationship, regardless of gender."

Herbert paused, allowing this to register.

"And so far as I'm concerned," he continued, "celebrating same-gender covenantal, self-giving relationships means that, when asked to do so, the Church should conduct same-gender marriages. What about you, Norman?"

"Well, Herbie, I'm surprised at hearing myself say this, but after reading the books you lent me, I was persuaded, albeit reluctantly, that the Church should do so. I've heard nothing this afternoon to cause me to change my mind."

"That mirrors my own position, Herbie," said Alice Burton.

Sensible and cautious, thought Herbert. When Alice speaks, it's worth listening. Her change of mind and Norman's bode well.

Richard Maxey cleared his throat, capturing the attention of the others.

"Herbie, I'm afraid I'm not convinced. My mind fastens upon gender complementarily. Medically it is irrefutable and it leads me to the conclusion that sexual activity of any description should only occur between persons of opposite gender. I accept that persons of the same gender can engage in faithful, self-giving, covenantal relationships, but I don't see why they need to be married to do so. They can enter civil partnerships instead. However..." and Richard Maxey shook his head sadly, "...from its inception, the Church of England has sought to play an inclusive role in the nation's life. I don't believe that its door should be closed to anyone, whatever their sexual preference or practice. If Christians can reconcile how they behave in private with their consciences, then who am I to say they're wrong? So, I won't stand in the way of same-sex marriages in church if that's what the Church of England decides should happen."

Herbert nodded slowly at Richard before glancing around the table, inviting comment with raised eyebrows, but encountering only a slight shaking of heads.

"So, what now, Herbie?" Gordon Slim asked.

"Gordon, we'll go through the motions this evening, after which I shall report the decision of the PCC to Bishop Julian. He's already told me that, as things stand at the moment, he won't sanction my conducting an unlawful marriage ceremony in the Abbey. At present, all that the Church of England authorises is what's called an order of *Prayer and Dedication after Civil Marriage* which falls far short of what Ralph and Pascal want. I've already explained that to them."

"But Herbie, aren't some incumbents conducting same-sex marriages and blessing services in church?"

"Richard they are. It seems that provided the consent of the bishop is not sought and provided the bishop isn't told about it, then even if the bishop is aware, an Episcopal blind-eye may be turned."

"Very pragmatic. Very English."

"Indeed, Gordon. But the trouble is that Ralph is so high profile that doing that would be very risky, not least to my position as Rector."

"Don't want to lose you," voiced Alice Burton firmly.

"Thank you, Alice. Well, we'll just have to play it by ear. Bishop Julian doubts whether Ralph's Bill will be passed in the Lords. But there's still the attitude of the newly elected General Synod."

"And when does that meet?"

"It's meeting today, Gordon, but same-gender marriage is not on its agenda. We'll have to see what happens when it meets in York in July."

There was a knock on the door.

"Come in."

Leela Malik entered, bearing a tray.

"Julie thought you might like a cup of tea and some biscuits," she said. Herbert looked at his watch. It was 5.15 p.m.

"Thank you, Leela. And please thank Julie too," which was echoed around the table.

Gordon Slim cleared his throat.

"It's odd, isn't it?" he said. "According women an equal status with men, which by the way I support, has legitimised male to male sexual intercourse? Or at least disposed of a time-honoured argument against it?"

"A good example, I suggest," observed Richard Maxey, "of the law of unintended consequences."

Laughter rippled gently along the table.

When Alfred and Reginald Wicken and Peggy Taplow entered the meeting room at 6.00 p.m., they were surprised to see Norman Callow already there. He had not told them he was going to attend the earlier discussion. Jack Driver and Julie Onion entered shortly after them. At the other end of the building, Leela was caring for Little Alice. Herbert summarised the discussion that had taken place earlier.

"Peggy, anything you want to say?"

"No thank you, Herbie. I'm against it."

"It?"

"Same-sex marriage."

"Okay. Reginald? No? What about you, Alfred?

"Yes, Herbie, there is something I want to say, if you don't mind?"

"Of course not, Alfred. Everyone's free to speak their mind."

"Well, that's just what I'm going to do."

Alfred unfolded a sheet of paper, laid it on the table in front of him and smoothed it.

"I've read the two books you suggested we should, Herbie."

Herbert registered mute surprise. Alfred looked up and noticed.

"Thought you might be surprised, Herbie, but I take this very seriously. Now, those books. They're a load of rubbish and I'll explain why."

He looked down again.

"The authors argue that the passages in Scripture that appear to condemn homosexual behaviour have to be interpreted in the light of a prevailing social context that considered women to be lesser creatures than men. But that context was a human construct. Those passages have to be interpreted within a much wider context, that of the natural and, I emphasise, God-created world. I'll explain. Men and women, like all animals, are made to procreate. I needn't go into detail. The point is obvious. That's our primary function, just as it is for cows, sheep, foxes, you name it. Right?"

Alfred glanced around the table. Heads were nodding cautiously. He looked down again at the sheet of paper.

"Each of us, like any other animal, has a duty to pass on the genes that our parents have bequeathed us. It's a duty imposed upon us by nature and continues the process of Darwinian natural selection. It's also a duty imposed upon us by God. God created us to reproduce, as it is stated in Genesis, chapter one, verse twenty-eight. Having created Adam and Eve in his own image, and I quote, 'God blessed them and God said to them, "Be fruitful and multiply" '. Anybody who has the physical capacity to pass on his or her genes through reproduction, but neglects to do so, is not only failing in his or her duty to the human race. He or she is disobeying God."

The Honourable Member for Pepynbridge

Reginald Wicken was thinking: What most of them sitting around this table, including Herbie, may not know is that Alfred got a 2:1 in Agriculture at Nottingham University, where the study of genetics is part of the degree course.

But Herbert did. As Rector, it was his pitch to know.

Alfred continued,

"Homosexual activity is unnatural, because procreative organs are being used for something for which they weren't designed. It's unnatural because it sabotages nature's plan for natural selection and genetic improvement. As both are God-given, it follows that it's sinful. But it goes further than that. These books suggest that homosexuals are not responsible for their orientation. That's tosh."

Goodness, thought Alice Burton. Alfred's language is uncharacteristically mild. He really is trying to convince us.

"Homosexual activity is a life-style choice," continued Alfred. "Some men may prefer having sex with each other but there's physically nothing to prevent them from having sex with women and, as I've pointed out, it is God's will that they should. Personally, I cannot imagine why men, or women for that matter, should choose to have sex with each other, but they don't have to and they shouldn't. It's self-indulgent and it's a sin. And it's typical of our 'anything goes' culture. We're not the Ancient Greeks or the Romans. Never have been. In this country, from the Middle Ages until recently, buggery was a crime. We should respect the wisdom of our ancestors and abide by it. The trouble is, if we go on behaving with a disregard for natural law, for what's right and wrong, we'll destroy ourselves. It's no wonder that religious fundamentalists like ISIS are fighting us. They understand the importance of obedience to God. We're ignoring God's will and it'll finish us just like it finished the Ancient Greeks and the Romans."

Alfred looked up.

"That's all I want to say about homosexuality," he announced.

"I agree with Alfred," said Reginald, nodding vigorously.

Herbert looked at Peggy Taplow, who warily exchanged a fleeting glance with Julie. Both were recalling the occasion when, just after Julie had arrived in Pepynbridge, Peggy had unsuccessfully propositioned her. Peggy had apologised and asked Julie not to tell anyone. Julie had promised not to and hadn't, not even Herbert.

"Peggy?" enquired Herbert.

Almost imperceptibly she shrugged her shoulders.

"Anybody else?"

Herbert looked at the others in turn, each of whom shook their head.

Gordon Slim was thinking: That was a well constructed argument that would grace any courtroom. Alfred could have made a living at the Bar if he hadn't inherited Pepynbridge Farm.

Jack Driver was thinking: Alfred's brighter than I gave him credit for. His presentation was good professional stuff, even if I don't accept his premise that human beings are no more than just animals. We have intellectual and emotional capacities that set us apart from the rest. Objectively, human beings have insights into themselves and the world that no other creature has. We have to judge our behaviour by our standards, not by theirs. But do I need to engage with Alfred? I won't change his mind, but what about the others? Jack looked around the table. I suspect that Norman's on-side, so there's only Reg and Peggy. Not worth it.

Herbert turned back to Alfred.

"Alfred, can I ask you this?"

"Go on, Herbie."

"The authors of the books you've read emphasise the Christian importance of covenantal, self-giving love. Relationships characterised by stability, fidelity and permanence. They argue that such relationships, so defined, can exist between people of the same as well as the opposite gender. Where does that fit into your analysis?"

"If you don't mind me saying so, Herbie," replied Alfred, "there's a lot of nonsense talked about love."

He looked again at his paper. He had anticipated and prepared for this, keeping his argument in reserve in case he needed to deploy it.

"Love, as you've just described it Herbie, is merely nature's mechanism for securing genetic survival and improvement. When we're born, we're helpless and require protection. Women provide the nurture we need, through breast feeding, care and so on. Men guard, protect and provide for their women and their children, and emphasise 'their children', against predation by other human beings, driven by the imperative of improving their own gene pool at the expense of rivals. That protection is secured by, as you put it Herbie, a covenantal and stable relationship. Or as I prefer, a secure and enduring bonding between father and mother that both recognise as essential for the survival of their off-spring, the carriers and potential transmitters of their genes. That's why Jesus condemned divorce as he did in Matthew, chapter five, verses thirty-one and thirty-two. He did so because divorce was then and still is inimical to God's plan of natural selectivity."

Nice one, thought Herbert. But wrong all the same. I acknowledge Alfred's scholarship, but just as the Nazis cited eugenics to justify spurious anti-Semitism, so Alfred's using genetics to support spurious homophobia. I've always classed Alfred Wicken as a bigot. Now I'm beginning to wonder whether he might be dangerous as well.

You know, thought Richard Maxey, there's a grain of truth buried within Alfred's unpleasant rhetoric. But I'll not say anything. I've said what I've said and I'll stick with it.

Norman Callow thought: Alfred worries me. He gets worse as he gets older.

Gordon Slim thought: The sooner Alfred's off the PCC the better.

Sylvia Slim thought: Outrageous.

Julie Onion thought: Poor Herbie.

Peggy Taplow thought: Alfred's wrong. I know he is. He's just plain wrong.

Alice Burton reflected what a deeply unpleasant man Alfred was. She wondered what Marigold would make of his description of their relationship as functional bonding? She concluded that it probably wouldn't surprise her. Nothing about Alfred, she thought, would take Marigold aback. She's a saint to stick with him. But I'm not going to let him get away with it.

"Alfred," she objected, "that doesn't stand the test today, does it? People are divorcing each other all the time."

"But it should do, Alice. It's when we forget what we were, where we've come from and how we've got here, that we lose the ability to see where we should be going. My point is simple. The ancient truths have served us well. We ignore them at our peril. Of course, these days, people live much longer. Once a couple's off-spring have grown up and no longer require protection, their parents' relationship is genetically superfluous. But when Jesus lived, that was academic. In his day, most parents died in their forties or early fifties. Divorce before they had raised their children to sexual maturity undermined God's purpose in creating genetically improved humans, able in their turn to pass on their enhanced genes."

"Alfred, thank you for your contribution to our debate," Herbert said. "Interesting, but I would argue, utilitarian and wrong. It ignores the basic teaching of our Christian faith that, at its heart, lies covenantal, self-giving love, irrespective of any genetic imperative. Still, it's refreshing to have both sides of the argument out in the open. Does anyone else wish to comment on what Alfred has said?"

Herbert looked at gently shaking heads around the table. "No? Shall we vote on it then?"

There was a murmur of assent.

"The issue is, are we in favour of conducting same-gender marriages in Saint Aidan's Abbey, if and when the Church of England permits it? All those in favour?"

Eight hands were raised.

"And against?"

Three hands went up. Peggy Taplow's only tentatively, Julie Onion and Alice Burton both noticed.

"Carried, then. I'll report that back to Bishop Julian. Anything else? No?"

With relief, Herbert closed the meeting. It was 6.45 p.m.

Afterwards in Station Road, Alfred and Reginald Wicken and Peggy Taplow paused.

"I'm confused," said Peggy.

"Confused?" exploded Alfred. "I'm bloody furious. It goes against everything I've ever believed in. Life was perfectly satisfactory before this. We all knew where we stood. If you behaved, you went to heaven. If you sinned, you went to hell and, in this country if you were caught, you were locked up and a bloody good thing too. Now, kids simply won't be safe. It's scandalous and it's all to do with bloody Herbie Onion. I knew we should rue the day he ever came here."

"I agree," said Reginald Wicken. "But there's nothing to be done at the moment, Son, so I'm off."

Reginald set off down Station Road towards the cottage where he had lived since he had handed Pepynbridge Farm over to Alfred.

"Me too," said Peggy, climbing into her Land Rover Defender, parked outside the Rectory.

As Alfred was driving his Land Rover Discovery along the road to Corbury, the thought that had entered his head four weeks previously returned and his resolve hardened. I'm going to do something about this if it's the last thing I do, he promised himself as he turned into Pepynbridge Farm. But I won't say anything to anyone. Not yet, I won't.

When Marigold and Sophie returned from Sophie's ballet lesson, he reported what had happened and that he disapproved, but, to the relief of Marigold and Sophie, he said no more. But later, as he sipped whisky, he thought: I might just give Shirley a ring.

"Well done," remarked Julie in the Rectory as she and Herbert were eating supper.

"Thanks."

"Have you told the bishop and Ralph?"

"Not yet. I'll ring them in the morning."

"It won't make any difference, will it? To Bishop Julian's decision that you shouldn't conduct their marriage in the Abbey?"

"No, it won't. Not at all. But it's an important step along the way. I would expect Ralph to put tonight's decision into the public domain."

"Will you mind?"

"Me? Mind? Not in the slightest."

"What did you think of Alfred's contribution?"

"Worrying."

"I agree, Herbie."

"I hope he doesn't do anything stupid."

"Oh, I doubt it. He's a lot of hot air."

"I hope you're right, my love."

"So do I, Herbie. So do I."

Julie reached across the table and squeezed Herbert's hand.

He gazed at her, taking in her light brown, shoulder length, silky hair, lightly freckled, triangular shaped face, grey eyes, straight nose, generous smiling mouth and pointed chin. His mind went back to the fateful July evening two years ago, when he had dined with Julie for the first time in School House, across the road from the Rectory. The same evening when Sophie Wicken had concocted the myth that he had made love to her at Pepynbridge Farm, the myth had led to Herbert's trial in Medborough Crown Court in the December. It had been shortly after his acquittal that he and Julie had made love for the first time and Alice had been conceived. Since then, Herbert's love for Julie had intensified so that, sometimes like this evening, it overwhelmed him.

"Upstairs?" he suggested.

Julie withdrew her hand.

"After we've washed up."

Herbert smiled ruefully.

"Of course."

In their cottage later that night, Richard and Mary were in bed together.

"So how did it go, darling?"

"Herbie handled it brilliantly. I can't praise him enough."

"So what do you think now about same-sex marriage?"

"I'm not persuaded, but if the Church says it's all right, I'll go along with it."

"I'm not surprised."

Mary smiled into the darkness.

"Good night, darling."

"Good night, Mary. Sleep well."

♦♦♦♦♦♦♦♦♦♦♦♦♦♦♦♦♦♦♦♦♦

Tuesday, 16 February

On the morning after the PCC meeting, Herbert rang Bishop Julian and reported its decision. As he anticipated, it made no difference to the bishop's refusal to condone him conducting a marriage ceremony in the Abbey for Ralph Waters and Pascal Legrand. Herbert refrained from raising the topic of a service of blessing. The time was not right, he decided. At the other end of the line, Julian Ross was relieved that Herbert had not done so.

Then Herbert rang Ralph Waters.

"Excellent, Herbie," was Ralph's response. "Excellent. I'll ask Edgar to issue a Press Release straightaway."

♦♦♦♦♦♦♦♦♦♦♦♦♦♦♦♦♦♦♦♦♦

Wednesday, 17 February

At breakfast in the Rectory the next morning, Julie looked up from the copy of *The Daily Telegraph* she was reading.

"Herbie?"

"Yes?"

"Look at this."

She passed the newspaper, open at page 6, over to Herbert, who read the headline.

Archbishops hint Church could give blessing
to same-sex marriage

Underneath, it reported that the Archbishop of York, Dr John Sentamu, had written a letter on behalf of himself and the Archbishop of Canterbury to someone called Jayne Ozanne to the effect that the Church's attitude to same-sex marriage was under consideration and hinted that it would be the subject of closed discussions at the July General Synod in York.

"Did you know about that, Herbie?"

"As a matter of fact, I did. Bishop Julian told me when I went to see him about Ralph and Pascal."

Julie was silent and, glancing at her, Herbert discerned a hint of resentment.

"Bishop Julian put me under a cloak of confidentiality which I promised I would not break, not even to you."

Julie smiled reassuringly.

"I understand."

Herbert continued to read. Then he said,

"Jayne Ozanne is a lay member of General Synod, an evangelical and a vigorous campaigner for gay rights."

"Didn't she have something to do with a letter signed by a number of high-up Anglicans, calling on the Church to apologise for its attitude towards gays?"

"That's right, she did. And this letter from the Archbishop of York was written in response to that letter."

"It's good news, isn't it, Herbie?"

"Well, I hope so. But the article concludes with a comment from Alan Wilson, the author of one of the books we've been studying, that the Church has been talking about homosexuality for thirty years and it's about time something was done. I don't get the impression that he's unduly optimistic that it will. We'll just have to hope and wait and see."

◆◆◆◆◆◆◆◆◆◆◆◆◆◆◆◆◆◆◆◆◆

Thursday, 18 February 2016

At 7.50 a.m., Alfred Wicken was in his office listening to the *Today Programme*. One of the two presenters announced,

"As listeners may know, in two thousand and thirteen, Parliament passed an Act legalising same-sex marriage. However, in the face of theological objections from the Church of England, the Church was expressly excluded from the operation of that law. As a result, gay and lesbian people may not marry in an Anglican church like straight couples. Ralph Waters, the Member of Parliament for Pepynbridge Forest, is currently piloting a Bill through

Parliament to change the law so as to enable the Church of England to conduct same-sex marriages in church. The Bill has successfully navigated its First and Second Readings in the House of Commons and on Wednesday last week it passed its Committee Stage. It should be considered by the Commons again on the fourth of March and, if it passes, it will then go to the House of Lords. Mr Waters is with us in the studio. Good morning, Mr Waters."

"Good morning. And thank you for inviting me onto your programme."

"Mr Waters, could you explain to our listeners why you're trying to legalise same-sex marriage in Anglican churches?"

In the minute or so allowed for him to make his case, Ralph Waters did so fluently and persuasively. Then followed the questioning. Why not leave it to General Synod? Is the Government supporting his Bill? Did he expect it to become law? To all of which, Waters supplied predictable answers.

"Mr Waters, you don't hide the fact that you're gay, do you?"

"Certainly not."

"And you have a partner, I believe. Is that right?"

"It is."

"And you live in your constituency of Pepynbridge Forest?"

"At weekends, we do. We live in London during the week."

"So you and your partner spend your weekends in Pepynbridge?"

"Yes, we do."

"If your Bill becomes law, I understand that you and your partner want to be married in Pepynbridge Abbey?"

"Yes, we do, but that's not why…"

"So what does the vicar think about that, Mr Waters?" interrupted the presenter.

"He's a rector…"

"Well, the rector then…" impatiently, "…but what's his attitude, Mr Waters, to your getting married in his church? Is he in favour?"

"As it happens, he is."

"And the Parochial Church Council?"

"Is also in favour. That was the decision it came to at its meeting last Monday."

"Really? Is that attitude typical of church councils?"

"I couldn't say, but public opinion polls have been consistently in favour of same-sex marriage these past few years, so it's hardly surprising that people in Pepynbridge are too."

Alfred, anger mounting, muttered,

"Not all of us are, Mr Bloody Waters. Not all of us are."

"And the Bishop of Medborough?" persisted the presenter. "Is he in favour?"

"I couldn't say."

"So Mr Waters, you're leading a revolution in the Church of England are you?"

"No, I wouldn't say that."

"I bloody would," growled Alfred.

"Wouldn't you, Mr Waters?"

A pause followed. Then,

"You're piloting a Bill through Parliament to force the Church of England to conduct same-sex marriages in church, aren't you, Mr Waters?"

"Yes, I am, and if I may say so..."

The presenter interrupted again.

"I come back to something we discussed earlier in this interview. Shouldn't that be for General Synod, the Church's Parliament, to decide?"

"In normal circumstances it should, but at the moment it isn't planning to. My Bill seeks to remedy what is manifestly the unjust treatment of the LGBT community by the Church of England."

"But your Bill is opposed, isn't it?"

"By some it is..."

Alfred nodded vigorously.

"...but, as I have explained, currently it enjoys Government support."

"Thank you, Mr Waters. That's all we have time for. We'll be talking to ..." the presenter named a celebrated opponent of gay marriage, "...at half past eight."

Alfred slammed his biro down onto his desk. Filthy bugger! Now he's making Pepynbridge a national laughing stock. Millions will have heard that interview. This used to be a God-fearing community and now look at us. We're being made out to be a load of sex maniacs. Us! Who've tried to behave all our lives. Who've built a community here that lived by the Bible. I owe it to generations of Wickens to do something. To put a stop to it. Anything, if it's the last thing I do.

Alfred's anger festered all morning as he went around the farm and chatted to John, his farm-worker, who was greasing and cleaning machinery in the grain dryer behind the farmhouse. He didn't say anything to John about it, but by the time he went home for lunch, he had made up his mind. After lunch, Alfred went into his office, brought up a name from the memory in his mobile and pressed the dial key.

"Yes?"

"Hello. Shirley?"

"Yes?"

"It's Alfred."

"Alfred?"

"Alfred Wicken."

"Alfred! What the hell do you want?"

After Marigold had left him in December 2014, Alfred, desperate to have a son to take over his farm when he retired, had met Shirley Moore through a dating agency on the internet. Shirley was a Londoner, living in Peckham with three children of her own. She had been deserted by their father, Colin, and had been looking for security within another relationship. Shirley had told Alfred when they first met that Colin had served prison sentences for robbery and violence and she was looking for a safe haven away from that sort of world for herself and her children. Alfred had reassured her that there was nothing remotely like that in his past. In a move that later she had bitterly regretted, she had moved in to live with Alfred at Pepynbridge Farm. It had been a disaster for her and for her children and the previous August, in the middle of harvest, she had returned to Peckham, leaving behind only the briefest of notes. She and Alfred had not spoken since.

"Shirley, are you all right?"

"Yes." Cautiously, "Alfred, it's all over between us, okay?"

"Yeah, sure, Shirley. That's not why I'm ringing."

"So why are you ringing, then?"

"Shirley, I need some help."

"What sort of help?"

"Can't talk about it on the phone. Look, it's nothing at all to do with us, okay?"

"Okay, then. What are you suggesting?"

"Shirley, I'd like to meet you in London. In a pub?"

"Oh, you and your pubs, Alfred."

"No, it's not like that. I've virtually given up drink. Marigold's come back."

"Has she now? That's good. Okay then. There's a pub in Peckham called the Fisher's Arms…"

"No," Alfred interrupted. "Not in Peckham. Somewhere in Central London?"

More anonymous, he thought.

There was a pause.

"Okay then. The Mill and Grit…" and Shirley named a street in the West End.

"When?"

Alfred thought. He'd need time to prepare Marigold for him being away from the farm for a whole day.

"A week today?"

"Okay. Thursday, the twenty-fifth. Time?"

"Noon."

"Okay, see you then."

The line went dead.

That, thought Alfred, was easier than I thought it would be. But I'm not committed. Not yet. Just exploring. Plenty of time to make up my mind, one way or the other.

◆◆◆◆◆◆◆◆◆◆◆◆◆◆◆◆◆◆◆◆◆

Friday, 19 February 2016

Alfred and Reginald Wicken and Norman Callow were at their usual table in the Blue Boar. It was the first time they had been together since the PCC meeting.

"I'm surprised at you, Norman."

"I thought you would be, Alfred. But let's not talk about it. It's not the first time you and I have disagreed about something and I'm sure it won't be the last."

"When did I disagree with you?"

Alfred's tone was aggressive.

"You have a short memory, Alfred. You accused me of lying when I intervened in the trial of Herbie for interfering with Sophie a year ago last December. Remember?"

Alfred flushed.

"I'm sorry, Norman. I'd forgotten about that. Let's not go there, if you don't mind?"

"Of course not Alfred."

The Honourable Member for Pepynbridge

They were silent for a little while. Then, with a mischievous smile, Norman ventured,

"What about the EU Referendum then? Any thoughts?"

Earlier that evening, the result had been announced of David Cameron's negotiations in Brussels on the terms of Britain's continued membership of the EU.

"Plenty," growled Alfred.

"And?"

"Bloody useless."

"What is?"

"Not what is! Who is! That bloody Cameron, that's who. Thinks he's done well, does he? Scored an own goal if you ask me. Nothing done about all those bloody Poles and Romanians coming over here and stealing our jobs."

Alfred paused.

"Nor about the Frogs and the Huns coming here willy-nilly either. Bloody disgrace, that's what it is."

"Fen farmers are very pleased to have Poles and Romanians crop-picking for them in the summer, Son."

"Yes, Dad, but I don't grow fruit and veg."

"So what's happening to the campaign group you've joined, Alfred? What's it called again?"

"Leave.EU, Norman. Last Tuesday, it changed its name to Grassroots Out. Well, not exactly changed its name. It's joined up with Grassroots Out and UKIP in a new group called the GO Movement."

"So, will it be the official Brexit campaign, Son?"

"Couldn't say, Dad, but I hope so. Nigel's basically in charge."

The conversation moved on to football and how well Leicester City was doing in the Premiership. Afterwards, driving back to the farm, Alfred resolved to keep his thoughts about same-sex marriage and Mr Waters to himself, not discuss it, pretend that he had accepted the situation. But, he told himself, I haven't. No way.

◆◆◆◆◆◆◆◆◆◆◆◆◆◆◆◆◆◆◆◆◆◆

Sunday, 21 February 2016
The twelve attending the 9.30 a.m. *Book of Common Prayer* Holy Communion in the Abbey sat, as they always did, in the choir-stalls. Herbert, arrayed in cassock, surplice and, because it was Lent, purple stole, pronounced the final blessing and walked to the west end of the nave to bid them farewell. As usual, their responses were mostly curt. The Puritan Remnant disliked Herbert's High Church ways and were not reticent in signalling their disapproval. A churchwarden always attended the *BCP* service. This morning it was Alice Burton. She walked from the choir down the nave with Peggy Taplow.

Alice and Peggy were the same age. They had both been raised in Pepynbridge and had played together as children. Alice regretted their disagreement over same-sex marriage. She was talking to Peggy about her farm, which Peggy was always happy to discuss. She was a careful farmer, had no debts and had avoided many pitfalls, like BSE in the 1980s and 90s. Her business was in good heart.

"Worried about grain prices, Peggy?"

"Not really. They've not been great, but there's plenty in the bank to tide me over."

I'm sure there is, thought Alice. As they passed Herbert, they exchanged brief but cordial farewells and left the Abbey by the south porch. Outside, the lawn in Abbey Close was white with frost.

"Peggy, I'm sorry that we don't agree about Ralph Waters."

"You mean, about him and his rugby player friend wanting to get married in church."

"Yes. It's difficult for you, I know. I just wanted to say that, whilst we don't agree, I'm sorry that the subject had to come up."

"Thanks, Alice. That's kind of you."

Peggy paused in her stride and Alice halted beside her. She sensed that her friend wanted to say something, but was finding it difficult.

"Alice, you know, don't you, that when I was a lot younger, sometimes girls, young women rather, used to come and stay with me on the farm?"

"Yes, Peggy, I do."

Alice guessed what was coming.

"Alice, I've not told many people this, but I'm a lesbian. That's why I never married."

Alice refrained from remarking that she had privately come to that conclusion years ago.

"Peggy, it was very brave of you to say that."

"Thank you, Alice. You see, if I had supported Herbie at the meeting last Monday, I was afraid that it would come out. My being a lesbian, I mean. Alfred and Reg and Norman have been good friends to me over many years. They wouldn't speak to me if they knew. That's why I didn't support Herbie. You understand that, don't you, Alice?"

Alice nodded sympathetically.

"You won't tell anyone will, you Alice?"

Alice shook her head vigorously.

"Of course I won't, Peggy."

"I haven't been in a relationship for years, but I just wanted you to know because we've been friends since we were little. Remember?"

Alice nodded again. There was another pause. Alice waited silently.

"Alice?"

"Yes, Peggy?"

"I don't agree with Alfred about love just being a means of protecting genetic propagation. One or two of those girls I loved in the way that Herbie said. It was self-giving. Expecting nothing in return. Do you understand, Alice?"

"Yes, Peggy. Of course I do."

Alice bent forward and kissed Peggy softly on the cheek. As she drew back, she noticed Peggy's lips were pursed and her eyes were glistening. Not since they had been children had Alice seen her friend close to tears.

They walked together through the archway into Station Road, where their vehicles were parked and bade each other farewell.

As Alice drove back to Summerhay, she reflected:

So now effectively Alfred and Reginald Wicken are isolated. I'm not worried about Reginald. He's old and tired. But I am concerned about Alfred. What he said last Monday at the meeting was troubling. There was a calculated intensity about him that I've never seen before. Bad temper yes, many times. But not how he'd presented at the PCC meeting. He had been controlled and chilling. He's not to be underestimated, she decided, especially since he's cut down on the drink. As well as being a bigot, there is, I suspect, a cruel side to Alfred. I fear he'll try and make trouble. But quite how, I don't know.

Alice would be returning to the Abbey later for High Mass at 11.00 a.m. When she did, would she share her concern about Alfred with Herbie? Or with Richard? Not now, she decided. Not yet, anyway. And come what may, she would keep her promise not to disclose what Peggy had just told her.

Two hours later, Alfred and Reginald Wicken and Norman Callow were sitting at their usual table in the Blue Boar.

"So…" observed Norman Callow.

He sipped at his beer and replaced it on the table.

"…it's the twenty-third of June, then."

"Bring it on." Alfred was smiling broadly. "Bring it on, I say."

"Do you think Boris will choose to campaign for Brexit?"

"Don't know, Dad, but I shall. What about you?"

"Too old, Son."

"Norman?"

The Honourable Member for Pepynbridge

The retired school teacher sat silent, his brow gently furrowed, his lips pursed. Finally, "Don't know, Alfred. Haven't made up my mind yet. Plenty of time to do so. And if I do decide to vote to leave, I won't campaign. Not after my stroke and at my age."

Alfred and Reginald nodded understandingly and their talk moved to farming.

That evening in Pepynbridge Farmhouse on the *BBC News*, Alfred and Marigold watched Boris Johnson outside his house in London declaring that he was in favour of leaving the European Union.

"Bloody good thing," declared Alfred.

"Will you be doing anything in the campaign, Alfred?"

"Yup. My UKIP branch is meeting next Wednesday and I'm sure we'll be discussing what we can do. What about you, Marigold?"

"No, Alfred. Not my thing."

"No, I suppose not."

Alfred rose, walked over to a sideboard and poured himself a generous whisky.

"A bit early for my nightcap," he said, "but there's something to celebrate."

◆◆◆◆◆◆◆◆◆◆◆◆◆◆◆◆◆◆◆

Monday, 22 February 2016

In the House of Commons, Ralph Waters and Edgar Templeton-Smith watched as David Cameron reported upon the result of his negotiations in Brussels and answered questions regarding Britain's future in the

European Union, should the electorate vote Remain on 23 June.

Afterwards, as they walked together back to Norman Shaw North, Edgar said,

"What do you think, Ralph?"

"About the referendum?"

"Yes. Have you made up your mind how to vote?"

"Edgar, I have. I have tried to keep an open mind up to now, but I confess I've been biased towards remaining in the EU. Having heard the PM this afternoon, I shall vote to stay in."

"Whatever the arguments?"

"I think so, yes. What about you, Edgar?"

"Ralph, at the moment, I don't know. Cameron impressed me, but I'd like to hear the arguments for and against before I make up my mind. What about the Party, Ralph?"

"Trouble ahead, I fear. Big trouble. We'll have to see how it pans out, but there are some big beasts in the Brexit camp like Michael Gove and Boris. I believe they, or folk on their behalf, are going to make trouble for the PM."

"Pity!"

"Indeed. Don't forget that I've only been in the House since last May, so I was not privy to what went on before, but for the Conservative Party, it's been a toxic issue since we joined the Common Market in the nineteen seventies."

"Before I was born, Ralph."

They both laughed softly.

◆◆◆◆◆◆◆◆◆◆◆◆◆◆◆◆◆◆◆◆◆

The Honourable Member for Pepynbridge

Thursday, 25 February 2016

It was raining gently as Alfred walked down a narrow, pedestrianised street in Soho, hemmed in by three-storey and slightly shabby eighteenth century buildings that had once been houses but now were pubs, bars, restaurants, and coffee and sex shops. Alfred spotted a sign ahead of him bearing an image of a millstone against a pile of gravel. Underneath was written, *The Mill and Grit*. Alfred stopped in front of a heavy glass door, flanked by low, black wooden panels and, above them, exuberantly engraved windows. He pushed open the door and walked into a poorly lit bar with small tables and stools scattered about. He recognised Shirley sitting at a table in a corner and wondered how she would be with him. He need not have worried. She was friendly. She would like a white wine, please. Alfred went to the bar, ordered it and a non-alcoholic beer for himself and took them back to the table.

"Beer, Alfred? You told me you were off alcohol."

"I am, Shirley, except on Fridays and Sundays."

No sense in complicating matters by mentioning the large whisky every evening.

"This is non-alcoholic."

Shirley wrinkled her nose.

"Horrid stuff," she pronounced.

"Well, it's not so bad if you're not drinking the real thing."

"How are Sophie and Marigold?"

"They're fine. I told Marigold I was going to look at some cattle today at Louth Livestock Market in

Lincolnshire. There's an auction there every Thursday. No one else knows I'm meeting you."

"Okay. So want do you want, Alfred?"

"Shirley, I don't want to offend you."

"Difficult, Alfred."

"Yes. Well, what I want to explore is..."

Alfred hesitated. Saying it out loud daunted him. Shirley looked at him, wondering. She decided to help.

"Okay, why the cloak and dagger stuff? Meeting like this I mean. Is what you want done dodgy?"

"Yes, Shirley it is."

"How dodgy?"

Shirley fixed him with a steady stare. Having shared a house and a bed with Alfred for six months, he was, she knew only too well, prey to powerful prejudices with a vindictive streak that ran through him like letters in a stick of rock.

"What's your problem, Alfred?"

"An MP, Shirley."

"An MP, for God's sake? You serious?"

"Yes, I am."

"So what do you want to do about this MP? Get him out of the way?"

"Do you know anyone who could do that?"

"Not exactly, Alfred. But I know someone who might know someone. You really want to put a contract out on an MP?"

"If I tell you, Shirley, I would deny ever saying so."

Shirley laughed softly.

"Oh, Alfred, that goes without saying. Where I come from, that's a given. But it'll cost you."

"What, the contract?"

"Oh, that for sure. But I'd need an introduction fee."

Alfred eyed her.

"How much?"

"A grand."

"As much as that?"

"Not a penny less, Alfred. It's no good trying to bargain with me. That's my price. Take it or leave it."

"How do I get it to you?"

"I'll let you know, Alfred, okay?"

Alfred nodded.

"Someone'll call you on your mobile. You'll get a call within the next few days. It might be me. It might be someone else. If it is, you'll know I've asked him to call you, okay? But don't try to contact me again, okay? I stored your number when you called me. If you ring me, I'll see it's you who's calling and I'll not answer. Whatever. 'Bye, Alfred."

She drained her glass of wine and they both rose to leave. Alfred's drink lay untouched on the table.

"Thanks, Shirley."

Shirley looked at him, tossed her head slightly, sniffed, turned and walked out of the bar.

When Alfred followed her into the street, the rain had turned heavy. He turned up his collar, pulled his cap low over his forehead and walked to Tottenham Court Road Underground Station.

Later,

"Did you buy a beast, Alfred?"

"No, Marigold. There was one I fancied, but it was too dear."

But, in the train from King's Cross, much as he resented it, Alfred had decided that Shirley wasn't too dear. He'd pay her price, if that's what he wanted to have done, But was it? He wasn't sure. Just dipping my toe in the water, I am. That's all I'm doing. Maybe Shirley was talking a load of hot air. Well, we'll see.

♦♦♦♦♦♦♦♦♦♦♦♦♦♦♦♦♦♦♦♦♦

Friday, 26 February 2016

The telephone rang on Herbert's desk. It was 4.30 p.m.

"Hello? Reverend Onion, Rector of Pepynbridge."

"Oh, Herbie, it's Sylvia here. Please could I speak to Julie?"

"She's not home yet, Sylvia."

Teaching at Saint Aidan's Primary School finished at 3.30 p.m., but Julie generally worked until 5.00 p.m. There was a privately run crèche at the school, staffed by a nurse, who cared for Little Alice and other infants belonging to teachers and parents of pupils.

"She should be home at five, but she has to feed Little Alice and put her to bed. Could you ring again after seven? Or I could take a message?"

"No thanks, Herbie. I'll ring after seven."

"All right. Oh, and Sylvia?"

"Yes?"

The Honourable Member for Pepynbridge

"I hope you don't mind, but, in future if you want to speak to Julie rather than me, could you please use our other land-line? I keep this one for parish business."

Herbert supplied the number.

Just after 7.00 p.m., Julie and Herbert were in the kitchen when the telephone rang in there.

"That'll be Sylvia," observed Herbert.

Julie picked up the receiver.

"Yes?" Pause. "Oh, hello Sylvia." Pause. "Well done." A much longer pause. Then, "Of course you can. When? Why not tomorrow morning? I don't work on Saturdays." Pause. "About eleven? Good. See you then."

Julie replaced the receiver on its rest.

"Sylvia's finished her novel."

"Well done, her."

"Yes. She's asked me to read it. I said I would when we were at the Templeton-Smiths on New Year's Eve."

"Did I tell you that she'd spoken to me about finding a publisher?"

"No?"

Herbert recounted his conversations with Sylvia and Joshua Cohen. Then he mentioned Joshua's email containing the names of publishers and added,

"I don't know whether she's done anything about that."

"She hasn't, Herbie. She's just told me that she wants me to read it and say what I think about it before submitting it to another publisher. She says there's no point in paying to have it published if it's no good."

The Honourable Member for Pepynbridge

"I doubt whether the sort of publisher that Josh recommended would anyway. They're collaborative publishers and share risk with the author."

Herbert laid the kitchen table while Julie prepared dinner. Then, as they sat eating,

"Did Sylvia ask you to edit it?"

"No, just to read it."

"Why don't you offer to edit it? It'll take a lot more time, but I'm sure Sylvia would appreciate it. It wouldn't be surprising if it's full of errors. Punctuation, typos, repetition, continuity, that sort of thing."

"I don't have time, Herbie. Anyway, not until the Easter holidays. And even then I shall have a lot to prepare for the summer term. I'm a busy girl, Herbie."

"Of course you are, my love."

Herbert thought for a moment.

"What about Leela? She's bright and being of South Asian heritage, she'll approach it from a different perspective. Her judgement is less likely to be distorted by English cultural assumptions."

"That's a good idea, Herbie. Do you think she would?"

"It wouldn't surprise me, but, to be fair, Sylvia should offer to pay her."

"How much?"

"I've no idea. I'll ask Josh. How long is it?"

"About a hundred and twenty thousand words, Sylvia told me."

When they finished their meal, Herbie went into his study and, after a few minutes, he returned.

"Josh says the going rate for a professional to proof-read a manuscript that long would be eight or nine hundred pounds. It would cost more for someone to copy-edit it, checking continuity and so on. Josh says ten pounds per thousand words, so twelve hundred pounds. Leela would be well able to do that. I would think that paying her less than the professional going rate would be fair. Sylvia would have to ask her."

"What about Sophie?"

"Sophie's not academic." Herbert paused. "Like her father, she's apt to rush at things, jump to conclusions. And she's quite self-absorbed. I think Leela would be a better bet. She's clever. And careful too. Remember how she saw through Ash's Islamist cover last year, when Sophie didn't. Leela's shrewd, possesses a keen critical faculty."

"That's true. Thanks."

In The Blue Boar, Alfred, Reginald and Norman were sitting at their customary table with their customary pints of beer. Their glasses had already been re-charged once and conversation was flowing freely.

"So, how did your UKIP meeting go last Wednesday, Son? It was last Wednesday, wasn't it?"

Alfred looked into his beer and said nothing for several seconds. Then he straightened up, sniffed hard and growled,

"Yes, Dad, it was. And it didn't go well."

"Oh? Why's that?"

"You may have read in the paper, or seen on the telly, that there's a row going on in UKIP about which Brexit campaign it should be supporting?"

"I certainly have," said Norman and Reginald nodded.

"Well, I can't answer for UKIP nationally, but the local branch is in a real buggers' muddle over it. Members are resigning."

"What about you, Alfred?"

"Norman, I haven't made up my mind, but I'm pretty pissed off."

All three pulled at their pints and the talk between them switched, as it invariably did these days, to Leicester City's remarkable run in the Premier League.

Edgar in Pepynbridge Hall and Ralph and Pascal in Coronation Cottage watched television as Wales defeated France nineteen points to ten in Cardiff. Pascal sighed deeply and shook his head.

"Not France's year, I fear," observed Ralph.

"*Je ne crois pas. C'est dommage.*"

Ralph chose to make no reply.

◆◆◆◆◆◆◆◆◆◆◆◆◆◆◆◆◆◆◆◆◆

Saturday, 27 February 2015

In the Rectory kitchen, Sylvia handed a slender ring-binder to Julie.

"The original is in font twelve and one and a half spacing," she explained, "but I've reduced it to font ten, single spacing, otherwise it would be too bulky. It may be too long. I don't know."

"Okay, I'll read it and let you know what I think. Have you thought about having it edited?"

"Oh, yes I have. I've been on-line, but it costs a lot. I was hoping that a publisher might do that for me."

"Sylvia, let me read it. I'll not do a detailed edit. I'll just tell you if I think it needs it. All right?"

"Thank you, Julie."

Sylvia left. Sitting at the kitchen table, Julie opened the folder. The title page announced, *A Tyrant's Best Friend*. She turned to the first page of narrative and read,

John Russell was just nineteen years old when his uncle, Thomas Trenchard, Governor of the Dorset Coast, sent for him. It was the tenth of January, in the tenth year of the reign of King Henry the Seventh, reckoned by the Julian calendar.

"John, three ships have sought shelter from storms near Weymouth. The crews have no English and the good folk of Dorset believe they be pirates. You have French and Spanish. Prithee go thither and discover their business."

"Aye, Uncle," said John...

Julie closed the folder, put it on a shelf and began to prepare Little Alice's midday feed. She would read Sylvia's novel when she could find the time. Had she been rash on New Year's Eve, when she had promised Sylvia she would do so? She hoped not. She liked Sylvia and was pleased that she had found something more to do than just ferry Roger to and from Corbury and care for him and Gordon and their house in Hall Close. But, Julie thought, if Sylvia was seeking something more productive and rewarding, writing a novel was an uncertain venture upon which to pin her hopes. I wonder if I could use her at school as a teaching assistant. I'll have to check the regulations. If it's a possibility, I'll clear it with Herbie. Sylvia would be good at something like that.

At the same time as Sylvia was handing Julie her novel, Edgar was travelling by train from Clapham to Twickenham. When he arrived, he met up with old rugby friends and they watched England beat Ireland, twenty-one points to ten. By chance Ralph Waters and Pascal Legrand were drinking in the same bar at the stadium where Edgar and his friends went for a beer after the match. Edgar introduced Ralph and Pascal to his friends and was pleased and relieved when they accepted the openly gay couple without demur. Did it help that Ralph bought an expensive round of drinks for all of them? Edgar hoped not.

Pascal was unhappy over France's poor form against Wales the previous day.

"I doubt France will win the Six Nations," he predicted, with which the others present mutely concurred.

◆◆◆◆◆◆◆◆◆◆◆◆◆◆◆◆◆◆◆◆◆

Tuesday, 1 March 2016

Manoeuvring a tractor fitted with a fork behind Pepynbridge Farmhouse, Alfred deposited a large round hay bale in the Atcost shed that had previously served as a dairy unit. Now it housed twenty store cattle. Before long, he would turn them out onto grass for the spring and summer. By autumn, they would be ready for slaughter. He was cutting the twine that bound the bale when, just after 9.00 a.m., his mobile rang.

"Yes?"

"Alfred Wicken?"

"Yes, that's me."

"Alfred, Shirley suggested I ring you. Know who I mean? Shirley?"

Alfred's heart skipped a beat and he caught his breath.

"Still there, Alfred?"

"Yes. Sorry."

"No bother. You want something done, yeah?"

"Yes, that's right."

"Okay, mate. We'll meet, yeah?"

"Okay. Where?"

"Toddington Services on the M One, southbound. Okay?"

"When?"

"Depends."

"On what?"

"Well, Alfred, if you turn up and I'm there too, you'll owe Shirley a grand, yeah?"

"Yes, if we meet, then I will."

"Yeah well, if we do, you bring it with you, okay?"

"Okay."

"In cash, Alfred. Don't draw it out of your bank all at once. In bits, yeah? That way, you'll cover your tracks. So it'll take you a little while, yeah? When you have it, text this mobile number with a date, a time and the make and registration number of your motor. If it suits me, I'll text you back and we'll meet up. Okay, Alfred?"

"Okay." Alfred paused. "What's your name?"

"Tell you if we meet. 'Bye."

Alfred's mobile went dead.

At about the same time, Herbert was disturbed by a knocking on the front door of the Rectory. He opened it to reveal a solidly-built man with a round, weather-beaten face, wearing jeans, a woollen check shirt, a high visibility vest and safety boots.

"Reverend Onion?"

"Yes."

"Good morning, Reverend. I'm Harry Wood and I work for Corbury Construction."

"You've come about the Abbey roof?"

"That's right. I've got a couple of lorries parked up the street. Mind if I bring them into the Close so we can start erecting the cover over the Abbey?"

"Not at all, Mr Wood."

"Harry," corrected the other.

"Yes, of course, Harry. How long will it take to get it up?"

"Oh, three or four days, maybe. We're putting scaffolding all the way up the sides of the building and then a plastic roof over the top."

"The work won't interfere with what happens inside, will it?"

"No Reverend. Not at all. Is it just Sundays you're in there?"

"No, no. There's usually something going on every day. Prayer meetings. Bible study groups. Piano practice. Choir rehearsals every Tuesday and Wednesday at six o'clock."

Sophie Wicken's voice had matured into a fine soprano and Herbert had moved choir rehearsals from Mondays to Tuesdays to accommodate her ballet lessons.

"We'll be off site by six, Reverend. Before then, we'll keep the noise to a minimum. Once the temporary cover is in place, it'll be quieter."

"Well, good luck with it, Harry."

"Thanks, Reverend."

A few minutes later, in the looking glass over his study door that reflected the Abbey, Herbert saw two flatbed lorries, loaded with scaffolding, enter Abbey Close and park on the grass. He winced. Inevitable, I suppose, but David won't be pleased. David was the Abbey's paid verger who, as well as his many other tasks, kept the Abbey Close lawns in good order.

◆◆◆◆◆◆◆◆◆◆◆◆◆◆◆◆◆◆◆◆◆

Wednesday, 2 March 2016

At 10.00 a.m., when Ralph Waters walked into his room in Norman Shaw North, Edgar looked up from his desk and wordlessly held out a sheet of paper. Ralph took it. It was a letter from the Medborough Conservative Association. Edgar had been selected for a preliminary interview for the Medborough West Parliamentary Constituency.

Medborough West Parliamentary Constituency encompassed the western half of the City of Medborough and was bounded on its east and west respectively by the divisions of Medborough East and Pepynbridge Forest. Ralph had known the letter was coming. He had been approached by the sitting Member of Parliament, Sir Ramsey Phillips, and by the Chairman of the Medborough Conservative Association, Emmanuel Sickle, Jack Driver's partner in the law firm, Driver and Sickle. Sir Ramsey had decided to retire on the grounds of ill-health at the next General Election in 2020. The Association was looking to adopt a prospective parliamentary candidate and Sir Ramsey and Emmanuel Sickle and then Party Headquarters had asked Ralph about Edgar. Ralph had recommended that he should be interviewed, praising his work as his parliamentary assistant and emphasising his local roots in Pepynbridge. Ralph had said nothing of this to Edgar. He handed the letter back to Edgar.

"Well done, Edgar. I know Sir Ramsey. Poor chap's been diagnosed with prostate cancer. He's had surgery and is having a course of radio-therapy. His majority is not huge..."

"One thousand, nine hundred and ten, Ralph," interrupted Edgar, struggling to contain his excitement. "I've looked it up on the internet."

"Yes, well they're selecting a prospective parliamentary candidate now in case Sir Ramsey retires before the next General Election in twenty twenty. There might be a by-election, but unless and until you hear it from someone else, please keep that to yourself, Edgar."

"I shall, Ralph. Thank you for telling me."

"And don't get too excited. You've only been chosen for a preliminary interview. You'll be one of many. When is it?"

Edgar glanced at the letter.

"Monday week. The fourteenth, at eleven thirty-six."

He looked up.

"Ralph, please may I have the day off? I can go there direct from home and come on to London either the same day or on the Tuesday."

"Of course, Edgar. And I'm delighted for you. First interview, isn't it?"

Edgar nodded.

"Well, good luck."

"Thanks, Ralph. Is the Report Stage and Third Reading of your Bill still next Friday?"

"No, Edgar. This morning, I had another meeting with..." Ralph again named the Minister of State he was in discussion with over his Bill, "...who told me that the

Government has decided it will keep it alive and see what General Synod decides to do next July about same-sex marriage in church, if anything."

"So, what happens?"

"I've been asked to withdraw it upon an undertaking that HMG will re-introduce it as a Public Bill in the next Session that begins after the State Opening on the eighteenth of May."

"And will you?"

"Will I what?"

"Withdraw it? Can you trust the Government?"

"Yes, Edgar, I shall withdraw it. And yes, I believe I can trust the Government. If they rat on me, I'll go public. As you know, the *Today Programme* is interested in the progress of my Bill. The BBC is no friend of the Tories and if I'm let down, I'll create a stink."

Edgar stared out of the window at Big Ben. Then, without shifting his gaze, he asked,

"Wouldn't that scupper your chances of a Government job?"

"Not interested, Edgar. Not remotely interested."

I wonder? thought Edgar, reading the time on Big Ben. I wonder? I would be.

◆◆◆◆◆◆◆◆◆◆◆◆◆◆◆◆◆◆◆◆◆

Sunday, 13 March 2016

On Saturday, 12 March at Twickenham, Edgar and his friends had celebrated England's defeat of Wales by twenty-five points to twenty-one, securing England's victory in the Six Nations Championship and fulfilling Pascal's prediction that, this year, it would not belong to France.

The same afternoon, Julie had finished reading *A Tyrant's Best Friend*. Now, on Sunday, as she returned to her place in the choir stalls after receiving communion, she rehearsed in her mind what she was going to say to Sylvia. The book was good. She had found it hard to put down. It would hold a critical reader's interest, as it had hers. The characterisation was sensitive, multi-dimensional and objective. Stereotyping was avoided. The narrative flowed well. Although there was no bibliography, so far as Julie, who was no historian, could tell, Sylvia had done a lot of research into John Russell, King Henry VIII and their contemporaries. However, there were continuity gaffes and typographic and grammatical errors. It needed a rigorous edit.

The Post-Communion Prayers prayed, the final hymn sung, Herbert pronounced the blessing from the high altar and enjoined all to,

"Go in peace to love and serve the Lord."

"In the name of Christ. Amen," came the rumbled reply.

As Jack Driver played the Allegro from Vivaldi's *Spring*, the choir, preceded by the crucifer and followed by Herbert, resplendent in a purple chasuble, heavily embroidered with gold, recessed from the east end of the Abbey through the chancel and, at the crossing, turned left towards the choir vestry in the south transept.

After disrobing, Julie made her way to the west end of the nave where two helpers were dispensing coffee, tea and biscuits from a trestle table, covered with a white cloth.

"Hello, Sylvia," she said, when she had collected a mug of coffee.

Sylvia turned and smiled at Julie.

"I've read *A Tyrant's Best Friend.*"

Anxiety clouded Sylvia's features.

"Yes?"

Her voice betrayed a want of confidence. It was a big moment. No one else had read it, not even Gordon.

"I liked it."

"Did you?"

Relief swept Sylvia's face.

"Yes, I did. It reads well, but I do have one or two comments. Have you time to come back to the Rectory now? Herbie and I lunch late on Sundays. Or perhaps this evening?"

Sylvia looked at her watch. 12.15 p.m.

"Julie, I'll come now. I'd better tell Roger."

Gordon did not sing in the choir, but Roger did. Two years earlier, his treble voice had been of a quality that Herbert, with his extensive musical experience, had never previously encountered. In January 2015, Roger's voice had broken and, for several months he had not sung in the choir. Herbert was conscious of the damage that can be done to a newly maturing adolescent voice when too much is expected of it too soon, but, just before last Christmas, he

The Honourable Member for Pepynbridge

had auditioned Roger and invited him to rejoin the choir as a tenor.

Now, mug of coffee in hand, Roger was chatting to fellow choir members, Sophie, Ash and Leela. Apologising, Sylvia interrupted them. Yes, Roger would tell his father that Sylvia would be coming home a few minutes late.

"Tell Dad that there's a stew with dumplings for lunch. It's in the warming oven and won't spoil. I'll cook the sprouts when I get home. They won't take long."

"Okay, Mum."

"And remind him I'm looking forward to a glass of fizz."

Roger smiled at her.

"Sure thing, Mum."

Minutes later in the Rectory, Sylvia and Julie were sitting at the kitchen table. Julie praised the narrative of *A Tyrant's Best Friend*, but raised concerns about errors.

"Sylvia, please don't be offended, but it needs editing."

"You, know, Julie, it's funny. I've read it through at least…"

Sylvia paused to remember, then went on,

"…Oh, at least four times and I thought I'd tidied it up."

Julie drew upon her experience as a teacher.

"The problem is that you're the author, Sylvia."

Sylvia frowned and tilted her head slightly.

"Look," said Julie, "I'll explain. Because it's your book, you're always going to read it subjectively. When you were writing it, you knew what you were trying to achieve. Whether it's continuity in the narrative, punctuation, dialogue, whatever it is, when you re-read it, you're re-visiting your own creation. As I've said, you read it subjectively and so it's inevitable that you miss unexpected errors. Errors that you never imagined for one moment you would make. Do you follow me?"

Sylvia looked silently at Julie and then away, through the window that looked out across Station Road towards the primary school. She struggled to understand what Julie had said, what she had meant. Then it dawned. She was too bound up with *A Tyrant's Best Friend*, too committed to it to read it as someone would, who had never met her.

She switched her gaze back to Julie.

"Thank you, Julie. I needed that."

"Like a hole in the head?"

Julie smiled at her.

"No. Not at all. You're right, Julie. It needs someone else to look at it critically. But who? I could engage a professional editor. I've been on-line. To edit a book this long would cost over a thousand pounds."

Julie decided not to mention that Herbert had spoken to Joshua Cohen, who had said the same. Instead, she suggested,

"Why not ask a non-professional to edit it. Someone bright, but who would have the capacity to be objective. I'd love to do it, but I don't have the time."

Sylvia looked at Julie through narrowed eyes.

"You've someone in mind, haven't you?"

"Yes, Sylvia, I have. Leela. Actually Herbie suggested her. She's bright and she comes from a different culture that would enhance her objectivity."

"Have you or Herbie spoken to her?"

"No, neither of us has. We thought you should, if that's what you want to do."

"Thanks, Julie. I can't thank you enough. How much do you think I should pay her?"

"You'd have to talk to her about that. And Sylvia?"

"Yes?"

"I should speak to Abi and Sabi as well."

"Yes, of course."

"Well, here you are, Sylvia."

Julie handed the folder back to her.

"And, good luck with it."

"Thanks, Julie."

Sylvia made to leave, but Julie remained seated.

"Sylvia?"

"Yes, Julie?"

"Before you go..."

Sylvia settled again.

"Sylvia, please don't be offended, but I was just wondering..."

Julie paused and Sylvia raised her eyebrows interrogatively.

"Would you be interested in helping me out over the road at the primary school?"

"I could be. In what way, Julie?"

"As a teaching assistant?"

"Which would entail what?"

Julie Onion rose, collected a sheet of paper from a welsh dresser and resumed her seat at the kitchen table.

"I'll quote from the *Times Educational Supplement* website."

She looked down at the computer printout.

"The role of a teaching assistant, it states, 'is varied and often includes the following: working one to one or with small groups of pupils, supporting pupils with learning difficulties or disabilities, preparing the classroom for lessons, e.g. setting up equipment, tidying up and keeping the classroom in good order, creating displays of pupils' work, and helping on school outings or at school events'."

Julie looked up.

"What do you think?"

Sylvia's upward, pensive glance and pursed lips betrayed interest. She lowered her eyes and looked at Julie.

"You know, Julie, since Gordon and I moved to Pepynbridge two years ago, I have been thinking about what to do with myself. I'm a qualified solicitor with a law degree from Bristol University. I worked for a law firm when we lived in London but I decided not join one here because, every weekday and most Saturdays during term-time, I have to ferry Roger to and from Corbury. I suppose that's why I've written *A Tyrant's Best Friend*. But the sort of work you've just described sounds really rewarding. Would it be flexible enough for me to go to and from Corbury twice a day?"

"I'm sure it could be arranged."

"So, what would I need to do?"

"I assume you've got GCSEs in English and Maths?"

Sylvia chuckled.

"Heavens, yes."

"Well, you won't need any other academic qualifications to start at Saint Aidan's, although you will need to pass a DBS check. Know what that is?"

Sylvia nodded.

"I'll arrange that," continued Julie. "But it would be a good idea for you to do a teaching assistant's course. There are a number on offer. They're non-residential and Saint Aidan's would pay the course fee. And you could do it while you're working. I've already cleared that with the Chairman of the Board of Governors..." Julie paused, grinned and added, "...Herbie, actually."

"Sounds good, Julie. I'm really grateful to you for suggesting it. When would I start?"

"My preference would be this September, the beginning of the academic year. If you can enrol on a course before then, so much the better."

Sylvia smiled broadly.

"Fantastic, Julie. I'll do that. If you help me choose a course, I'll start straightaway."

Julie smiled and nodded.

"And we'll pay you, as well."

"Really?"

"Of course. I'll ensure it's on the agenda for the next meeting of the Board of Governors after Easter and let you know. Teaching assistant salaries start at about twelve and a half thousand a year and rise to about fifteen and a half."

Which is a lot more than I'm likely to earn from *A Tyrant's Best Friend*, reflected Sylvia.

They pushed back their chairs and rose. Sylvia walked around the table and hugged Julie.

"Thanks Julie."

Her voice sounded unsteady.

"Not at all, Sylvia. I'm delighted for you. And, once again, good luck with the book."

Sylvia cleared her throat.

"Thanks Julie. You're a good friend."

They exchanged affectionate kisses and, as Sylvia left, Julie thought:

She'll be fine. A good job done, my girl. Herbie'll be pleased.

It was after 2.00 p.m. when Sylvia let herself into the house in Hall Close she shared with Gordon and Roger.

"Not much fizz left, darling," Gordon joked.

"Yes, I'm sorry it took so long."

"Don't worry. Tell us about it."

"What about the sprouts?"

"Oh, never mind the sprouts. Tell us what Julie said."

When Sylvia had done, Gordon said,

"Your father would be chuffed."

Sylvia's father had been a head teacher before he had retired.

"You mean about my becoming a teaching assistant?"

"I do. I think it's a splendid idea. Good for Julie."

The Honourable Member for Pepynbridge

"Yes, Mum, I think so too."

"Thanks Roger."

"And good luck with the publishers," Roger added. "I think it's really, really exciting. Your book, I mean." Gordon took the bottle of *cava* to the dining table and they settled down to stew with dumplings, but no sprouts. After lunch, Julie rang the Maliks.

Watching television in Coronation Cottage, Pascal's disappointment at France's failure to win the Six Nations by reason of England's triumph at Twickenham the day before, was compounded by France's defeat in Edinburgh by Scotland, twenty-nine points to eighteen, despite a redeeming try by Guilhem Guirado, the French captain. All that remained now to salvage Gallic pride would be a win in Paris against England the following Saturday, depriving England of the Grand Slam. On that score, intuition provided Pascal with little comfort.

◆◆◆◆◆◆◆◆◆◆◆◆◆◆◆◆◆◆◆◆◆

Monday, 14 March 2016

The preliminary interviews of those seeking nomination as the prospective parliamentary candidate for the constituency of Medborough West took place in the Conservative Office in Medborough. Following the intervention of Party Headquarters in Millbank, over a hundred applicants had been pared down to twenty-one, each of whom had been given a time to attend between 10.00 a.m. and 6.00 p.m. There was one interviewing panel and twenty minutes had been allocated for each applicant. Seventeen minutes for the interview. One minute for the changeover of candidates. And two minutes for discussion and decision. The panel was to short-list four applicants from those it had seen.

Edgar was sitting in a waiting room, from which three doors led off, the one through which he had entered from the street and two on the other side of the room. At 11.00 a.m. precisely, one of them opened. An applicant emerged and smiled diffidently at Edgar. Edgar's name was called and he walked into a room where seven men and women were sitting behind a table. On Edgar's side of the table, nearest the door, was a high backed chair.

"Good morning," said a man, sitting in the middle of the others. "Edgar Templeton-Smith?"

"Yes, Sir."

"Edgar, do take a seat."

He indicated the high backed chair.

"I'm Ian. And this is..."

He introduced the other panel members.

"How do you do?" said Edgar.

He smiled at each in turn as his greeting was returned and sat on the chair.

"Now, Edgar..." started Ian.

The interview lasted precisely seventeen minutes that Ian timed by a clock on the wall above the door behind Edgar. Questions dealt with Edgar's education, his knowledge of politics generally, his political views, which Edgar described as mildly right of centre economically but socially liberal, how he anticipated nursing the constituency pending his election, what he thought about the current leadership of the Party, and were there any particular issues about which he felt strongly? Edgar mentioned the war in Syria and Iraq, terrorism and education. He said nothing about the EU Referendum or same-sex marriage. He would have done had he been asked, but he wasn't.

"Thank you, Edgar," concluded Ian. "It's been a pleasure to meet you. We'll let you know next Friday how you've done. If you are short-listed, you will need to be at the Orchid Conference Centre the following Tuesday, the day after Easter Monday. We'll let you know the time. Know where it is? You do? Good. Any questions, Edgar?"

Edgar shook his head.

"No, Ian and thank you."

"Not at all. Goodbye."

Edgar rose and left the room.

◆◆◆◆◆◆◆◆◆◆◆◆◆◆◆◆◆◆◆◆◆

Tuesday, 15 March 2016

Alfred had been careful withdrawing £1,000 for Shirley. Using ATMs, he had taken out no more than £200 at a time and yesterday, a fortnight after the call from Shirley's contact, he had the whole amount. He had texted that he could meet him on Tuesday, 15 March, at Toddington Services at 11.00 a.m. He would be driving a Land Rover Discovery and gave its index number. The reply was,

2moro at 11 in the car park by the moto building southbound

The Honourable Member for Pepynbridge

Now Alfred was sitting in his Discovery, parked next to a retail hall, bearing the legend "Moto". It was raining.

A man in a hooded parka jacket and jeans approached from behind the Discovery and tapped on the passenger window. Alfred motioned to him to get in, which he did. Alfred looked at him. He was fortyish, his hard-featured face partly concealed by a hood.

"You Alfred?"

"Yes."

"Okay. Just call me Jim, okay?"

"Okay, Jim."

"You're looking to disappear someone?"

"Yes."

"Who?"

"An MP called Ralph Waters."

Jim looked at Alfred in astonishment and gave a low whistle. Shirley hadn't mentioned the target.

"An MP? Why?"

"Don't ask."

"Okay, but that'll cost you."

"How much?"

Jim thought for a moment.

"Ten grand?"

Alfred nodded. He was expecting more.

"When?" Jim asked.

"No hurry. July or August, maybe?"

"Okay. We'll have to do some detective work. Who is it again?"

"Ralph Waters."

"Ralph Waters?"

"Yes, that's right."

"Where does he live?"

"In London somewhere. And in Pepynbridge at weekends."

"Where's that?"

Alfred explained.

"Okay. Got Shirley's grand?"

Alfred handed an envelope to Jim, who removed a wad of twenty pound notes and counted them, twice.

"Okay. Cool. Now the deal is that we'll meet again and you'll hand over five grand, okay? You text me that you've got the five grand and I'll text you the date and time we meet. It won't be here. Too dangerous."

Alfred raised his eyebrows.

"CCTV and face recognition. Very sophisticated these days. I've got a mate in the business. A computer-aided long lens can pick out a pre-programmed face in a crowd from a long way off. Tricky, mate. We'll meet out in the countryside. Safer. No cameras. You hand me the five grand then and the rest when the job's done. I should start getting it together now, okay? And take your time, yeah? When the job's done, the fuzz will be all over anyone who might have had a reason for getting rid of this..." he paused, "...Ralph Waters?"

Alfred nodded.

"And you have a reason, haven't you? Otherwise you wouldn't be talking to me, yeah?"

Alfred nodded again.

"How will I know where the next meeting will be?"

"Got a sat-nav?"

Alfred gestured towards the dashboard. Jim reached into a pocket in his parka, drew out a slip of paper and gave it to Alfred.

"OS co-ordinates. Put them into your sat-nav, follow them and they'll take you to a cottage in the middle of a wood. I'll be there. After you've handed me the five grand, I'll give you another piece of paper with another set of co-ordinates, which is where you'll hand over the other five grand when the job's done. Okay?"

"Okay. But it's all a bit mysterious."

"Got to be, Alfred. As I just said, can't be too careful these days. Now, I know who you are, but you don't know who I am and you'll never know. Jim's not my real name. And you'll never know who's done the job, but it won't be me, okay?"

Alfred nodded.

"Okay, Alfred. 'Bye."

Jim left the Discovery, shut the passenger door and walked away, out of the view from Alfred's rear mirrors.

Alfred started the Discovery and, as he drove back to Pepynbridge, he thought: It's not like slaughtering a bullock. I'm going to have to think about it. No need to hurry. And if I change my mind, it'll have only cost me a grand. Anyway, where the hell am I going to find ten grand?

Then Alfred remembered the Wicken Necklace.

◆◆◆◆◆◆◆◆◆◆◆◆◆◆◆◆◆◆◆◆◆◆

The Honourable Member for Pepynbridge

Friday, 18 March 2016

At 9.30 a.m. in his room in Pepynbridge Hall, Edgar opened and read an email from Robert Burgess, the Conservative agent for both Medborough constituencies. Edgar called Ralph's mobile.

"Ralph?"

"Yes, Edgar?"

"Ralph, I've got an email from Robert Burgess, the Medborough West agent."

"Yes?"

"I've been short-listed."

"For Medborough West?"

"Yes."

"Well done. And you've accepted?"

"I shall do."

"Does Bob Burgess say how many are on the short-list?"

"Four."

"What's he asking you to do, Edgar?"

"He wants me to attend the Orchid Conference Centre in Medborough at ten o'clock on the Tuesday after Easter, the twenty-ninth of March. It's on the outskirts of the city."

"Yes, I know it."

"I'm asked to give an address, which should last about twenty minutes, and then those present will ask me questions. The whole thing will last an hour."

"Does the agent say who'll be there?"

"Yes, he does. Members of the Medborough Conservative Association on the electoral roll for West Medborough. A list of them with their email addresses is attached to his email. I take that to be a suggestion that I should email them all, saying why I'm the right person for them."

"That's about right, Edgar. Why don't you draft it and run it past me before you send it out?"

"That's kind of you, Ralph."

"Not at all. I'm leaving London at ten thirty this morning to see my mother in Saint Albans."

By 10.00 a.m., Edgar had drafted and emailed his draft statement to Ralph. Fifteen minutes later, after making minor amendments suggested by Ralph, he attached it to the 132 emails he then sent to everyone on Burgess' list, as well as replying to his email, confirming he would attend at the Orchid Conference Centre at 10 a.m. on Tuesday, 29 March.

In Elsie's bungalow in the grounds of Temple Grange, mother and son had been chatting amiably together for nearly an hour, cradling cups of coffee and eating cupcakes, before Ralph told her about Edgar. Elsie detected warmth and pride in her son's voice.

"That's lovely for you, darling. You're pleased, aren't you?"

"Ma, I am. He's just the sort of person we need in the House."

"Fond of him?"

Ralph eyed his mother shrewdly. She didn't miss much.

"Yes, Ma, I am. But not too fond."

"Could you be?"

"You mean, is he gay?"

She nodded.

"Yes, he is, but I'm very happy with Pascal."

Although it's a pity he's black, thought Elsie, but did not voice it. Ralph was aware of her reservations about his partner.

"Darling, what are you doing for Easter?"

"I'm staying in Pepynbridge, Ma. And you?"

"What I always do, darling. The usual Good Friday observances at Saint Stephen's and then Mass on Easter Day. And afterwards, as you know, there's a big Easter lunch in the church hall."

Saint Stephen's was the Roman Catholic Church nearby, where Elsie attended Mass every Sunday and on major Christian festivals when they fell on a weekday. Ralph and Elsie had not spent Christmas or Easter together since Ralph had converted to Anglicanism at Oxford. Elsie had disapproved. It had cast a shadow between them that had persisted until, accepting that it was permanent, she had reconciled herself to it, but only up to a point. She preferred to spend the two great Christian festivals in the year with fellow Roman Catholics rather than with Anglicans, from whom she felt alienated by her lifetime of unwavering Catholic observance. Besides, if she stayed with Ralph over Easter, Pascal would be there as well.

The House of Commons was due to recess on Maundy Thursday, 24 March. Ralph knew that on Good Friday, his mother would be at Saint Stephen's attending The Passion of the Lord and praying the Stations of the Cross followed by the Three Hours Agony. All of which, he remembered from his childhood, would last from 10.00 a.m. until 3.00 p.m. Ralph would not be visiting Elsie over Easter.

"Well, as I shan't be seeing you again until after Easter, may it be a blessèd one for you, Ma."

"Thank you, darling. And for you as well."

They rose. Elsie kissed Ralph on the lips and he left to join Pascal in the Range Rover.

"To Pepynbridge, Boss?"

"Yes, please, Pascal."

On the way north up the A1,

"Boss, I'm off to Paris tomorrow."

"England versus France?"

"It is. If England wins, they complete the Grand Slam."

"And if not?"

"They'll still be Six Nation champions, but France will be happy."

"Will France win?"

Pascal shrugged his shoulders. He doubted they would.

"When are you off?"

"Tomorrow morning. I'm going with Edgar."

"Good. I hope it goes well, although you can imagine who I should prefer to win. And Edgar too, I imagine."

Behind the wheel, Pascal chuckled softly.

◆◆◆◆◆◆◆◆◆◆◆◆◆◆◆◆◆◆◆◆◆

Saturday, 19 March 2016

Edgar and Pascal drove to Paris via the Channel Tunnel in Edgar's VW Golf. During the journey, their conversation, interspersed with diffident silences, focussed upon sport, the rugby union World Cup that had concluded in the United Kingdom the previous October, the Six Nations Championship, and the test cricket series between England and South Africa in December and January.

In Paris, Pascal directed Edgar to the *Quatorzième Arrondissement* and a small hotel in *Montparnasse* with underground parking. Pascal had booked a double room furnished, to Edgar's relief, with twin beds. They showered, changed and left for the *Stade de France*, arriving at 8.00 p.m. CET. The match, which started at 9.00 p.m. CET, was decisively won by England, achieving the Grand Slam by scoring three tries, two converted and four penalties to seven penalties by France. Thirty-one points to twenty-one. As they left the stadium, Pascal's reaction was philosophical and complimentary of England.

"Eddie Jones is doing a good job," he remarked.

"Indeed he is. It'll be good for all Northern Hemisphere rugby union if England can beat the Southern Hemisphere nations."

"England goes to Australia this summer, *Oui?*"

"We do."

"*Bonne chance.*"

"*Merci. Et France en Argentine, n'est pas?*"

"*Oui.*"

"*Alors, bonne chance aussi.*"

In a *brasserie* near the hotel, Pascal and Edgar ordered *steak frites* with red burgundy, followed by a *digestif* of

Armagnac. Watching the match and sharing the meal left them relaxed and assured in each other's company.

At Pascal's prompting, Edgar recounted his education, his upbringing as a Roman Catholic, his time at Oxford when he had won a rugby Blue, and his political ambitions. Pascal listened sympathetically, intervening now and then for clarification or elaboration.

Finally, Edgar enquired,

"And what about you, Pascal? Were you brought up in France?"

Pascal took a sip of *Armagnac* and, adopting an uncharacteristically sombre look, he shook his head and began. He had been born the eldest of four siblings on Easter Sunday 1980, in what was then Zaire, he told Edgar. His family had lived in a village with no electricity and just one water well. He and his father, Lushiku, had tended a small patch of maize, large enough to feed the family. Along with other men from the village, Lushiku had hunted to supplement their diet with bush meat. Then, in 1996, came the First Congo War. One day, Pascal had returned from a neighbouring village to discover the corpses of every member of his family, together with many others from the village, murdered by immigrant Tutsis from Rwanda. He descended to no detail and Edgar did not press him.

Pascal went on to describe how he had used his family's savings, hidden under the burnt ruins of the hut that had been his home, to smuggle himself into France. Arriving in Marseilles, he had survived through male prostitution until he had met a doctor, Étienne Montaigne, who was gay. Montaigne had taken Pascal into his home. They had not entered a sexual relationship, but Montaigne had enrolled Pascal in a *lycée*, where Pascal had shone at rugby. A talent scout had spotted him and Pascal had graduated to playing first class rugby union for the *Top 14* club in South West France. He had kept in touch with Montaigne until the doctor had died from AIDS in 2002. Pascal's name in Swahili, Pasaka Kubwa, translated into French as Pascal Legrand, which he had adopted. It was after Pascal had played in a match against *Stade Français* in Paris in 2004 and was drinking in a gay bar in the city that he had met Ralph Waters. Shortly afterwards, Pascal had suffered the serious neck injury that had required surgery. Whilst he had been convalescing, Ralph had visited him in South West France. He had suggested that they embark upon a relationship and that Pascal should live with him in London. Pascal had been advised by the surgeon who had operated on his neck that he should retire and, regretfully concluding that his professional rugby union career was over, he had agreed.

"And, *comme on dit en anglais*, the rest is 'istory."

"So you and Ralph have been together now for twelve years?"

"Nearly. It's been good."

"And are you French or Congolese?"

"I have been a French citizen since two thousand and two. It would have taken longer if I had not studied at the *lycée* for two years."

So, you could have played for France if you hadn't been injured, was Edgar's unspoken reflection. He warmed to Pascal. His unaffected modesty, touched by humility, and coupled with a powerful physique, bestowed upon him a dynamic to which Edgar felt drawn. But, he reminded himself, Pascal belongs to Ralph and that's somewhere I'd be mad to go.

"You have no partner, Edgar?"

"No, Pascal. But I don't rule it out if I met the right sort of guy."

"Like me, *mon ami?*"

Humour danced in Pascal's eyes.

"Yes, Pascal. Just like you, but not while Ralph's around."

"*Bien sûr que non. Ça n'était que ma plaisanterie. D'accord?*"

"*D'accord, mon ami. Mon cher ami.*"

"*On y va, oui?*"

"*Bien sûr. Je vais regler.*"

"*Non. On partage, oui?*"

"*D'accord.*"

As they walked back to the hotel, Edgar anticipated that the journey back to England would be more relaxed than the one out. And so it proved. A friendship had been born.

◆◆◆◆◆◆◆◆◆◆◆◆◆◆◆◆◆◆◆◆◆

Easter Sunday, 27 March 2016

After the House of Commons had risen on Maundy Thursday, Ralph, Pascal and Edgar had travelled together to Pepynbridge where they planned to remain until Parliament re-assembled on 11 April.

On Easter Sunday in Saint Aidan's Abbey, Herbert had mesmerised the congregation with a *tour de force*, marking what he regarded as the most important festival in the Christian year. The choir had sung Mozart's Mass in C Major, the *Coronation*, to which, as the composer's sublime melodies and harmonies, suffused with incense, had coiled about the ancient building's sacred space, the pellucid soprano notes of Sophie Wicken and Leela Malik had added an elusive numinousness.

Sylvia had arranged to visit the Maliks after High Mass. When it was over, with a ring-binder containing the font ten typescript of *A Tyrant's Best Friend* under her arm, she walked with Ash and Leela to their house in Abbey Gardens, accompanied, as Ash always was, by Craig Miller, who had been sitting unobtrusively but alert at the back of the nave.

The previous autumn, in the wake of his betrayal of *IstishhadUK* and profound disillusion with Islam, Ash had converted to Christianity, but Leela remained an observant, albeit liberal Muslim. She had persuaded herself that singing in the choir was not *harām*, or forbidden, a view endorsed by some Islamic scholars. Ash and Leela's parents were non-observant, styling themselves, "secular Muslims".

Abi Malik, South Asian and in his late forties, was tall, generous of girth with a round bald head, chubby cheeks with laughter creases stretching out from his eyes. He cared for patients in mental health units in Medborough and another town some miles away, as well as nurturing a lucrative private practice. Abi had qualified as a doctor at the Lahore Medical and Dental College, where Sabi had been a nurse. They had married and Sabi had abandoned nursing when Ash had been born. Leela had arrived two years later and, in 2004, the Maliks had left the Punjab for London. In 2010, Abi had secured his psychiatric consultancy and the family had moved, first to Medborough, and then, a year ago, to Pepynbridge.

Sabi Malik, aged forty, was a slim, pretty, South Asian woman, short of stature, softly spoken with a gentle, but capable air about her. She was content devoting herself to the care of Abi, Ash and Leela and their home and sought nothing more from life.

Sylvia sipped tea with the Maliks in their sitting room and explained the purpose of her visit. Abi turned to Leela.

"Well, Leela, how does that strike you?"

Leela was sixteen. Pretty like her mother, she was short and slim, with long, glossy, black hair and wide-set, large brown eyes set in a strong, triangular face ending in a pointed chin. She sat silent, digesting what she had heard. She wondered whether she was up to the task and how long it would take her. At Medborough Academy, she was sitting ten GCSEs in the coming summer. Spring Term had ended a week ago and Summer Term would start on 11 April. There would be little time to finish the edit by then. Half term at the end of May lasted only three days. Summer holidays didn't start until 21 July. Finally, she spoke.

The Honourable Member for Pepynbridge

"Mrs Slim…"

"Leela, please call me Sylvia."

"Thank you, Sylvia. How quickly do you want the job done?"

"As long as it takes you, Leela."

"Well, Sylvia, I could start it now, during the holidays, but I have to revise for my GCSEs coming up next term. I mustn't fluff them."

"I wouldn't want you to."

"After my GCSEs are over in June, there won't be a lot going on at the Academy for the rest of Summer Term. We break up towards the end of July. There won't be any homework after the exams, so I'll try to get it done by July, but I can't promise."

"So it attracts you, Leela, does it?"

Abi's voice was warm, encouraging. It would be a good exercise for his clever daughter.

"Oh, yes Dad, it does. I'd love to do it."

Excitement shone from her eyes.

Sylvia mentioned payment.

"How much would a professional editor charge?" asked Abi.

When Sylvia told them, he observed,

"I wouldn't think that Leela would be looking at anything like as much as that."

"No, I wouldn't. In fact, Dad, I don't want to be paid anything at all. I'd do it as a favour."

"Are you sure, Leela?"

"Yes, Dad, I am."

She turned to look at Sylvia.

"Sylvia, I like you and would love to help you with your novel. It won't be a chore. It'll be fun. I don't want to be paid for having fun."

"Leela, that's very kind of you, but…"

Leela interrupted her.

"No, Sylvia. If you don't mind, I really do not want paying."

Her look and tone were firm.

"Thank you, Leela. But if you change your mind once you've started and seen the size of the task, you must let me know."

Leela nodded.

"Happy with that, Leela?"

"Yes, Dad."

"Sabi?"

"Yes, fine."

"Ash?"

"Lucky Leela," was Ash's response. "But," he added, "I've got A Levels and after that the trial in London in June, so I couldn't do it, even if I had been asked."

Ash smiled at Sylvia to reassure her he was not offended.

Sylvia handed Leela the ring-binder.

"Thanks, Leela."

"No, thank you," responded Leela, emphasising "you".

Leela opened the ring-binder and then looked up at Sylvia.

"Yes?" enquired Sylvia.

"The text is on your computer, isn't it?"

"It is."

"I wonder. Could you let me have a copy in a larger font, say twelve, with one and a half spacing?"

"Of course, Leela. No problem. I'll drop it by later today. I think I've got enough paper."

"Thanks. It'll make it easier for me to edit."

Leela handed the ring-binder back to Sylvia.

Later, over lunch in Hall Close, after Sylvia reported her conversation with the Maliks, Gordon observed,

"You know, we really ought to reward Leela if she does a good job."

"I agree," replied Sylvia, "but how?"

"How about inviting her to join us when we go to Spain in August?"

"That's a good idea. What do you think, Roger? It's as much your holiday as ours."

"Fine by me."

Roger, who had never had a girlfriend, found the prospect of spending time with Leela in Spain intriguing.

"Okay," concluded Gordon. "Let's see how she does."

Sylvia had sufficient paper, as well as toner, and later that day she took a bulkier ring-binder around to Abbey Gardens.

◆◆◆◆◆◆◆◆◆◆◆◆◆◆◆◆◆◆◆◆◆

Tuesday, 29 March 2016

When Edgar arrived at the Orchid Conference Centre Shortly before 10.00 a.m., he was handed a folder containing a schedule of interviews and the CVs of himself and the other three candidates, a man and two women. His interview was listed first. The others had all contested the General Election of 2015. The last to be interviewed had also fought the one in 2010. Two were currently employed as special advisers to cabinet ministers. The other worked for a City bank, not his father's. Edgar guessed that the candidates' track records had determined the order of interviews and that, as the first, he was seen as the least likely to be selected. That settled his nerves. When his name was called and he entered the conference hall, he felt unexpectedly relaxed, even light-headed. What the hell, he thought. Let's enjoy it. And, taking his seat on the stage behind a table between Emmanuel Sickle and Robert Burgess, he did.

After Sickle introduced him, Edgar stood and gave a brisk twenty-minute address, focussing on current political issues and why he argued that he was well qualified to represent West Medborough in the House of Commons. After that, the mind that had secured a first-class honours degree at Oxford framed with ease, answers to questions, even before they concluded. He replied with *brio*, interlaced with humour. After a while, he sensed the audience, numbering he thought about sixty, was with him. When he was asked about his views on the EU Referendum, he remarked that he was listening to the arguments and had not yet made up his mind.

"However, if I am elected as your MP in twenty twenty, by then it'll be academic. Whichever way the country votes on the twenty-third of June, we'll just have to make the best of it."

That seemed to satisfy the meeting, but then came the question that Edgar would have preferred not to answer.

"Mrs Nancy Cornwell," announced a large woman in her sixties, rising to her feet. She was wearing a hat, a floral cotton suit and a pearl necklace.

"Mr Templeton-Smith," she continued in a deep, cultured voice, "in the old days we always thought that it benefitted the constituency if its Conservative Member of Parliament had a wife to support him and fill in for him when he was unable to attend functions. We see that you're not married."

"No, Mrs Cornwell, I am not."

"In the old days," she persisted, "the candidate used to bring his wife or..." she paused for emphasis, "...his fiancée along to a final interview, so we could see her and judge whether she would fit in."

Ignoring a low groan of disapproval that sounded from parts of the hall, she fixed Edgar with a steady gaze.

"Do you have a girlfriend, Mr Templeton-Smith?"

"No, I do not."

"Any particular reason, Mr Templeton-Smith?"

"Mr Templeton-Smith," interrupted Emmanuel Sickle, "you needn't answer, if you prefer not to."

"But Mr Chairman," protested the egregious Mrs Cornwell, "it's a perfectly proper question."

"Not these days it isn't, Mrs Cornwell. As you've hinted yourself with your references to the 'old days', it's not like that any more."

Mrs Cornwell remained on her feet, openly defiant, lips compressed and brow knitted. The embarrassed silence that followed Sickle's intervention gave Edgar time to think. You know what? he thought. If I answer her question truthfully when I've been told I needn't, it might just gain me a brownie point.

"That's all right, Mr Chairman. I'm happy to answer Mrs Cornwell's question."

Edgar looked directly at her.

"Mrs Cornwell, the reason I don't have a girlfriend is because I'm gay."

An expression of triumph crossed her features.

"And you know what?" Edgar continued, his voice rising slightly. "That shouldn't matter a damn these days."

She shook her head.

"You may disagree, Mrs Cornwell, but most of this country, and especially the young, don't and it's the youth vote we need. We've got the grey vote, but it's the young we want to vote Tory and join our campaign for a better, kinder and more tolerant Britain. Homophobia simply alienates them."

"Hear, hear," someone called out and the room burst into spontaneous applause.

Edgar smiled at Nancy Cornwell, who, registering angry disgust, sat down. Edgar transferred his smile to embrace the whole assembly and, when the applause died down, he thanked them.

"Mr Templeton-Smith?"

"Yes, Mr Chairman?"

"If we select you, and I'm not saying we shall, we have three more applicants to interview, all of them excellently qualified, but if we select you, we shall issue a Press Release to the Press Association and *The Medborough Post* this evening. Would you have any objection if it mentioned that you're gay?"

"Not at all."

As the words left his lips, Edgar thought how difficult a card the public disclosure of his sexual orientation had been to play. But, he sensed, he'd played it well. Now it was out in the open, he remembered what Herbie had said. This was the occasion to have played it.

"Any more questions, anyone? No? Well, thank you Mr Templeton-Smith, we'll email our decision to you later today. No problem with that?"

"None at all, Mr Chairman."

"Good. Well, goodbye."

Edgar left the conference hall, pursued by a low murmur of approval.

Edgar decided not to go to London until the next morning. If he were selected, he would need to alert his parents and his brother and sisters, home from school for Easter, to the expected disclosure in tomorrow's newspapers.

Augusta met him in the cavernous hall.

The Honourable Member for Pepynbridge

"Well, how did it go, darling?"

"Not bad, Mum."

"When will you know?"

"Later today."

It was a mild, sunny, spring day and Edgar went for a walk. In the Park, leaves were beginning to break on the trees and early swallows were darting above, seeking puddles for wet mud to construct nests under the eaves of the Hall. He breathed in the sweet air and strode past the Pavilion into the woods, carpeted with bluebells. To his delight he heard a cuckoo's call echoing through the trunks as if in a cathedral. Which in a sense, reflected Edgar, it is; God's creation, a natural sacred space. It's my faith again, he thought, coming and going like Magic FM in the Chilterns. He was confident that the morning had gone well and began to construct in his mind the speech he might make at his formal adoption meeting, were it to happen.

An hour later, Edgar returned to the Hall and joined Augusta for a light lunch in the conservatory. Then he went up to his room and, sitting at a desk, opened and answered emails and browsed news sites. After a while, the tension and excitement of the morning induced a fatigue that overwhelmed him. Uncharacteristically, he lay down on his bed and drifted into a light sleep.

Edgar was woken by a bleep from his laptop. He rose, sat in front of it and opened Microsoft Outlook. There was an email from *r.burgess@medboroughconservatives.com*, inviting him, on behalf of the Medborough Conservative

Association, to be the prospective parliamentary candidate for West Medborough at the next General Election in 2020. There would be a formal adoption meeting at the Conservative Club in Medborough on the following Friday, 1 April, at 6.00 p.m. Would he please indicate whether he accepted, preferably by this evening? And, if so, whether the date and time of the adoption meeting were convenient? Attached was the press release that would be issued, which mentioned that Edgar was gay.

Edgar suppressed an urge to holler and emailed his acceptance immediately, saying he would attend on 1 April and approving the press release. Then, he emailed Ralph.

At 7.30 p.m., he joined Alistair and Augusta downstairs in the drawing room and accepted a gin and tonic from Cyril.

"Where are the others?" he asked.

"They'll be down in a minute, darling," said Augusta.

That's good, Edgar thought. He'd rather tell his parents first, while they were on their own.

"How did it go, today, Edgar?"

"Pretty well, Dad…"

Edgar paused for dramatic effect.

"I've just learnt that I've been selected."

"Wonderful, dear boy. What good news. Cyril?"

"Yes, Sir?"

"Champagne please."

"Of course, Sir."

Cyril left the room.

"Dad, Mum. There's something I need to tell you."

"Yes, darling?"

Augusta's voice betrayed uneasiness.

"A press release will be issued tomorrow, reporting my selection as the Conservative candidate for Medborough West."

Edgar paused again.

"Yes?"

Alistair prolonged and raised it.

"I was asked this morning about my love life."

"Well, darling, as you told me the other day, you don't have a girlfriend at the moment."

"No, Mum, I don't. Well, there was this tiresome woman who persisted in asking me why not."

Alistair guessed what was coming. He had suspected it since before Edgar had left Beaufort School at eighteen. It was something he had already discussed with Augusta.

"And what did you say?"

Edgar gazed into the blue wells of Augusta's eyes, reflecting his own apprehension. He had always loved Augusta, but in the eternity of this moment and detached from everyone and everything save her sweet face, the strength of his love for her shocked him. He hated what he was about to do, because of the hurt he knew it would cause her. But he had no choice. Edgar took a deep breath and summoned up as much calm as he was able.

"I told them I was gay."

There was a sharp intake of breath from Augusta.

"Oh no, Edgar!"

"'Fraid so, Mum. I'm sorry."

"Nothing to be sorry about, dear boy."

Edgar looked at his father with surprise and relief.

"Thanks, Dad."

"I've suspected it for some time," Alistair went on. "Remember the conversation around our table last New Year's Eve? It happens. It's always happened. And we have to accept that it happens. All I say to you Edgar is that, if and when you find a partner, I hope that you'll find happiness with him."

"Alistair!" exclaimed Augusta. "What about Catholic teaching?"

"Augusta, the Church is changing."

"It didn't change last October," objected Augusta. "The Synod on the Family in Rome rejected homosexuality as a life choice."

"Much, it was hinted, to Pope Francis' regret. The tide is turning. Anyway, Edgar is our son. We love him dearly. We may wish that his orientation were otherwise, but we must learn to live with the fact that it isn't."

Edgar and Augusta looked at each other. Then unexpectedly, for it was the first time Edgar had witnessed it, his mother's eyes filled with tears. She crossed the room, embraced him, and kissed him on the cheek.

"Darling, I love you and I always will."

Edgar, his composure slipping, was rescued by the arrival of Cyril, bearing a magnum of Pol Roger, closely followed by Edgar's brother and sisters.

Alistair announced Edgar's adoption, champagne was poured and Edgar accepted excited congratulations from his siblings.

Taking Edgar to one side, Alistair murmured,

"Will you tell the others?"

Edgar reflected for a moment. Then,

"Of course, I shall. One of them's sure read it in *The Post* tomorrow."

"Good man."

Over dinner, when Edgar announced that he had come out as gay, Joseph said,

"So what? I guessed it."

Martha said,

"No big deal."

And Antonia said,

"Well done, Edgar. That must have been hard for you."

Slowly and barely perceptibly, Augusta shook her head in surprise and privately resolved not to be the only one in the family left behind.

After dinner, when Edgar went upstairs to his room and opened his laptop, there was an email from Ralph, congratulating him and inviting him to dinner at Coronation Cottage the following evening.

◆◆◆◆◆◆◆◆◆◆◆◆◆◆◆◆◆◆◆◆◆

Wednesday, 30 March 2016

The Medborough Post was published every Wednesday and Alfred always collected a copy from the village shop before breakfast. As Neville, the shop-keeper, handed it to Alfred, he said,

"Good news about Edgar Templeton-Smith, Alfred."

"What's that?"

"He's been chosen by the Conservatives to fight Medborough West at the next election."

"Hmph," grunted Alfred. "I'll not be voting for him."

"Why not? He's a good bloke."

"He's Conservative and I'm UKIP."

"Oh, well," observed Neville and sighed. Awkward chap, Alfred. I'd have thought he'd be pleased that a local lad had been chosen. He turned to serve his next customer.

Alfred went home for breakfast. Marigold and Sophie were in the kitchen waiting for him. He sat at the table and, as Marigold fetched his breakfast of bacon, eggs and sausages from the cooker where she had been keeping it warm, he opened *The Medborough Post*, found the piece about Edgar and began to read.

"Bloody hell!"

"What's the matter, Dad?"

"Another poofter wants to be an MP."

Marigold placed the plate in front of Alfred.

"Who's that, Alfred?"

"Edgar Templeton-Smith."

"Edgar?" cried Sophie excitedly. "That's great. He's lovely."

"Huh! He's a poofter."

"What do you mean, Dad?"

"He's queer. That's what it says here."

"You mean gay?"

"Not my word, Sophie, but that's what *The Post* says. This village is full of 'em. That MP and his fancy black boy and now Alistair's lad. Horrible."

Silence fell as Alfred started to eat. Sophie looked at Marigold and raised her eyebrows interrogatively. Marigold, standing behind her husband, shrugged her shoulders and gently shook her head.

Later, when Alfred had left for the farm and Marigold and Sophie were washing up, Sophie asked,

"Mum, what do you think?"

"What about, Sophie?"

"About Edgar being gay?"

"I think it's a shame. Like you, I think he's a lovely boy. Or man, rather. Good looking, clever, ambitious. He'd make a wonderful husband..."

For a brief moment, Marigold reflected upon how different life might have been if Alfred hadn't got her pregnant at seventeen and instead she'd married someone like Edgar Templeton-Smith.

"...but it's not to be," she concluded. "So that's that."

"What do you think about gays, Mum?"

"I'm not bothered, Sophie. It's just one of those things. It happens to us as well, you know. But not to me. Nor to you. You've got Ash, lucky girl."

Sophie nodded.

"He'll be around in a moment."

"Off for the day?"

The Honourable Member for Pepynbridge

"Yes, going to Southwell Races. And Craig's coming too. I like him. He's nice."

"That's good, Sophie. It's a pity you've got to wait so long to marry Ash. When will it be?"

"Well, as you know, he's taking his A Levels this year. In September he starts a two-year agriculture course at a college in King's Lynn. He'll finish in June twenty eighteen. We're thinking about getting married then. He'll be twenty and I'll be nineteen, nearly twenty."

Sophie's birthday was on 27 July.

"Two years older than I was when I married Dad."

"Well, yes Mum. But…"

"I know what you're going to say, Sophie, so don't say it. You're not going to make the same mistake, are you?"

"No way, Mum. No way."

They were silent for a moment, lost in private thought. Then Marigold asked,

"Would you like a white wedding, Sophie?"

"Oh, yes I would, Mum. If Dad can afford it."

"I'm sure he can. And in the Abbey?"

"Why not, Mum?"

"No reason why not."

Marigold paused.

"Sophie, has Dad told you about the Wicken Necklace?"

"The what?"

"The Wicken Necklace."

"No, he hasn't. What is it?"

"Let's sit down again for a moment. I've something to tell you."

They resumed their places at the kitchen table.

"Sophie, a long time ago…"

Marigold thought for a moment. Then she remembered.

"…during the Crimean War, a Wicken called Sophie, the daughter of one of your forebears called Paul, married a Templeton by the name of Roderick…"

"So I'm related to the Templeton-Smiths, then?"

"No, you're not. But hear me out please, Sophie."

"Sorry, Mum."

"The Templetons gave Sophie an emerald and diamond necklace as a wedding present. She wore it when she was married in the Abbey. Roderick Templeton was a Hussar. Not long after the wedding, he went with his regiment to fight in Crimea, and…you've heard of the Charge of the Light Brigade?"

"Yes."

"Well, Roderick Templeton was in it and he was killed."

"How awful. What happened to Sophie?"

"There were no children and she never remarried. She died a few years later. From TB it was said. A lot of folk did in those days. So the connection with the Templetons was broken. Sophie, the reason I know all this is because your dad told me about it before we were married. And it's why we called you Sophie."

Sophie's eyes widened in surprise.

"Wow. So what happened to the necklace?"

"It's in Dad's safe in the office. After Sophie died, the Wickens offered to return it, but the Templetons wouldn't hear of it. And I was thinking, how wonderful it would be if you wore it on your wedding day, just like the other Sophie Wicken did all those years ago."

Sophie nodded vigorously.

"What does Dad, think?"

"Haven't spoken to him about it yet and, as you've just said, there's plenty of time. But I shall. And it would be better coming from me rather than you. I'm not sure I should have told you really. Okay?"

"Okay, Mum. Won't breathe a word. But it would be amazing."

They were silent for a moment.

"Mum?"

"Yes?"

"Did you wear it when you got married?"

"No, Sophie. I didn't."

"Why not?"

"It didn't suit me. But it would suit you."

"Why?"

Marigold looked at her daughter, appraising afresh the long fair hair framing a round face with blue eyes, pert nose and generous lips. Marigold reflected with pride that Sophie, seventeen in July, with a slim body, honed fit by ballet, understated breasts and a face that would grace the cover of Vogue, was growing into a beautiful woman.

"Because I'm a brunette and not pretty and you're blonde and beautiful."

"Thanks Mum. You've never told me that before."

"Well, I've told you now, so don't let it go to your head. All right?"

"No chance, Mum. And thanks again."

Sophie rose, walked around the table and kissed Marigold on the cheek. It was something they rarely did to each other.

"Be off," retorted Marigold, but Sophie saw that her mother was smiling.

She liked Marigold, which is more than she could say of Alfred. But at least these days he was treating her with respect, which had not been the case before she and Ash had decided to get married.

"Oh and Mum?"

"Yes?"

"The other day, Ash and I were talking about being married. Ash knows how important it is for Dad to have family running the farm."

Sophie paused.

"Go on," demanded Marigold, impatiently. Her way was direct and she expected it from others.

"Well, Ash suggested we do what the Templeton-Smiths did when they got married."

Marigold waited. She had no idea what was coming.

"Mum, Ash thinks that when we get married, we should hyphenate our names. So we'll be Mr and Mrs Wicken-Malik. Or maybe Malik-Wicken. That sounds better, don't you think? We haven't decided yet."

"That's a wonderful idea. Your dad will be really, really pleased. Well done the pair of you."

This time they exchanged kisses. As they did, they heard Ash calling from the front door.

The Honourable Member for Pepynbridge

"Mum, I must go," said Sophie.

Marigold watched her as she left the kitchen. A good girl is our Sophie, she said to herself, wiping her eyes on a tea towel.

As Alfred, driving a tractor and spreader, was top dressing a field of winter wheat with ammonium nitrate granules, his thoughts were seething. Edgar, of all people. Brilliant rugby player. Bright. Sensible. In line to inherit the Pepynbridge Estate, either on his own, or with Joseph, Alfred supposed. Not with the girls, though. No, not with Martha or Antonia. Not unless Alistair had gone soft in the head. But Edgar a queer. A poofter. So, no children. Just buggering other blokes instead.

Alfred shook his head. I just don't understand it. He allowed his thoughts to wander on until...It's that faggot Waters' doing. That's what it is. Edgar's gone to work for him and now look. It's like a contagious disease. Like...what's it called in the Bible? Leprosy. That's right. You catch it from another poofter. Who knows what the three of them, Waters, his black boyfriend and Edgar, get up to in London? Three in a bed, I don't doubt. Or even more. Alfred's imagination conjured up and lingered over the prospect until a stirring in his groin at first startled and then angered him. So, not just contagious, but infectious as well. That's what they do and it should be stopped. Nipped in the bud. He banished the homoerotic imagery and revisited his meeting with Jim. You know what? Alfred told himself. Maybe I should do something about it after all.

Before that faggot Waters infects other nice young lads like Edgar Templeton-Smith.

On the headland at the end of the field, Alfred deftly turned the tractor and spreader around and, guided by a GPS signal at its preset working width, the tractor retraced its tracks, parallel to the strip just fertilised. Alfred continued to ruminate. Doing something about Waters would be risky. There must be another way? But I can't think of one. In Grand-dad's day, a call to the cops would have done the trick. But now…undecided, Alfred continued spreading fertiliser on the field. When he finished and was loading the spreader with more fertiliser for a neighbouring field, he thought: What I'd like to do and what I ought to do are two different things. Different altogether. I've driven under the influence, but apart from that, I've always kept on the right side of the law. It would be a huge step, and if I got caught, it'd be life. And then what would happen to the farm? It would have to be sold. Shaking his head again, he finished loading the spreader and drove into the next field.

In Pepynbridge Hall, Edgar's mobile rang.

"Yes?"

"Edgar Templeton-Smith?"

"Yes?"

"The Bishop of Medborough's assistant speaking. Are you able to speak to the bishop?"

"Of course."

"Hold on, please."

After a pause,

"Hello, Edgar. Bishop Julian here."

"Hello, Bishop."

"Edgar, first of all, may I congratulate you on your selection as the prospective parliamentary candidate for Medborough West."

"Thank you, Bishop."

"The other matter I wanted to talk to you about briefly is same-sex marriage and the General Synod."

"Yes, Bishop?"

"Well, I said that I would keep you posted on what's happening. You've probably read about the Shared Conversations that have been going on?"

"I have, Bishop."

"Well, they're progressing well. As you probably also know, they will continue in a two day closed session in York next July when Synod meets."

"Yes, Bishop, I am aware."

"Edgar, I know that Ralph Waters wants to maintain pressure on the Church of England with his Bill, but the discussion format the archbishops have decided upon takes the issue out of our hands. I can say, in confidence, that the bishops are largely in favour of permitting same-sex marriages in church, but there's serious opposition building amongst the evangelicals. At present, the outcome in July is completely unpredictable."

Julian Ross paused.

"Yes, Bishop?"

"And I should add that even if the Shared Conversations result in a consensus, I doubt anything will happen quickly. It's far more likely that, in those circumstances, the archbishops would want there to be a further period of reflection and consultation. So, it's all a bit inconclusive. I thought that you and Mr Waters should know."

"Thank you, Bishop. I'm seeing Ralph this evening and I'll pass on what you've told me. And Bishop?"

"Yes, Edgar?"

"Thank you for keeping me in the picture."

"Not at all. And good luck at the next election."

"Thank you, Bishop."

That evening in Coronation Cottage, Ralph, Edgar and Pascal celebrated Edgar's selection over *roulade de saumon aux crabes des neiges*, followed by *cotolettes d'agneau à la provencale* and ending with cheese, all accompanied first by white and then by red burgundy. Edgar congratulated Pascal on his cooking.

"*Merci. Mais pas du tout, mon vieux. Pas du tout. C'est mon passe-temps favorit.*"

Edgar related his conversation with Bishop Julian earlier that day.

"Thank you, Edgar. I shall urge the Government to keep up the pressure. I think it will. I'm confident of a sympathetic ear in Number Ten."

Afterwards, as they drank coffee and sipped *Armagnac*, Ralph and Edgar discussed what he might say at his adoption meeting two days later. Then Ralph continued,

"Edgar, it wouldn't surprise me if Sir Ramsey steps down before twenty twenty. I was chatting to him in the Members' Smoking Room the other day. He's obviously not well and he told me he's not improving. Very sad. He's a loyal Member, but he doubts he'll make it to the end of this Parliament. I thought I should let you know."

"Thanks, Ralph..."

Edgar paused and the others watched him, sensing that there was more he wanted to say.

"You know, I really cannot thank you both enough for the kindness you've shown me since we first met last Christmas."

"Both of us?" responded Pascal, surprised.

"Yes, both of you. You've been good friends to me and will be, I hope, for many years to come."

"We'll drink to that."

Ralph raised his brandy balloon. Edgar and Pascal did likewise and they drained them.

Edgar rose.

"How about a run tomorrow morning, Pascal?"

Since Paris, it was something that Edgar and Pascal had been doing together frequently.

"Bon idée, mon vieux. A quelle heure?"

"À neuf heures?"

"D'accord. D'où?"

"D'ici?"

Pascal nodded.

"Et tu?" Edgar turned to Ralph, who smiled.

"Non, merci."

Edgar departed and, as he walked back to the Hall, he reflected upon how well life seemed to be turning out for him. He crossed his fingers.

◆◆◆◆◆◆◆◆◆◆◆◆◆◆◆◆◆◆◆◆◆

Friday, 1 April 2016

Edgar had prepared carefully for the adoption meeting. He had run his acceptance speech past Ralph, who had praised it and had suggested no changes.

The meeting room in the Conservative Club in Medborough was crowded and poorly lit. Norman Callow, who belonged to the Pepynbridge Forest Conservative Association, had contacted Edgar and asked if he might attend. Edgar had agreed, but although Edgar looked for him, he failed to spot Norman standing amongst the crowd at the back. Edgar's speech was well received and afterwards he accompanied Emmanuel Sickle, Robert Burgess and a frail Ramsey Phillips to the bar, where Edgar was introduced to other Association officers. Meanwhile, Norman Callow slipped out and walked to Medborough Bus Station.

At 8.30 p.m., the last bus from Medborough to Corbury drew to a halt at the bus-stop outside Pepynbridge Rectory. Norman Callow stepped off and walked the few metres to his cottage in Abbey Way, where he ate a simple supper. Shortly after 9.00 p.m., he joined Alfred and Reginald Wicken next door in the Blue Boar.

"I've just been listening to Edgar Templeton-Smith," he announced as he sat down, holding a pint of bitter.

"Why's that?" asked Alfred.

"Well, I'd read in *The Medborough Post* that Edgar had been selected for Medborough West, so I rang the Hall and left a message asking if I could attend his adoption meeting. Edgar rang back and said I could, although he couldn't give me a lift because I wanted to be back here by eight thirty. So I caught the bus to Medborough and listened to him and caught the bus back. He was impressive."

Alfred grunted angrily.

"But he's a poofter, Norman."

"And so is our Member of Parliament, Alfred. It doesn't stop Waters from doing his job and it won't stop Edgar from doing his, if he's elected."

"Well, I just don't think it's right. Poofters ought to be locked up. What do you think, Dad?"

"I agree with you, Alfred, but I'm an old man."

"What do you mean? What difference does that make, eh?"

"Alfred, I was born in nineteen forty-five. It was a very different world then and a lot's happened since. I can't be bothered with things like homosexuality. No point at my age. Nothing I can do about it anyway."

But there is something that I could do about it, thought Alfred.

"Norman?"

"Yes, Alfred?"

"You know that this Waters bloke is trying to change the law about poofters getting married in church?"

"I do, Alfred."

"It's called a Private Member's Bill, am I right?"

"You are, Alfred."

"So what happens if a Member of Parliament like Waters, who's trying to get his Bill through Parliament, dies before it's passed?"

"No idea, Alfred, but…"

Norman Callow, who had a good knowledge of history and more than a passing interest in politics, pondered Alfred's question for a while, before continuing,

"I think it would depend."

"On what, Norman?"

"Well, I don't know anything specific about procedure in Parliament, but I imagine that if a sponsor of a Private Member's Bill dies, but support for it remains, someone else takes it on."

"What about Waters' Bill, then?"

"I would doubt it."

"Why?"

"It's very personal, isn't it? Whatever Waters says about it, he wants to marry his partner in the Abbey. Of course, if his Bill passes, it would have a wider application, but I doubt anyone else in the House of Commons would want to spend time and effort trying to get it through Parliament. It doesn't exactly smell of roses, does it? But that's just my personal view. I really couldn't say for certain, Alfred."

But, thought Alfred, that's another reason why it might be a good thing if Waters, as Jim had put it, was "disappeared". It's a pity I can't share my thoughts with someone like Norman, but…no way.

"Thank you, Norman."

"Anyway, Alfred, what makes you think that Mr Waters might die?"

"Oh, nothing in particular, Norman. I just wondered what would happen, that's all."

Alfred moved the conversation onto the weather, the state of his crops, grain prices and, after those topics had been exhausted, Norman Callow ventured upon the EU Referendum.

"Well," commented Alfred, "I'm still going to UKIP branch meetings. The last one was the Wednesday before Easter, but they're still squabbling about which Brexit campaign we should be backing. Bloody ridiculous, if you ask me."

As Norman and Alfred discussed the referendum, Reginald Wicken, who knew his son better than Alfred did himself, looked at him and pondered the line his conversation about Ralph Waters had taken. He wouldn't put it past Alfred to be so driven by prejudice as to do something really stupid. It would be in character. Should I ask him? Reginald decided there was no point. If he was contemplating something criminal, Alfred would lie. He never welcomed criticism. Just gets bloody cross, he does. Should I tell the police? No. They would dismiss anything I said as an old man's fears, the product of early dementia, perhaps. Or beer talk. But, I do worry about Alfred. I really do.

Norman too was troubled by what Alfred had said about Waters. Like Reginald, he had known Alfred all his life. He had taught him at St Aidan's Primary School and watched him grow up. There was a worrying streak of unpredictability in Alfred. And a serious want of judgement too.

Later, standing outside the Blue Boar after Alfred had left to drive precariously back to Pepynbridge Farm, Reginald and Norman shared their concern. Norman agreed with Reginald that, when as had happened in the past, Alfred was carried away, he was capable of doing something seriously silly,

"...like going into milk when he didn't need to and knew nothing about it."

"And now?"

"And now? Paying someone to do away with Waters?"

"Christ, Norman, I hope not."

"So do I, old friend. But knowing Alfred, I wouldn't put it past him."

"How could we stop him?"

"We couldn't, because we wouldn't know, would we? If we told the police, they would just dismiss it as beer talk. Which it might be, but I don't think so."

"Bloody hell, Norman."

Tuesday, 5 April 2016

At 10.00 a.m., Alfred Wicken parked his Land Rover Discovery in a multi-story car park next to the Cathedral Shopping Mall in Medborough. Earlier, after Marigold had gone shopping in Corbury and Sophie had left with Ash and Craig, to go where, Alfred neither knew nor cared, he had opened the safe in his office and taken from it a small, flat, heart-shaped, red-leather case. Opening it, he had reminded himself of the cascade of brilliant white diamonds and bright green emeralds that was the Wicken Necklace. When his dairy venture had failed, Alfred had rescued the farm by selling land in Pepynbridge to a developer who had built Abbey Gardens and Hall Close. He had not sold the necklace. He treasured it as a Wicken heirloom, even though Marigold had declined to wear it because, she had told him, it was "too posh".

"It makes me out to be someone I'm not, Alfred," she had told him shortly before they had married and it had remained in the safe.

She won't miss it, thought Alfred. Hasn't even mentioned it since we were married. It's a pity to sell it, but needs must, he told himself. It's different from my money troubles when I sold the land. That only affected me. What Waters is up to brings the whole of Pepynbridge into disrepute. And not just Pepynbridge. And if no one else is going to stop him, then I, Alfred Reginald Oliver Wicken, landowner and farmer, bloody well am. Not for nothing have the Wickens upheld for centuries Christian Biblical principles in Pepynbridge. It's time for me to act.

In its case, the necklace was nestling in a pocket of the old tweed coat he used to wear out shooting before he had bought the Schöffel. Alfred walked through the shopping mall as far as Ridley's Jewellers and rang a bell. He heard a click and pushed. The door opened and he stepped inside.

The Honourable Member for Pepynbridge

Behind a glass-topped counter displaying an array of jewellery, stood a tall, overweight, untidy man wearing large spectacles, with dark curly hair, a pale, round face and red, wet lips.

"Good morning, Sir."

"Good morning. My name's Alfred Wicken. I'm interested in selling this."

Alfred slid the case across the counter. The other opened it and removed the necklace, running it through his hands sensuously and touching some of the gemstones to his lips to check they weren't glass. No, he decided, they were cold and genuine. He removed his spectacles and, fixing a magnifying loupe in his right eye, he examined the necklace, gem by gem, making notes on a pad on the counter. Finally, he removed the loupe, put on his spectacles, looked at his notes and then at Alfred.

"Mr Wicken, this is a very fine example of an early nineteenth century necklace. Do you mind telling me how it came to be in your possession?"

His tone was cautious. When Alfred related the story of the marriage of Sophie Wicken and Roderick Templeton, the other relaxed, reassured.

"Well, Mr Wicken, in the saleroom I estimate this could fetch as much as twenty-five thousand pounds…" Alfred's heart missed a beat, "…but if you want to dispose of it now, I'll buy it from you for fifteen."

Alfred yielded. It was more than enough and there was no way he was going to draw attention to himself by selling at auction.

"Thank you. Any chance of having it in cash?"

"No problem, Mr Wicken. It'll take a little time, that's all."

The jeweller was familiar with sellers seeking to avoid capital gains tax. It wasn't his job to prevent or report them. And it might suit him too. Time would tell.

"Next Tuesday all right for you?"

"Fine."

The jeweller pulled a mobile out of his pocket.

"Mr Wicken, I just need to photograph it."

"Why?"

"To check it's not stolen goods."

Alfred's face darkened. The other held up a hand.

"Just a routine precaution, Mr Wicken. Nothing personal, I assure you."

"Oh, all right then."

After he had photographed the necklace, he replaced it in its case and handed it back to Alfred.

"Next Tuesday, then. Goodbye Mr Wicken."

"Goodbye," replied Alfred.

After he left the shop, Alfred realised that he had not asked the jeweller his name. Ridley probably, he thought, but not that it matters. Next Tuesday it would be then.

In Abbey Gardens, Leela was enjoying *A Tyrant's Best Friend*. She had been five when she had arrived in England. Her memories of the Punjab were sketchy. Although she clung loyally to her Muslim faith and, so far as was possible in the quintessentially English rural community that was

Pepynbridge, to Islamic culture, she had become aware within herself, at school at first and then through browsing the internet, of a fascination with the history of her adopted country. She had divined that the way England was today owed much to its Tudor monarchs. The civic and religious society that Queen Elizabeth the First had bequeathed to the house of Stuart, afterwards tempered in the furnace of the Civil War, had matured into a liberal, pluralist democracy. Leela firmly rejected Islamism, which her brother, Ash, had embraced last year, based as it was upon a literalist interpretation of the *Qur'ān*. It was, she decided, wholly possible to observe her faith bereft of fundamentalist deviancy, which she deplored. She hoped that one day, perhaps even in her lifetime, Islam would come to mirror the tolerant Christianity of the West, and particularly of England.

Harbouring these sentiments, Leela embarked upon the edit of Sylvia Slim's book. And, as she read the story featuring John Russell, King Henry VIII's best friend, she fell in love with it. Armed with a red biro, she attacked the text with relish, correcting, wherever she found them, typographical mistakes, grammatical solecisms and continuity howlers.

◆◆◆◆◆◆◆◆◆◆◆◆◆◆◆◆◆◆◆◆◆

Tuesday, 12 April 2016
    "Are you sure you want to sell this?"
    "I am," insisted Alfred. "Are you Mr Ridley?"

"My name is Cornelius Ridley," explained the other, ponderously. "My great-grandfather founded this business in nineteen hundred and ten. He was called Cornelius. So was my grandfather. And it's my father's name as well. Family tradition," he supplied, unnecessarily.

Ridley had removed the necklace from its case and was examining it once again with the magnifying loupe. He replaced it in its case, snapped it shut and, reaching under the counter, he drew out a large brown envelope.

"I checked on the internet that the necklace is clean, Mr Wicken. So..." he handed the envelope to Alfred, "...I suggest you go into my office and count this."

Ridley raised a wooden flap at one end of the counter and pointed to a doorway at the back of the tiny showroom. Alfred walked through the counter and into a small office, furnished with a desk and two chairs, one on either side of it.

"Do sit down and take your time, Mr Wicken."

"Thank you," responded Alfred.

It took Alfred ten minutes to count the 300 fifty pound notes, twice over. He replaced them in the envelope and walked back into the shop. It was empty, save for Cornelius Ridley.

"All there?"

"Yes, all there, thank you."

"Not at all."

Ridley never enquired why someone outside the trade was selling him a piece of jewellery, however valuable. There were all sorts of reasons, not all of which would bear scrutiny by the law enforcement authorities. It was one of his tasks to keep on right side of them and he had discovered that ignorance was the best way of doing so. He was not registered with HMRC as a High Value Dealer. His books never recorded sales for cash, let alone for cash in excess of €15,000, which the money laundering regulations stipulated was the threshold for registration. Not that it mattered on this occasion, as he was buying the necklace. He would sell the necklace to a dealer he knew in London. But not just yet. Sellers like Wicken sometimes changed their mind and asked to buy back what they had sold him. It was an easier way for him to turn a profit than by going to London. For now, the purchase would not appear in his books. If Wicken did decide to buy it back, Ridley had no wish to draw the notice of HMRC to the transaction. Any more, he suspected, than Wicken did.

He handed Alfred a hand-written receipt, headed "Ridley's Jewellers".

"You should have this, Mr Wicken. I've signed it, but I've not kept a copy."

"Thank you."

Alfred pocketed the receipt, bade Ridley farewell and returned to his Discovery. It was twelve noon. Sitting in the driving seat, he removed 100 fifty pound notes from the envelope, folded them in half and slid them into the inside pocket of his jacket. He put the envelope containing the rest of the money into the glove pocket, closing and locking it. Then, from another pocket, he retrieved the slip of paper that Jim had given him and tapped the co-ordinates into his sat-nav. The destination, he saw, was near Thetford, Norfolk, seventy miles and one hour, twenty minutes distant. He tapped a text into his mobile. A reply arrived almost immediately.

meet me today at half one

Alfred started the engine and travelled east out of Medborough. Eighty minutes later, he was driving along a quiet lane through Thetford Forest. The sat-nav told him to take the next turning to the left. It led into Forestry Commission woodland. A quarter of a mile further on, it announced that he had arrived at his destination. In front of the Discovery was a small, dilapidated cottage, its windows dirty and broken, its thatch uneven and blackened. Alfred parked the Discovery and stepped out. As he approached the cottage, the front door opened and Jim emerged.

"We'll do the business in your motor."

They climbed into the front, Alfred in the driving seat. He drew the folded notes from his jacket and gave them to Jim, who counted them twice over, just as Alfred had done.

"Okay, mate. That's good. What happens next is that we'll check Waters out. Find out where he lives. What his patterns are..."

"His what?"

"Patterns. Where he goes and when. Is it regular? Know any?"

"Well, he attends the House of Commons when it's sitting. And I've found out that he lives with his queer boyfriend in Barton Street in London. Know it?"

"Yeah. What else?"

"He spends most weekends in Pepynbridge in a cottage in the grounds of a big house called Pepynbridge Hall."

"Anything else?"

Alfred thought and then remembered something he'd been told...by whom? He couldn't remember. Perhaps he'd heard it in the Blue Boar? Or maybe he'd read it in *The Medborough Post*.

"He spends time in Spain."

"Much?"

"He's got a house there, I think."

"Know where? Spain's a big place."

"I could find out."

"Don't bother. We'll find it."

Alfred looked at Jim and raised his eyebrows.

"Don't ask, mate. But it would help if you let me know when he's going there, if he does."

"I reckon I could find that out."

"Okay. When you know, just text me the dates out and back, okay? And these are the co-ordinates for when we meet next."

Jim handed Alfred another slip of paper, slipped out of the Discovery and walked towards the cottage.

Funny, thought Alfred. Can't see a vehicle. Wonder how he got here?

On the way back to Pepynbridge, Alfred pondered how he could find out about Waters' visits to Spain. Then, listening to the 2.00 p.m. Radio 4 *News*, Alfred was angered to learn that that the Electoral Commission had chosen Vote Leave in preference to the GO Movement as the official

Brexit campaigner. So, I backed the wrong horse, he reflected. He wondered what UKIP's reaction would be.

That evening over dinner, he asked,

"Do either of you know when Waters and his black friend go to Spain?"

Sophie shook her head, but Marigold said,

"No, but I could find out. As you know, Alfred, I sometimes help out at the Estate Office. Someone there may know. But what's it to you, Alfred?"

"Never mind, Marigold. Just interested, that's all."

As Alfred ducked his head and forked food into his mouth, Marigold and Sophie exchanged puzzled looks across the table.

◆◆◆◆◆◆◆◆◆◆◆◆◆◆◆◆◆◆◆◆◆

Thursday, 14 April 2016

Sir Ramsey Phillips, seventy-one years old, since 1979 Member of Parliament for Medborough West and knighted for services to politics in 1997, died during the night of Tuesday, 12 and Wednesday, 13 April, the day after Parliament had returned from its Easter Recess.

His passing had been peaceful, a spokesman had informed the media. He had gone to bed in his London house at ten in the evening and Lady Phillips had been unable to rouse him the next morning. There would be a post-mortem, but nothing untoward was suspected.

Ralph Waters and Edgar Templeton-Smith were sitting at their desks in Norman Shaw North.

"I spoke with the Chief Whip yesterday evening, Edgar."

"And?"

"The House of Commons returns after the EU Referendum on Monday, the twenty-seventh of June. He's going to move the writ for the by-election the same day. The Summer Recess starts on the twenty-first of July and the by-election will take place on Thursday, the twenty-eighth of July. The PM wants to have it as soon as practicable. Elections in August are not welcome and September is party conference season. So, polling will be on the twenty-eighth of July."

Ralph paused for a moment, pondering his next remark, before deciding to make it.

"The PM expects you to win, Edgar."

"That's encouraging, Ralph."

"With the Labour Party in the mess it's in, you shouldn't have a problem, Edgar. Mind you..." he paused.

"Mustn't be complacent, Ralph?"

"Precisely. Couldn't have put it better myself."

They smiled at one another.

"What about UKIP, Ralph?"

"It'll take votes from both Labour and Conservative. And I doubt the Lib Dems will bother you. You should be all right, Edgar."

"If I do win, when would I take my seat?"

"Traditionally, newly elected Members take their seat on a Tuesday. The House rises for the Summer Recess on Thursday, the twenty-first of July, so you will have to wait until after it returns on Monday, the fifth of September. The Chief Whip and I have agreed that, if you are elected, you should take your seat the next day. In the meantime, I'll be dealing with Medborough West constituency matters in the House..." he paused, before adding dryly, "...in which endeavour, you will be perfectly placed to assist me."

"But, I'll be campaigning."

"You will, but not until the end of June. And then so will I. And so will the PM. And so will other members of the Government."

"Wow."

"Yes. You'd better behave yourself."

Again they smiled at one another.

"Ralph, Emmanuel Sickle has called a meeting this evening in the Medborough Conservative Office."

"Edgar, whenever you are required to be in Medborough, there's no need to ask me. Just tell Jane..." he gestured at his secretary sitting at the other desk "...or leave me a message."

"Thank you, Ralph. I have a lot to thank you for."

"Leave that for now. Let's see what happens. Oh, and another thing about taking your seat. You will need two sponsors and it would be a privilege for me to be one of them."

"Of course, Ralph. And the other sponsor?"

"Usually a whip. So, fair wind, Edgar. Sadly, there's a downside. There always is."

Edgar looked quizzically at the older man.

"If you win, I'll have to find myself another parliamentary assistant."

All three laughed.

"Bet he won't be as good–looking as Edgar," said Jane.

"But he's gay," joked Ralph.

"Couldn't care less."

Jane smiled broadly at Edgar. She had grown fond of him and, whilst she regretted he was gay, she felt unthreatened by him.

Edgar looked at her, amused.

"Well, Jane, now that I shall be leaving Ralph's employ, it wouldn't be unprofessional for me to take you out."

"And it'd be safe too. For both of us."

They broke into more laughter.

That evening, Edgar was closeted in the Medborough Conservative Office with Emmanuel Sickle, Robert Burgess and local Party officials. Edgar informed those present of the dates of the writ and of the by-election, although Sickle and Burgess had already been given the same information earlier that day by Conservative Campaign Headquarters in Millbank. Sir Ramsey's memorial service, it had been announced, would take place in Medborough Cathedral in May. It was agreed that Edgar should attend, together with the principal officers of the Association.

"I've been in touch with Noel Murray, the Acting Returning Officer," announced Robert Burgess. "Nominations will close on Tuesday, the fifth of July. If it's okay with you, Edgar, we'll open our campaign with a public meeting in the Orchid Conference Centre on

The Honourable Member for Pepynbridge

Thursday, the seventh of July. It'll be a big do. The nationals should be there, so..." Burgess left the implication hanging in the air.

"I won't let you down, Robert."

"Of course you won't," remarked Emmanuel Sickle, smiling. "Wouldn't have chosen you, Edgar, if we'd thought you would."

"Oh, and Edgar?"

"Yes, Robert?"

"Call me Bob, okay? Everybody does."

"Okay, Bob."

They mapped out a campaign plan. Social media, a personal website, when and where they should hold public meetings, press conferences, slots on local radio and television and visits to local businesses, especially factories, which would be provisional as appearances by national Party figures in the constituency would be scheduled by Headquarters and everything else organised around them.

"And," added Robert Burgess, "we shall need an Election Address from you, Edgar."

"I'll draft something tomorrow and email it to you."

"Fine. And we'll need photographs of you as well."

"You have one, Bob. I emailed it you after I was adopted."

"You did. It's not the greatest shot of you. We should have some more. I'll fix up a studio session here in Medborough and let you know when and where. Okay? And, Edgar?"

"Yes, Bob?"

"You'll base yourself locally during the campaign, will you?"

"Of course. I'll be staying in Pepynbridge."

"Anything else, the rest of you?" asked Burgess. "No? Okay. Let's call it a day. Meet again when?"

The following Friday was fixed.

"Right," said Emmanuel Sickle. "Next door for a drink?"

Everyone nodded. The Conservative Club was next to the Conservative Office and before long the bar was filled with the buzz of excited anticipation. There is nothing a local constituency association and its agent, of whatever political colour, enjoy more than a parliamentary election campaign. And a by-election conducted, as this one would be, with no shortage of funds and in a blaze of national publicity, is icing on the cake.

In the kitchen at Pepynbridge Farmhouse, Alfred, Marigold and Sophie were eating dinner.

"Alfred?"

"Yes, Marigold?"

"You wanted to know when Mr Waters is going to Spain."

"I did."

"Do you mind telling me why?"

"Just interested, that's all."

"Nothing else, Alfred?"

"Why should there be?"

Alfred's tone was intimidating.

The Honourable Member for Pepynbridge

Oh well, thought Marigold, anything for a quiet life. Why ever did I marry such a disagreeable man? Then she remembered. That damn pregnancy, which, she reflected as she had many times before, had been as much her fault as his. She glanced at the result. Sophie looked up and smiled at her. A good girl, was our Sophie, Marigold re-assured herself. So, not all bad then. Better humour Alfred in the interests of preserving harmony. But his interest in Waters and his partner is odd and not a little worrying.

She reached into a pocket and drew out a scrap of paper.

"According to what I've been told, Ralph Winters and Pascal Legrand are flying out to Spain on Thursday, the twenty-sixth of May and returning on Sunday, the fifth of June. Then, in the summer, they're flying out again on Friday, the twenty-ninth of July for about five weeks. No one could tell me the date when they return. Some time in September, I imagine."

"Thanks, Marigold. Could you pass me that note, please?"

Later that evening, Alfred texted the dates to Jim. There was no reply.

Jim, or Neil, his real name, decided that Spain was where to do the business. Safer than in the UK. He'd already arranged two successful contracts with Tony in Marbella. May or June was too soon. Alfred had said it didn't need to be done before July or August. So, plenty of time to sort it. He sent Tony a text. After a little while came a reply. Yes,

Tony was interested. Like the other times, would Neil send him details by encrypted email?

◆◆◆◆◆◆◆◆◆◆◆◆◆◆◆◆◆◆◆◆◆◆◆

Friday, 15 April to Thursday, 26 May 2016

Over the next six weeks, Edgar worked with Ralph in Westminster from Monday to Thursday and nursed Medborough West Constituency on Fridays and Saturdays. He drafted his Election Address and visited a studio in Medborough to be photographed.

During the same period, Ralph attended the House of Commons until the Prorogation of Parliament on 12 May, visited his mother on Friday mornings and, together with Pascal, spent the weekends in Pepynbridge. Shortly before the Prorogation, Ralph issued a Press Release announcing that he had withdrawn his Bill upon an assurance by the Government that it would re-introduce it in the Commons or the Lords following the State Opening of Parliament on 18 May.

Pending the outcome of the General Synod in York on 8 July, there was no further discussion about same-sex marriage at meetings of the Pepynbridge PCC. When, as they were bound to, having served for three years, Alfred and Reginald Wicken, Peggy Taplow and Norman Callow stepped down at the Annual General Meeting on 24 April, only Norman Callow was re-elected. The other three vacancies were filled by parishioners supportive of Herbert Onion.

The Honourable Member for Pepynbridge

To everyone's surprise and relief, work on the Abbey roof progressed with remarkably little disturbance of the activities beneath.

Alfred attended UKIP branch meetings in Medborough on 27 April and 25 May. After the GO Movement, of which UKIP was part, had failed to secure its appointment by the Electoral Commission as the official Brexit campaign, Nigel Farage had announced that UKIP would continue to campaign to leave Europe. However, Alfred thought its capacity to do so would be limited and privately concluded that Farage had been marginalised. But did he care? Not really. Alfred's enthusiasm for Brexit was faltering. In April, he attended a regional meeting organised by the NFU, where a dispiriting picture had emerged of the consequences for British agriculture if the EU Referendum were to result in a vote for Leave. Alfred was not concerned about the three percent fall in agricultural land values between January and March, but uncertainty over payments post-Brexit to replace those received by farmers under the Common Agricultural Policy un-settled him. At the NFU gathering, he had discovered he was not alone. On 18 April, the NFU announced that it backed remaining in the EU. As the Leave campaign was being led by Vote Leave, UKIP did not invite Alfred to address public meetings.

On 2 May, Leicester City became champions of the Premier League and, on Tuesday, 3 May, Alfred suspended his rule of abstinence and spent the evening celebrating in the Blue Boar with Reginald and Norman.

At the UKIP meeting of 25 May, Alfred contributed little and wondered afterwards whether he would attend the next one on Wednesday, 22 June, the day before the referendum. In the Blue Boar, Reginald and Norman noted Alfred's loss of interest and talked of other things.

On the farm, Alfred and John, his farm-worker, sprayed crops, mended fences and machinery, and cared for the cattle, which by then were grazing meadows behind the farmhouse. Alfred waited for some communication from Jim, but none came. He stopped talking about Ralph Waters, which allayed Marigold and Reginald's anxiety. Familiar with Alfred's volatility, they hoped that his antipathy towards homosexuality in general and Waters in particular had subsided. They were wrong, but Alfred said nothing to disabuse them. Whenever the topic was raised in the Blue Boar, Alfred changed the subject, but Norman Callow remained uneasy. With his experience, garnered over a life-long teaching career, of human nature in general and of Alfred in particular, the reluctance of his former pupil to engage was out of character.

Sylvia, guided by Julie, enrolled in a twelve-month ABC Level Two Teaching Assistant correspondence course and discovered she enjoyed studying for a Certificate of Achievement from ABC Awards and a Learner Unit Summary.

Summer Term at the Academy began on 12 April, and Sophie, Ash and Leela were all revising hard. Ash for A Levels, Sophie for AS Levels, and Leela for GCSEs. Leela's examination timetable, which began with Spanish on 20

May, would stretch until late June. Roger was not sitting any public examinations that summer.

◆◆◆◆◆◆◆◆◆◆◆◆◆◆◆◆◆◆◆◆◆◆

Thursday, 26 May 2016

On Thursday, 26 May, Parliament rose for the Whitsun Recess and later the same day, Pascal Legrand and Ralph Waters drove to Luton Airport. After a two and a quarter hour flight to Alicante and a drive in a hired Europcar Audi A4 for an hour north along the AP7 toll motorway, at 6.30 p.m. CET, Pascal turned off at the exit signed to Javea. Twenty minutes later, the Audi drew up outside a single storey villa built high on the Cabo de la Nao headland, eight or so kilometres south of Javea by road. Its rendered exterior walls were painted pale pink and letters carved in a stone set into its gable-end announced it as *Casa Rosa*.

Looks were deceptive. *Casa Rosa* comprised two single storey villas, the one built above the other on a precipitous hillside and inter-connected by a staircase, quarried through the soft limestone that separated them. Below the lower villa, the slope steepened into a sheer drop to waves breaking on rocks a hundred or so metres below. At both levels, terraces overlooked a shimmering Mediterranean, across which white sails meandered. On the horizon, a merchant ship appeared almost stationary. Pascal pressed a remote control and wrought iron gates slid back. He drove in and parked. Then he left the Audi, unlocked the front door and disabled the alarm.

"I'll fetch the cases in, Boss."

"Thank you, Pascal."

Ralph walked into the villa. The gates slid to behind Pascal as he carried two briefcases, bulging with books and papers, into the house and closed the front door. There was no other luggage. Both kept clothes and toiletries at *Casa Rosa*.

From a Seat Ibiza parked in the *carril*, or narrow lane, that led to *Casa Rosa* and its neighbouring villas on the headland, a lean, middle-aged man, dressed in a T-shirt and jeans, with a baseball cap above a tanned, square, hard-featured face, had observed the arrival of Ralph Waters and Pascal Legrand. He then drove downhill to the junction of the *carril* with the *carrer*, or street, that ran through *urbanización*, or estate, and parked in a space reserved for residents' cars. The *carril* leading to *Casa Rosa* was a dead end. From his vantage point at the junction, the man in the Seat could track the comings and goings of Ralph Waters and Pascal Legrand. If only one went out in the Audi, the other had no means of transport. Keeping track of the Audi would disclose the pattern of activity of the two who had just arrived at *Casa Rosa*.

Inside the upper villa, Pascal took a bottle of *cava* from the fridge, opened it and took it, together with two tall-stemmed glasses, out to Ralph on the top terrace. Dressed in shirts and chinos, they sipped as the sinking sun cast the lengthening shadow of the villa at their backs across the glass-topped table and the wicker chairs in which they were sitting. The day, they sensed, had been hot but now was cooling, with a gentle breeze from the sea.

"Gym, tomorrow, Pascal?"

"Yes, Boss, if it's all right with you?"

"Of course. So off by ten?"

"Yes. Then I'll go shopping in the *Mercadona* in Javea and stock up. That'll take time. I should be back by one. Renata has left bread, butter, jam and milk in the fridge. And there's coffee and tea as well."

"We'll eat lunch here tomorrow."

"Sure, Boss. What would you like?"

"Oh, fresh bread, *jamon serrano, manchega* and olives?"

"No problem, Boss."

"And wine?"

"Of course, Boss."

They finished the *cava* and, in the Audi, went to dine at a restaurant in Javea.

The man in the Seat followed them there and, much later, back again. Then, after the wrought iron gates had slid to, he went and ate at a different and cheaper restaurant in Javea before letting himself into the one-bedroom apartment that, using a forged identity card in the name of a fictional Spaniard, he had rented for two weeks. He would maintain his surveillance of Waters and Legrand until they returned to England on Sunday, 5 June. Then he would report back to Neil, who would fly out to meet him in Alicante a day or so later.

◆◆◆◆◆◆◆◆◆◆◆◆◆◆◆◆◆◆◆◆◆◆

Thursday, 2 June 2016

Leela made better progress with *A Tyrant's Best Friend* than she had anticipated. By the beginning of Summer Term on 11 April, she had edited over three-quarters. Since then, at her desk in her room in Abbey Gardens, she had occasionally looked longingly at the ring-binder on the shelf above her desk, but self-discipline had always won, bending her head anew to her revision.

Half term had started on Saturday, 28 May, and would end on the following Friday. There were more GCSE exams for Leela to sit after she returned. However, confident that she was sufficiently prepared for them and believing that last minute, panic-driven revision would only cloud and confuse her mind, she decided that completing the edit would be a diversion that would better prepare her for the challenges awaiting her in the examination hall.

So it was that, at 5.00 p.m. on Thursday, 2 June, Leela rang Sylvia. Could she come and see her? Of course she could. Now, they were sitting at the Slims' kitchen table in Hall Close. Leela laid the ring-binder in front of Sylvia.

"Finished," she announced proudly, smiling broadly.

"Well done, Leela."

"Sylvia, if you agree with my edits, I'm afraid there's quite a lot of work for you to do. Spelling, continuity, punctuation, that sort of thing."

"Have you suggested altering the narrative?"

"Hardly at all. I loved it."

"Did you really, Leela?"

Sylvia's voice betrayed anxious hope.

"Sylvia, I loved it. Truly I did. Whether it will sell, I couldn't tell, but if I hadn't already read it, I'd buy it."

"Thank you, Leela. And I really can't thank you enough for all the work you've put into it."

"You'd better look at my edits first. You may not like them."

"I'm sure I shall."

Sylvia paused and Leela watched her, sensing she was holding something back.

"Leela, when Gordon and I were discussing this in the spring, we decided we should like to reward you."

"But, Sylvia..." protested Leela.

Sylvia raised her right hand.

"No, Leela. Please hear me out. You know, don't you, that we own a house in Spain?"

Leela nodded. Disconcerted, she suspected what might be coming.

"Gordon and I would very much like it if you were to come and spend some time with us in Spain when we're out there in August. It's lovely. There's a swimming pool and we're not far from the sea."

Leela was ready with her response.

"Sylvia, that's very kind of you and I'd love to come. But..."

"But, what, Leela?"

"Sylvia, you know that I'm an observant Muslim, don't you?"

"You're worried about Roger being there as well? About being alone with him?"

Relief swept Leela's features. She nodded.

"With Roger, yes. And with Gordon as well, when you're not there."

"That's fine, Leela. We've thought of that. Do you think that Ash would come as well? He'd be a suitable chaperone, wouldn't he?"

"Wow, that's really kind of you. Yes, he would. But what about Sophie?"

Sylvia smiled.

"The house sleeps six. Gordon and me in one bedroom. You and Sophie in another. And the boys in the third. All right?"

Leela made no effort to hide her excitement.

"Awesome, Sylvia. But would Ash and Sophie come as well?"

"We'll ask them, Leela. Leave that to Gordon and me. Don't say anything to Ash for the moment, okay? And once again…" Sylvia tapped the ring-binder with a forefinger, "…thanks. I'll mention you in the acknowledgements."

Leela left and Sylvia opened the folder. As she noted Leela's corrections, her head nodded again and again. The girl was bright. How wise of Julie to have suggested that Leela should edit it.

She was still reading when Roger came in from playing tennis and later, when Gordon arrived back from London. She suggested that they go out to dinner at the Templeton Arms, the hotel and restaurant at the bottom of the village, with a lawn beside the River Pepyn. They ate outside, bathed in evening sunshine, and happily discussed the prospect of Leela, Ash and Sophie staying with them in Spain next August. Much more fun than just the three of them. They had forgotten about Craig Miller.

♦♦♦♦♦♦♦♦♦♦♦♦♦♦♦♦♦♦♦♦♦♦

Sunday, 5 June 2016

"Have you got a moment, Ash?"

"Sure, Sylvia."

High Mass was over and Sylvia, Roger and Ash were walking down the nave of the Abbey from the choir vestry in the south transept. At the west end, Sylvia would normally collect a cup of coffee and chat, but today she had asked Gordon to wait for them outside the south porch.

"Where's Sophie?"

"She'll be along on a minute."

"And Leela?"

"She'll be going home to help Mum get lunch."

Together with Craig Miller, who joined them from the back of the nave, they waited at the west end for Sophie to join them. When she did, they walked out into warm sunshine to meet Gordon. Because he was not in the choir, Sophie and Ash hardly knew him.

"Hello, Sophie."

"Hello, Mr Slim."

"Oh, please call me Gordon."

"Okay. Hello, Gordon, then."

"Hello, Ash. And please, you call me Gordon as well."

"Hello and thank you, Gordon."

"Fancy a drink at the Blue Boar?"

They walked from Abbey Close through the archway between the Rectory and Abbey Hall, turned right up Station Road and into the garden of the Blue Boar. Gordon and Ash went into the bar and bought drinks. A beer each for the two of them, a white wine for Sylvia, and soft drinks for Roger, Sophie and Craig. As they walked back through the bar, they acknowledged Alfred and Reginald Wicken and Norman Callow, sitting at their usual table in a corner with partly drunk pints of bitter in front of them.

Outside, all six sat at a wooden picnic bench under a large green parasol and Gordon Slim canvassed the idea of Ash and Sophie spending a week or so in August with Sylvia, Roger, Leela and him at their house in Spain. It was in return for Leela editing Sylvia's novel, Gordon explained, but Leela was rightly insisting on a chaperone and would not go without Ash. Ash and Sophie looked at each other. Then Ash spoke.

"I'll have to clear it with the police first."

He looked at Craig, who nodded slightly.

"If that's okay, then if Mum and Dad agree that Leela should go, there'll no problem about me going, provided I'm not playing cricket for Northants. What about you, Sophie? What will your mum and dad say?"

Sophie was quiet for several moments before she replied, "Ash, Mum'll be okay, I'm sure. But Dad's a different matter. He's..." she paused "...it's difficult to know which way he'll jump."

"Unpredictable, you mean?"

"Yes, Gordon. Very. Look, I'd love to come but I'll see what Mum says. Whether we ask Dad…" she shrugged her shoulders "…I don't know."

"So, no point in going into the bar and asking him now?"

Sophie laughed scornfully.

"No, Gordon. Dump something like that on him without warning and he'd be far more likely to say 'no' than 'yes'. He's stuck in his ways. Doesn't welcome surprises."

"Well, Sophie," Gordon explained, "assuming you can come, we'll book you, Ash and Leela on a flight from Luton or Stansted and collect you from Alicante Airport. We'll be driving out. We sail on the ferry from Portsmouth to Bilbao on Wednesday, the twenty-seventh of July, arriving at the house the next day and staying there until the end of August. Sophie, can you let us know?"

"Of course I shall. I'll just have to clear it with Mum first. What about the fare?"

"Don't worry about that. We'll sort that out."

"You know, that's really kind of you, Gordon."

"Not at all, Sophie. We're looking forward to seeing you all there…" Gordon paused and turned to Craig, "…with or without you. There's a camp bed we can set up in the sitting room."

Craig Miller smiled.

"Let's wait and see, shall we?" he said. "The trial may go short. If it does, then Ash's security status will be reviewed and I may not need to be there."

"And I'll let you know if and when I'm playing cricket for Northants, Gordon."

"Thank you, Ash."

The conversation turned to the trial of the Islamists, due to start the next day in Woolwich Crown Court. Ash was not looking forward to giving evidence. Except when he was at home, he had been guarded by Craig Miller and other armed plain-clothes police officers continuously since the arrest of the other nineteen members of *IstishhadUK* the previous September. Craig had recently dropped a hint that Ash's evidence might not be needed, but had not elaborated.

"Will you be going to Court tomorrow, Ash?"

"No, Gordon. I'm sitting my final A Level tomorrow. If I'm required to give evidence, I shall be going to London on Tuesday. But..." and he turned to look at Craig, "...Craig has told me that I might not have to appear in Court after all. It'll be a hell of a relief not to."

Craig Miller's face was a mask.

"Well, good luck, Ash. With the exam and with the trial."

"Thank you, Gordon."

They spoke of other things and, shortly afterwards, went their separate ways. Sophie pedalled back to Pepynbridge Farm, arriving before Alfred. He'd stay drinking in the Blue Boar until closing time at 2.30 p.m.

Marigold was in the kitchen preparing lunch.

"What a lovely idea, Sophie. Of course you must go." was her reaction when Sophie asked her about Spain.

"What about Dad?"

Marigold gazed out of the kitchen window at the trees at the bottom of the garden. The sun was high now and the light was strong. Alfred wouldn't like it, she knew. He would react instinctively and probably negatively. Later, he might be persuaded to change his mind, but by then, it could be too late. Flights had to be booked and the end of July and beginning of August, Marigold knew, was a busy time.

"We won't mention it to him."

"Mum?"

"We'll say nothing. If we ask him now, he'll probably say 'no'. Let's leave telling him until..." she paused "...after you've gone?" Her voice rose interrogatively. "He won't be happy, mind. And not for the first time."

They laughed softly.

"Okay, Mum. But what if he hears from other people that I'm going?"

"Tell them to keep it a secret."

There was a scrunch of gravel on the drive. When Alfred entered, Sophie was helping Marigold lay the kitchen table for lunch.

Later, Sophie telephoned Ash and then the Slims to say that she could go to Spain in August, but warning them that no one else in Pepynbridge should know and explaining why. Ash and Sylvia Slim separately assured Sophie that no one else in Pepynbridge had been told and that no one else would be.

◆◆◆◆◆◆◆◆◆◆◆◆◆◆◆◆◆◆◆◆◆

The Honourable Member for Pepynbridge

Monday, 6 June 2016

On Monday afternoon in the Sports Hall at Medborough Academy, Ash finished writing his final A Level paper, Economics. He was reading through it when the bell sounded for work to be handed in. Ash took his to the desk and left the hall. Through double doors, Craig Miller and two other men were waiting in the lobby. Ash recognised Sergeant Andrew Hay and Cedric Fane from the previous summer. Andrew Hay, in his thirties, shaven-headed, square-jawed and tight-lipped, with small blue eyes set in chubby features, was attached to the Eastern Counter Terrorism Intelligence Unit. He had been the lead officer in charge of the investigation into *IstishhadUK*. Cedric Fane from MI5 had been a member of the same team. Slender, with a boyish face and a shock of straight mousy hair falling over his forehead, Ash thought he still looked absurdly young for one employed as he was.

"Hello, Ash."

"Hello, Andrew. Hello Cedric. How are you?"

"I'm fine, Ash. And you?"

"As well as can be expected, given what I'm supposed to be doing tomorrow."

"Rest easy, young man," said Hay. "Where can we talk?"

"Outside on the playing field?"

Ash pointed to an expanse of grass, visible through glass double doors at the far end of the lobby. The four of them walked out and onto the perimeter path.

"You're not needed tomorrow, Ash," announced Hay.

"Why not?"

"Let's just recap, okay?"

Ash nodded.

"There are four main Islamists, yes?"

"Yes, that's right. Zed and…"

Ash paused, struggling to remember.

"Don't worry about names, Ash. And there were sixteen others, including yourself, yes?"

"Lesser fry," supplied Cedric Fane.

"That's right," broke in Ash. "They'd done nothing except talk before they were arrested."

"Well, yes. But they were talking about causing multiple deaths in twenty Christian places of worship at midnight last Christmas Eve."

"True, Andrew, but they were not as important as the other four. They weren't the leaders."

"No, Ash, they were not. Well, I'll tell you now. The CPS and our QC have been in discussions with the defence lawyers for several days and this morning, the fifteen lesser fry, as Cedric's just termed them, agreed a basis of plea with the prosecution."

Ash stopped walking and, eyebrows raised, turned to look at Hay. The others paused in their stride.

"A basis of plea," explained Hay patiently, "is a version of facts, agreed between the prosecution and the defence, upon which the judge is invited to sentence defendants if they plead guilty. Regarding the fifteen, after the basis of plea had been settled with the prosecution, their briefs went to see the judge who indicated that each of them would be sentenced to no more than four years if they pleaded guilty on that basis."

"Can the judge do that?" queried a surprised Ash.

"Yes, he, or as it happens in this case, she can. It's called a Goodyear indication. But never mind about that. That's what's happened. But that's not all. What the judge wasn't told was that the fifteen were willing to give evidence against the four ring-leaders. What's called turning Queen's evidence."

He paused for dramatic effect and to allow what he regarded as highly significant to sink in. Then he continued,

"When the briefs for the four ring-leaders heard that the rest were going to turn Queen's evidence, they also agreed a basis of plea with the prosecution and went to see the judge. The judge gave them an indication that if their clients pleaded guilty, she'd pass life sentences, but with a minimum term to be served of no more than sixteen years."

"That's a long time."

"It is, Ash, but not nearly as long as they would have got if they protested their innocence and were found guilty. Which they would have been. The evidence against them, not least of your kidnapping, is overwhelming."

"So, what happened?"

"No trial. This morning, everyone pleaded guilty at Woolwich Crown Court. They'll be sentenced in three weeks time. The judge ordered reports on them."

"Why?"

"In case there are individual circumstances that would justify a lesser sentence."

"Like what, Andrew?"

"Mental health issues. That sort of thing. So, Ash, no need for you to go to London tomorrow. And, as a result of what's happened, we shall be reviewing your level of security. I'll let you know about that."

"So, I might be able to play this summer for Northants, Andrew?"

"Maybe. We'll let you know by the end of the week. So, it's goodbye for now, Ash."

"Goodbye Andrew. And thank you for everything."

"It's not over yet, Ash."

"Well, whatever. And thank you too, Cedric."

"Don't mention it, Ash," replied Cedric Fane, grinning boyishly. "All in the line of duty. And good luck with the cricket."

They shook hands and left, Hay and Fane in an unmarked car, and Ash with Craig Miller in the unmarked police car that had transported him between home and Medborough Academy since the beginning of the Autumn Term.

◆◆◆◆◆◆◆◆◆◆◆◆◆◆◆◆◆◆◆◆◆

Tuesday, 7 June 2016

Neil and Tony, the man in the Seat, were sitting in a small, back-street bar in Alicante. It was noon. Outside the temperature was edging towards thirty Celsius. Inside the thick walls of the bar, it was cool. On the table between the two men were a plate of *tapas* and two tall narrow glasses, *cañas*, canes in English, suggested by their shape, full of cold, pale beer.

Tony was talking.

"Every weekday morning, the Afro goes to a gym in Javea. He leaves the house at ten and, if he's not shopping, he gets back at about twelve. He and the target...Waters is it?"

"Yes."

"Well, the Afro and Waters usually eat lunch at the house. They either stay in during the afternoon or they go out. They eat out every evening. I've spoken to the Spanish guy who runs the gym. It's the same when they're out here in the summer."

"What's the house like?"

"Using a false name, I discovered from the Spanish Land Registry where it is. The day before they arrived, I drove up there. Granadella it's called. I walked into the grounds of the villa next door, which was empty, climbed over a low wall that separates the properties and into the garden belonging to Waters. His place is two villas, one built above the other."

"CCTV?"

"No. None in the street and not at the villa either. I was surprised. I suppose he hasn't got around to it yet."

"Did you get inside?"

"No. Alarmed and well locked and bolted. But I could see in through the windows. Big windows they are. There's a staircase at the back between the top and the bottom level.

Each has got a terrace overlooking the sea and there's a swimming pool beside the lower one. The top terrace juts out almost as far as the one below."

"What do you think, Tony?"

"Easy, mate. One morning, after the Afro had gone to the gym, I climbed over the wall and watched Waters sitting on the upper terrace, reading. He'd no clue I was there."

"And?"

"He's tiny. Seen him?"

Neil shook his head.

"Well he is. The work of a moment to walk across the terrace behind him, pick him up and threw him out over the edge. He'd clear the bottom terrace and then it's almost sheer all the way down to the sea. Just some rocks at the bottom. Long way down. Know what I mean?"

"Certain?"

"Certain, mate. Accident, pure and simple. Could have done it then, but I wanted to clear it with you first."

"You go for it, mate. They're coming out again for a month or more from Friday, the twenty-ninth of July. You okay for that?"

"No problem. The day before I sort it, I'll get a mate to mind the bar and I'll drive up here from Marbella. Next morning, after the Afro's gone to the gym, I'll climb over the wall..." he paused and, after drawing deeply on the straw coloured liquid in his *caña*, he wiped his mouth with the back of his hand and pronounced quietly, "...and it'll all be over. Job done. I'll be back in Marbella by night-time. I'll text you when it's done. What about the dosh?"

"Five grand in sterling for you when you've done the job, okay?"

"Sure, mate. Like you said in your email. Money for old rope. But can I be sure?"

"I've not let you down yet, have I?"

"No, mate. But there's always a first time. You rat on me, and I'll find you. Or one of my mates will. Nasty, they are. Know what I mean?"

"I know that, Tony. Don't worry. I'll not let you down."

"Better not, Neil. Better not."

"I'll be in your bar in Marbella with the five grand within seven days of the British Press reporting Waters' death. I'll have to get the money off the client first."

"Blimey! You ain't got it?"

"Not all of it. But I will. No worry. And don't you get caught."

"No chance. Haven't yet. This'll be the sixth job I'll have done. Three for a guy in Manchester and two for you, plus this one. Always make it look like an accident. A fall, car crash, drowning in a swimming pool, whatever. The Spanish police, *Guardia Civil* they're called, they're clueless. They come into Bar Toni, that's my bar, and I give 'em a drink. Nice guys. But clueless."

"You speak Spanish, don't you?"

"Fluent, mate. Born here. Mum and Dad are Brits. Lived all my life here and I own and run that little bar in

The Honourable Member for Pepynbridge

Marbella. A pillar of the ex-pat community, I am. Bloody pillar, mate."

They had been picking at the *tapas*. Now they drained their *cañas* and left in the Seat for the airport. Neil's plane was due to land at Gatwick at 11.25 p.m.

◆◆◆◆◆◆◆◆◆◆◆◆◆◆◆◆◆◆◆◆◆

Thursday, 9 June 2016

On Wednesday, Alfred had been out on the farm when his mobile had pinged. He had stopped the Discovery and drawn the mobile from his pocket.

meet me tomorrow at 12

Alfred had texted back,

ok

Now Alfred and the man he knew as Jim were sitting together in the Discovery near a brick-built shed in another part of Thetford Forest. Like the first time, Alfred could see no other vehicle and wondered how Jim had got there. He decided not to enquire.

"It'll happen in August."

"But he'll be in Spain in August. I told you that."

"Yeah, I know that, mate."

Alfred looked the man he knew as Jim, his face registering surprise. Then, after a pause, almost in a whisper,

"So, in Spain then?"

The other nodded.

"Why?"

"Safer, Alfred. Over here, he's nearly always got someone with him. Either that Afro or someone else. Big strong bugger the Afro is. And anyway, it's difficult to disappear someone in the part of the Smoke where he hangs out. Westminster and round there. Too bloody dangerous. And in Pepynbridge? Well, you wouldn't want that, would you Alfred? Too close to home, eh?"

Alfred nodded and looked away.

"I've got a good contact in Spain. Clever. Discreet. Nothing to connect him with the target. Much safer. Done it before. No come back. Good news, eh?"

Alfred nodded again, still looking through the windscreen.

"How?"

"Not telling. You'll read about it in the Press when it's happened. It'll look like an accident, yeah? And that's when you'll give me the other five grand, right?"

"Yes, of course."

"I'll text you. No messing mate, okay?"

Alfred shook his head.

"You mess me about and there'll be big trouble. Very big. Read me, Alfred?"

Turning and looking into the hard face of the man he knew as Jim, Alfred nodded slowly. Suddenly he felt remote. Remote from Jim, remote from his surroundings, remote from everything. Am I really here? he wondered. Did I really hear what I've just heard? It's unreal.

"Okay, that's all. August, right? You be ready."

The Honourable Member for Pepynbridge

The man Alfred knew as Jim handed him another slip of paper.

"Different place. You be there when it's done and dusted, okay?"

"Okay."

"'Bye Alfred."

Jim left the Discovery and disappeared behind the shed. Probably where his vehicle is, thought Alfred, noticing faint tyre marks in the damp ground. He started the Discovery and, trancelike, he drove away.

As he followed his sat-nav out of Thetford Forest and back to Pepynbridge, unwelcome reality intruded. Had he really done what he had just done? Arranged the death of another human being? Alfred shivered. His palms were damp on the steering wheel. Am I being a bloody fool? What would Dad think? An image of Reginald floated across Alfred's consciousness, not as Reginald was now, old and diminished, but robust as he had been when Alfred had been a child. He'd be livid. Beside himself. And what about Marigold? And Sophie? Or, for that matter, Ash?

It was a troubled Alfred who drove through the gateway into Pepynbridge Farm later that afternoon. Still, August was some eight weeks away. Plenty of time for me to change my mind, he reassured himself. Then, with dismay, he realised he hadn't asked Jim about that.

◆◆◆◆◆◆◆◆◆◆◆◆◆◆◆◆◆◆◆◆◆

Friday, 10 June 2016

It took Sylvia several days to review Leela's edits. She incorporated nearly all of them into the draft on her laptop. It was not just a question of incorporation. Some of Leela's suggestions had required slight re-ordering of the narrative. When Sylvia had finished, she read it through, she hoped for the last time, and was satisfied. On Friday morning, she brought up Joshua Cohen's email with the names of collaborative publishers. She re-visited their websites and, after some hesitation, chose *LineByLine Publishing*, based in Coventry. *LineByLine's* website had spaces to enter her name, her email address, her telephone number and the title and brief description of her book. She entered her personal information and, into the last space, she pasted her synopsis of *A Tyrant's Best Friend*.

On the screen, her cursor hovered over *"Submit"*. She had clicked the mouse so many times when submitting to publishers and dreaded yet another disappointment. She took a deep breath and pressed. The screen went blank. There, it was done.

Ash was sitting in Andrew Hay's office in Medborough Police Station. Opposite him sat Chief Inspector Paul Evans from SO15, the counter-terrorism unit based at Scotland Yard, whom Ash remembered from last year, together with Andrew Hay. Craig Miller was standing by the door.

"Ash, we've reviewed your security requirements."

Evans' air was solemn.

"We've decided that the level of threat to you can be lowered. Over the nine months since the arrests, we've received no intelligence suggesting that you've been at risk from AQAP."

AQAP was the acronym for Al Qaeda in the Arabian Peninsular, the erstwhile sponsor of *IstishhadUK*.

"What with Paris last November and Brussels in March and other shenanigans elsewhere, our assessment is that AQAP and ISIS, or Daesh, have adopted an altogether different *modus operandi*, if you know what I mean?"

Ash nodded.

"They're random targeting large crowds of civilians in Europe, the Far East and the US and we don't believe they'll bother with individuals like you."

"What about lone operators? We hear a lot about them?"

"We do, Ash, but in our estimation you're at no greater risk from a loner than almost anyone else in the UK. Remember, there were only twenty members of *IstishhadUK*, all of whom, apart from you, are now safely locked up..." he paused, "...and will be for some time. So, we've decided that it's safe to withdraw your protection officer and the marked car to take you around. We'll leave you with your personal alarm and the fixed alarm in your parents' house, okay?"

Evans allowed himself a thin smile. Above, his eyes were cold, detached.

"And playing cricket?"

"We've thought of that. You've got a professional contract with Northants, haven't you?"

Ash nodded.

"Go and have fun, Ash."

Now Evans' smile was more genuine, almost avuncular.

"Thank you, Sir."

Hands were shaken and Ash exchanged email addresses with Craig. They had been together a lot over the past nine months and had become good friends.

"Good luck, Ash. I'll come and watch you playing for Northants,"

"Thanks Craig. Look forward to seeing you there."

Ash was driven back to Pepynbridge by a uniformed officer in a marked police car. Now he had finished his A Levels, he would not attend Medborough Academy again, except for Speech Day on Saturday, 2 July at the end of Summer Term. In September, if he secured his projected A-Level passes, he would start at the agricultural college in King's Lynn. In the meantime, he would play cricket for Northants and work for Alfred Wicken on his farm.

When he arrived home, Ash telephoned Kevin Wood, Northants head coach, and arranged to attend the County Ground on the following Monday morning for nets practice and, if required, on weekday mornings after that whenever he was free. Wood agreed that, if Ash were picked for the County Firsts, he would not be required for the match against Glamorgan on Wednesday, 3 August, so he could go to Spain so long as he was back in time to play against Leicestershire at home on Saturday, 13 August. Later the same evening, he rang Gordon Slim and confirmed that he would come to Spain with Sophie, provided he was back in

England by 12 August. And that Craig Miller would not be with him.

"Excellent, Ash. I'll book the flights."

In bed that night, Ash reflected that the removal of police protection probably owed more to the fact that his evidence was no longer needed, than to any personal concern for him. Hardly surprising, he admitted, since I was a member of *Istishhad* before I betrayed the others. He slipped into untroubled slumber.

◆◆◆◆◆◆◆◆◆◆◆◆◆◆◆◆◆◆◆◆◆

Saturday, 11 June 2016

Since Paris, the friendship between Edgar and Pascal had deepened. As well as running together, they had taken walks in St James's Park and in the woods around Pepynbridge. They had drunk in pubs. They had been to the theatre. They had eaten out. Ralph had sometimes been with them, at other times, not. Politics was not an interest they shared. But sport was. Not just rugby football, but all physical sport was a recurring topic of their conversations. Despite the attraction that Edgar felt for his gentle giant of a friend and of which Pascal was aware, Edgar did not let it intrude, for which Pascal was grateful. Pascal's life with Ralph Waters met his emotional and physical needs and he was well content. It was a pity that Elsie Waters disapproved of him, but there was nothing he could do about that.

On a warm and sunny Saturday morning, Pascal and Edgar were walking through the woods that lay behind Pepynbridge Hall.

They shared and rejoiced over the news that, the day before, the Scottish Episcopalian Church, a member of the Anglican Communion, at a meeting in Edinburgh of its General Synod, had approved by ninety-seven votes to thirty-three a motion removing the doctrinal clause stating that a marriage is between a man and a woman.

Then Pascal enquired,

"Are you taking a holiday in the summer, Edgar?"

"Hadn't thought about it, Pascal."

"You know about Ralph's house in Spain?"

"Not really. I know he has one, but he's never talked to me about it."

Pascal described *Casa Rosa* in detail, its situation and the nearby towns of Javea, Moraira, Denia and Calpe.

"Sounds great."

"It is, Edgar. I just wonder, would you like to come and stay with us there in August? As you know, we were out there last week. Ralph mentioned it and I said I'd ask you."

"Thank you, Pascal. I should like that very much. The by-election campaign will be over by then and, whether or not I'm elected, I'm sure I could do with a break."

"We're flying out on Friday, the twenty-ninth of July. I'll ask Ralph to book you on the same flight."

Edgar thought for a moment.

"Thanks, Pascal. That's very kind. But the twenty-ninth of July is the day after the by-election. The count will start on Thursday night and go into the early hours of Friday. And there's bound to be a gathering afterwards, whether I win or lose. I'll be knackered. Tell you what? I'll fly to Alicante on the Sunday and hire a car."

"Okay, Edgar. But you needn't hire a car. We can fetch you."

"Thanks, Pascal, but if you don't mind, I would prefer to have my own transport out there. Then we won't be tied to one another if we want to do different things or go to different places. For example, when you go to the gym in the mornings?"

"Edgar, I quite understand. Ralph won't mind, I'm sure."

"And I'd like to be back in England by the middle of August."

"That's fine, Edgar. I'm so glad you're coming."

They exchanged affectionate smiles,

Back at Coronation Cottage on Sky Sports One they watched England triumph over Australia in Brisbane, thirty-nine points to twenty-eight.

"A good win, Edgar."

"Indeed, Pascal."

"I'm happy for England."

"You know what, Pascal? So am I."

They chuckled companionably.

The same morning, Ash rang Alfred on his mobile and Alfred agreed that, until Ash began college in September, he should help him out on the farm every week-day after nets practice in Northampton. He would start on the following Monday. Ash did not mention that he would be going to Spain in August.

◆◆◆◆◆◆◆◆◆◆◆◆◆◆◆◆◆◆◆◆◆
◆◆◆◆◆◆◆◆◆◆◆◆◆◆◆◆◆◆◆◆◆

FIESTA
(Celebration)

Monday, 13 June 2016

In the kitchen at Pepynbridge Farmhouse, Alfred and Marigold Wicken had eaten supper and were drinking coffee. Sophie was out with Ash. In a moment, Alfred would turn on the television and, accompanied by a large whisky and water, watch it until he went to bed. It was a good moment, Marigold thought, to broach the question of the Wicken Necklace. As always when embarking upon a topic with Alfred, the usually direct Marigold decided upon an uncharacteristically oblique approach to keep him calm, to avoid arousing his inherent mistrust of anything she suggested, simply because she had suggested it and was a woman. Like his other prejudices, Alfred's view on the place of women was rooted in antiquity.

"We're lucky, aren't we, Alfred?"

Alfred looked at her suspiciously. What does the woman want?

"I mean, what with Sophie and Ash being an item," she supplied.

"Mmmm?" murmured Alfred, noncommittally.

"I'm looking forward to their wedding."

"Long time off, Marigold."

"Yes, it seems so now, but time flies. I was talking to Sophie about it the other day. They plan to get married in twenty-eighteen when Ash has finished college. That's only two years away."

"So why talk about it now?"

"Well, we could begin to think about the sort of wedding she might have."

"It'll depend on the harvest, Marigold."

"Alfred, she's our only child. She'll be getting married to the man who'll be running the farm with you. And, if they're more fortunate than we were, there'll be lots of children. Sophie's told me that's what they want. Hopefully, there'll be some little Wicken boys."

"Malik boys, they'll be."

"Not according to Sophie."

"What do you mean?"

"Sophie's told me that when she and Ash get married, they're going to call themselves Mr and Mrs Malik-Wicken, or Wicken-Malik."

Alfred looked at Marigold in astonishment.

"You don't mean that, do you, Marigold?"

"Yes, I do Alfred."

"Like the Templeton-Smiths?"

"Yes, that's right."

"Well, bugger me. That'd be bloody marvellous."

"Yes, Sophie and I thought you'd be pleased. It makes it all the more special, don't you think? The wedding, I mean."

"What are you getting at, Marigold?"

Okay, thought Marigold, in for a penny, in for a pound.

"Alfred, I think that Sophie should have a white wedding in the Abbey and a reception here afterwards."

"In the old dairy?"

Alfred was smiling now, teasing her. With a trace of irritation, Marigold riposted,

"Let's see, shall we. A marquee would be better, but if you can't afford it..."

"Yeah, let's see."

"And Alfred, she's grown into a beautiful young woman."

"She has, but so what?"

"Don't you think that, with her fair skin and hair and her blue eyes, if she wore a white wedding gown, perhaps off-the-shoulder, the Wicken Necklace would look lovely on her? She has the same first name as the last Wicken who wore it?"

Alfred looked away and drew in a very deep breath. Bugger! Should have seen this coming. Bloody fool, I've been. And what am I going to say when she asks why I sold it. Sod it, Alfred, you're in the shit.

"Can we just look at it, Alfred, while Sophie's out? I haven't seen it since before we got married."

Marigold's voice seemed to be coming from far away.

"It's not here."

"Not here, Alfred?" Marigold's voice rose in surprise. "But you used to keep it in the safe in the office."

Alfred thought furiously. He needed time to work something out, anything.

"I put it in the bank for safe keeping."

"Safe enough here, Alfred."

"The NFU Mutual didn't agree," he lied.

"Our insurers?"

Alfred nodded.

"But surely you can get it out?"

"I could, but I'd have to clear it with the NFU first and then warn the bank."

"So when?" persisted Marigold sternly.

She wasn't sure whether to believe her husband and was determined to pin him down.

"When can I see it, Alfred?"

Now her voice carried a note of menace.

I can't bluster my way out of this one, thought Alfred. I cannot for the life of me think of why Sophie shouldn't wear it on her wedding day. Marigold won't be fobbed off, that's for sure. She's left me once. I don't want her to leave again.

"I'll see if I can bring it home next week. Next Monday, okay?"

Marigold surveyed Alfred through narrowed eyes and nodded. There's something odd going on here, she thought. I don't trust him one bit, she realised. Not one little bit.

◆◆◆◆◆◆◆◆◆◆◆◆◆◆◆◆◆◆◆◆◆◆◆◆

Tuesday, 14 June 2016

Alfred pressed the doorbell of Ridley's Jewellers and, hearing the click, pushed open the door.

"Good morning, Mr Wicken."

"Good morning Mr Ridley."

"Another necklace to sell, Mr Wicken?"

Alfred looked angrily into the amused eyes of the jeweller. He wasn't finding this funny at all, but he bit back the retort that rose to his lips.

"No, Mr Ridley."

Alfred paused.

"Yes...?" said Ridley expectantly.

He guessed what was coming, but he wasn't inclined to make it easy for Alfred, to whom he'd taken a dislike. He couldn't quite put his finger on why, but he had. Instinct, he supposed. Jewellers tend to be perceptive judges of character. They have to be to survive in the trade.

"Have you still got the necklace I sold you?"

"You're very lucky, Mr Wicken. I have. I was just about to take it to London. I emailed a photograph of it to a dealer up there and he's very eager to buy it."

The lie slipped easily past Ridley's red, moist lips. He was enjoying this.

"Would you like to buy it back?"

"Yes, please, I would."

"Hmmm..."

Ridley pretended to reflect.

"It'll cost you, I'm afraid."

"How much?"

"Twenty thousand."

"Twenty thousand? But Mr Ridley," Alfred protested, "you bought it from me for fifteen."

"Mr Wicken, I'm doing you a favour. The dealer in London has offered me twenty-five. I told you that's what it would fetch at auction."

Alfred looked at Ridley, unsure whether he was telling the truth. But there's no way I can find out, he realised. The bastard's got me over a barrel.

"Yeah, okay then."

"Twenty thousand pounds, Mr Wicken?"

"Yes, all right. I haven't got it all now, but…"

"A week today?"

Alfred was silent as the other watched him. The fish was on the hook. Plenty of time to play him. So, be gentle with him. There's anger lurking inside him. Don't lose him, Cornelius. Easiest five grand you'll make in a long time.

I've still got £10,000 in cash, thought Alfred. So, I need to raise another £10,000. Last year's wheat's all sold. I could sell this year's crops forward, but prices are still low and I reckon, given the poor summer, they'll improve this coming harvest. The bank? This time of the year the overdraft's at its limit. I'll ask, but if the bank won't play ball, then what about the store cattle? Yes. They would do. There are twenty of them. They were worth…he remembered figures he'd seen in last week's *Farmers Weekly*. Eighteen month old steers in good condition were fetching about £750. He did a quick mental calculation. If I sold fourteen, that would raise enough. Could I do that this week? Doubtful. But I should be able to get them into Melton Market by next week.

"Cash or cheque or electronic transfer?"

"Cash, please."

"How about two weeks today?"

The Honourable Member for Pepynbridge

"Done, Mr Wicken. It's a pleasure to do business with you."

Alfred nearly exploded, but, exercising unusual restraint, he presented outwardly calm. He thanked Ridley and left the shop.

It was when he was walking back to the Discovery that Alfred remembered that he was going to have to find another £5,000 for Jim when the job was done. So, he needed to raise £15,000, not £10,000. On his mobile, Alfred rang the branch of the bank where he banked in Medborough. Yes, the accounts manager just happened to be free this morning. He could see Alfred now if it was convenient. The branch was but a short walk from the Cathedral Shopping Mall and fifteen minutes later, Alfred was sitting in the accounts manager's office. Alfred struggled unconvincingly to explain why he suddenly needed an increase of £15,000 in his overdraft limit at a time when his crops had been drilled and fertilizer and sprays bought and paid for. His request was politely refused. Alfred had expected the decision and accepted it calmly. He could not afford to upset the bank.

"Sorry we can't be of help, Alfred."

"That's all right. I quite understand. Thank you for seeing me at such short notice."

"Not at all, Alfred."

Alfred did a quick mental calculation. To raise £15,000, all twenty stores would have to go. Would make more sense, really. Why get rid of fourteen and keep six?

"I've got some cattle I can sell. I'll put them into Melton Market next week. When the money comes into my account, I'd like to draw it out in cash, if that's all right?"

The accounts manager scrutinised Alfred curiously, but decided not to enquire further. The provenance of the money would be recorded, so no question of it being laundered.

"Perfectly all right, Alfred. If you tell me when you would want it, I'll make sure it's ready for you here in the branch."

"I shall sell the cattle on…" Alfred reached into an inside pocket, drew out a diary and consulted it. "…Tuesday, the twenty-eighth of June. The proceeds of sale should be transferred into my account the same or the next day. So, to be on the safe side, shall we say, Friday, the first of July?"

"Friday the first then. The cash will be here for you."

"Fifteen thousand?"

"If it's in your account, then of course. Fifties all right, Alfred?"

"Yes, please."

"No problem."

Alfred thanked the accounts manager and left.

Back in Pepynbridge Farmhouse, Alfred arranged transport for the cattle to be auctioned at Melton Mowbray Livestock Market on 28 June.

That evening at supper, Sophie was out again with Ash and Alfred announced to Marigold that he would bring the Wicken Necklace home at the end of the month. Marigold decided not to enquire why so long. They ate in silence for a while before Alfred said,

"I've decided to go out of cattle."

"Why?"

"The price is good at the moment. I'm selling them at Melton Market in a fortnight."

Marigold looked at him and frowned. Had he pawned the necklace and, now that she had mentioned Sophie wearing it when she got married, had decided to redeem it? But if so, why had he pawned it? If that's what he'd done. And if he hadn't, why did he suddenly need all that money? All right, she knew from doing his books that last year's harvest had sold badly, but not that badly. The overdraft was entirely accounted for by the cost of this year's cultivation and it should be cleared after harvest. There really is something very odd going on, she thought, and I don't like it. In fact, I'm afraid. I'm not going to challenge Alfred or mention it to Sophie, but I need to talk to someone.

That night in bed, Marigold decided to go and see Norman Callow. Norman taught me when I was at Pepynbridge Primary School, she reasoned. And he taught Alfred as well. Norman's an odd ball, but he knows us both very well and I trust him, which was more than I can say of my husband right now.

◆◆◆◆◆◆◆◆◆◆◆◆◆◆◆◆◆◆◆◆◆

Wednesday, 15 June 2016

When Norman Callow had retired as head teacher of Saint Aidan's Primary School, he had moved out of School House into a small cottage in Abbey Way next to the Blue Boar. On Wednesday morning, just after he had finished breakfast, he heard a gentle knocking on his front door. When he opened it, he was surprised to see Marigold Wicken standing on the threshold. So far as he could recall, she had never called on him before.

"Hello, Marigold. Come in."

The front door opened directly into a tiny sitting room. Narrow stairs in one corner led up to a bedroom. Through an open door at the back of the sitting room, Marigold could see into the kitchen. And, she knew, there was a lean-to off the kitchen, which she guessed housed a bathroom and lavatory. They sat in easy chairs on either side of a fireplace and an unlit gas fire.

"So to what do I owe the honour of your visit, Marigold?"

Marigold decided to come straight to the point.

"Norman, I'm worried about Alfred."

"I'm not surprised."

Marigold looked at Norman quizzically. He continued,

"He's been displaying a level of animus against Ralph Waters and Pascal Legrand that's very worrying."

Marigold looked puzzled.

"Animus, Norman?"

"Hostility. He's been half hinting at doing something to or about Waters and, unusually for Alfred, he's not elaborating. Not saying what. He's playing his cards close to his chest. Is that what's worrying you, Marigold?"

"Partly," replied Marigold. "He hates Waters and everything he stands for. But there's more."

She told Norman about the necklace and the sale of the cattle.

"He's been raising money that he doesn't need. Why? That's what I'd like to know."

"Marigold, thank you for telling me that."

Norman paused, wondering how far he should share his fears about Alfred with Marigold.

"Coffee, Marigold?"

"Thank you, Norman. Yes, please."

Norman went into the kitchen. Marigold sensed that Norman was taking her seriously and was relieved that she had come to see him.

Norman brought in two mugs of coffee, gave one to Marigold and sat down. He had made up his mind. Danger was threatening and the best way of confronting it was to be open about it, with Marigold anyway. He looked at her directly.

"Marigold, I believe Alfred wants to harm Ralph Waters. And the money you say he's raising may be to pay someone to do so."

Marigold looked shocked. She knew Alfred well enough, but had never thought him capable of something as serious as that. She hesitated for a moment before asking,

"How, Norman?"

"I don't know. It could be a sting."

"A sting?"

"Yes. An operation to trap Waters and record him saying something or agreeing to something he shouldn't. Journalists try and do it all the time with politicians."

"Would Alfred pay someone to do that?"

"No idea, but if that's all it is, it's nothing to worry about. Waters wouldn't be the first politician to be trapped like that. And," Norman added, smiling thinly, "he won't be the last."

"So, what would be something to worry about, Norman?"

"If Alfred's paying someone to harm Waters physically."

Marigold was horrified.

"He wouldn't do that, would he?"

"Marigold, I've known Alfred all his life. I taught him as a child. I wouldn't put it past him to do something really daft if his dander's up. Inside, he's like a coiled spring. Always has been."

"Tell me about it, Norman. How can we stop him?"

"Until we know what he's up to, we can't, Marigold. We'll just have to keep our eyes and ears open and, if it is that serious, hope we can find it out before it's too late."

"The police?"

"Wouldn't listen. Not enough there. They don't know him. We do, but they'll not act on what we suspect he's capable of."

"Thanks, Norman. At least I wasn't imagining things."

"You weren't, I'm afraid, Marigold. You weren't. But keep your eyes and ears open. And keep in touch."

"Norman, I shall. Believe me."

They finished their coffee and Marigold left.

◆◆◆◆◆◆◆◆◆◆◆◆◆◆◆◆◆◆◆◆◆

Friday, 17 June 2016

When Gordon Slim arrived home from London for the weekend, Sylvia greeted him with,

"Gordon, good news. *LineByLine* emailed me today asking me to send them the first three chapters of *A Tyrant's Best Friend*."

"And have you?"

"Of course I have."

"Have you told Roger?"

"Yes. He's upstairs doing his home-work. He's so pleased for me."

"And so am I, my darling."

Gordon took Sylvia into his arms and they kissed.

"Not now, darling," protested Sylvia as mutual passion ignited. "Dinner's nearly ready."

"Okay darling. We'll celebrate later," announced Gordon, looking down into Sylvia's eyes. "I really am pleased for you, but you're not there yet, you know. *LineByLine* could still turn you down."

"Of course they could. But you know, a premonition tells me they won't."

"Oh, Sylvia. You and your premonitions. We'll see. I hope you're not disappointed."

They laughed happily, disengaged and went into the kitchen.

In the Blue Boar, Alfred and Reginald Wicken and Norman Callow were sitting at their usual table. Before Alfred had arrived, Norman had told Reginald about his conversation with Marigold. They had agreed to confront Alfred and that Reginald should take the lead.

"I hear you're selling your store cattle, Son?"

"Yes, that's right, Dad."

"Why?"

"Well, the prices are good and I need to raise some money."

"But why would you want to be doing that, Alfred?"

Norman's tone was deliberately neutral. Alfred had anticipated the line the conversation might take.

"My accountant advised me to."

Neither of the others spoke. They watched Alfred, willing him to elaborate. Alfred realised that he needed to say more.

"My Sophie and Ash are going to be married. And there's a cottage to be done up for them. When I told my accountant that I needed to raise a fair bit of cash in a couple of years' time, he suggested that if I could get a decent price for my cattle now, the stock market's cheap and it might pay me to invest the money. He recommended that I talk to a stockbroker, mentioned his name, so I rang him and his advice was the same."

Do you know, thought Norman Callow, I don't believe a word of it. The stock market isn't that cheap. He says he doesn't need the money yet. He could just as easily sell his cattle when they're ready for slaughter. He glanced at Reginald, who responded with an openly sceptical look.

Norman picked up his glass, drank deeply from it, put it back on the table and wiped the back of his hand across his lips. Alfred, unnerved by their silence, looked from one to the other. He sensed the need to convince them, to deflect any suspicion they might be harbouring about him.

"You do know that our Sophie's getting married?"

They both nodded, slowly.

"I know it'll only be when Ash has finished at college in twenty eighteen, but Marigold says they'll have to have a white wedding in the Abbey and a reception afterwards in a marquee. I agree. But I reckon that'll cost me thirty grand. That's what I told my accountant. And that's why I'm selling the cattle."

More silence.

"I'll invest the proceeds in a portfolio of shares."

A raft of questions occurred to Norman Callow, but, he thought: It's not worth asking them. If Alfred's lying, and I think he is, he'll go on lying.

"Ah, well, Alfred," Norman finally said, "if that's the advice you've received, so be it."

If Alfred had responded with, well what would you do? or something similar, Norman thought, I might have given him the benefit of the doubt. But Alfred did not. Instead, he changed the subject.

After Alfred left them to drive home, Norman Callow and Reginald again shared their concern, but agreed that, for now, there was still nothing they could do.

◆◆◆◆◆◆◆◆◆◆◆◆◆◆◆◆◆◆◆◆◆

Saturday, 18 June 2016

In Coronation Cottage, Ralph, Edgar and Pascal watched television as England defeated Australia in Melbourne twenty-three points to seven. They discussed the murder of Jo Cox MP and Ralph said that he would be attending the House of Commons on Monday to hear tributes to her. There was no reason for Edgar to attend. Ralph would be back in Pepynbridge the same evening.

"Made up your mind how to vote in the referendum, Edgar?"

"Yes, Ralph. I shall vote Remain."

"Good man. I expect Remain to win."

"Hope so, Ralph."

"*Et, qu'un français, moi aussi.*"

Pascal and Edgar exchanged broad smiles.

◆◆◆◆◆◆◆◆◆◆◆◆◆◆◆◆◆◆◆◆◆

Sunday, 19 June 2016

At lunchtime, Alfred, Reginald and Norman were nursing their pints in the Blue Boar. Reginald and Norman had agreed it would be pointless to revisit the sale of Alfred's cattle.

"A bad do last Thursday," observed Reginald.

"What was, Dad?"

"That nice young MP, Jo Cox, being killed in her constituency."

"Birstall," supplied Norman.

"Yes, I suppose so," remarked Alfred. "But she was a Remainer."

"So?" enquired Norman, his voice edged with contempt.

Alfred recognised the warning signs.

"Yeah, well, okay. It was horrible, I agree."

"Still supporting Brexit, Alfred?"

"Think so, Norman. As you know, I was all for it, but I'm worried about the effect on farming. My head says Remain. My heart says Leave. What about you?"

"I've changed my mind. I shall vote Remain," answered Norman. "But I don't want to argue about it, if you don't mind. It'll spoil the day."

"Dad?"

"Leave, I am. No worry."

Their conversation moved onto the European Cup.

"So, we knocked off Wales on Friday. Slovakia next, then?"

"Yes, Son. Slovakia next."

"When is it?"

"Tomorrow."

"No problem."

"Don't let's count our chickens," cautioned Norman.

◆◆◆◆◆◆◆◆◆◆◆◆◆◆◆◆◆◆◆◆◆

Friday, 24 June 2016

On Wednesday, 22 June, Sylvia had received an email from *LineByLine*, asking her to email the complete typescript of *A Tyrant's Best Friend* to them as an attachment, which she had done immediately.

At the UKIP meeting the same evening in Medborough, Alfred had been fired up by rousing declarations of support for Brexit. In Pepynbridge Village Hall the next day, his heart had won and he had cast his vote accordingly. Neither he nor Marigold had stayed awake to hear the result, but on Friday morning, together with millions around the world, they awoke to learn that fifty-two percent had voted Leave and forty-eight percent had voted Remain. At least, I've got something right, Alfred reflected as he shaved. We'll celebrate in the Blue Boar this evening.

In Pepynbridge Hall, Edgar, who had voted Remain, was surprised and perplexed. Gloomily, he watched David Cameron announce on television that he was resigning as Prime Minister and that there would be an election for a new Leader of the Conservative Party to be in place before the party conferences in September.

Later Edgar went to the Conservative Office in Medborough and discovered that, in the two Medborough parliamentary constituencies, sixty-one percent had voted Leave and only thirty-nine percent Remain.

"Not good, Edgar."

"Why not, Bob?"

Robert Burgess screwed up his features.

"UKIP is strong in Medborough. These figures will encourage their supporters to get out and vote in the by-election."

"But they don't know how I voted, Bob."

"So how did you vote, Edgar?"

"I voted Remain."

"I'm afraid you'll be asked and you'll have to tell the truth."

"Of course I shall."

That evening, he called on Ralph Waters at Coronation Cottage. After commiserating over the result of the referendum, Edgar asked,

"It won't make a difference will it? Cameron resigning?"

"No, Edgar, it won't. If you win the by-election, he should still be in post when you're sworn in on the fifth of September. Even if he isn't, it'll make no difference."

"Who do you think will succeed him?"

"Too early to tell. Nominations close on the thirtieth of June. I expect Boris will run and probably Theresa May as well. But beyond that, it's anyone's guess. Because Parliament's not sitting, it's difficult for me to discover what's happening. We'll find out soon enough."

Andrew Hay emailed Ash that the Islamists were to be sentenced at Woolwich Crown Court on the following Monday, and would he like to attend? If so, the Medborough Police would pay his return fare to London. Ash replied, thanking Hay, but refusing.

Just after Sylvia returned with Roger from Corbury, her laptop pinged. When she opened Outlook, there was another email from *LineByLine*. She hesitated to open it. So many disappointments. Is this going to be yet another? Finally, she clicked her mouse over it.

Dear Sylvia,
I love A Tyrant's Best Friend and should be delighted if
you would commission LineByLine to publish it.
Peter Gleave, Proprietor

Sylvia firmly suppressed a whoop of joy. She had been this far last January with the vanity publisher. A draft contract was attached to the email. She opened it. As well as the usual clauses about copyright and the like, for the sum of £1,300, half of which was to be paid on her signing and returning the contract, *LineByLine* would do everything necessary to publish her book in paperback and marketing it on Amazon and through Gardners, book wholesalers in Eastbourne. The balance of £650 was to be paid after she approved the proof and before it was sent to the printers. A cover design would follow shortly. If she had any ideas about what it should look like, *LineByLine* would be pleased to consider them. *LineByLine* would price her book at nine ninety-five for the paperback and four ninety-five for the digital version. Sylvia would receive fifty copies, free of charge. She breathed in and out deeply, several times, and then, raising two clenched fists above her head, she cried,

"Fa-a-a-ntastic!"

When Gordon arrived home later in the afternoon, he read and approved the terms of the contract. Sylvia signed it, scanned it and sent it to *LineByLine*. Then she transferred £650 electronically into *LineByLine's* bank account, details of which were in the contract. Within minutes, she received an email from Peter Gleave, thanking her for the return of the contract and the transfer of £650 and informing her that she would receive a PDF proof within a few days. Provided she made no significant alterations, *A Tyrant's Best Friend* would be published and available on Amazon and from Gardners from Monday, 25 July. Her fifty copies would be couriered to reach her, Peter Gleave anticipated, on the same day. Two days, she reflected happily, before she, Gordon and Roger would be setting off for Portsmouth and Spain. She'd take them with her.

That evening, Gordon opened a bottle of champagne and Roger was allowed a glass. After dinner, Gordon and Sylvia went on-line and, finding portraits of the main characters in *A Tyrant's Best Friend*, they decided that the cover might feature an adolescent and easily recognisable Henry VIII and a youthful John Russell, facing and stretching their hands towards each other in a gesture of friendship. Sylvia mocked it up and emailed it to Peter Gleave.

In the wake of the result of the EU Referendum, the mood in the Blue Boar was celebratory, and not just confined to Alfred, Reginald and Norman. The bar was crowded, mainly with elderly and middle-aged Brexit supporters. Fred, the landlord, had announced free drinks all round. The noise level was high.

"Bloody good thing. Don't you agree Dad?"

Alfred struggled to make himself heard above the laughter and excited voices.

"I do, Son, although I suppose you're not so happy, Norman?"

"Well, Reg, I voted Remain, but not enthusiastically, I must admit. I was in two minds, really. What next d'you think, Alfred?"

"We should get out as quickly as possible. Right now, I say. No messing about. Let the bloody Frogs and Huns stew."

"Hmmm…" Norman's tone was thoughtful. "I doubt it's going to be that easy. We shall have to see."

The three sat silent as they pondered about how Brexit would be realised. It was hard to say. Alfred decided to change the subject.

"Iceland tomorrow, then. That'll be another win for us."

They discussed England's form.

"I'm not sure it'll be a walkover, Alfred."

"Get real, Norman. They're tiny. If we can't beat Iceland…" Alfred's voice tailed off.

"Is there another game tomorrow?"

"Yes, Dad, Spain against Italy."

As "Spain" passed his lips, Alfred's mood darkened. He stared up at a hunting print on the wall above where Norman was sitting. There's still time to stop it, he thought. I could text Jim. But not just yet, even if I want to and I'm not sure I do. Far from sure, I am. I need more time to think. Waters isn't going to Spain until…when was it? The end of July? Better check when I get home. I've got Marigold's note … somewhere. Do I really want it to happen? Oh, come on Alfred, of course you do. It's already cost you six grand. But there again… Alfred's palms were clammy.

"You all right, Alfred?"

Norman's voice broke into his thoughts. Alfred blinked, wiped his palms against his trousers, and looked at him.

"Yeah, fine. Why do you ask?"

"You were away with the fairies, that's why."

Not exactly the fairies, thought Alfred. More like devils...my devils. He shook his head briskly to clear his gloom. Come on, he told himself. We're here to celebrate, aren't we?

Norman observed Alfred shrewdly and suspected his inner struggle. But, he reflected, I can't help unless he asks. I wish he would, but I can't force him to. It'll have to come from him and I'm far from sure it will. If I raise Waters again, he'll just clam up. Norman drew deeply on his glass.

Reginald had also been watching Alfred. It was all really, really worrying. Pity his mother's not still alive. She was the only one who could get through to him when he's like this. Stubborn, he is. Bloody stubborn. Been like it since he was tiny.

◆◆◆◆◆◆◆◆◆◆◆◆◆◆◆◆◆◆

Saturday, 25 June 2016

In Pepynbridge Hall, Alistair, Augusta, Edgar, Ralph and Pascal watched with growing excitement as in Sydney, after a thrilling display by both teams, England beat Australia by forty-four points to forty. At 12.45 p.m., Cyril, who had been watching the match with the rest of the staff on a television in his pantry, entered the drawing room with a magnum of Pol Roger.

"Champagne, Sir?"

Alistair grinned at Cyril.

"Indeed, Cyril. Good news, eh?"

"Indeed Sir. Lunch will be served at a quarter past one."

Later over lunch, all who had watched the match discussed the result of the EU Referendum, in which, Alistair ruefully disclosed, all the Templeton-Smiths had voted Remain, the election for the leadership of the Conservative Party, the return of Parliament on the following Monday and the European Championship match between England and Iceland the same day.

◆◆◆◆◆◆◆◆◆◆◆◆◆◆◆◆◆◆◆◆

Monday, 27 June 2016

From the *BBC News* website, Ash discovered that the judge at Woolwich Crown Court had passed the sentences that Andrew Hay had predicted she would. That chapter in his life, Ash hoped, was now closed. When the "lesser fry", as Cedric had called them, were released after serving two years, which Hay had warned Ash they would be, Ash doubted whether they would bother with him. As for the ring-leaders, it would be sixteen years before they came out of prison, but only, Hay had explained, if the Parole Board thought it was safe to release them. If not, they would stay inside. Sixteen years was too far ahead to concern Ash. It was time for him to start living his life as he chose, not as others directed.

Just before 10.00 p.m. in Pepynbridge Farmhouse, Alfred watched in dismay and disbelief as Iceland eliminated

England from the European Cup by two goals to one, after which he poured himself an extra large whisky. Marigold, anticipating her husband's reaction, had retreated upstairs just before the final whistle. Sophie, who had no interest in football, was in her room, surfing the internet.

◆◆◆◆◆◆◆◆◆◆◆◆◆◆◆◆◆◆◆◆◆◆

Tuesday, 28 June 2015

At Melton Mowbray Market, Alfred was beside the ring as his cattle were auctioned. Alfred disliked selling at auction. He preferred to finish his stock himself and sell them for slaughter to the butcher in Bury St Edmunds he'd dealt with for many years. At auction, there was no opportunity to haggle, at which he excelled. As each animal came under the hammer, he was nervous. He need not have been. All twenty sold well and, at the end, after deducting the seller's commission of three and three-quarters percent, the net proceeds amounted to just over £15,000. He provided the auctioneer's assistant with details of his bank account and left.

Back home, Marigold asked,

"How did it go, then?"

"All right. They sold well in fact."

"So how much?"

"Just over fifteen thousand."

"And what are you going to do with that, Alfred? Clear the overdraft?"

"No, Marigold. I'm taking it as drawings."

"As drawings, Alfred? What do you need all that for?"

"I'm investing in some stock."

"Livestock?"

"No, Marigold, shares on the stock market."

"Why?"

"Because my stockbroker advised me I could get a better return on the stock market than from the cattle."

"I didn't know you had a stockbroker, Alfred."

"Well I have, and if you don't mind, Marigold, I'd like to leave it there. If it comes off, I'll tell you."

"And if it doesn't?"

"It won't," said Alfred, adopting an aggressive tone of defiance.

Marigold, reading the signs, decided not to press him further. But it did nothing to lessen her concern. Instead, she said,

"Can we talk about Sophie's wedding?"

"Not now."

"Why not, Alfred? I would just like to know whether Sophie and Ash can count on having a white wedding in the Abbey and a reception here afterwards."

"Wait and see," was Alfred's response and he went into his office.

Marigold shook her head sadly. He was lying, she was sure. She turned her attention towards the evening meal.

♦♦♦♦♦♦♦♦♦♦♦♦♦♦♦♦♦♦♦♦♦♦

The Honourable Member for Pepynbridge

Friday, 1 July 2016

Alfred collected £15,000 in fifty pound notes from his bank and walked to Ridley's. When the door clicked, he walked in. It was twelve noon. Cornelius Ridley was alone.

"Ah, Mr Wicken," exclaimed Ridley. "Hold on a moment."

He disappeared into the office behind the counter, opened a safe and took out the red leather case. Returning, he placed it on the counter and opened it. Inside lay the necklace, exactly as Alfred remembered it.

"Have you got the receipt I gave you?"

Alfred produced it and Ridley tore it into tiny pieces.

"Won't need that any more, eh?"

He smiled at Alfred, but received a stony glare in return. Alfred drew a large envelope from an inner pocket in his coat and handed it to Ridley.

"Wait there, please, Mr Wicken."

Ridley went into his office and closed the door. After what seemed to Alfred to be an age, but was only eight minutes, Ridley emerged.

"All there, Mr Wicken, thank you."

Alfred closed the case on the necklace and picked it up.

"Goodbye, then," he said.

Ridley's face was expressionless. The deal was done, the profit made. And tax-free too. Nothing in the books.

"Goodbye and thank you, Mr Wicken."

Alfred pocketed the necklace, turned on his heel and left. His palms were damp, as they had been after his last meeting with Jim. And in the Blue Boar a week ago.

The Honourable Member for Pepynbridge

Alfred arrived back at Pepynbridge Farm in time for lunch.

"You wanted to see this," he announced, putting the case on the kitchen table and sitting down.

Wordlessly, Marigold took it and opened it. Then, as she gazed at the necklace, she said softly,

"You know, Alfred, I'd forgotten just how beautiful this is. It will look absolutely stunning on Sophie."

Despite all that it had cost him, Alfred experienced a sudden and unexpected surge of relief, of joy even. First the referendum. Now this. It seems I'm getting things right after all. As he watched Marigold remove the necklace and run it through her fingers, for the first time for as long he could remember, Alfred took stock and acknowledged how lucky he was. Lucky to have a loyal wife like Marigold. Lucky to have a beautiful daughter like Sophie. And lucky to have Ash. Clever, brave and a fine cricketer, waiting in the wings to help him on the farm and one day, to take it over...Pity he's black, he added privately as an afterthought.

Then he remembered Jim and his euphoria evaporated. Had it really been such a good move to set up the contract?

Marigold replaced the necklace in its case.

"I'll put it back in the office safe, Marigold."

"Will that be all right?"

"Oh, yes. I've cleared it with the NFU."

Have you really? wondered Marigold, or had that just been a lie to cover up whatever you'd done with the necklace?

When Alfred returned to the kitchen, they ate sausages and mashed potato in silence. Then Alfred pushed his empty plate away.

"Marigold?"

"Yes?"

"If I can afford it, Sophie can have her white wedding."

"And a reception?"

"And a reception..." Alfred paused, "...in a marquee. That's why I've sold the cattle."

But he wasn't sure how he was going to pay for it. Sell off some more land, perhaps? Or take out a mortgage? And, in addition, there would be the cost of refurbishing the cottage for Sophie and Ash. Alfred baulked at the prospect of finding so much money.

Marigold was suffused with relief. So that's all right then. Norman and she might be wrong after all. Thank heavens.

"Thank you, Alfred."

Marigold smiled at Alfred across the table, a smile that Alfred sheepishly returned.

◆◆◆◆◆◆◆◆◆◆◆◆◆◆◆◆◆◆◆◆

Thursday, 7 July 2016

The Orchid Conference Centre was packed. All the seats set apart for the Press were occupied and more had been demanded and provided. There was a hum of expectation as everyone waited for the platform party to emerge from a side door onto the stage. First out was Robert Burgess, followed by Emmanuel Sickle and next by Joyce from Party

Headquarters in London. All sat behind a long table except Sickle, who remained on his feet. Chatter died.

"Ladies and gentlemen, welcome to Medborough. It is a privilege to play host to such a distinguished gathering. But you've not come here this evening to listen to me. Without further ado, I am delighted to welcome onto the stage the Conservative Parliamentary Candidate for the forth-coming by-election..." he paused before raising his voice, "...Edgar Templeton-Smith."

As Sickle sat down, Edgar strode onto the stage to polite applause.

"Good evening," he cried, his arms outstretched. "Welcome. Great to see you all here."

Edgar lowered his arms and walked to the gap at the table between Robert Burgess and Emmanuel Sickle. Standing, he continued,

"It is an enormous privilege and honour to be your Conservative Candidate for the by-election on the twenty-eighth of July. Tonight and for the next three weeks of this campaign, I shall be seeking, not just your votes, but the votes of everybody on the electoral roll in this Parliamentary Constituency of Medborough West. And here's why..."

Edgar spoke for fifteen minutes. Any longer, Ralph had warned him, and however good his speech, he would begin to lose his listeners.

"And remember this, Edgar."

"What's that, Ralph?"

The Honourable Member for Pepynbridge

"The most effective part of your performance will be the question and answer session after you've spoken. It's like a game of tennis. Balls are served to see if you can bat them back over the net. It's a sport that holds the attention of your audience. Do well in that, and you're on your way, Edgar."

When Edgar finished speaking and sat down to applause, Emmanuel Sickle invited questions. They kept coming. At the end of each, several would stand, hoping to be called to ask the next. To every question, Edgar responded with *brio* and occasional quips, which, as the evening wore on, were greeted with ever louder laughter. They're with me, he thought. Great! Asked who he would support as the next leader of the Conservative Party and Prime Minister, Edgar observed that he would await the final shortlist of two and, as a member of the Party, make up his mind then for whom to vote. He added that he would serve loyally under whoever the Party chose.

Five rows back in the audience, a middle-aged woman, sporting a blue rosette, turned to another middle-aged woman sitting next to her, also wearing a blue rosette, and whispered,

"You know what, Florence? He's just like David Cameron."

"I agree Ethel. Looks like him. Sounds like him. A gentleman. He'll be alright."

"I shall vote for him."

"Oh yes, Florence. Me too."

Eventually, Emmanuel Sickle glanced at Robert Burgess and then at Joyce, both of whom nodded. Sickle rose and brought the meeting to a close, thanking everyone for their attendance and encouraging them to vote for Edgar on Thursday, 28 July. As the platform party rose to leave, enthusiastic applause broke out and then shouts of,

"Good luck, Edgar."

"Go for it, Edgar."

"Well done," said Joyce as they left the stage.

"So far, so good," replied Edgar.

"Let's hope the rest of the campaign goes as well," remarked Robert Burgess.

"No reason why not," said Joyce.

They went to the bar in the foyer for a drink and discussed the first round of voting to fill the vacancy created by the resignation of David Cameron, and then the departure of Nigel Farage as leader of UKIP.

"Will Farage's going make any difference in the by-election?"

Edgar sounded anxious.

"Too early to tell, Edgar. Hope not," was Robert Burgess' reply, invested with an outward confidence he doubted. They finished their drinks and left.

Later, on regional television in his room at Pepynbridge Hall, Edgar watched clips of him speaking at the meeting. The Labour candidate, Philip Jones, would launch his campaign the next day and Monty Felickson, the UKIP candidate, and Anthony Bond, the Lib Dem, the day after that. In the interests of balance, clips from their opening meetings would receive similar coverage. But Edgar's were the first to be broadcast, giving him, as Robert Burgess was to tell him the next day, "momentum".

Later still, Edgar learnt from the *BBC News* website that, in the second round of voting for the leadership of the Conservative Party, Theresa May had topped the poll, Andrea Leadsom had come second and Michael Gove had been eliminated. Edgar decided that he would vote for Theresa May.

♦♦♦♦♦♦♦♦♦♦♦♦♦♦♦♦♦♦♦♦

Sunday, 10 July 2016

On Friday, 8 July, the General Synod of the Church of England had convened in York. On the same day, Sylvia had opened her emails to discover that *LineByLine* had sent her, as an attachment, the proof of *A Tyrant's Best Friend*. In order to edit it, she had converted it from PDF to Word. She had started to skim-read it, but then, remembering what Julie had said to her about the author being too bound up in a work to spot mistakes, Sylvia had sighed and decided to ask Gordon to look at it when he came home later that day.

On Sunday afternoon, Gordon looked up from Sylvia's laptop.

"Finished," he announced.

"Great! You're a star."

"Sylvia, you haven't forgotten, have you, that this is the first time I've read it?"

"Gordon, I'm so sorry. I should have asked you before."

"Not at all. I think it's brilliant, darling. You're a very clever girl and I'm very proud of you."

For a moment, Sylvia feared she would break down. She crossed the living room to Gordon, sitting with her laptop on his lap, bent down and kissed him on the forehead.

"Love you, darling."

"Me too, Sylvia."

"Many typos?"

"A few. I've corrected them in red."

"I'll look at it again in the morning before I send it back to Peter Gleave."

"Can I read it too, Mum?"

"Of course you can."

Roger Slim took the laptop and went upstairs to his room.

◆◆◆◆◆◆◆◆◆◆◆◆◆◆◆◆◆◆◆◆

Monday, 11 July 2016

Edgar spent the morning with Robert Burgess and two volunteers canvassing electors in Medborough. He was disconcerted to discover a mixed mood amongst the traditional Conservative supporters he encountered on doorsteps. Those who declared that they had voted Remain were angry with the Brexiteers and fearful over the result of the referendum. Those who had voted Leave were triumphant and contemptuous of the Remainers. The Leavers were united by the hope, and in the case of some, expressed the certainty, that Andrea Leadsom, a Brexiteer, would be elected Leader of the Conservative Party and

Prime Minister. Some Leavers even declared that if Theresa May, who had campaigned for Remain, won, they would vote for the UKIP candidate, Monty Felickson.

Back in the Conservative Office for lunch, Edgar observed,

"Our people are deeply divided, Bob, aren't they?"

"I'm afraid they are, Edgar. It's worrying. The trouble with by-elections is that they encourage protest voting. The referendum was the same. I'm sure that many who voted Leave were convinced it was the right thing for the country. But others decided to give a bloody nose to what they regard as the metropolitan élite, epitomised by David Cameron and George Osborne."

"They certainly did that."

"And that mood prevails. Still, you're an attractive candidate, so don't give up hope."

Edgar and Bob's feelings were mixed when they switched on the television in the Office and learned that Andrea Leadsom had withdrawn, leaving Theresa May as Leader of the Party and Prime Minister elect.

"Personally, I'm deeply relieved," observed Edgar.

"So am I, but it's not going to make our task any easier. It'll alienate some who voted Leave."

"Will there be an early general election?"

"May says not and I doubt it. Why not see what your friend Waters thinks?"

"I shall, Bob. And thank you."

"Okay. Now finish your sandwich and let's start pounding the streets again."

◆◆◆◆◆◆◆◆◆◆◆◆◆◆◆◆◆◆◆◆◆◆

Wednesday, 13 July 2016

On Edgar's bedside table, his mobile rang and awoke him.

"Yes?"

"Edgar Templeton-Smith?"

"Yes."

"Mr Templeton-Smith, my name is Corinne Atkinson. I'm a journalist with *BBC Radio Cambridgeshire*. Would you be prepared to comment on something that the UKIP candidate, Mr Felickson, said at a public meeting last night?"

"Depends on what he said."

"He said that he was against gay marriage and civil partnerships and thought it was a pity that homosexuality had been legalised…still there Mr Templeton-Smith?"

"Yes, I am. I've only just woken up. Would you mind calling me back in an hour?"

"Well, we rather hoped that we could interview you over the phone for our *Breakfast Show*."

Edgar looked at his clock radio. 6.30 a.m.

"In half an hour then?"

"Okay. Call you back at seven."

As Edgar shaved, showered and dressed, he thought: Too early to phone Ralph or Bob. My first big test. Well, if I'm going to be an MP, I'd better be ready for stuff like this.

At seven o'clock, his mobile rang and, when he answered, an interview followed. Yes, it was correct that he was gay. No, he did not have a partner, although he hoped he might one day. Felickson's comments, which had been recorded, were played back to him and he was asked for his reaction.

"I'm afraid Mr Felickson's remarks were wholly inappropriate for someone aspiring to become a Member of Parliament. Homosexual acts have been legal for over fifty years and seeking to change that would not only be an affront to social justice, but betrays the attitude of someone who wants to walk backwards in history."

"And what do you say about gay marriage?"

"Legalising it was one of the defining acts of David Cameron's premiership. It's supported by our new Prime Minister, who voted for it and it's here to stay."

"So, why do you think Mr Felickson said what he did, Mr Templeton-Smith?"

"You'll have to ask him, but whatever his private view might be, mentioning it as part of his campaign amounts to nothing more than reprehensible dog-whistling. He should be ashamed of himself. What we should be talking about is the future of post-Brexit Britain, not the discarded prejudices of yesteryear. I'm fighting a clean campaign and I urge him to do the same. We need to restore the public's trust in politics."

"Mr Templeton-Smith, do you think it was a personal attack against you because you're gay?"

"People must draw their own conclusions, but I'm confident the voters in Medborough West won't have any truck with mud-slinging."

"Thank you, Mr Templeton-Smith."

His mobile went dead.

Two hours later in the Conservative Office, Robert Burgess remarked,

"I heard your interview. It'll have done you no harm at all, Edgar. Many voters will agree with you. Well done. Oh, and something else. The PM's coming to the constituency a week on Friday. I've booked the Orchid Conference Centre for eight o'clock. She'll speak and you'll add a few words of your own. This is the first electoral test of her support in the country and it's hugely important that you win."

Edgar smiled wryly.

"Thanks Bob. Just what I need."

In the Rectory study, Herbert was sitting behind his desk with a half empty mug and four stapled sheets of A4 paper in front of him. It was a piece he had printed off the *Church Times* website, headed,

Synod members thanked for staying on
to talk about their differences

Alice Burton and Richard Maxey were in the leather wing armchairs with two more half empty mugs on a small table between them. They were holding copies of the same piece that Herbert had given them when, half an hour earlier and at his invitation, they had arrived at the Rectory. They had both read it.

Following two days spent in Shared Conversations, the July meeting of the General Synod had ended the day before. The excerpt from the *Church Times* included part of an official Press Release with enigmatic remarks by the

Archbishop of Canterbury. It went on to report the views of ten of those who had participated in the Shared Conversations.

"What do you think, Herbie?"

"Alice, my take is that not much seems to have changed, I'm afraid. Despite the moderate tone of the comments, they seem to reveal that deep differences remain."

"What about..." Richard glanced down, turned over a page and continued "...what Andrew Foreshaw-Cain said and I quote, 'I came away with the strong sense that Synod is ready for a change.'?"

"He's ordained and a campaigner for gay recognition by the Church, Richard. He upset the hierarchy two years ago when he married his male partner. If you read the comments by the Revd Doctor Ian Paul, an assistant professor at Nottingham University and a member of the Archbishops' Council, you'll find a rather different take."

Richard and Alice searched and found the passage.

"He's predicting the Church will split over same-sex marriage, Herbie."

"Well, Alice, not quite. He talks of a serious division and possibly a split."

"So, where does that leave Ralph Waters..." Richard Maxey paused "...and you, Herbie?"

Herbert had thought long and hard after reading the piece from the *Church Times* and he had spoken to Bishop Julian on the telephone before inviting Alice and Richard to the Rectory.

"Richard..." he paused, "...and Alice. Much as I'd like to help Ralph and Pascal, I've come to the conclusion that, as matters presently stand, I should not. I telephoned Bishop Julian yesterday evening on his return from York. He was not happy. It was, I sensed, with reluctance that he made it clear that he could not sanction my conducting a service of blessing along the lines of the American model. If I did and it became public knowledge, he would have to consider my position as Rector of Pepynbridge."

"And it would become public knowledge, wouldn't it?"

"It would Richard. And actually I don't believe that Ralph Waters would want to go through with it, anyway. His campaign is to get the law changed so that he and others like him can be legally married in church. Nothing less will do. To participate in a service of blessing that led to my dismissal would deprive him of respect and credibility. I haven't spoken to him yet. I wanted to discuss the situation with you first and I shall contact him after we're done."

"It's a terrible shame, Herbie. That's what I think."

"Alice, so do I. In my opinion, for what it's worth, the Church of England will come around to it. After all, other denominations are. Only last Saturday, the General Assembly of the United Reform Church voted overwhelmingly to permit the conduct of same gender marriages in their churches."

"And meanwhile?"

"Ralph will have to press on with his Bill. Good luck to him, I say."

"So do I," responded Alice Burton and Richard Maxey in unison.

They finished their coffee and left.

Herbert opened a small book on his desk and turned its pages until he found Ralph Waters' telephone number which he dialled. A recorded message informed Herbert that Ralph Waters MP was attending the House of Commons and invited the caller to leave a message. Herbert did, suggesting they meet when Ralph Waters was back in Pepynbridge. Later, Waters rang back and they arranged to meet in Coronation Cottage the following evening.

◆◆◆◆◆◆◆◆◆◆◆◆◆◆◆◆◆◆◆◆◆

Thursday, 14 July 2016.

When Herbert Onion went to see Ralph Waters and Pascal Legrand on Thursday evening, it was just as Herbert had predicted. Waters accepted that, for the time being, he must continue with his campaign.

"I've spoken to a senior member of the new Government, Herbie, and I am assured that my Bill will be re-introduced in the House of Commons before it rises on the twenty-first of July."

"What will happen to it then, Ralph?"

"The First Reading is a formality that will take place when the Bill is re-introduced. The Second Reading, I'm told, will be scheduled soon after the House returns in November, following the party conferences. The minister I spoke to said that the Bill is regarded as talismanic of the new Government's liberal commitment to social justice, so I'm optimistic."

"And in the meantime?"

"Pascal and I shall carry on as we have been doing these past twelve years. Another glass of wine, Herbie?"

"Yes please, Ralph."

Pascal silently appeared with a carafe and re-charged their glasses.

"Oh, and Herbie?"

"Yes, Ralph?"

"No reason why St Aidan's should wait any longer for its organ to be re-tuned. Pascal, please pass this to the Rector."

Herbert took a slip of paper from Pascal, glanced at it and saw that it was a cheque made out to St Aidan's PCC for £250,000. He opened his mouth to speak.

"No need, Herbie," said Ralph smiling. "You'll see that I've dated it the twenty-eighth of July. That's because, I had to give fourteen days notice to my broker to transfer the funds into my bank account, which I did earlier today."

Herbert looked at the cheque and nodded.

Ralph continued,

"I'm confident that we shall be married in the Abbey before too long and we have decided that we shall have Handel's sixth organ concerto while we sign the register. So, you'll need to have the organ re-tuned before then, because there'll have to be an orchestra as well."

Herbert laughed softly.

"Well, Ralph, that may well solve the problem."

"Why?"

"Because Harrison and Harrison of Durham, who will be doing the work, have told me they can start this October and that, if they do, it will take twelve months. So, why don't we provisionally fix your marriage for October next year?"

Ralph smiled, drew a diary from his jacket pocket and looked at the 2017 calendar printed at its front.

"The Conservative Party Conference is likely to take place next year between Sunday the first and Wednesday the fourth of October, so let's say Saturday the seventh of October? What do you think, Pascal?"

"*Parfait, mon vieux.*"

"Herbie?"

"Fine by me, provided the Church of England has legalised same gender marriage by then…"

"Or Parliament has, Herbie."

Herbert smiled and continued,

"…and the retuning of the organ is complete. Let's keep it under review. And, Ralph?"

"Yes?"

"Thank you for the cheque."

Ralph Waters waved away Herbert's thanks.

Later, after Herbert had returned to the Rectory for dinner, he told Julie and then telephoned Alice Burton and Richard Maxey with the news, cautioning that nothing was certain until same gender marriage in church had become legal.

◆◆◆◆◆◆◆◆◆◆◆◆◆◆◆◆◆◆◆◆◆

Friday, 15 July 2016

At 9.00 a.m., Edgar, Robert Burgess, Emmanuel Sickle, Joyce from Headquarters and three Medborough West Constituency Association vice-chairmen, one of them a woman, were sitting in a collection of high-backed and easy chairs in the Medborough Conservative Office to review how the campaign was going. After briefly discussing Theresa May's election as Leader of the Party and Prime Minister, they turned their attention to the by-election. Burgess wore an unhappy expression.

"Bad news, I'm afraid, Edgar."

"What's that, Bob?"

"Internal poll commissioned by HQ. It has you on thirty-two percent. Felickson on thirty-one percent, Jones on twelve percent and Bond on seven percent. The rest are undecided."

Silence, while those present digested the bad news. Bad, Edgar realised, because it put the UKIP candidate within reach of victory. The undecideds accounted for only eighteen percent, which was tight. If they voted, it could go either way. For him, or for Felickson.

"Medborough voted overwhelmingly for Brexit and Felickson is benefitting from the dissatisfaction that Theresa May was a Remainer. You've not said anything yet about that, have you Edgar?"

"Bob, I haven't, but I shall."

The Orchid Conference Centre had been booked for an open election meeting on the following Monday.

"I support Theresa May and shall say so. There's no point in being mealy-mouthed about it. She's parked her tanks on Labour's lawn, championing the sort of things I believe in. Shareholder control over excessive salaries. Broadening our appeal to encompass the least advantaged in our society. Trident. And same-sex marriage."

"Really? Same-sex marriage?"

"Yes, Bob, really. I've looked up the voting figures for the Second and Third Readings of the Marriage (Same Sex Couples) Act, Two thousand and thirteen. Theresa May voted in favour on both Readings."

"Well, we'll just have to ride the wave and hope for the best, Edgar."

"Indeed. Actually, I'm optimistic, even if you're not."

"Did you talk to Waters about a General Election?"

"I did, Bob. Ralph told me that the common view amongst Conservative colleagues at Westminster is that it is extremely unlikely before twenty twenty."

"Good. Oh, by the way, Edgar, I had Paddy Austin, Felickson's agent, on the phone yesterday. He told me that his man refuses to take part in any face-to-face debates, whether on television or the radio."

"Why not?"

"He didn't say, but I think it's a mistake. The voters won't like it."

"So not all bad, then, Bob."

"No, Edgar. Not all bad, although I attended a meeting of Felickson's earlier this week and you'd have wiped the floor with him. Superior, he is. Not attractive."

"Not attractive like me, you mean?"

Those present laughed.

That evening, in Coronation Cottage, Edgar dined with Ralph and Pascal.

"Well, you've created quite a stir, Edgar."

"How's that, Ralph?"

"I heard the interview of you on *BBC Radio Four News*."

"On *BBC Radio Four News*? But I was interviewed by *BBC Cambridgeshire*."

"You were, but what your opponent said was toxic and Radio Four rightly decided it should be given a wider audience. Senior people in Westminster are very impressed, I can tell you. Now, all you've got to do is to win."

"You're not the only person who's telling me that, Ralph. No pressure then."

In the Blue Boar, Norman enquired,

"Did you hear the interview of Edgar on the *BBC News*?"

"Yeah," growled Alfred. "Bloody poofter, he is. I was at the meeting where the UKIP bloke said what he did. Quite right, he was. It's about time our politicians started to talk common sense like that."

"Like what, Son?"

"Didn't you hear it, Dad?"

Reginald shook his head.

"Well, the UKIP bloke…what's his name?"

"Felickson, Alfred. Monty Felickson."

"Thanks, Norman. That's right. Felickson. Well he said that gay marriage should be banned and queers should be locked up. Quite right, I say."

"I agree, Son."

"Yeah. Pity we can't vote for him. Wrong constituency."

Norman decided not to engage.

"How's the harvest going, then?"

"Not started yet, Norman. The weather's improving, so I'm hopeful. But prices are still bloody awful. It makes no sense. At least we're out of Europe now..."

"Or will be."

"Norman, we voted for Brexit and that Theresa May's said that Brexit means Brexit. Bloody good thing too."

"Another beer, Alfred?"

"Yeah, thanks, Norman."

"You too, Reg?"

"Why not?"

On the way back to Pepynbridge Farm, Alfred's thoughts turned once again, but uneasily, to Jim and the contract. Edgar Templeton-Smith's comments on the *News* had reminded him of how Alistair's fine son, and a good shot too, had been corrupted by the vile, unspeakable Ralph Bloody Waters. I've been having second thoughts, he admitted, and no wonder. But not any longer. Made up my mind I have. Disappearing Waters can only do good and, as Jim told me, no chance of getting caught. And, his thoughts ran on, that black bugger might be disappeared at the same time. They're always together. Bloody good show. Buy one, get one free. I'll not phone Jim. Let it ride. Alfred smiled to himself. That night, he slept well.

◆◆◆◆◆◆◆◆◆◆◆◆◆◆◆◆◆◆◆◆

Monday, 25 July 2016

Just after 2.00 p.m., there was a knock on the front door of the Slims' house in Abbey Gardens. Roger opened the door. A delivery van was parked outside and a man was standing at the door, holding a large cardboard box.

"Sylvia Slim?"

"Hold on. I'll call her. Mum?"

"Yes?" came the reply from the kitchen.

"Parcel for you, Mum."

Sylvia came into the hall and when she saw the box, a thrill mixed with relief passed through her. My books, she guessed. They've arrived in time. Roger took the package, while Sylvia signed the PDA. Then, she closed the door.

"In the dining room, please Roger."

"Okay, Mum."

Roger placed the package on the table.

"Like me to open it for you?"

"Thanks, Roger."

When he had done, Sylvia reverentially drew out a volume, looked at the cover, turned it over, opened it, closed it, put it to her lips and kissed it.

"Well done, Mum."

Roger walked over and hugged Sylvia, who nodded and lowered her head to hide her tears.

♦♦♦♦♦♦♦♦♦♦♦♦♦♦♦♦♦♦♦♦♦♦

Wednesday, 27 July 2016

At 10.30 a.m. at Portsmouth International Port, the Slims drove their Skoda Octavia onto Brittany Ferries' *Cap Finistère*. Inside the car, as well as their luggage, were the fifty copies of *A Tyrant's Best Friend*. Ralph Waters had invited them to a barbecue in *Casa Rosa* on Monday evening to celebrate its publication. Sylvia had no idea how many guests would be there, but she planned to sell as many copies as she could persuade them to buy.

The *Cap Finistère* had sailed at 11.45 a.m. and now, at 7.00 p.m., Gordon, Sylvia and Roger were dining in the *Restaurant du Port*. A bottle of champagne had been drunk and a bottle of burgundy was half empty. As a special treat, Roger had been allowed a glass of each. Their mood was celebratory.

Gordon drew out a piece of paper from an inside pocket of his cream, light-weight blazer.

"Sylvia, I thought you'd like to see this."

He passed Ralph Waters' cheque for £250,000 to her. She took it and gasped. As she gave it in turn to Roger, she exclaimed,

"Wow, where did you get this, Gordon?"

"Herbie phoned me yesterday on my mobile on my way back from London and asked to call in at the Rectory. When I did, he told me that Ralph and Pascal had decided to postpone their marriage ceremony until October next year, provided the Church of England has recognised and authorised same-sex marriage. Whether it will have done is anyone's guess, but Herbie told me that Ralph seemed confident. Apparently the Government is still supporting his Bill. We shall have to wait and see."

"That's wonderful news, Gordon. Takes the pressure of all of us, especially Herbie. But what about the cheque, Gordon?"

"Well, as you know, the organ needs re-tuning and Ralph wants that done before he and Pascal get married in the Abbey. Ralph gave Herbie that cheque and, because I'm the Treasurer, Herbie gave it to me and asked me to pay it into the PCC's bank account."

"So, why haven't you paid it in?"

"Take a closer look at it, Sylvia."

Roger passed the cheque back to his mother who studied it intently. Suddenly, her eyebrows rose in surprise.

"It's dated wrong," she exclaimed. "It's dated two thousand and fifteen. What a silly mistake."

"We all make them, darling. I only noticed last night when I was writing out the paying-in slip to post it to the bank on our way to Portsmouth. It was too late to call Ralph and too early this morning, because we had to leave home at seven o'clock. When we see Ralph at the barbecue on Monday, I'll ask him to re-date it, or write a replacement. Then I'll post it to the PCC's bank in Medborough. Herbie wants to give Harrison and Harrison instructions to start the work on the organ and, when he does, he may need to draw on it for a deposit."

"Golly! Well, I hope nothing happens to Ralph Waters in the meantime."

"Why should it, darling?"

"Well, you never know, Gordon. Strokes and heart attacks can come at any time."

"Don't be so gloomy, Mum."

"It's okay for you two, but sometimes I get premonitions. I can't explain it, but I do. Right now, I've got a bad one about Ralph Waters. Sometimes they're right. Sometimes they're not."

"Let's hope this one's wrong, darling."

"Indeed. Anyway, I'm delighted Ralph Waters and Pascal whatever his name is have made their decision. I approve."

"So do I," Gordon and Roger pronounced in unison.

When they had finished their meal, the three of them walked on the deck for a while. The night was warm and, in the darkness, they watched lights on the coast of Brittany drifting past to port. Then they went to their outside four-berth cabin and slept. The *Cap Finistère* was scheduled to dock at Bilbao the next day at 12.45 p.m. CET.

◆◆◆◆◆◆◆◆◆◆◆◆◆◆◆◆◆◆◆

Thursday 28 to Friday 29 July, 2016

Approaching midnight, it was hot and stuffy in Medborough Town Hall, crowded as it was with Noel Murray, the Acting Returning Officer, his deputies, ballot counters sitting at tables, supervisors, accredited observers, the four candidates, their agents and guests. On the ballot counters' tables, piles of ballot papers were being sorted by candidate, counted and placed in bundles of a hundred, each with a slip attached, bearing the candidate's name. Deputy returning officers were wandering about, collecting the bundles and placing them in separate piles, one for each candidate, on the table at the end of the hall behind which Noel Murray was sitting. The candidates stood to one side, watching as the piles grew higher.

Curious, Edgar glanced at Monty Felickson, the UKIP candidate. It was the first time he had seen him in person, rather than pictured on a poster board. Of medium height and lean, he looked to be in his forties, was almost completely bald and his thin, pale features betrayed arrogance and disdain. Beside him hovered a heavily made-up, slim and, Edgar acknowledged, an undeniably beautiful woman, he guessed in her thirties, elegantly dressed in blue denims, silk blouse and wool and cashmere poncho incorporating a hood and shawl. His wife, he mused. Or maybe his trophy? High maintenance, whichever. Wonder what she thought of his views on gays? Probably approved.

While the piles of votes cast for Philip Jones and Anthony Bond remained reassuringly modest, Edgar and Robert Burgess noted with alarm that Monty Felickson's pile was the same height as Edgar's. As soon as a bundle of ballot papers was added to Edgar's pile, Felickson's acquired another and matched his.

Just before 2.00 a.m., Noel Murray called the four candidates and their agents to his table. The count was over. All the ballot papers were piled on his table. Murray displayed the spoilt ballots, securing agreement that they should not be counted. Then, glancing at a sheet of paper he was holding, he said,

"The provisional result is that Anthony Bond has three thousand and twenty-one votes. Philip Jones has three thousand, seven hundred and sixty votes. Monty Felickson has fourteen thousand, five hundred and thirty-two votes and Edgar Templeton-Smith has fourteen thousand, five hundred and forty-five votes."

He turned towards Felickson's agent.

"Mr Austin?"

"One moment, Noel. Monty, come with me, please."

The two of them stepped away from the table and conferred. When they returned to the Acting Returning Officer's table, Austin demanded a recount.

It was nearly 4.00 a.m. before the recount was completed. Edgar remained marginally in the lead and, on behalf of Felickson, Austin conceded defeat. Noel Murray, accompanied by the four candidates and their agents moved onto a platform at one end of the hall. Doors were opened and, despite the hour, a crowd surged in. Noel Murray insisted that members of the Press, equipped with camcorders, should be at the front. Then he announced,

"I, Noel Rupert Murray, Acting Returning Officer for the Parliamentary Constituency of Medborough West hereby declare that in this by-election, held on the twenty-eighth of July two thousand and sixteen, the number of votes cast for each candidate was as follows. Bond, Anthony James, the Liberal Democrat candidate, three thousand and thirty. Felickson, Montmorency Deloitte, the United Kingdom

Independence Party candidate, fourteen thousand, four hundred and ninety votes. Jones, Philip Eric, the Labour Party candidate, three thousand seven hundred and fifty-seven. Templeton-Smith, Edgar Francis, the Conservative Party candidate, fourteen thousand and five hundred and eighty-one."

After a momentary pause, a roar of approval rose in the hall.

Noel Murray waited for it to subside before continuing,

"And I hereby declare that Edgar Francis Templeton-Smith is elected the Member of Parliament for West Medborough."

This was greeted with renewed cheering.

After each candidate had delivered the short speech customary on such an occasion, Edgar stepped off the platform. Ralph and Pascal approached him and Pascal hugged Edgar.

"Excellente, mon cher ami. Excellente."

Ralph held out his right hand which Edgar shook.

"Well done, Edgar. Very well done. The PM will be delighted..." pause "...and relieved too."

"Thank you, Ralph. I thought you were flying to Spain."

"We are, but later today."

"There'll be a gathering after this in the Conservative Office to celebrate."

"I know, but please forgive us. It's past four already. Our flight leaves Luton at seven forty this evening and I need to call on my mother first. But Pascal tells me we're seeing you on Sunday. Is that right?"

"Ralph it is and I'm really looking forward to it. My plane gets into Alicante from Luton at eleven fifteen in the evening local time. As you know, I'm hiring a car so I should be with you by about one in the morning."

"You know how to find us?"

"Er...No, I don't actually. Pascal explained to me roughly where you are."

"I'll email you directions. And once again, well done. On Monday evening, we're having a barbecue at *Casa Rosa*. The Slims and their guests, Ash, Leela and Sophie and some of my local ex-pat friends will be there. Sylvia has just had her novel published. Ash has scored his first century for Northants. And you've won the by-election. So plenty to celebrate, Edgar."

"Indeed, Ralph."

When Edgar arrived back at Pepynbridge Hall at 7.30 a.m., he was surprised and delighted to be greeted in the hall by Alistair and Augusta. And by Cyril bearing a bottle of Pol Roger.

"I know you've been at a party in Medborough, Edgar, but as you've driven home, I expect you haven't had much to drink, so we thought we'd put that right. Congratulations."

"Thanks Dad. Where are the others?"

"In bed, asleep. We all stayed up until after four."

Augusta approached Edgar and kissed him on the cheek.

"Wonderful, darling. I'm so proud of you. And I wasn't in the least upset by the interview you gave about being gay. I've reconciled myself to it."

Edgar returned the kiss.

"Thanks Mum. You don't know how much that means to me."

"More than winning the by-election?"

"More than winning the by-election, Mum."

Cyril opened the bottle and poured into three glasses on a table against a wall.

"What about you, Cyril?"

"Thank you, Sir, but I never drink before six in the evening. Drink has ended many a good butler's career. Whenever you're ready, Sir, breakfast is served in the dining-room."

Later, in his room, before he went to bed, Edgar opened two emails. One was from Ralph, with directions to *Casa Rosa*. The other read,

Dear Edgar,

Congratulations!

I work as a clerk in the House of Lords and look forward to renewing our friendship after you've taken your seat in the Commons.

Tristram x

You know what? thought Edgar. So do I, and he emailed a reply saying so.

Just after eleven o'clock, Ralph was sipping coffee and nibbling a cupcake in Elsie's bungalow at Temple Grange.

"You must be delighted, Ralph."

"Ma, I am. Edgar's a splendid chap who'll go far. Barring disaster, I anticipate he'll be offered a job after the next election in twenty twenty."

"What about you, darling?"

"We'll have to wait and see."

"Would you take one?"

Ralph smiled.

"Justice Secretary or Attorney General would be good."

"Aren't you aiming a little high, darling?"

"Well, Solicitor General, perhaps. Actually, Ma, the truth is that I'm really not interested in a job. I was joking."

"Really, darling?"

"Yes, really, Ma."

Elsie smiled.

"So, you're off to your place in Spain?"

"Today, Ma. Do you know, I'm quite tired. I've bought some good books to read. The weather out there is fabulous."

"Too hot for me, darling."

"Yes, Ma, it would be, but, as you know, I love the heat and so does Pascal."

Elsie decided not to spoil the occasion with a remark about Pascal Legrand being well used to it, given his origins.

"Well, darling, I'm sure you've earned your break. When are you back?"

"Sunday, the fourth of September. The day before the House of Commons returns."

Ralph did not break the news to her about him and Pascal marrying. Time enough for that. Mother and son continued to chat companionably until it was time for Ralph to leave. After she kissed him on the lips, holding his face between her hands, Elsie looked anxiously up into his eyes.

"Darling, do be careful with all these terrorists around."

Ralph Waters laughed.

"No fear Ma. I'm not important enough for anyone to wish me harm. Provided the plane doesn't drop out of the sky, I'll be okay."

"And don't drink too much. That's what they do in Spain, isn't it?"

Ralph smiled.

"I won't, Ma."

"Well, *bon voyage!* Is that what they say where you're going?"

"No, Ma. They say *¡buen viaje!*"

"Oh, that's far too difficult for me to say. 'Bye, darling."

"'Bye, Ma."

At 5.30 p.m., Ralph Waters and Pascal Legrand walked into the Departure Hall at Luton Airport and joined the queue waiting to check in on easyJet flight EZY2227 to Alicante, departing at 7.40 p.m. After they had checked in, they made their way upstairs through the security gates and into the Departure Lounge. At 11.30 p.m. CET, after an event-free flight, Ralph Waters and Pascal Legrand found the Europcar dark blue Audi A4 they had hired in the airport car park and set off along the AP7 *autopista* in the direction of Javea and Granadella.

♦♦♦♦♦♦♦♦♦♦♦♦♦♦♦♦♦♦♦♦♦

Sunday, 31 July 2016

Shortly after breakfast, the sun was shining and Alfred left Pepynbridge Farmhouse in his Discovery with a packet of sandwiches and a vacuum flask of tea. He and John would spend the whole day until nightfall harvesting. It was almost the only imperative in Alfred's life that trumped the Blue Boar.

At 6.00 p.m. in Abbey Gardens, Sophie collected a suitcase from the back of Marigold's car. Her mother was sitting in the driving seat.

"When will you tell Dad?"

"Tomorrow morning. He'll not be in until late this evening. When are you leaving?"

"We're leaving Pepynbridge at three thirty in the morning."

"Wow, that's early. What time's your flight?"

"We take off from Luton at ten past six. The Slims will have checked us in on-line and Dr Malik is driving us to Luton, arriving at five."

"I'll break the good news to your father at breakfast."

"God, I hope he doesn't hit you, Mum."

"Your dad's done a lot of unpleasant things during our marriage, but he's never done that, Sophie. I told him before we married that if he did, I'd leave him."

"I don't think I'll need to tell Ash that, Mum."

"No, I don't think you will. 'Bye, Sophie."

"'Bye, Mum."

"Have fun."

"Don't worry, I shall."

Leela was standing in the open front door. As Marigold drove away, Sophie turned and went inside.

After a six-hour drive from Marbella, at 2.00 p.m. CET Tony had booked into a small hotel in Javea under a false name, using his forged identity card. Then he had driven to Granadella and, checking there was no car at *Casa Rosa*, he had parked his Seat in the space at the bottom of the *carril* and waited. Now, at 8.00 p.m. CET, he watched the Audi A4, driven by the Afro with the target...Waters, he reminded himself...with Waters sitting beside him, approaching down the *carril*. As he had done earlier in the year, Tony followed them to a restaurant in Javea. Then he went to another, cheaper restaurant, ate a meal and returned to his hotel, reassured that there were only the two of them staying at *Casa Rosa*.

At 11.15 p.m. CET, easyJet flight EZY2227, the same one that Ralph and Pascal had taken the previous Friday, settled onto the runway at Alicante Airport. Half an hour later, Edgar collected his rented Europcar VW Polo from the airport car park and, having memorised the directions Ralph had emailed him, he arrived at Granadella shortly before 1.00 a.m. CET. As Ralph had advised, he parked the VW in the unofficial space for residents' cars at the bottom of the hill leading up to *Casa Rosa* and walked up, carrying his suitcase. When he reached *Casa Rosa*, he pressed the intercom door bell on one of the gate pillars.

"Yes?"

Edgar recognised Pascal's voice.

"Pascal, it's Edgar."

"Okay."

The gates began to slide open and Pascal emerged from the front door.

"Welcome, Edgar. Ralph's gone to bed."

They walked into the house.

"Would you like something to eat?"

"No thanks. I had something to eat at Luton Airport."

Pascal showed Edgar to a bedroom and wished him good night.

"Breakfast whenever you like," were his closing words.

◆◆◆◆◆◆◆◆◆◆◆◆◆◆◆◆◆◆◆◆◆

Monday, 1 August 2016

The Airbus A319 carrying Sophie, Ash and Leela touched down in Alicante at 9.45 a.m. CET. They collected their cases from a carousel, met Gordon at the barrier and walked out into bright sunshine and an ambient temperature of twenty-seven degrees Celsius.

"It's hot," remarked Sophie.

"Not as hot as it'll be later," Gordon responded happily.

"And not as hot as Lahore," added Ash, remembering. Leela nodded.

The Honourable Member for Pepynbridge

They found Gordon's car with its British plates in the airport car park and Gordon drove out of the airport and onto the AP7 northbound.

From 6 a.m., Alfred had been out on the farm, cleaning the filters on his combine and afterwards, because a stiff overnight breeze had inhibited the formation of dew, harvesting with John. A few minutes before 9.00 a.m., Marigold heard his Discovery drive into the yard and cracked two eggs into the frying pan to accompany the bacon and sausages she had cooked earlier.

"Where's Sophie?" asked Alfred, as he started his breakfast.

"In Spain, Alfred."

Alfred, fork halfway to his mouth, said,

"What? In Spain? You're joking."

"No, I'm not. She slept last night at the Maliks and this morning, she, Ash and Leela flew out to Spain."

"Who's she staying with?"

"With the Slims."

"Not with that poncey MP then?"

"No, although Sophie told me that they're all going to a barbecue at Mr Waters' house this evening."

The fork clattered onto Alfred's plate, blood drained from his face and he stared aghast at Marigold.

"At Waters' place?" he whispered.

"Yes. That's what Sophie told me."

Alfred gripped the edge of the table with both hands. Then, with a rush, his colour flooded back. Eyes bulging, he shouted,

"Why didn't you fucking well tell me, Marigold?"

Marigold stared at her husband steadily, before replying calmly,

"Because you would have stopped her from going."

"Too fucking right I would."

Alfred pushed his plate away, rose and stumbled into his office, slamming the door behind him.

Sitting at his desk, Alfred was gripped by fear. The others don't matter a damn, but Sophie and Ash do and they're in mortal danger. And why? Because I've fucking well paid for someone to kill Waters. And I have no idea how it's going to be done. It could be a fire. Or a bomb. Or a hail of bullets. He closed his eyes and an image of Sophie's bloodied corpse lying beside Ash's cracked his mind. He opened his eyes and stared at the opposite wall. No! Bloody hell! No! What a balls-up! You bloody fool, Alfred! So what are you going to do about it, eh? What the fuck are you going to do, Alfred? He sat still for several minutes before slowly pulling his mobile from his pocket. He tapped in,

cancel the contract

For several minutes, he stared at the screen, struggling to reconcile what he longed to happen to Waters with what he knew he had do to safeguard Sophie and Ash. He had no choice. No choice at all. He brought up Jim's number, inhaled deeply, held his breath and pressed *"Send"*. Seconds later, when the screen told him the message had gone, he exhaled and sank back in his chair, submerged by relief. You know what, Alfred? On and off, you've been wondering whether to do that for a while now. Well, whatever. Had no choice when it came to it. Maybe you've done the right thing after all. Getting to be a habit. He glanced at the clock on his desk. It was precisely 9.00 a.m.

At 10.00 a.m. CET, Tony was sitting in his car below *Casa Rosa* in the residents' parking place. There were several cars parked there and he took no notice of the Europcar VW. He watched as Pascal drove the Audi down the hill and passed him on the way to Javea and the gym. Tony pulled on latex gloves to prevent him shedding DNA, left his car and walked up the *carril*. At the gates of *Casa Rosa*, he checked there was no other car there. The neighbouring villa, he knew, was empty. He climbed over the low wall into its garden. He stopped and listened. No sound came from next door. He walked a little way down the garden and then climbed over the boundary wall into the narrow space between it and *Casa Rosa*. Again, he stopped and listened. No sound. Along the back of the villa, he knew, there was a veranda between it and the terrace, enclosed by the extended side walls of the villa. Tony walked silently to the end of the wall beside him and looked around it.

Ralph Waters, wearing shirt, shorts and a straw hat, was sitting reading a book in a wicker chair facing seawards on the terrace, some four paces from the balustrade at its edge. Tony eyed him intently. He would walk silently forward and tap Waters on the shoulder. Waters would stand up and turn towards him. Tony would place his right arm between Waters' legs and grab Waters' right arm with his left hand and haul him over his shoulder in a fireman's lift. Then, walk to the balustrade and, with a heave, thrust Waters out over the edge, beyond the terrace below, down to the sea and the rocks. Tony turned the plan over and over in his mind until he was confident he knew exactly what he was going to do. His mouth was dry, the palms of his hands were damp within the latex gloves and his heart was racing. He took several deep, slow breaths to calm himself. Then, he stepped out onto the terrace.

"Can I help?"

Tony froze and looked to his right, in the direction of the voice. In the shade at the back of the veranda stood the tall, lean, athletic figure of Edgar Templeton-Smith, dressed only in swimming shorts. In the corner of his eye, Tony noticed Ralph Waters rise from his chair and turn towards him. Tony instantly gauged Edgar's physique. He was no match for him. Stuffed! How it had happened, he did not know. But he had to get out and get out fast before the man on the veranda could stop him.

In impeccable Spanish, Tony said,

"*Lo siento señores. Estoy en la propiedad equivocada. Lo siento. Voy a salir de inmediato.*"

He turned on his heel, vaulted both walls, ran down the hill, got into his car and drove away. As he did so, his mobile pinged. When he left the *urbanización*, he pulled over and read,

contract cancelled see u friday

¡Mierda! thought Tony. Just as well I stopped. Well, I want my bloody money. But I'll leave it until I see Neil on Friday. He tapped and sent,

ok collect u malaga airport friday

He joined the *autopista* and drove south in the direction of Murcia.

At *Casa Rosa*, Ralph ventured,

"What was all that about?"

"Not sure, Ralph."

"I didn't understand what he said, Edgar."

"Nor did I, really. Something about being in the wrong house, I think. A burglar, maybe? He was wearing latex gloves. Pascal's taken your car and mine is parked down the hill, so he must have thought the house was empty."

"Hmmm...I think I'll have some security fences installed."

"Good idea, Ralph. And maybe CCTV as well. It would act as a deterrent if nothing else."

Waters nodded.

At about the same time, Alfred's mobile pinged. Jim's text read,

ok

Alfred thought some more and tapped in,

what about my money?

He pressed *"Send"* again. After waiting half an hour for a reply, he recovered Jim's number from the mobile's memory and called it. There was no ring sound. An automated voice informed him,

"This number not in use."

Alfred sat back in his chair.

So! Ten grand he'd just lost. Five to Jim. And five to that pompous bugger Ridley. Oh, and another grand to Shirley. Worth calling her? Alfred remembered she wouldn't answer. No point. Eleven grand gone. Gone for fuck all. Alfred, you're a fucking idiot.

His eyes strayed to the grey gun safe in the corner of his office. It would be quick. Just take a shotgun and a cartridge and drive out onto the farm, load it, put the barrels in his mouth and then, *pouff*! He'd feel nothing. He was sure of that.

There came a light knocking on the door.

"Yes?"

The door opened, and Marigold peered anxiously around it.

"You all right?"

Alfred looked at her steadily and recalled how he'd felt after he'd recovered the Wicken Necklace and shown it to her. You know, you are lucky, you old bugger. A good wife. A lovely daughter. And a splendid son-in-law-to-be who'll take over the farm. He breathed deeply in and out and a profound calmness settled over him.

"Yes, Marigold, I'm fine. I was just taken unawares, you know?"

Marigold nodded.

"Well, better get back to the harvesting."

He rose, kissed her softly on the cheek, something he's not done for years, Marigold reflected, left the house and drove out to the field of oil-seed rape where John was combining.

Marigold let her thoughts run on for a while before deciding to call on Norman Callow.

"Come in, Marigold. Coffee?"

Marigold nodded and sat in the tiny sitting room while Norman was busy in the kitchen. When he joined her, bearing two mugs, and sat down, Marigold recounted what had happened earlier that morning in the farmhouse over breakfast and afterwards. When she had finished, Norman sat silent for a while.

"You know, Marigold, I believe that was a crisis for Alfred. It sounds to me that he's wrestled with it and won. And now he's come out the other side, a wiser man."

"And happier, Norman."

"And happier, thank God. I don't know how long it'll last, but for the time being, Marigold, I believe we can stop worrying."

At 11.00 a.m. CET, Gordon drove into an *urbanización* of villas, built on the side of a hill in the Marina Alta, and drew to a halt under an ivy-clad car-port. Sophie, Ash and Leela got out of the car and paused, taking in the scene. Steps led down from the car-port, past a villa, to a terrace and a swimming pool, glinting blue in the strong sunlight. Beyond, a valley, edged by mountains, stretched into the distance.

"Wow," exclaimed Sophie. "There's fun to be had here."

"There is indeed," replied Gordon. "Come and meet Sylvia and Roger."

An hour later, the temperature had climbed to thirty-two degrees Celsius. Everyone was in swimwear, with Sylvia insisting that they should anoint themselves with factor twenty sun block, even Ash and Leela. Now they lay on sun-beds reading, chatting and, from time to time, dipping into the pool to cool off.

Roger, who from across the chancel in Saint Aidan's Abbey had observed Leela many times in the choir stalls, was struck by how different she presented in her one-piece swimming costume. In England, Leela dressed modestly in loose fitting clothes that revealed little apart from her face, hair and hands. Now Roger noted her slim figure, her small delicate breasts and her long slender legs. He was suddenly overcome by an emotion he'd only ever read about in novels. He would have to tread carefully, he realised, because of Leela's insistence on maintaining her Islamic faith and culture. But, he decided, tread I certainly shall. He dived into the pool, embarrassed by an incipient stirring in his groin.

The blistering day had become tropical night, warm, velvety and still. On the terrace of *Casa Rosa*, lit by soft, low energy lamps, Pascal was slow-roasting a *cabrita*, the carcass of a goat she-kid, over a gas-fired barbecue. On a table were bowls of salads and fresh fruit, jugs of cream, and a board laden with Spanish and French cheeses. On another table, two huge china bowls, loaded with ice, held bottles of Bollinger champagne, white and *rosado* wine and cans of beer. Beside them, stood bottles of red wine from Spain's Ribera del Duero and two large glass jugs of iced fruit juice. Sylvia was sitting behind a third table, on which there was a pile of *A Tyrant's Best Friend*. In front of her, people were queuing to buy a copy for twelve euros, each of which Sylvia dedicated and signed. Around the same terrace, smaller tables were laid for dinner. As well as the Slims and their house-party, there were twenty or so other guests, mostly British expatriates, whom Ralph Waters had befriended over the years he had owned *Casa Rosa*. The wine and the chatter flowed easily under stars that shone vividly in the unpolluted air of the Costa Blanca.

When the Slims had arrived, Ralph had unhesitatingly apologised to Gordon for misdating the cheque and wrote out another.

"I'll post it to the UK tomorrow, Ralph."

"Good. As I'm sure you know, Gordon, it'll take several days to arrive."

"Yes, of course. But, as they say here, *estamos en españa.*"

Ralph Waters laughed.

"You know, apart from *mañana*, 'We're in Spain' is about the only Spanish I understand."

He paused for a moment before deciding not to spoil the party by recounting the intrusion that morning at *Casa Rosa*. Ralph, Edgar and Pascal had agreed to keep it to themselves.

At one point, Ralph called for silence and made a short speech congratulating Edgar on winning his seat in

Parliament, Sylvia on the publication of *A Tyrant's Best Friend*, and Ash on the century he'd scored for Northants. Following applause, each replied with a short speech of thanks.

Then Ralph called Pascal over to him and announced that they had decided to be married and, all being well, their marriage would be solemnised in Pepynbridge Abbey on 7 October next year, upon which there was more applause and Ralph and Pascal smiled happily.

Pascal returned to the barbecue. The *cabrita* was ready, so he carved and served it and everyone sat and ate.

Afterwards on the top terrace, Leela, her long black hair reaching down almost to her waist and dressed in a loose, ankle-length cotton shift, leant against the balustrade and gazed out into the darkness at the lights of two ships, moving across the horizon. After a while, she was aware of Roger beside her. They stood, saying nothing for several minutes, before Roger's hand closed over hers where it lay on the balustrade and he said,

"Leela, I like you."

It had not happened before to Leela, but a strange excitement spread through her and she resisted the temptation to remove her hand, leaving it covered by Roger's. Then she ventured quietly,

"Roger, I like you too."

"In fact, Leela, I like you a lot."

Leela wondered whether to reply, but then threw caution to the winds.

"Me too. But Roger?"

They turned their heads and looked into each eyes.

"Yes?"

"We mustn't be alone together. You understand that, don't you?"

"What never?"

Leela turned away and gazed again out to the sea, exploring her feelings, wrestling with her conscience. Then she looked back at him.

"Well, not just yet, Roger."

She removed her hand, put it over Roger's and squeezed it.

"Let's see how we go. Okay?"

"Can't ask for more than that, Leela."

◆◆◆◆◆◆◆◆◆◆◆◆◆◆◆◆◆◆◆◆◆◆

Friday, 5 August 2016

It was 1.00 p.m. CET, and Tony and Neil were sitting in Bar Toni in Marbella, drinking ice cold *cañas* and nibbling *tapas*. Tony had reported what had happened at *Casa Rosa* the previous Monday.

"Sorry about that," remarked Neil, "but the punter got cold feet."

"How much did you get off him?"

"Five grand in sterling. He was going to pay me another five when the job was done. Five for you and five for me."

"So, fifty-fifty, then."

"Yeah."

"I'll settle for two and a half, Neil."

Neil smiled with relief. He had expected that. He reached into a jacket pocket, drew out a bundle of fifty pound notes and passed them to Tony, who counted them. When he had finished, he said,

"As usual, Neil, it's been a pleasure to do business with you. Need a bed for the night?"

"That'd be kind. My flight leaves Malaga tomorrow afternoon at ten to three."

"Yeah, well, we'll go to the best restaurant in Marbella tonight and celebrate, okay? Fifty-fifty?"

"Sounds good, Tony."

They exchanged broad smiles.

An hour later, as Tony and Neil were enjoying exquisitely cooked seafood in a restaurant overlooking the Mediterranean, in the Blue Boar, Alfred, Reginald and Norman were nearing the end of their second pint of bitter.

"Alfred, you're in a better mood this evening than I've seen for months. What's happened? Harvest going well?"

"Not too bad, Norman. We've finished the oil-seed rape and the barley. The wheat's not quite ready. That's why I'm here and not out combining. But prices aren't good. Feed wheat's a bit better at a hundred and thirteen pounds a ton, but feed barley's only ninety-eight, would you believe. Sometimes, I wonder why I bother."

Alfred looked down into his beer, his brow furrowed.

"So, what's brightened you up..." pause "...anything to do with Ralph Waters?"

Alfred looked up suspiciously and took in Norman's critical appraisal.

"Reg and I have been very worried about you, you know."

Alfred decided to say nothing and let Norman continue. But it was his father who spoke.

"Son, we think that you've been planning to do Waters some harm."

Alfred opened his mouth to reply, but Reginald waved him down.

"Or you've paid someone else to do him harm. Serious harm, Son."

Silence stretched between them.

"We're not expecting you to say anything, Alfred," continued Norman, "but if anything untoward had happened to Waters or his partner, given your attitude over these past few weeks, I'd have found myself in an awkward position."

"What do you mean, Norman?"

"Well, speaking for myself and not for your father, if anything had happened to either of them, depending upon what it was, I'd have felt obliged to report my suspicions to the police. I'm sorry, Alfred. I like you, but that's where my duty would have led me."

Alfred drained the last of the bitter from his glass.

"Another?"

Reginald and Norman finished their drinks and nodded. Alfred collected the glasses and had them refilled at the bar. He paid and returned to the table.

"It's not going to happen," he announced.

"What never?"

"Not if it's down to me, Norman."

Alfred paused.

"I've learnt my lesson."

"Cost you, Son?"

"Yes, Dad."

"How much?"

"I'd rather not say. But what I will say is that..."

He paused while the others watched him. Then clearing his throat, he continued hoarsely,

"...is that I'm bloody ashamed of myself and nothing like it will ever happen again."

All three drew deeply on their beer.

"Some lessons are hard, aren't they, Alfred?"

"Yes, bloody hard, Norman."

"Well, we'll say no more about it, okay?"

Alfred nodded and, unexpectedly, his eyes filled with tears. He wiped the back of his hand across them.

"Thanks, Norman."

"Not at all, old friend."

"And you too, Dad. Thanks."

Reginald reached over and squeezed Alfred's arm.

"I'll say this for you, Son."

"What's that, Dad?"

"When all is said and done, you're a bloody good farmer."

"Thanks, Dad. I take after you."

The three of them laughed gently.

The Honourable Member for Pepynbridge

All was well once more in Pepynbridge.